Holmes
FOR THE
Holidays

EDITED BY
Martin H. Greenberg,
Jon L. Lellenberg, and
Carol-Lynn Waugh

BERKLEY PRIME CRIME, NEW YORK

HOLMES FOR THE HOLIDAYS

A Berkley Prime Crime Book
Published by The Berkley Publishing Group
200 Madison Avenue, New York, NY 10016

The Putnam Berkley World Wide Web site address is
http://www.berkley.com/berkley

Book design by Irving Perkins Associates

First Edition: November 1996

Library of Congress Cataloging-in-Publication Data

Holmes for the holidays / edited by Martin H. Greenberg, Jon L.
    Lellenberg, and Carol-Lynn Waugh.—1st ed.
        p.   cm.
    ISBN 0-425-15473-4
    1. Holmes, Sherlock (Fictitious character)—Fiction.   2. Detective
and mystery stories, American.   3. Detective and mystery stories,
English.   4. Private investigators—England—Fiction.   5. Christmas
stories, American.   6. Christmas stories, English.   I. Greenberg,
Martin Harry.   II. Lellenberg, Jon L.   III. Waugh, Carol-Lynn Rossel.
PS648.D4H66   1996
813'.0108351—dc20   96-19798
                                                                      CIP

Printed in the United States of America

10   9   8   7   6   5   4   3   2

ACKNOWLEDGMENTS

Grateful acknowledgment to Dame Jean Conan Doyle for permission to use the Sherlock Holmes characters.

"The Watch Night Bell" copyright 1996 by Anne Perry.
"The Sleuth of Christmas Past" copyright 1996 by Barbara Paul.
"A Scandal in Winter" copyright 1996 by Gillian Linscott.
"The Adventure in Border Country" copyright 1996 by Gwen Moffat.
"The Adventure of the Three Ghosts" copyright 1996 by Loren D. Estleman.
"The Adventure of the Canine Venetriloquist" copyright 1996 by Jon L. Breen.
"The Adventure of the Man Who Never Laughed" copyright 1996 by J. N. Williamson.
"The Yuletime Affair" copyright 1996 by John Stoessel.
"The Adventure of the Christmas Tree" copyright 1996 by William L. DeAndrea.
"The Adventure of the Christmas Ghosts" copyright 1996 by Bill Crider.
"The Thief of Twelfth Night" copyright 1996 by Carole Nelson Douglas.
"The Italian Sherlock Holmes" copyright 1996 by Reginald Hill.
"The Christmas Client" copyright 1996 by Edward D. Hoch.
"The Adventure of the Angel's Trumpet" copyright 1996 by Carolyn Wheat.

CONTENTS

S herlock Holmes is an admirable man, but whatever coziness he possesses comes mostly from the Baker Street scene— the light and warmth inside holding the cold and dark outside at bay, Mrs. Hudson hurrying upstairs with food and drink at the tinkling of a bell, and of course comfortable old Dr. Watson in the armchair before the fire, reading the latest issue of *The Lancet* or writing up one of Holmes's cases for the *Strand* magazine. Perhaps Holmes is hard at work looking up some telltale data in his commonplace books, or conducting an experiment in his chemical corner that will prove a man's innocence or guilt. Or perhaps he is unoccupied at the moment, and at leisure, a condition he detested—moodily passing the time by playing the violin until a frantic knock at the door and rush of footsteps up the stairs brings him his next client and case.

It is easy for us to imagine Holmes and Watson that way. It is far less easy for those who have read the stories carefully to imagine much more jollification at Baker Street. Not even at Christmastime, for Holmes and Watson are proper, reserved English professional gentlemen of the late Victorian age. They address each other by their surnames, not their Christian names, they observe the proprieties of their era and class, they maintain a reticence about their personal lives and feelings that is scarcely understandable to the modern world of today, where public display of feeling and emotion is hard to avoid even by those who would wish to.

So it is with the Christmas adventure of Sherlock Holmes that we have from Dr. Watson's pen. "The Adventure of the Blue Carbuncle" appeared in the *Strand* magazine for January 1892. And it was, as Christopher Morley, founder of the Baker Street Irregulars, Holmes's greatest admirers, wrote, "a Christmas Story without slush." It takes place not on Christmas itself, but two days after, and Watson, married at the time and living elsewhere, stops by Baker Street to call upon his friend and wish him "the compliments of the season." Just that: the compliments of the season. No caroling, no gaudily wrapped presents, "no lachrymous Yuletide yowling," to quote Morley again. Even at Christmastime, their sense of restraint is well in place, and Watson never lets the Christmas spirit that animates this story get out of hand.

Even so—and perhaps because of that—"The Blue Carbuncle" is one of the best tales in the Holmesian Canon. There is a lost hat, from which Holmes is able to make the most striking deductions about its owner. There is a Christmas goose, lost along with the hat the night before by the unknown man, that turns up with a precious jewel in its crop. And there is the certainty, when the owner of the hat and goose shows up to claim them, that he knows nothing whatever about the blue carbuncle, which has been stolen from the Countess of Morcar at the Hotel Cosmopolitan. The goose came from the goose club at the Alpha Inn, near the British Museum. And so, through the cold and frosty streets of London that night go Holmes and Watson, on a journey of detection that takes them to the Alpha Inn, Covent Garden market, and back to Baker Street before the mystery is solved, and an innocent man, in jail accused of the theft, is set free.

The true culprit is also set free, by Sherlock Holmes. "After all, Watson, I am not retained by the police to supply their deficiencies," says he. "Besides, it is the season of forgiveness. Chance has put in our way a most singular and whimsical problem, and its solution is its own reward."

Sherlockian scholars love to analyze Watson's stories, and "The Blue Carbuncle" is no exception, particularly since it seems to harken back to earlier Christmases. When Holmes and Watson visit the Alpha Inn to learn where its goose club procured its birds, they depart with a remarkably hearty farewell to the pub's proprietor, from Holmes, of all people. "Here's your good health, landlord, and prosperity to your house!" One scholar has pointed out that the Alpha Inn—believed to be the Museum Tavern, at the corner of Museum and Great Russell streets—may have been Holmes's own local during his early years in London, for he had lived in that neighborhood then, he told Watson elsewhere, in Montague Street around the corner from the British Museum. Holmes was in active practice as the world's first consulting detective for twenty-three years, and Watson was associated with him for seventeen of those, but several of them were before Watson came onto the scene—solitary years for the young Holmes, living in a rented room there in Bloomsbury, studying the various aspects of his unshaped profession at the British Museum and at St. Bartholomew's Hospital, and learning on foot the geography of the world's largest city. Holmes was alone and poor then, and Christmas is the time of year, Charles Dickens tells us in "A Christmas Carol," when want is most keenly felt. Perhaps a few of his first Christmases in London were spent at the Alpha Inn nearby, where some company could be borrowed, and cheer purchased, for an hour or two at a time. It was only later, when Watson came along, and they took rooms together in Baker Street, and Mrs. Hudson saw to their wants, that Christmas was no longer as solitary as it once had been.

"The Adventure of the Blue Carbuncle" is a Christmas story that has stood the friends of Mr. Sherlock Holmes and Dr. John H. Watson in good stead for over a century now. But there is no denying the fact that it is only one Christmas of the many that the two great friends and companions shared. Perhaps the stories in this volume are some of the others.

Jon Lellenberg
Christmas 1995

THE WATCH NIGHT BELL

Anne Perry

y friend and colleague Sherlock Holmes had not a high
regard for the logical nature of women. Indeed he considered their virtues to lie in an entirely different area,
one with which he personally had little to do, being a man not
attracted to the domestic life. He was a creature with a most brilliant intellect which was constantly in need of stimulation, or he
fell into a state bordering upon melancholy. He felt that women
tended to see everything on a personal and emotional level. The
abstract joys of pure reason lay beyond their grasp.

Indeed if the young woman who sat in our rooms in Baker Street
that chilly morning three days before Christmas was typical of her
sex, then I could offer him no argument. She was everything he
found most irritating: small, almost childlike in stature, fussy of
dress and manner. She fiddled constantly with her fur muff, strok-
ing it as if it were an animal, plucking at it with her fingers. Worst
of all, she seemed unable to sustain a thread of thought or finish
a sentence, but was constantly interrupting herself.

I could see Holmes growing close to losing his temper. He had
agreed to see her because he was bored, and her letter had indicated an extreme urgency and peril.

Our visitor had so far told us of the delights of Christmas in

1

Northumberland, the crisp snow, the roaring fires, the magnificent countryside. She had described the excellence of the larder and the cellar, and the general festivities of Christmas. She had interrupted herself to mention the stables and the conservatory, and the pleasantness of the gardens—even at this time of year.

Finally Holmes could bear it no longer.

"Miss Bayliss!" he said levelly. "Be good enough to come to the point! So far you have described an idyllic situation. What is it you fear? If all is as you say, what brings you to London? Above all, what brings you to me?"

She looked quite startled. "Oh! Oh, dear. I am so sorry, Mr. Holmes. You have been most kind, and I have been so upset I have rambled on and wasted your time, without properly explaining myself!" She gazed at him, full of apology.

"The point, Miss Bayliss," he said with barely concealed impatience.

She began to look very distressed, her hands plucking at her muff, her bosom rising and falling rapidly. I wished to offer her some refreshment—perhaps in part to distract her mind from her anxiety and help her express herself, for she was obviously labouring with a profound emotion—but I feared with any further delay Holmes would abandon her altogether.

"Are you in personal danger, Miss Bayliss?" I asked gently.

She turned to me from the large armchair where she was sitting, her face filled with gratitude.

"Oh, no, Dr. Watson, not I! It is my father."

"And what is it you fear may happen to your father?" Holmes asked.

"That he may be murdered, sir," she replied succinctly.

Holmes's interest was not quite caught. He regarded her as a hysterical and overimaginative woman whose fancies were likely to be irrational.

"What makes you fear such an attack, Miss Bayliss? Has he received some threat, or has an attempt been made already?"

"Oh, no!" She almost laughed, as if the idea were absurd, if only we could understand it. "You do not know my sister, Mr. Holmes, or you would not even ask!"

"Your sister?" His eyebrows rose in slight surprise. I knew him well enough to realize he did not believe her that there was in fact any danger. "Do you mean that your sister poses some threat to your father's life?"

"Indeed yes." She bowed her head. "It is a terrible thing to have to say, and it shames me more than you can know." Her voice was very soft, but quite distinct. "That is one of the reasons why I can hardly approach the local police. They would never believe me, for which I cannot blame them. Alyson seems on the outside to be everything sweet, obedient and dutiful. Only I know her well enough to see what she is really intending. . . ."

The last hope of interest died from Holmes's eyes.

"I am sorry, madam, but I am not qualified to intervene in a family disagreement."

She perceived instantly that she had lost him. Her face crumpled in despair. She gazed downwards, and I thought she was hiding tears.

"If you knew what a noble man my father is, Mr. Holmes, you would not dismiss it so. He is one of the finest and bravest soldiers our country has known. He fought in the Zulu war . . . at Rorke's Drift. He seldom talks about it, but even I, who have never been to Africa, can be moved to tears of wonder and respect for the man who fought in those campaigns. I expect you know the history of it, Dr. Watson, and will not be surprised to hear that he carries the scars, and the pain of the Zulu spear to this day."

"Indeed not!" I said heartily. Naturally, like any other soldier in Her Majesty's forces, I was familiar with the story of the small military hospital at a mission station on a crossing point of the Buffalo River, where 104 men had withstood attack after attack from some four thousand Zulu warriors. It was one of the most heroic and disastrous events in our colonial history. No encounter has ever won so many of the highest awards for valour. Every man who was there must surely deserve not only our respect, but any assistance we could possibly offer, should he need it.

I looked at Holmes, expecting to see reflected in his lean face some of the emotions I felt, and to do him justice, I was not disappointed. He was as sceptical of Miss Bayliss as ever, but his attitude had altered significantly. He no longer brushed her aside.

3

"No man who survived such a battle should fall at the hands of his family, Miss Bayliss," he said more gently. "Please tell me why it is you believe your sister would wish him harm."

I too listened intently. She must surely have some desperate reason, and there must be proof of it, or how could anyone believe such a monstrous thing?

She began speaking very quietly, and for once she did not ramble, but was completely coherent.

"My sister Alyson is older than I, Mr. Holmes. We live a fairly lonely life. My father owns the largest house for some considerable distance. We have friends, of course, but the circle of our acquaintances is small, and there are not many gentlemen from among whom either Alyson or I could choose a suitable companion for our lives."

"I see," Holmes said quickly. "And has Alyson fallen prey to someone your father does not care for?"

She looked up at him, her eyes bright. "I see you understand very well. I am afraid that is precisely what has happened. Except that in a sense it is already too late. Alyson married him a year ago." Her small face fell into an expression of great anger and sadness. She seemed to be speaking as much to herself as to either of us. "He is very handsome, and his manner is charming. I could not fault him, when he is with Alyson, or my father. But he takes me for a fool, and has not bothered to hide his true self from me. He is reckless, and greedy, Mr. Holmes. He has squandered his own small means, and now looks to Alyson's inheritance to repair his fortunes. My father's name carries great weight . . ."

"It would do," I agreed hastily. "A man with such a history must be held in honour by all who know him. Is this man also a soldier?" I asked because I wished to form a picture of him in my mind.

"Oh, no, Dr. Watson." She shook her head fiercely. "He has never risked anything in the service of others, nor has a concept of duty. He loves the comforts of life and deplores hardship of any kind."

"With such a father, what can your sister find in him to attract her?" I asked incredulously.

"A smooth tongue," she replied. "An attentive manner. He can talk well of art and ideas. He is widely read. Alyson has learned

4

THE WATCH NIGHT BELL

too much of the army and foreign travels and the abilities of lead-ership. She would sooner have a husband who will remain at her side and keep her constantly entertained."

Holmes made no remark, but I could see his disdain quite plainly, and indeed my own feelings may have been as clear in my face.

"Your father cannot approve the match," I said earnestly. "He must regard your sister's future with some trepidation. Is that why you fear he may be in danger? Surely that is still a very desperate measure to take, actually to do him harm?"

"Of course it is," she agreed simply. "But Theodore needs the money which Alyson will inherit upon my father's death, and be-lieve me, sir, it is a great deal. Perhaps I have not made that plain enough. I am speaking of one of the finest houses in Northum-berland, and the means to maintain it, and to live in the style of a gentleman for the rest of his life. That is a very considerable prize for any man."

"Then it is Theodore whom you fear?" Holmes corrected her earlier statement.

"No, Mr. Holmes, it is Alyson who will perform the act, under his influence. They are to stay with us over the Christmas period, for at least three days, arriving on Christmas Eve. His situation is already financially precarious. He is in severe debt, but will not curb his spending. He must act soon, or his creditors will foreclose. Of course he will take care to be able to prove himself elsewhere, in case he were to fall suspect in any way. No one but you or I would suspect Alyson herself."

She looked up gravely. "That is why I need you, Mr. Holmes; a man who is not blinded by beauty or charm, and who can deduce logically from facts, no matter what they say, or how repugnant the conclusion may be. Your reputation for clarity of thought and acuity of perception is known, even as far north as the borders of Scotland. It is also known that you fear nothing, and are totally impartial, and are a match for anyone's brains." She said this with such directness of manner that it seemed a mere statement of fact, and in no way intentionally a compliment.

"Your father's name, madam, and style of address?" Holmes asked.

5

She did not yet dare to assume his consent.

"Colonel John Bayliss, sir, of Allenbury Park, near Alnwick," she responded. "You . . . you will help me, Mr. Holmes?"

I could not bear to think of Colonel Bayliss suffering such a death, and at the hands of his own child. I took the initiative from Holmes without even thinking what I was doing.

"Of course we will, Miss Bayliss! Give us directions how we may reach you, and we shall be there. And you may rest assured, if any man on earth can save your father, it is Sherlock Holmes."

"I know it, Dr. Watson," she said fervently. "That is why I came here."

Holmes took my impetuosity in very good part. He smiled a little dryly. "There is one more thing we shall require, Miss Bayliss."

"What is it? Anything I can provide . . ."

"Some reasonable explanation for our arrival at your father's home on Christmas Eve when we have not his acquaintance, and barely have yours."

"Oh! Oh, yes, of course." She was thrown into confusion again, her hands flying to her muff and beginning to twist and turn.

I struggled to think of any plausible reason, and nothing came to my mind. I was still afraid Holmes might use this difficulty to avoid the case, even at this stage.

"I would be willing to call upon him briefly, simply for the honour of meeting a man who was at Rorke's Drift," I said impulsively. "We could improvise from there. He would surely at least invite us in for a glass of punch. If we then claimed a lame horse, or some other impediment to our continued journey . . ." I blushed as I said it, it seemed so poor a suggestion, but Miss Bayliss seized upon it.

"That is excellent, Dr. Watson. Please, only arrive, and I shall be able to find a way, if I have to disable your carriage myself!"

So thus it was that as the vast sky darkened over the moors beyond Alnwick the afternoon of Christmas Eve, Holmes and I were sitting huddled in the bitter cold, driving a rented carriage towards the looming bulk of Allenbury Hall, and seeing its glimmering lights ahead.

We were received most civilly, in spite of having appeared from nowhere, and without the slightest introduction from anyone. Colonel Bayliss was a vigorous man in his early sixties, white-haired, his skin burned to a rich brown by many years in Africa. He walked with something of a limp—perhaps the Zulu spear wound his daughter had spoken of—but his handshake was hearty and he seemed in excellent health.

One did not need Holmes's deductive powers to see at a glance that Allenbury Hall enjoyed great prosperity. Decked in Christmas finery, coloured-paper chains, bright ribbons, lights everywhere, wreaths of holly and painted pinecones, it was a sight to lift the heart of any man.

I made the speech I had carefully prepared, expressing my admiration for Colonel Bayliss, and he received it with becoming modesty, sweeping it away before I could complete it, and making us both welcome.

"My dear fellow, it is a delight to have unexpected guests so near to Christmas. Is it not the best thing a man could ask for? I fear it might snow. It often does this time of year, if the wind drops. We shall have a white Christmas! May I take the liberty of having my coachman take your horses into shelter?"

"That would be most civil of you, sir," Holmes accepted, and I knew at that moment we should certainly stay for dinner, and probably for the night as well.

And so it transpired. An excellent table was set, gleaming with crystal and fine linen, silverware, superb candelabra blazing with lights, and a most beautiful arrangement of holly, bright with berries and the white splash of mistletoe. A log fire crackled in a huge inglenook hearth, warming the whole room, and the aroma of roasted haunch of venison and steaming vegetables greeted us before we had even found our places and sat down to soup.

There were but six of us around the long table. At the head was Colonel Bayliss; at the foot his younger daughter, the diminutive Millicent, our hostess in more than one sense; on the far side Alyson, who was, as we had been told, both beautiful and charming in manner, although I thought I detected in her a certain wilfulness, as though she were used to being the centre of attraction. Theodore Franklyn was also as Millicent had described him, handsome of face and a trifle glib of tongue. It seemed to me he strove a trifle too hard to please, in conversation being all things to all men, and too little true to himself. But possibly I was prejudiced, seeing that I believed him to be party to the proposed murder of his host, and a man for whom I had formed an instant liking, quite apart from my regard for his reputation.

Holmes and I occupied the fourth side, and I was cold enough and hungry enough after our long train journey, to enjoy the meal heartily.

The conversation turned from one subject to another. I confess I did not listen to it all, but rather watched the faces of Alyson and Theodore, which I could do quite naturally since they sat opposite me, and both spoke animatedly. She seemed to defer to him in opinion on any subject of gravity, and he to her in matters of taste. They never disagreed. Nevertheless, I formed the decided impression that her feeling towards him was warmer than his for her.

I noticed also that he had a ready appreciation for the luxuries which Allenbury Hall offered. He spoke of the shooting, the riding, the fishing, the hunting, specifically of the meet he expected on Boxing Day, and enquired what time it would be. He seemed to me to engineer himself into being offered an extremely good mount for the occasion, which was to be after the servants and tenant farmers were offered their gifts which gave the day its name.

As expected, it began to snow; Colonel Bayliss invited us to stay for the night. It was not becoming for Millicent to intervene, but I caught her eye and saw her immense relief. Almost immediately afterwards she rose and excused herself, saying that she felt a little unwell, and would prefer to retire for the evening, if we would forgive her.

"Will you not come to the Watch Night service, my dear?" the colonel asked her, then turned to Holmes and me. "We have our own small chapel here," he explained. "It is something of a tradition. It is very simple." He smiled self-deprecatingly. "No very splendid music, I'm afraid, just a few hymns unaccompanied, and a prayer. Then, as master of Allenbury, I ring the chapel bell on the stroke of midnight. I am not very good, but it is a fine sound nonetheless, and carries for miles. A joyous thing, if I may say so, a peal of bells across the snow the moment of Christmas morning."

"It sounds marvellous," I said enthusiastically. "I should be most pleased to attend."

"I too," Holmes agreed, surprising me with his eagerness. Surely he could not imagine Alyson Bayliss would attack her father at such a time!

"Millicent?" Bayliss asked with a pucker of concern across his brow.

"Thank you, Papa, but perhaps not. I shall lie down for a while. I'll have Dora stay with me. I am sure I shall be quite well in the morning. I am probably no more than overtired."

"Your journey to London and back was too much for you," Alyson said sympathetically. "Two such long train rides in so short a time would exhaust anyone. It seemed hardly worth your going."

"It was important I see Lady Muriel," Millicent replied from the doorway. "She is my godmother, and she was seriously ill. It was the least I could do." She turned to Holmes and me. "I hope you will find everything to your liking, and sleep well. Good night and . . . merry Christmas." And with a hasty smile, she was gone.

It was only eight o'clock, and the Watch Night service would not start until twenty minutes before midnight. We sat at the table another quarter of an hour, then Alyson also excused herself to speak to the cook about tomorrow's arrangements, and to the housekeeper about the guest rooms for Holmes and me. We four men were left alone. It promised to be a long evening, but I looked forward to it. I hoped Colonel Bayliss might be persuaded to tell us something of his African experiences.

And it was all I had thought; however, I was troubled by the seeming impossibility of our task. Miss Bayliss had told us that Theodore was to be a guest until December 27, and during that time Alyson would surely make her attempt upon her father's life. But how could we possibly remain at Allenbury Hall throughout the period? Surely he would merely wait until we had gone?

"Have you some plan to dissuade him?" I asked Holmes.after we were shown upstairs to our rooms to refresh ourselves before joining the others for the short walk to the chapel. "Colonel Bayliss seems to be quite unaware of any danger whatsoever."

9

"Nevertheless, I think he does not like Theodore," Holmes replied. We were standing in the room prepared for him, a handsome chamber overlooking the lawns at the back of the house, where the snow was already dusting the ground in a film of white. A fire had been lit for his comfort, and it was extremely agreeable.

"What makes you say that?" I had noticed nothing. "He seemed the essence of courtesy toward him."

"Precisely," he said with a little shake of his head. "He had the manner of a man who takes the utmost care to make no error whatsoever, lest it be taken advantage of. He was not at ease with him, as one is with a friend."

"You are right, and I missed that," I admitted. Looking back, I perceived exactly what he meant. It was the care one gives a guest that one does not trust to overlook a flaw and before whom one's pride must remain whole. I have never been so guarded in the company of someone I naturally liked. "I should have noticed that," I said aloud.

"Never mind, Watson." Holmes smiled at me. "He quite clearly took to you, my dear chap, and to that I think we owe the likelihood of being invited to remain. If Miss Bayliss is correct, her sister will act soon, perhaps tonight or tomorrow."

"Do you have any idea yet how?" I asked urgently. I was most concerned we should foil the plot, and it grieved me to think of how Colonel Bayliss must feel when he realized who lay behind it, but it was not something we could keep from him.

Holmes's face grew thoughtful. "Well, certain things are apparent," he replied. "Since their purpose is to inherit her share of his fortune and, since she is the elder, this house, it must appear to be either an accident or natural causes. She cannot afford an investigation. The former seems most likely."

"A fall downstairs?" I suggested. "Or an accident during the hunt on Boxing Day? Perhaps that is why Theodore was so eager to know its time and place! He has specifically asked to borrow a mount for the occasion."

"Indeed," Holmes mused. "And yet if he abhors danger and discomfort, as Miss Bayliss said, perhaps he knows that he will not need to make good his words. I think, Watson, the attempt will be made before then, and when we are less likely to expect it. Be wary, my friend. Alyson Franklyn may be cleverer than even her sister suspects. Now, take a few moments to refresh yourself, then collect your coat and hat and we will join the family and servants for the Watch Night service."

At half past eleven we met in the hallway, Colonel Bayliss, Alyson, Theodore, Holmes, and I. Millicent was still indisposed and in her bedroom. The colonel led the way and we went out of the great front door and walked across the new snow towards the tiny chapel, which lay a mere fifty yards away. The clouds had cleared, driven by a bitter wind, and now the sky was dazzling with stars. Our footsteps crunched on the frozen gravel of the driveway. It was a magnificent night, and I looked forward greatly to hearing the voices raised in singing and the peal of the bells across the sleeping parkland and the fields and cottages as they rang in the Christmas morning. I was very sorry Miss Bayliss was so weighed down by fatigue, and perhaps distress, that she was not able to join us, but it did not surprise me.

We came into the chapel, a most simple stone building, like the main house. It was wretchedly cold, but our good spirits sustained us. There were already a dozen servants waiting for us, and five more arrived the moment after, presumably retainers from cottages nearby, gardeners, grooms, and so forth. They tipped their hats and bade the colonel good evening, and a merry Christmas, to which he responded warmly.

We were all met, and stood together before the altar, muffled in coats and scarves, the men bare-headed, the women with best hats on. The colonel offered a prayer of thanksgiving, then led us all in singing carols and hymns of joy.

A few moments before midnight, checking his gold watch, he moved to stand under the tower and reached for the bell rope. We all waited expectantly. It must be the stroke of midnight. The first peal of renewed hope for the world would ring out over the land, and we would wish each other happiness, perhaps shake hands, and return home through the starlight to the house, and the warmth of our beds.

The colonel looked up into the shadows above where the bell hung from the cross beam. He reached for the rope.

The butler, who also had out his watch, nodded gravely.

Holmes glanced at the floor where the colonel's feet stood braced to throw his weight on the rope, and then without warning he dived forward and flung himself on the colonel, carrying him to the ground just as the bell plummeted down with a terrible rending crack, splintering the floorboards and sending jagged shards of wood in the air.

One of the maids screamed.

Alyson Franklyn was as white as the snow outside.

Theodore stood as if frozen to the spot.

No one moved, until awkwardly Holmes climbed to his feet and held out his hand to assist the colonel.

"How did you know?" I gasped, moving forward as well. "How could you possibly . . ."

"Sawdust," Holmes replied. "Sawdust on the floor. Thank God I saw it in time."

"My dear Holmes . . ." The colonel looked extraordinarily shaken, but with an effort he mastered his emotion. "You have saved my life by your observation, your quick thinking, and your courage. I am immeasurably in your debt." He held out his hand, and I noticed it shook very slightly.

Holmes grasped it and wrung it firmly.

"A piece of good fortune," he said modestly. "Any man would have done as much."

Bayliss hesitated, but made no further comment. With a level smile he turned to the staff and wished them a happy Christmas, then, declining assistance from the butler, he turned and walked out into the icy night.

Holmes looked at the great chunk of rafter which had broken and come down with the bell, and now lay amid coils of rope. He bent down and without attempting to move anything, peered at the whole tangled mass.

I knelt beside him.

"Sawdust?" I said very quietly so as not to be heard by the remaining servants. I peered at the sawn wood. "It does not look sawn to me, rather more like woodworm."

"Of a gigantic size, Watson," Holmes replied with a downward twist of his lips.

"Gigantic size?" I replied curiously. "Surely they do not . . ."

Then I observed what he meant. I followed the line of his gaze, and saw the remnants of the holes where the beam had split. They were indeed very large for a worm, especially such a tiny creature as that known as woodworm. An earthworm would have been more the size to cause such devastation. I looked up at Holmes.

"A drill, I think," he said softly. "Someone has very carefully made these holes where the pressure is greatest, so the slightest pull on the beam would bring it down."

"How long would such a thing take?" I asked.

"Perhaps two hours," he replied, counting the number of bore marks he could see. He turned towards the servants still waiting, watching him. "When was this last inspected?"

"S'afternoon, sir," one of them replied. "I always look at it Christmas Eve, jus' to make sure, like. Master always rings it, Christmas Night, New Year, an' for births, marriages, and deaths on the estate."

"At what hour did you examine it?"

"Ha' past five, sir. Up there wi' a lantern, I was. Was fair and safe then."

"Then it was done since half past five," Holmes answered, rising to his feet. He thanked the man, and together we set out back to the house.

"Theodore?" I said as soon as we were out of earshot.

"Possibly," he replied, frowning and bending his head forward. "Or Alyson. It does not require a great deal of strength to use an auger and bit, simply a supple wrist. Any competent horsewoman could manage it without difficulty."

"Then it could be either of them," I answered as we strode under the stars, the frost sharp beneath our feet.

Holmes did not reply. I imagined he was thinking, as I was, of the task ahead of us of informing Colonel Bayliss of the truth.

"Drilled?" he said in disbelief as we stood together in the library before the dying fire. "Surely you must be mistaken!" But it was barely a protest. In his eyes he knew it was the truth. Holmes would not speak such a thing unless he were certain.

"Have I your permission, sir, to search for the drill?" Holmes asked.

Bayliss hesitated. Holmes did not need to say that it must be someone in the household. No stranger could have entered the chapel, nor was it reasonable to suppose any but those closest to him would have motive for such an act, or the knowledge that it was he, and only he, who would ring the bell.

"Yes, I suppose it must be done," he conceded. "Whoever took it will not have been able to return it to the toolshed, since it is locked at night. I shall help you. Where do you propose to begin?"

"With Mr. and Mrs. Franklyn's room," Holmes answered soberly.

"Theodore was with us all evening!" Bayliss protested, then his face became so much paler I feared he may suffer some constriction of the heart. But his courage did not desert him. With a great effort he composed himself and straightened his shoulders. "I cannot think my daughter would do such a thing. The sooner we can clear her of even the faintest suspicion, the better."

Together we three went up the great sweeping stairway and along the corridor to Alyson and Theodore's bedroom. Colonel Bayliss knocked sharply, and a moment later it was opened by Theodore, looking curious. He was still fully dressed.

"What is it?" he asked on seeing Holmes and myself as well. "Has something further happened?"

Briefly the colonel explained what had transpired, and that he must make a thorough search of all the rooms.

"Of course," Theodore agreed, but his mouth was pinched with annoyance. "I regret you consider it necessary, but perhaps it will serve to clear your mind."

Without answering, the colonel went in, and Holmes followed him, and apologized to Alyson Franklyn, who was seated in a chair by the dressing table. Holmes and I began to search while Colonel Bayliss stood motionless in the centre of the room, his face a mask of grief.

It was Holmes who found it, wedged under the bed, into the corner so that it was suspended between the side and the foot. He brought it out, complete with the bit still in place, and held it up.

No explanation was possible. The sawdust of the beam was still in the grooves of the bit. It had not even been cleaned.

Alyson and Theodore stared at each other in horror.

My concern was for Colonel Bayliss. He looked as if he had been struck with a mortal wound. The Zulu spear all those years ago cannot have hurt as this must have. I moved over to him.

"Come, sir," I said gently. "There is no more purpose to be served here." I offered him my arm. He did not take it, but I knew from his brief glance at me that he was sensible of my tenderness towards him.

"I shall tell Millicent what has happened," he said huskily. "She will need to know . . ."

"I will do that," Holmes offered. "She is deeply concerned for you, Colonel. It was she who invited Holmes and myself here, in order to forestall any attempt upon your life. She at least is utterly loyal to you."

Bayliss attempted to smile, and found it beyond him. He nodded his acceptance, and walked away, his shoulders bowed, his feet heavy.

Holmes and I went to Millicent's door and knocked. I intended to remain only long enough to give her the news, and then see if I could offer the colonel something to help him sleep, and perhaps steady his heart.

The door was opened by the ladies' maid.

"Yes?" she enquired.

"I must speak with Miss Bayliss," Holmes replied. "It is a matter of the deepest importance, or I would not disturb her. There has been an attempt upon her father's life."

The maid stared at him in a moment's horror, then collected her wits.

"Is . . . is the colonel all right, sir?"

"Yes, he is quite well, but naturally he was profoundly upset by the event. Will you please fetch your mistress."

"Yes, sir." And obediently she disappeared and Holmes and I waited impatiently in the landing.

Miss Bayliss arrived at the door in her nightgown and robe, her hair loose about her shoulders. She looked from Holmes to me and back again.

"It happened!" she said in a whisper. "Where? What did she do? Dora says Papa is all right. Are you sure?"

This last question was addressed to me.

"Indeed he is quite unhurt," I said as kindly as I could. "Except in spirit, of course. Perhaps your presence will be of comfort to him."

"Of course. I'll go to him immediately. Does he know yet that it was Alyson?"

Holmes explained very briefly what had occurred.

"I see," she said solemnly. "I cannot thank you enough, Mr. Holmes. You have saved the life of a brave man. I wish you had not had to do it at such a cost." She looked very pale, as if in spite of her own foreboding, the actuality had still shocked her.

"Are you sure you are well enough?" the maid asked uncertainly, then looked at me. "Miss Millicent has been in bed all evening, sir. I know because I never left the dressing room. Please do see to it she's cared for. It's a horrible thing, and such a shock!"

"I will," I promised, and stepped back to allow Miss Bayliss to pass. As she did so Holmes suddenly stiffened, then shot out his hand and grasped her by the wrist, almost wrenching her to a stop.

She let out a cry of pain and surprise.

"What is it?" she gasped. "Whatever is the matter, Mr. Holmes?"

"Is there a fire in your room, Miss Bayliss?" he demanded.

"Of course," she replied.

"And is it lit? Has it been lit all evening?"

I was about to protest, but something held me back, some trust in his judgement deeper than any conscious thought.

"Yes it is lit," she said, facing him boldly. "Why do you ask?"

"At what hour was it lit?" he pressed.

"I . . . I don't know . . ."

"About half an hour ago, miss," the maid replied for her. "You said particular not to light it earlier, as you were already too warm."

"What on earth does it matter, Holmes?" I was bewildered.

Holmes, who was still holding Miss Bayliss by the wrist, with his other hand pulled back the heavy curtain of her hair and showed several dark marks on her neck, behind her ears, and on her scalp.

"Soot," he said with a bitter smile. "It is not easy to wash off. It gets into everything. I have seen small boys who climb up chimneys to clean them, with marks such as these." He turned to her.

"Only you went up not to clean but to escape your room, to drill through the beam which held up the chapel bell, and to leave the auger and bit in your sister's room, while she was out. Thus you could dispose of your father and your sister in one blow, and use us as your cat's-paw. You did not succeed, Miss Bayliss. Your father is alive and well, and your sister will have her full inheritance, whatever she may choose to do with it!"

She stared at him with her chin high, her eyes blazing.

"She will squander it on that worthless husband!" she said in contempt. "And he is worthless, Mr. Holmes, a deceiver and a cheat. I know that better than you may imagine, because he courted me first!"

Holmes did not reply. He had misjudged both her subtlety and the bitterness of character and the strength of her nerve, and he knew it. He had allowed his prejudice to sway him, and only his keen observation and his deductive power had saved him from being precisely the tool in her plan that she had intended.

It was a sobering thought, and one which caused him to display an unusual humility that strange and quiet Christmas in Allenbury Hall. It lingered even into Boxing Day.

In fact it was New Year's Eve, and we were back in Baker Street, before he gave me permission to write up the affair, with a rueful suggestion that next time a woman's silliness caused him to disregard her, I should discreetly mention the name of Miss Millicent Bayliss to him, and he might reconsider his judgement.

THE SLEUTH OF CHRISTMAS PAST

Barbara Paul

Never had I seen Holmes in so buoyant a mood; he was like a man from whose shoulders an onerous weight had been lifted . . . as indeed he was. Only the day before had he concluded his investigation into the affair of the clock that ran backward—a lengthy, strenuous investigation which at times I feared was exacting a toll on my friend's health. But all had been concluded satisfactorily, and discreetly; not only had Holmes been remunerated handsomely, but he was also enjoying the sweet euphoria that only the successful solution of a knotty problem can bring.

"Shall we take a stroll to Manchester Square, Watson?" Holmes asked. "I'm of a mind to listen to the carolers."

"Ah," I said, taken by surprise. "Then you intend to celebrate Christmas this year?"

"I always celebrate Christmas," he replied flatly. "But not always at the same time others do. Christmas is a state of mind, Watson! Come, let us be off. Today is Christmas."

It was, as a matter of fact, only the twenty-first of the month, in the year 1887. But if Holmes was inclined to celebrate the holiday four days early, who was I to say him nay? I wrapped my black wool muffler over my head before donning my hat; I'd been disposed toward the earache lately.

Manchester Square was only three streets away. The crisp December day was invigorating, and I was pleased my companion had suggested an outing. In the past he'd displayed a tendency to stay cooped up in our rooms at Baker Street when he had no case pending; it was heartening to learn that Sherlock Holmes, of all men the most impervious to sentiment, was as susceptible as the rest of us to the joyous appeal of the holiday season.

The carolers were all children. Their dulcet young voices floated through the clear air to bring a smile to the faces of all who passed by. All but one, I noticed. A tall man in a brown greatcoat stood scowling at the children as they sang. "I say, Holmes," I ventured, "isn't that . . . ?"

"Our Mr. Curtis," he agreed. "And looking every inch a man who abominates Christmas or child singers or both. I wonder what dismays him so."

Curtis and Company was a prosperous chemist's shop on Crawford Street, the nearest such to Baker Street; Holmes and I both frequented the establishment on a regular basis. On every occasion of my own visits, Curtis had been quite affable, clearly a man at peace with himself and the world. His present thunderous visage made him almost unrecognizable.

He did not notice our approach. "Are you not enjoying the music, Mr. Curtis?" Holmes asked.

The chemist started and with an effort focused on our faces. "Oh, Mr. Holmes," he said in a distracted manner. "Dr. Watson, good day. The music? Yes, yes, quite nice. Quite nice indeed."

"Yet I fear you may be frightening the children," Holmes persisted in a playful manner, "glowering at them in so fearsome a way."

"Was I glowering?" Curtis looked toward the carolers and smiled and nodded, as if to compensate for any earlier lapse in goodwill. "I was preoccupied, Mr. Holmes. Another matter entirely was demanding my full attention."

"No trouble, I hope?"

He hesitated. "I am uncertain. You know of our Merchants Association's Christmas Charities Fund? Oh, what am I thinking—of course you know. And I want to thank you again for your generous subscriptions, both of you."

"You are most welcome," I said. "Is the Fund not doing well?"

"Exceedingly well, Dr. Watson," Curtis replied. "That is not the problem. It's only that—" He broke off abruptly, apparently changing his mind about telling us. "But I don't want to trouble you about a matter that is undoubtedly only a misunderstanding. Gentlemen, I wish you the joy of the season."

"And to you, sir."

We watched as he hurried off in a direction opposite to that of his place of business. "He suspects someone of stealing from the Fund," Holmes remarked. "Or of planning to."

"From a charitable fund?" I objected. "Surely no man would be so low as to steal from the poor at Christmastime."

Holmes looked at me with a glimmer of amusement. "I fear I cannot share your faith in the essential goodness of mankind, my friend. To many among us, perhaps to most of us—money is money. It does not matter where the money comes from or where it is intended to go. By all means let us hope that Curtis is mistaken and his fund is in no danger of being misappropriated. But at the same time let us not assume that all is well."

I had heard Holmes make similar cynical pronouncements before and knew from past experience that argument was futile. Holmes liked to claim that expecting the best of people was to assure that one lived a life of constant disappointment. To avoid listening to the repetition of a dogma that was distasteful to me, I said the only thing one can say in such a situation. "Tea?" I suggested.

"An excellent idea! Chatterby's, I think."

"Very well." I started walking toward Wigmore Street, where we would be most likely to find a hansom cab for hire.

"No, Watson—this way!" Holmes called. "We walk!"

"But Chatterby's is over two miles distant!" I protested.

"Just enough to get our blood circulating! The tea will taste all the sweeter afterward. Come, Watson. We walk."

We walked.

*   *   *

Upon our return to Baker Street (by hansom cab, I might add), we were met at the door by Mrs. Hudson with the news that a young woman was waiting for us in our rooms.

"I hope you don't mind that I let her in," the housekeeper said. "The poor young thing had been crying, and it's so bitterly cold outside that I didn't have the heart to send her away."

"It's not that cold, Mrs. Hudson," Holmes said, "but you did right. Thank you."

She looked at him, surprised. "It's turned near freezing, Mr. Holmes."

He returned her look. "No, it hasn't."

"Yes, it has," I interposed. "We don't all have your natural immunity to cold, Holmes."

"Ah." He said no more but led the way upstairs.

Our visitor was very young . . . not more than eighteen, I would venture. And she had indeed been crying, normally a fact to make Holmes impatient rather than sympathetic. But the holiday season was still upon him; he spoke to her gently and offered refreshment, which she declined.

"I don't know whether you can help me or not, Mr. Holmes," she said in an anguished voice. "But I am in desperate need of advice and I have no one to turn to."

"No father or mother? No other relative?"

"None. My mother died when I was a child, and my poor father met with an unfortunate accident not two months hence. There are no others, except my fiancé, and he . . . he is part of the problem for which I seek advice."

I said, "Perhaps you would tell us your name."

"Oh! Forgive me. My name is Amy Stoddard. I still live in my father's house in Bayswater Road."

"Your father was an importer of spices?" Holmes asked. "And you assisted in the business—perhaps in keeping the accounts? Or in sending out the bills?"

Her eyes grew large with astonishment. "How ever did you know that, Mr. Holmes?"

"I detected a slight scent of cinnamon when I first entered the room," he answered in an offhand manner. "And the middle finger

21

of your right hand has a callus at the point where one normally grips a pen—a more pronounced callus than can be accounted for by the writing out of school exercises."

"I copied all my father's correspondence for him, as well as sending out the bills." She smiled sadly. "I was the only one who could read his handwriting."

"Well, now. Suppose you tell us the problem for which you seek advice and the part your fiancé plays in it. First, what is his name?"

"Thomas Wickham. He is the youngest son of a viscount who incurred his family's displeasure by going into trade. My father met him through the Paddington Merchants Association. They were to work together on the Christmas Charities Fund until . . . until my father . . ."

"So it was your father who introduced you," Holmes interjected quickly, not revealing by so much as a twitch of the eyelid that this was the second mention of the Christmas Charities Fund we'd heard that day.

"Yes. As my husband, Thomas will oversee the operation of my father's business, as soon as certain legal matters are attended to. But it is not about the importing of spices that I consult you, Mr. Holmes. It concerns a totally unrelated matter."

"Proceed."

Miss Stoddard paused a moment to gather her thoughts. "Last week Mr. John Fulham, a friend of my father's, took me to see Sir Henry Irving's new play at the Lyceum Theatre. As we were leaving at the end of the performance, we encountered purely by chance Thomas's business partner, Etienne Piaget. I introduced him to Mr. Fulham, and then Monsieur Piaget said a most re-markable thing. He expressed regrets that I would not be able to spend Christmas with my fiancé.

"I asked him whatever did he mean? I was planning a Christmas Eve dinner for Thomas and some friends, and Thomas had been helping me with the arrangements. Mr. Fulham spoke up and said that was quite true, that he had received his invitation two days earlier." She paused. "Then an expression came over Monsieur Piaget's face that I can describe only as the look a Frenchman gets when he realizes he's committed an inexcusable faux pas."

"Aha!" Holmes exclaimed. "I know that look."

22

"He was quite embarrassed," the young woman said. "He murmured something about being mistaken, that he only thought he saw a ticket for passage on the *Mary Small* for the twenty-third of the month. It had to be something else he'd seen lying on Thomas's desk. He started bowing and backing away—the poor man practically fled."

"Tell me, Miss Stoddard," Holmes asked, "what business do Mr. Wickham and Monsieur Piaget pursue?"

"They are wine merchants. Monsieur Piaget buys the wines in France, and Thomas administers the London side of the business."

"I see. Pray continue. You asked your affianced about the ticket for passage on the *Mary Small*?"

"I did. He was astonished. Thomas said he could not imagine what was on his desk that his partner should mistake for a steamship ticket."

"A simple error, surely," I offered. "Not a cause for concern."

"Ah, but, Watson," Holmes said, "Miss Stoddard has not finished her story—am I correct?"

"You are." She paused. "Earlier today Thomas called at my house. At my request, he has been looking through my father's papers, searching for any unfinished business that should be seen to. He'd come across the draft of a letter that he could not read—I believe I mentioned my father's penmanship did not measure up to normal standards. The letter simply requested a change of shipping dates for a consignment of ginger and other spices, an ordinary commercial transaction.

"Thomas laughed when I finished reading him the letter, amused that I could decipher what no one else could. Then he said, 'You can read a dreadful scrawl that's fully illegible to the rest of us, but can you write it? Have you ever tried imitating such an idiosyncratic hand?'

"I had, in fact, done just that upon several occasions. Once I left a note for my father in 'his' handwriting, to tease him . . . and he later complained he couldn't read a word! When Thomas heard that, he wanted to see a demonstration. He took a paper out of his pocket and asked me to copy it in my father's handwriting. I did, and Thomas was so pleased with the result that he took the copy with him to show to Monsieur Piaget. He left the original behind.''

Our visitor took out a folded piece of foolscap. "It was only later that I began to wonder about the nature of what I had copied." She handed the paper to Holmes. "Please tell me what you think."

I joined Holmes at the window and we both read the passage Wickham had given his fiancée to copy. It was brief, only two sentences:

It is my intent that the governance of my affairs be placed in the hands of one who is most qualified to oversee them. Determining who that person is has occupied much of my attention during the past year.

"Your father left a will?" Holmes asked sharply.

"Yes, and I am to inherit all."

Holmes flicked the paper with a long forefinger. "Is this Thomas Wickham's handwriting?"

"No, that writing is unfamiliar to me."

"Quite possibly because a deliberate attempt has been made to disguise it. Look here, Watson." He pointed to the word *my*. "See the large loop beneath the line of writing for the letter *y*? And here in the *g* and the *p*? Yet twice—here, and here—there is only a straight descending line instead of the large loop. There's a similar inconsistency in the way the letter *r* is written . . . wide and square in most places, but narrow and ill formed in the words *during* and *year*. This letter was written by an inexperienced forger, I daresay."

"But . . . but why?" I asked. "This is no legal document." I looked to Amy Stoddard. "Did you sign your father's name to the copy?" She said no. "Then how can this be a threat to her inheritance, Holmes?"

"Yes, how? That is the question we must endeavor to answer. Miss Stoddard, have you told anyone of your suspicions?"

"No, no one."

"Not even Mr. John Fulham?"

"Mr. Fulham was my father's friend. I felt I needed the advice of an impartial listener."

"A wise conclusion. Continue to maintain your silence until I speak to you again." Holmes walked across the room to pick up a small leather writing desk to be held on the lap; he handed it to our visitor. "Beneath the hinged lid you will find pen and paper," he said as he removed the cap of the inkwell. "I want you to write the addresses of yourself, your fiancé, Monsieur Piaget, and Mr. John Fulham. Business addresses as well as residential, if you please."

"I believe Monsieur Piaget stops at a hotel when he is in London," she said, "but I fear I don't know which one."

"Very well, only the business address for him."

I moved over to stand behind Amy Stoddard as she bent to her task. Her handwriting was a graceful, well-formed calligraphy, attaining a level of elegance without resorting to curlicues or other forms of gaudy ornamentation. It was not difficult to understand why her father had wanted her to copy his correspondence.

I could see that Holmes too appreciated the beauty of her penmanship when she handed him her list of addresses. "What should I do, Mr. Holmes?" she asked. "I pray that my suspicions of Thomas are without valid foundation, but the two circumstances of the steamship ticket and the wording of that passage have been some cause of alarm to me. Am I being unjust to Thomas?"

"I hope to have the answer to that before too many more days have passed, Miss Stoddard. For now, I advise you to remain at home with the doors locked. Invent some pretext for not seeing Mr. Wickham until next we speak. And make certain the servants are instructed not to admit him to the house."

Her mouth trembled. "Do you think I am in danger?"

"I think that is quite likely. Return home immediately, and do not leave until I call on you." He noticed how shaken she was and added, "Miss Stoddard, we will get to the bottom of this matter. That I promise you."

Slightly reassured, she bid us a faint-voiced farewell. I accompanied her to the street and secured a cab for her; when I returned, Holmes was standing by the fireplace lighting his pipe. "Well, Holmes, what do you make of that?"

25

"Tell me your impression," he countered.

I shrugged. "A young, vulnerable heiress, alone in the world . . . easy prey for an unscrupulous suitor."

"And yet her father approved the marriage."

"Fathers have made mistakes before." I warmed my hands at the fire. "This Wickham sounds like a rascal of the first order."

"He does indeed. But what a curious course of action he has chosen to pursue." Holmes sat down in one of the armchairs by the fireplace. "The penniless youngest son of a viscount so desirous of obtaining money that he is willing to alienate his family over the issue. He goes into a respectable trade. He courts and wins the hand of an attractive young heiress." Holmes pointed his pipe at me. "Why not stop there? He has what he wants. Why proceed with this deception of the disguised handwriting? And why book passage on the *Mary Small*? Unless Piaget truly was mistaken."

I took the other armchair. "Perhaps something happened that forced him to change his plans."

"Quite possibly. But let us proceed with caution, Watson. We know none of these people—a circumstance we set out to rectify early tomorrow morning. We will begin, I think, by inspecting the business premises of Wickham and Piaget, Wine Merchants."

As it turned out, we did not begin with Wickham and Piaget after all. My earache had returned in a most raging intensity; and after a near-sleepless night I arose early and dressed. I had carelessly failed to replace my special mixture of oils and medicinal herbs that I have found to be the most efficacious treatment of otalgia.

"You are going out before we have breakfasted?" Holmes asked in surprise.

"Just to Crawford Street," I replied. "I need to pay our Mr. Curtis a visit."

Holmes understood immediately. "Oh, my dear fellow! The walk to Chatterby's brought back your earache! And I insisted. . . . I am responsible for your discomfort!"

"Nonsense, Holmes. I could have refused to walk. I did not."

"Sit down, Watson. No, no argument! I will go to Mr. Curtis's establishment and procure your medication myself. Do not protest so, Watson. I am going, and that's the end of the matter." He hurried off to his room to dress.

I sank down gratefully into my chair by the fire. Damned decent of Holmes, when it was my own fault for not refilling my prescription. Physician, heal thyself indeed.

Holmes was gone in a trice, and soon after there came a knock at the door. It was Mrs. Hudson, with a tray.

"Mr. Holmes said he would eat shortly, but I was to bring you your breakfast straightaway," she informed me.

"Thank you, Mrs. Hudson," I said as she put down the tray. "Bananas and cream? Wherever did you find ripe bananas this time of year?"

"Oh, they ripen on the boat, Dr. Watson. We should be having bananas all year round now, the greengrocer tells me. Some new trade agreement with one of those places in South America."

What excellent news. When she'd gone I poured my first cup of tea of the day and immediately began to feel better. The bananas and cream were a delicious accompaniment to the porridge, the only proper meal with which to begin a cold winter day. Kippers and kidneys are all very well, but they don't coat the stomach lining the way a good bowl of porridge does.

I was just finishing my third cup of tea when Mrs. Hudson once again appeared at the door. "It's one of *them*," she said with disapproval. "Urgent, he says."

I knew whom she meant. "Send him in."

In came one of the street urchins Holmes frequently employed as errand runners and observers. This one was unfamiliar to me. "Mr. Holmes is not here," I said.

"It was Mr. Holmes wot sent me," the lad replied. "He says you're to come quick like, 'cause Mr. Curtis, the chemist—somebody's done murdered him."

"Good heavens!" I cried, rising hastily. Mr. Curtis, murdered? I found a tuppence piece in my pocket and gave it to the boy. "Run along, now."

"Thankee, gov'nor," he said with a big grin. He started to leave but stopped. "Ow, I'm forgetting." He pulled a small package out from under his jacket. "Mr. Holmes says give you this."

It was my earache medicine. I shooed the boy out and warmed

the oil at the fireplace before doctoring myself. I stuffed my ear with a piece of cotton batting, wrapped my muffler over my head, and set out for Mr. Curtis's shop. I was halfway to Crawford Street before it occurred to me to wonder how Holmes was able to have my prescription made up when the chemist lay dead.

The entrance to the shop was barred by a burly peeler until Inspector Lestrade appeared and instructed him to let me in. "How did it happen, Lestrade?" I asked. "Could it have been self-inflicted?"

"He was shot, Doctor. And it can't have been suicide, because there's no gun to be found."

Conclusive. "Who found his body?"

"His clerk, who summoned us. We arrived only a few moments before Mr. Holmes came strolling in."

"Watson," Holmes called from where he was standing by the body, "come take a look, will you?"

Curtis lay on the floor not behind his counter, but sprawled in front of a display of dental hygiene appliances. I knelt beside his body and examined the two bullet wounds, one in his chest and one in his head. "Small-bore pistol," I said. "Someone wanted to make sure he was dead. Either shot was enough to kill him."

"The chest shot?" Holmes asked.

"Without a postmortem dissection, I can't be positive. But it looks to me as if the bullet penetrated the heart."

Holmes nodded, satisfied. "You've questioned the clerk, Lestrade?"

"As well as I could," the policeman said. "He's too shocked to make much sense. Look at him."

We all looked over to where the clerk stood huddled in the corner, guarded by another peeler. He was shaking, and his mouth was moving soundlessly. His eyes traveled everywhere except to the body on the floor.

"Nevertheless, we must try," Holmes said. The three of us approached the cowering clerk, who shrank even farther into his corner. "What's his name?"

"Grimes," said Lestrade.

"Come, Grimes, you must pull yourself together," Holmes said briskly. "Your employer has been murdered this dark day, and we need to ask you questions."

"I didn't kill him!" the clerk blurted out.

"Of course you didn't," Holmes replied in a matter-of-fact tone. "Has anyone accused you?"

"Not yet." Grimes glared at Lestrade. "But they will."

Lestrade scowled. "Why do you say that?"

"Because you will find out. . . . I am telling you now, so you can't say I tried to keep it from you."

"Keep *what* from us?"

The clerk swallowed hard and muttered, "Four years in Newgate Prison. For thieving. Mr. Curtis was the only one who was willing to give me a chance at an honest job. He said I was quick to learn and I kept myself clean, and if the till ever came up short he'd box my ears for me! But it never did. I never stole from Mr. Curtis, not in all the six years I've been working here. And I didn't kill him! Why would I kill the only man who's ever been decent to me?"

"Why indeed," Holmes murmured. "Now, my good man, no one is going to haul you back to Newgate Prison. But perhaps you can help us find the killer."

Grimes looked puzzled. "How?"

"Tell us first of all if Curtis had any personal enemies."

The clerk shook his head vigorously. "Not Mr. Curtis, no, sir. He was one of them people that everybody likes."

"The very impression I had of him," Holmes remarked. "What about business rivals?"

"None that I know of. We're the only chemist's shop hereabouts."

"And the business itself? Prospering?"

"Oh, yes, sir, doing very well. Mr. Curtis, he gave me a rise just last month."

"And was your employer worried about anything these past few weeks?"

Grimes squinted his eyes and stuck his tongue in the corner of his mouth, thinking back. "If he was, he kept it to hisself. He seemed the same as usual to me."

"No more than I expected," Holmes said with something like

a sigh. "Thank you, Grimes . . . you've been most helpful."

The three of us left him and stepped outside into the cold sunshine. Lestrade jerked his head back toward the shop. "What about that Grimes, Mr. Holmes? What do you think?"

"Oh, the man is clearly innocent," Holmes replied indifferently. "You would be much better advised to direct your investigations toward the Paddington Merchants Association and, more specifically, to their Christmas Charities Fund."

"I gave to that Fund," Lestrade commented, surprised. "What about it?"

"Curtis suspected that someone was stealing from the Fund, or perhaps was planning to abscond with the entire account. I have no details to give you, but perhaps Curtis confided his suspicions to someone else. Was he married?"

"Eh? Er, yes, he was married."

"Then Mrs. Curtis would seem the logical person to ask first, would she not? Once she has had sufficient opportunity to absorb the shock of her husband's untimely death."

Lestrade was nodding. "That's a good notion, Mr. Holmes. I thank you for pointing out that line of inquiry."

"My pleasure, Lestrade." Holmes took one final look back at the body on the floor. "I am sorry about Curtis." Then he turned on his heel and strode off down the street.

Lestrade and I exchanged a look and I hurried off after Holmes. "Didn't Amy Stoddard say that Thomas Wickham was involved in the administration of the Christmas Charities Fund?" I inquired of my companion. "Could he possibly be the one Curtis suspected?"

"If he is," Holmes replied, "then he is most likely a murderer as well. We cannot allow that young girl to enter into a marriage with a killer. Are you feeling well enough to accompany me to the establishment of Wickham and Piaget? How is your earache?"

"Considerably abated," I said truthfully. "In fact, it is almost gone. I say, Holmes, how were you able to obtain the medicine? That clerk Grimes was in no condition to mix the oils and the herbs."

"Oh, I looked in Curtis's prescription drawer and found the directions you'd written out. I mixed your concoction myself. I must say it has a most pleasing aroma."

I stopped walking in astonishment. "You mixed the prescription?"

He waved a hand dismissively. "A simple matter. Shall we proceed to York Place? There we should find a coachman and a sturdy horse to take us to our destination."

Amy Stoddard's list told us that Wickham and Piaget's business establishment was located in Coldharbor Lane, which we were surprised to learn was in the center of one of the less desirable sections of London. The streets were narrow and dirty, the cheaply constructed buildings old and shabby. Small groups of presumably unemployed men crowded around metal drums in which they'd built fires. Our coachman was only too happy to discharge his passengers and be on his way.

The rough-looking men warming themselves at the fires eyed Holmes's and my clothing and muttered among themselves. There was not a woman or child in sight anywhere; I could see only groups of hardened men with no money and with time on their hands. I grew uneasy, wondering if we were safe here. Holmes walked confidently ahead down Coldharbor Lane, seemingly oblivious to his surroundings; but I knew his keen eye had taken in every detail.

Our search took us to a heavily padlocked warehouse. "Is this what we're looking for?" I asked. "Did Miss Stoddard not understand we wanted the address of the offices, not the warehouse?"

"One moment." Holmes darted around to the side of the warehouse and a moment later called out, "Here, Watson!"

I followed. He had discovered a narrow door upon which hung a sign proclaiming **Wickham & Piaget. Fine Wines.**

"Surely these are not the offices!" I exclaimed.

"Let us find out." Holmes tried the door, which opened onto a narrow ascending staircase. Another door at the top of the stair was locked. Holmes knocked.

I'd had in my mind that the suitor Mr. Stoddard had endorsed as his daughter's future husband would be an older man of some substance, with visible signs of his prosperity on display. The bad

31

neighborhood we found ourselves in had disabused me of my second assumption, and the opening door at the business premises of Wickham & Piaget dispelled the first.

"Yes, gentlemen?" The figure standing in the open doorway was slight, with reddish brown hair, and undeniably an Englishman . . . not Piaget. And he was young, no more than twenty-three or twenty-four.

"Mr. Thomas Wickham? My name is Sherlock Holmes and this is Dr. Watson. May we have a few moments of your time?"

Young Wickham's expression showed he was familiar with Holmes's reputation. "Certainly, Mr. Holmes. Please do come in. Is there some way I may assist you?"

The offices were makeshift, occupying an enclosed partial floor with a large window overlooking the warehouse below. I could see crates of wine in neatly stacked rows, plus a few larger wooden crates that appeared not yet to have been opened.

"Do you own a pistol?" Holmes snapped out.

Wickham looked startled by the question but answered willingly enough. "We keep a pistol here in the offices." He smiled wryly. "I'm sure it did not escape your notice that this is not the safest of neighborhoods."

"Then why do you remain here?"

The young man's eyes showed a flicker of irritation but he retained his courteous manner. "Financial necessity, Mr. Holmes. My partner and I had only a small amount to invest in our new business. We had a choice to make. We could lease elegant offices and present a good face to the world, but then we would be forced to import only cheap wines with the money we had left. We decided instead to build a reputation first as merchants who can be relied upon always to deliver quality wines. The elegant offices can come later. Now, Mr. Holmes, will you please tell me why I am being questioned?"

"First, the pistol. Where is it?"

He looked as if he were about to protest, but he went to a desk and pulled open a desk drawer. He made a sound of surprise and started opening other drawers. "It is not here! I don't understand."

"I think I do," Holmes murmured. "Tell me, you are acquainted with a chemist named Curtis?"

"Yes, indeed. Mr. Curtis is a member of the Merchants Association committee that administers the Christmas Charities Fund."

"A committee of which you are also a member."

"My partner and I both are members."

"Piaget also?"

"Piaget assumed the duties of another member who recently passed away."

"Mr. Stoddard, you mean."

Wickham looked more puzzled than ever. "You are correct. Mr. Holmes, I really must insist upon an explanation."

Holmes's dark eyes bored into his. "Curtis was murdered early this morning. A pistol shot to the heart and another to the head."

Wickham staggered. "Mr. Curtis . . . is dead?" After a long moment, he sank into the nearest chair and buried his head in his hands. A minute or so later he raised a tormented face and said hoarsely, "Oh, Mr. Holmes, you don't know what doleful news you bring me! I . . . my father and I are estranged. I have often suffered from the lack of his sage advice." He ran one hand nervously through his reddish brown hair. "But when I first joined the Merchants Association, two older men welcomed me and encouraged me, even directing new business my way. Without even knowing they were doing so, they took the place of the father that is lost to me. And now . . . now they are both gone!"

Stoddard and Curtis. I moved over next to him. "I am sorry, Mr. Wickham."

He acknowledged my sympathy with a nod. "Was it a burglary?" he asked.

"Nothing was taken," Holmes replied, watching Wickham narrowly. "It was a heartless, deliberate murder."

"But why?" Wickham cried, rising shakily from his chair. "Mr. Curtis was the kindest-hearted of men! Who would want him dead?"

"The man who was stealing from the Christmas Charities Fund," Holmes answered with a cold deliberation.

Wickham looked dumbfounded. "Stealing? From the Christmas Fund? Who?"

"Do you not know?"

"I? No! Are you certain there has been a theft of funds?"

"Not I," Holmes replied. "But Curtis suspected someone of chicanery. And that seems to be the only reason for removing him from the scene. Our Mr. Curtis was a threat to someone's continuing safety."

"Oh, dear God!"

I asked, "Curtis said nothing of this to you?"

"Nothing! Oh, the poor man!"

Holmes changed his tack. "Monsieur Piaget is not present, I see. Where may we find him?"

Wickham had to force himself to concentrate on the question. "He is presently stopping at the Red Lion near Piccadilly Circus. But he sails to Bordeaux tomorrow."

"Aboard the *Mary Small*?"

Wickham was beyond further surprise. "If you already know the answer, why do you ask the question? Yes, he has passage on the *Mary Small*. Is there something ominous in that?"

"Well," I began, "he did say he saw—"

"Watson." Holmes's voice cut me off. "Mr. Wickham, I daresay we will meet again. But we will leave you now." Without further ado he opened the door and started down the stairway. I cast a glance at the stricken young man whose peace of mind we had disturbed, murmured something, and closed the door behind me as I left.

Holmes was waiting for me in Coldharbor Lane. "Well," he said with an air of exasperation, "that is the most likable young murderer I have ever encountered. Ethical, industrious, respectful. Did you notice his hands, Watson? Heavily callused. Our wine merchants cannot afford to pay warehouse workers. Young Mr. Wickham has been doing the heavy labor of loading and unloading crates himself."

"Do you still think he is a murderer?" I asked. "Surely his grief over Curtis's death was genuine."

"Either that, or that young man more properly belongs in the Lyceum as a member of Sir Henry Irving's company of players."

"Do you think he was acting?"

Holmes did not answer immediately. "Curious," he finally said. "I knew instantly this morning that Curtis's clerk Grimes was not acting. Yet with Wickham, I could not be certain. He seemed truly distressed—yet we cannot ignore what we know about him. The *Mary Small*, the passage he had Miss Stoddard copy in her father's handwriting."

"Holmes, why did you stop me from mentioning that Piaget said he'd seen a steamship ticket lying on Wickham's desk?"

"Ah, my friend, because the only way we would know about that was if we'd heard it from Miss Amy Stoddard. And we don't want Wickham knowing we'd visited him on her behalf, do we? Not so long as there is the slightest chance that she is in danger from him."

"Oh. Of course. You're right."

"Now, where are we?" We'd left Coldharbor Lane, but there was not a hansom cab in sight. "Let's try down this way." He strode off at a brisk pace. "Watson, we must divide our efforts at this point. Do you think you could learn from Inspector Lestrade whether Curtis had told his wife whom he suspected of pilfering from the Christmas Fund?"

"Yes, certainly."

"Good. When you have done that, return to Baker Street and dose your ear with more of that sweet-smelling oil. I shall be along later and we can share what we have learned."

"Where are you going?"

"To the Red Lion in Picadilly. Monsieur Piaget and I are due for a little chat."

I returned to Baker Street in a state of nervous excitement. Lestrade had related to me that Curtis had not told his wife the name of the man he suspected, but had instead referred to him only as a wine merchant. Ah! Wickham or Piaget? There was no real question. I was convinced that Wickham's grief over Curtis's death was authentic and not simply a performance staged for our benefit. Piaget was the villain we were seeking.

It was teatime before Holmes made his appearance. When I told him what I had learned from Lestrade, he nodded thoughtfully. "I myself have discovered a matter that would support your somewhat emotional declaration of Wickham's innocence."

"Indeed? What did Piaget have to say?"

"I did not speak to him. Monsieur Piaget is no longer stopping at the Red Lion. He settled his account this morning and told the innkeeper he was returning to France."

I frowned. "But Wickham said Piaget was sailing tomorrow, on the twenty-third."

"And Piaget said the steamship ticket he saw on Wickham's desk was made out for the twenty-third."

I shook my head in confusion. "I don't understand."

"Nor did I," Holmes admitted. "One of the two men was clearly lying. That there is a ticket for passage aboard the *Mary Small* on the twenty-third of December, there is no doubt. But which one of them bought it? It was essential to find out. So I paid a visit to the steamship ticket offices."

"Excellent, Holmes!"

"There I had a stroke of luck. The Kerward line, which owns the *Mary Small*, is not a large company, as steamship lines go, and only one ticket-seller is employed for the entire line. He is a most agreeable fellow who told me straightaway that yes, he had sold a ticket for December twenty-third on the *Mary Small* . . . to one Thomas Wickham."

"*What?*" I was so startled that I spilled my tea.

Holmes handed me a napkin. "I questioned him closely, but he showed me the passenger list and Wickham's name was right there. That seemed to settle the matter, but then the good man said, ' 'Oi remember 'im all roight, Mr. 'Olmes. Oi couldn't hardly maike out wot 'e was saiyin', with that frog accent an' all.' "

I put down my cup. "A French accent?"

"Indeed. So I asked him if Wickham was thin, clean-shaven, and with hair that was a reddish brown. He answered no, he was average-sized and had black hair and a mustache."

"It must have been Piaget," I gasped. "He bought the ticket in Wickham's name!"

"Exactly, Watson. And now we have a rough description of what Monsieur Piaget looks like. But where is he? There are dark enterprises afoot, Watson, of which we have caught only glimpses. I fear Miss Stoddard may be in even graver danger than first I anticipated."

"But not from Wickham," I insisted. "It's clear Piaget's purpose was to make Miss Stoddard suspicious of her fiancé. First he buys the steamship ticket in Wickham's name, and then he tells her a lie about seeing the ticket on Wickham's desk. Surely Wickham is exonerated?"

"Only half-exonerated. There is still the curious passage that Wickham had Miss Stoddard copy in her father's hand."

I poured us both another cup of tea. "Yes, alas, there is still that."

Holmes ignored the tea and began to pace. "Doesn't anything strike you as peculiar about that passage, Watson? 'It is my intent that the governance of my affairs be placed in the hands of one who is most qualified to oversee them,' " he quoted from memory. "A simple declaration of intent, followed by: 'Determining who that person is has occupied much of my attention during the past year.' A statement of what he has done toward realizing that intent. But where is the conclusion? He names no one, he specifies no instructions for how his wishes are to be carried out. Don't you see it, Watson? What Miss Stoddard copied was merely an excerpt from a longer document!"

I failed to see his point. "But to what purpose?"

"A test, Watson! It was a test! To see if she could indeed reproduce her father's eccentric writing!" Holmes pulled up a chair close to mine and perched on the edge. "The plan is to come up with a document, perhaps a will, that was written *after* the will that leaves Mr. Stoddard's entire estate to his daughter. It is a plot to disinherit Amy Stoddard! But how ironic! The villain is thwarted in his plan by a species of penmanship that no one can either read or reproduce—*except* the very person he is trying to rob of her inheritance!"

I looked him directly in the eye. "Are we speaking of Piaget or Wickham?"

"Aha! That's the puzzle, isn't it! Since Piaget tried to discredit Wickham with his lie about the steamship ticket, perhaps he had designs on Miss Stoddard himself and was trying to eliminate the competition? Yet it was Wickham who asked Miss Stoddard to copy the excerpt from the new will, not Piaget."

"But Wickham has no need to disinherit the young lady. She has promised to marry him."

"Perhaps he fears she will change her mind. Piaget may be nothing more than an underhanded suitor who is now crawling back home, defeated, having lost the lady to his partner and rival. I was careless, Watson. I should have recognized Piaget's story about the steamship ticket as a lie the moment I heard it."

"How so?"

Holmes leaned forward from the edge of his chair. "Put yourself into a real situation similar to that fabricated by Piaget. Say you make a social gaffe by mentioning to Miss Stoddard that you saw Wickham's steamship ticket. She is astounded! 'Why, what do you mean?' she cries. 'He is spending Christmas Eve with me!' " Holmes's eye gleamed. "Now, Watson—what do you say?"

I raised my eyebrows at him. "I say I must be mistaken."

"And? What else?"

What else? "That I'm sorry."

"And?"

The man really could be exasperating. "And . . . nothing else! I was mistaken and I'm sorry. That's all."

"Exactly!" Holmes cried in triumph. "You say *nothing else.* You do not, for example, name the ship. Nor do you casually let slip the day of the month on which that ship is scheduled to weigh anchor. Piaget wanted to plant a doubt in Miss Stoddard's mind. He wanted her to know the ship and the date . . . in the hope that she would check at the ticket office and find young Wickham's name on the passenger list!"

"Ah, I see!" What a wicked thing for Piaget to have done. "But instead of going to the ticket office, she came to you."

He sat back in his chair, a satisfied smile on his face. "Precisely. Piaget may have had some additional depraved plan in mind, to culminate before the twenty-third of the month—in addition to pilfering from the Christmas Fund. But if all his plotting were to fail, he has ready and waiting a steamship ticket through which he can effect his escape."

Now it was I who leaned forward in my chair. "So you *do* believe in Wickham's innocence?"

"It would appear that Wickham has been more the victim of a deception than the perpetrator of it—except for that one unexplained detail. It was Wickham who had Miss Stoddard copy the excerpt from what has every appearance of being a fraudulent will. Piaget did not do that, Watson."

Nor did he. There was no explaining that away.

It was almost dark when we left shortly after for Grosvenor Square, where Mr. John Fulham maintained a residence. "Mr. Fulham is in a position to verify or refute one detail of Thomas Wickham's story," Holmes said as we rode in the brougham we had hired for the evening. "He will know whether his good friend Stoddard stood *in loco parentis* for the young man or not."

John Fulham was a handsome man in his mid-fifties who welcomed us cordially. When Holmes said he had been consulted by Miss Amy Stoddard, Fulham was immediately concerned.

"Is she having difficulties?" he asked worriedly. "I have been trying to watch out for her as well as I can, for her dear father's sake as well as her own."

"You and Stoddard were close friends?"

"Yes, quite close. We knew each other for near to thirty years. But why did Amy consult you, Mr. Holmes?"

"She was experiencing a few last-minute doubts about her fiancé," Holmes answered glibly. Not a total untruth. "That is why I am here, Mr. Fulham. You are, of course, acquainted with Mr. Thomas Wickham."

"I am." Was there a note of disapproval in his voice?

We were seated in an attractive drawing room, drinking the best glass of sherry I had tasted in many a month. Mr. Fulham wore his success easily, a man used to living well.

Holmes said, "Mr. Wickham claims that Mr. Stoddard took him under his wing when the former joined the Merchants Association. Is that true?"

"Yes, he and Curtis both became his mentors." Fulham suddenly frowned. "That is a terrible business about poor Curtis. The *Times* claims the police are baffled as to who could have killed him and why."

"For the moment," Holmes said. "That will soon change, I warrant. But you say both Stoddard and Curtis did help young Wickham to establish himself in business."

"That they did." Our host sighed deeply. "I'll confess, Mr.

Holmes, that they saw something in Wickham that I could never
see. Do you know where he maintains his offices? In a neighborhood I would not venture into even in broad daylight!"

I coughed.

"A young merchant just starting out cannot be expected to
maintain fully appointed offices, surely," Holmes said mildly.

"No, of course not. But there are certain standards to be maintained, standards that are endorsed by the Merchants Association,
I might add. But Wickham struck me as merely a well-mannered
opportunist willing to take advantage of two softhearted men in a
position to be of assistance to him." He shook his head. "I don't
know, Mr. Holmes. Perhaps I do the young man an injustice. I
have nothing to go on except my own instincts."

"And your instincts tell you . . . ?"

"That young Wickham is not to be trusted. As you may imagine,
I was not overjoyed when Stoddard informed me that Amy and
Wickham were to be wed."

"Did you attempt to dissuade him from permitting the union?"

"Only once. Stoddard made it quite clear that such argument
was unwelcome, and I never repeated the attempt."

There was something I had to ask. "Do you know, Mr. Fulham,
if Wickham's partner was equally interested in marrying Miss
Stoddard?"

"Piaget?" Fulham smiled. "That's not very likely, Dr. Watson,
not with a wife waiting for him in Bordeaux. Why do you ask?"

I felt my face redden. "I didn't know Piaget was married."

"For some years. It's my impression that he and Amy barely
know each other."

Holmes asked if Fulham had anything to do with the administering of the Christmas Charities Fund; Fulham said no. "One
final question, Mr. Fulham, if you don't mind, and then we'll leave
you in peace. If Amy Stoddard were your daughter, would you
forbid her to marry Thomas Wickham?"

"Forbid?" He thought about it. "No, she is of age. But what I
would do is find a way to persuade her to postpone the wedding
until I had consulted you, Mr. Holmes—to discover everything
about the young man that you possibly could."

Holmes nodded in acknowledgement. True to his word, he

asked no more questions. We bade Fulham good night and took our leave.

Back in our hired brougham, I said, "That was a curious interview. Fulham both cast doubts upon Wickham's character and verified his claim that Stoddard and Curtis had acted as his mentors."

"I am interested only in Fulham's facts," Holmes replied, "and they say that Wickham told the truth about Stoddard and Curtis. Mr. Fulham's opinions, on the other hand, we need not treat as of equal import. Now we shall pay a brief visit to Miss Stoddard, to inform her of what we have learned. And then our day's work will be done."

But when we reached the Stoddard house in Bayswater Road, we found something of a ruckus at the door. Thomas Wickham was pounding at the door, red-faced, agitated, the very picture of the frustrated lover. "Why will you not let me in, Amy?" he cried.

"She will not let you in, Mr. Wickham," Holmes said, stepping out of the brougham, "because I instructed her not to."

Wickham whirled around. "Mr. Holmes! Why are you here?"

"All in good time." He stepped up to the door. "Miss Stoddard! Are you there?"

"Mr. Holmes?" came her voice through the door. "Is that you?"

"It is I, and Dr. Watson is with me. You may open the door now."

We heard the sound of a bolt being drawn, and the door opened slightly and Amy Stoddard's worried young face peered out at us. "Is Thomas still there?"

"Amy!" he cried, and tried to push his way in.

I held him back. "All in good time," I admonished.

"You have nothing to fear, Miss Stoddard," Holmes reassured her. "I have one question to ask Mr. Wickham—to which I think I know the answer—and much should be made clear. May we come in?"

She stepped back from the doorway and permitted us to enter. Wickham was the very picture of misery; when he tried to approach his fiancée, she stepped back from him, uncertain how to react. She led us into a drawing room even more elegant than the one in Grosvenor Square that we had just left.

When the young people and I were seated, Holmes stood in

front of Wickham. "Now, sir. Recently you gave Miss Stoddard a brief passage to copy in her father's handwriting."

"Yes." He glanced fondly at the young woman. "And she did so perfectly."

"Why did you give her that particular passage?"

With an effort, Wickham tore his gaze from Miss Stoddard to look at Holmes. "Why, what was it? It was just something Piaget handed me. I didn't even read it."

"Aha! As I thought. And whose idea was it to discover whether Miss Stoddard could imitate her father's handwriting?"

Wickham frowned. "I believe Piaget first suggested it . . . but I thought it a splendid game. I had abandoned any hope of deciphering the draft of a letter Mr. Stoddard had left among his papers and announced my intention of asking Amy to read it for me. Piaget wondered if she could reproduce Mr. Stoddard's penmanship. He handed me a piece of paper and said to see if she could copy that. I slipped the paper into a pocket without looking at it."

"And that completes the picture!" Holmes said with a touch of smugness. "Now I pray you both listen very carefully. I have a great deal to tell you." He began with Curtis's murder and proceeded step by step through what we had learned that day. When it became clear that Wickham was the victim of a plot to discredit him in her eyes, Miss Stoddard gave a little cry and rushed to the side of her fiancé. "So I am happy to say," Holmes concluded, "that your father's judgement of Mr. Wickham was entirely correct."

I am not certain the two young people even heard him, so deeply were they involved in their reconciliation. Holmes gestured to me, and we left the house quietly.

I could not resist. "Are you quite certain that it is safe to leave her alone with him?"

"Oh, no doubt of it, Watson! Mr. Wickham is an admirable young man, and I have every confidence their union will be a long and happy one." He pretended not to see me smiling at him.

We had one more call to make that night. We informed Inspector Lestrade that a Frenchman named Etienne Piaget had shot and killed Mr. Curtis with a pistol taken from the business premises of Wickham & Piaget, wine merchants, and that he could most likely be apprehended aboard the *Mary Small* before it sailed the next day.

We were sitting down to our midday meal on the day of the twenty-third when an enormous clamor erupted outside our door; we could hear a frenzied voice calling out Holmes's name. Holmes opened the door to a wild-eyed Wickham and an upset Mrs. Hudson pleading with him to desist. Holmes reassured the housekeeper and drew the young man inside.

"She is gone, Mr. Holmes! Taken from her room during the night! Amy has been abducted!"

"Calm yourself, Wickham. Did the servants summon the police?"

His eyes darted back and forth between us. "They did not even know she was missing until I arrived—they assumed she was still sleeping since she had not left her room! Mr. Holmes, what are we to do?"

Holmes slumped down disconsolately on a chair. "And I was arrogant enough to think this affair was concluded! How did her abductors get into the house?"

"I don't know!"

"Think back. In what condition was her room?"

"In disarray. A chair was overturned, a vase was broken—Amy fought them." He choked back a sob. "Glass! There was window glass on the floor!"

"So they knew which room was hers. At least one of the blackguards was familiar with the house." He rose and began to pace. "I blame myself. I should never have left her there as long as Piaget is at large. But this latest escapade is senseless! What could he hope to gain? A forced marriage is out of the question, since he already has a—" Suddenly he broke off and stopped dead in his tracks, his eyes wide and his mouth open.

"Holmes?" I said.

"I am a fool!" he shouted. He struck his forehead with the palm of his hand. "An utter fool!" He whirled toward Wickham. "Go immediately to the police and ask for Inspector Lestrade. Tell him Amy Stoddard is being held prisoner in the house of John Fulham in Grosvenor Square."

"Fulham!"

"Go now! Not a moment is to be wasted!"

Wickham left at a run. "Fulham abducted her?" I said incredulously.

"Or had her abducted. Watson, bring your pistol. We must make all haste."

Snow had begun to fall. Unfortunately, we had discharged our hired brougham the night before and thus wasted precious minutes finding a hansom cab. Holmes urged the driver to utmost speed.

"But why Fulham?" I asked as the horse did its best through the snowy streets. "Why do you conclude he is Miss Stoddard's abductor?"

"Watson, do you remember the young lady's words in her narration of the chance encounter with Piaget at the Lyceum Theatre? She said: 'I introduced him to Mr. Fulham.' If the two men were meeting for the first time...then how did Fulham know Piaget has a wife in Bordeaux?"

"Good God!" I exclaimed. "You are right!"

"That was no chance meeting," Holmes continued. "It was arranged by the two men, so Piaget could make his gaffe about the steamship ticket. Don't you see, Watson? It's not Piaget who wanted to marry our young heiress—it was Fulham! Piaget is merely his henchman." Holmes's mouth was bitter. "Her father's 'friend.'"

"But Piaget did kill Curtis?"

"Oh, yes. Piaget is a scurrilous fellow who can pass up no opportunity to line his pockets, and Curtis was getting too close to the truth. Fulham must have been furious with his accomplice. To risk the larger reward to gain a lesser? Inexcusable. But Fulham evidently concluded that his plan to separate the two young lovers had less chance of success than he'd anticipated, so he abandoned it in favor of another plan. Compel Amy Stoddard to forge a new will in her father's handwriting, naming Fulham administrator of Stoddard's estate. It would be a license to steal."

We were both silent a moment, thinking our separate thoughts. I said, "After Amy Stoddard does what Fulham wants, what happens to her then?"

Holmes's face was grim. "Yes, what happens to her then? Fulham can hardly leave her alive to bear witness against him. I only hope we are not too late."

At last we reached Grosvenor Square. We dismissed the hansom cab and approached Fulham's house cautiously. "A ladder was needed to reach Miss Stoddard's room," Holmes said. "Let us see if we can find it." We made our way to the rear, looking through the half-open drapes into the ground floor of the building; no one was in sight.

The ladder was there. Fulham's house had an attic, but the ladder reached only to the first story. Holmes chose a window at random and we put the ladder in place. It was unnerving, climbing that slippery ladder with the wind and the snow blowing in our faces, but we reached the top without mishap. Holmes turned his face away and used his elbow to break the glass.

Inside, we found ourselves in what appeared to be a guest bedchamber. We paused a moment, long enough to ascertain that the sound of breaking glass had not been heard elsewhere in the house. Then we began a systematic search of the rooms on that floor. Once a servant appeared carrying bed linens, but we stepped quickly into one of the rooms and avoided detection.

Holmes silently pointed upward. We located the backstairs leading to the attic. We tested each step before putting our weight on it. At the top was a door that Holmes opened cautiously; it led to an attic room like any other attic room, full of trunks and boxes and semi-discarded items. At the far end was another door. I drew my pistol.

Just as we reached the second door, we heard a scream. "Never!" cried Amy Stoddard's muffled voice from the other side of the door. "I'll never do it!"

Holmes threw open the door. "Unhand her, you blackguards!" he cried.

Amy Stoddard lay huddled on the floor, with John Fulham and a black-haired man with a full mustache bending over her. Upon our entry, the latter immediately pulled a pistol from his pocket—but with a bound, Holmes was upon him before he could fire.

I pointed my own pistol at John Fulham. "If you value your life, Fulham," I said, "you will not move." He stood motionless, shock and disbelief written on his handsome face.

I risked a glance toward the two struggling men. At last Holmes succeeded in disarming his opponent.

"*Chien d'un chien!*" his adversary spat.

"And to you as well, Monsieur Piaget," Holmes replied, panting slightly from his exertions. Pointing Piaget's own pistol at him, Holmes knelt by the recumbent girl. "Miss Stoddard! Are you able to stand?"

"Oh, Mr. Holmes!" she cried. "Never have I been so happy to see someone!" With Holmes's assistance, she struggled to her feet. "*He*," she declared, pointing an accusing finger at John Fulham, "was trying to force me to write a new will in my father's hand!"

"But you resisted," Holmes said, "giving us the time to learn of your abduction and to take action. You have much courage, Miss Stoddard. You, Piaget! Go stand by your . . . master."

The Frenchman muttered under his breath but took his place at Fulham's side.

"And you, John Fulham, what do you have to say for yourself?"

Fulham had had time to think of a defense. "It was what Stoddard wanted," he said with a tremor in his voice. "He told me so. But he died before he could write the new will."

"Oh, that's to be your excuse, is it?" Holmes said with a sneer. He stepped up close to the other man. "Fulham, you are a truly despicable example of humanity. To betray a friendship of nearly thirty years' standing because your greed knows no bounds? Unthinkable! And to do so in such a loathsome way, by persecuting the innocent! It is our duty to protect our young, not exploit them. John Fulham, you are little more than a brute. I cannot begin to express my contempt for you!"

Personally, I thought he'd done quite well at expressing his contempt; but before I could say anything, an uproar broke out belowstairs. Leaving me to guard the two villains, Holmes went to the top of the stairs and shouted down to come to the attic.

In a trice Lestrade and Wickham were crowding into the attic room where Amy Stoddard had been held against her will; Lestrade had brought a number of peelers with him, who wasted no time in hauling Fulham and Piaget away. Wickham had an arm wrapped about Miss Stoddard, furious at what had been done to her but simultaneously relieved that she was unharmed.

Lestrade asked, "Did they torture you, miss?"

"I was struck two or three times," she said, "but not tortured. They told me I would receive no food or drink until I complied with John Fulham's wishes."

The inspector shook his head. "You're fortunate Mr. Holmes was able to deduce where you'd been taken."

She looked at Holmes. "I owe him a debt I will never be able to repay." Her face clouded. "My father trusted John Fulham. He considered him an honorable man."

"Well, miss," Lestrade said. "Men of goodwill can be deceived by those who aren't."

"Why, Lestrade," Holmes said with a laugh, "you're a philosopher now?"

"No, Mr. Holmes, I'm just a policeman trying to do his job. Mr. Wickham here told me something of what's been happening, but details are missing. I take it you would not be averse to accompanying me and relating the whole story?"

"The pleasure," Holmes said expansively, "is truly all mine."

Many young ladies would take to their beds following so harrowing an experience; but Miss Amy Stoddard was planning a Christmas Eve dinner, and a Christmas Eve dinner she would have. She invited—nay, urged—Holmes and me to attend; we were happy to accept.

Ours was not a large party, only ten of us. The company was congenial, the food was good, and the wines were excellent— Wickham had seen to that. After we'd dined, we gathered in the vicinity of the open front door to listen to the carolers in the street.

Amy Stoddard placed a hand on Holmes's arm. "You made all this possible, Mr. Holmes. You gave me my life as a Christmas present."

Holmes tut-tutted. "You look happy, Miss Stoddard."

She laughed softly. "How could I not be happy? I'm with the man I am to marry, surrounded by old friends and new friends as well. Mr. Holmes and Dr. Watson—you are always welcome in this house. I will be grateful to both of you until my dying day." With a smile she glided away to join Wickham.

A servant moved among us with a tray filled with glasses of port.

"Well, Watson," Holmes said, taking a glass, "this is one of the most satisfying conclusions to our adventures within recent memory, would you not agree?"

"Most assuredly. You realize, do you not, that you yourself have acted *in loco parentis* for Miss Stoddard?"

"I? How so?"

"You gave her the protection her father was unable to provide."

Holmes smiled and lifted his glass. "Happy Christmas, my friend."

A Scandal in Winter

Gillian Linscott

At first Silver Stick and his Square Bear were no more to us than incidental diversions at the Hotel Edelweiss. The Edelweiss at Christmas and the new year was like a sparkling white desert island, or a very luxurious ocean liner sailing through snow instead of sea. There we were, a hundred people or so, cut off from the rest of the world, even from the rest of Switzerland, with only each other for entertainment and company. It was one of the only possible hotels to stay at in 1910 for this new fad of winter sporting. The smaller Berghaus across the way was not one of the possible hotels, so its dozen or so visitors hardly counted. As for the villagers in their wooden chalets with the cows living downstairs, they didn't count at all. Occasionally, on walks, Amanda and I would see them carrying in logs from neatly stacked woodpiles or carrying out forkfuls of warm soiled straw that sent columns of white steam into the blue air. They were part of the valley like the rocks and pine trees but they didn't ski or skate, so they had no place in our world—apart from the sleighs. There were two of those in the village. One, a sober affair drawn by a stolid bay cob with a few token bells on the harness, brought guests and their luggage from the nearest railway station. The other, the one that mattered to Amanda and me, was a streak of

49

black and scarlet, swift as the mountain wind, clamourous with silver bells, drawn by a sleek little honey-coloured Haflinger with a silvery mane and tail that matched the bells. A pleasure sleigh, with no purpose in life beyond amusing the guests at the Edelweiss. We'd see it drawn up in the trampled snow outside, the handsome young owner with his long whip and blonde moustache waiting patiently. Sometimes we'd be allowed to linger and watch as he helped in a lady and gentleman and adjusted the white fur rug over their laps. Then away they'd go, hissing and jingling through the snow, into the track through the pine forest. Amanda and I had been promised that, as a treat on New Year's Day, we would be taken for a ride in it. We looked forward to it more eagerly then Christmas.

But that was ten days away and until then we had to amuse ourselves. We skated on the rink behind the hotel. We waved goodbye to our father when he went off in the mornings with his skis and his guide. We sat on the hotel terrace drinking hot chocolate with blobs of cream on top while Mother wrote and read letters. When we thought Mother wasn't watching, Amanda and I would compete to see if we could drink all the chocolate so that the blob of cream stayed marooned at the bottom of the cup, to be eaten in luscious and impolite spoonfuls. If she glanced up and caught us, Mother would tell us not to be so childish, which, since Amanda was eleven and I was nearly thirteen, was fair enough, but we had to get what entertainment we could out of the chocolate. The truth was that we were all of us, most of the time, bored out of our wits. Which was why we turned our attention to the affairs of the other guests and Amanda and I had our ears permanently tuned to the small dramas of the adults' conversation.

'I still can't believe she will.'

'Well, that's what the headwaiter said, and he should know. She's reserved the table in the corner overlooking the terrace and said they should be sure to have the Tokay.'

'The same table as last year.'

'The same wine, too.'

Our parents looked at each other over the croissants, carefully not noticing the maid as she poured our coffee. ('One doesn't notice the servants, dear, it only makes them awkward.')

'I'm sure it's not true. Any woman with any feeling . . . .'

'What makes you think she has any?'

Silence, as eye signals went on over our heads. I knew what was being signalled, just as I'd known what was being discussed in an overheard scrap of conversation between our parents at bedtime the night we arrived. ' . . . effect it might have on Jessica.'

My name. I came rapidly out of drowsiness, kept my eyes closed but listened.

'I don't think we need worry about that. Jessica's tougher than you think.' My mother's voice. She needed us to be tough so that she didn't have to waste time worrying about us.

'All the same, she must remember it. It is only a year ago. That sort of experience can mark a child for life.'

'Darling, they don't react like we do. They're much more callous at that age.'

Even with eyes closed I could tell from the quality of my father's silence that he wasn't convinced, but it was no use arguing with Mother's certainties. They switched the light off and closed the door. For a minute or two I lay awake in the dark wondering whether I was marked for life by what I'd seen and how it would show, then I wondered instead whether I'd ever be able to do pirouettes on the ice like the girl from Paris, and fell asleep in a wistful dream of bells and the hiss of skates.

The conversation between our parents that breakfast time over what she would or wouldn't do was interrupted by the little stir of two other guests being shown to their table. Amanda caught my eye.

'Silver Stick and his Square Bear are going ski-ing.'

Both gentlemen—elderly gentlemen as it seemed to us, but they were probably no older than their late fifties—were wearing heavy wool jumpers, tweed breeches, and thick socks, just as Father was. He nodded to them across the tables, wished them good morning and received nods and good-mornings back. Even the heavy sports clothing couldn't take away the oddity and distinction from the tall man. He was, I think, the thinnest person I'd ever seen. He didn't stoop as so many tall older people did but walked upright and lightly. His face with its eagle's beak of a nose was deeply tanned, like some of the older inhabitants of the village, but unlike them it was without wrinkles apart from two deep folds from the nose to the corners of his mouth. His hair was what had struck us most. It clung smoothly to his head in a cap of pure and polished silver, like the knob on an expensive walking stick. His companion, large and square shouldered in any case, looked more so in his ski-ing clothes. He shambled and tended to trip over chairs. He had a round, amiable face with pale, rather watery eyes, a clipped grey moustache but no more than a fringe of hair left on his gleaming pate. He always smiled at us when we met on the terrace or in corridors and appeared kindly. We'd noticed that he was always doing things for Silver Stick, pouring his coffee, posting his letters. For this reason we'd got it into our heads that Square Bear was Silver Stick's keeper. Amanda said Silver Stick probably went mad at the full moon and Square Bear had to lock him up and sing loudly so that people wouldn't hear his howling. She kept asking people when the next full moon would be, but so far nobody knew. I thought he'd probably come to Switzerland because he was dying of consumption, which explained the thinness, and Square Bear was his doctor. I listened for a coughing fit to confirm this, but so far there'd been not a sign of one. As they settled to their breakfast we watched as much as we could without being rebuked for staring. Square Bear opened the paper that had been lying beside his plate and read things out to Silver Stick, who gave the occasional little nod over his coffee, as if he'd known whatever it was all the time. It was the *Times* of London and must have been at least two days old because it had to come up from the station in the sleigh.

Amanda whispered: 'He eats.'

The waiter had brought a rack of toast and a stone jar of Oxford marmalade to their table instead of croissants. Silver Stick was eating toast like any normal person.

Father asked: 'Who eats?'

We indicated with our eyes.

'Well, why shouldn't he eat? You need a lot of energy for ski-ing.'

Mother, taking an interest for once, said they seemed old for ski-ing.

'You'd be surprised. Dr. Watson's not bad, but as for the other one—well, he went past me like a bird in places so steep that even the guide didn't want to try it. And stayed standing up at the end of it when most of us would have been just a big hole in the snow. The man's so rational he's completely without fear. It's fear that wrecks you when you're ski-ing. You come to a steep place, you think you're going to fall and nine times out of ten, you do fall. Holmes comes to the same steep place, doesn't see any reason why he can't do it—so he does it.'

My mother said that anybody really rational would have the sense not to go ski-ing in the first place. My ear had been caught by one word.

'Square Bear's a doctor? Is Silver Stick ill?'

'Not that I know. Is there any more coffee in that pot?'

And there we left it for the while. You might say that Amanda and I should have known at once who they were, and I suppose nine out of ten children in Europe would have known. But we'd led an unusual life, mainly on account of Mother, and although we knew many things unknown to most girls of our age, we were ignorant of a lot of others that were common currency.

We waved off Father and his guide as they went wallowing up in the deep snow through the pine trees, skis on their shoulders, then turned back for our skates. We stopped at the driveway to let the sober black sleigh go past, the one that went down the valley to the railway. There was nobody in the back, but the rugs were ready and neatly folded.

'Somebody new coming', Amanda said.

I knew Mother was looking at me, but she said nothing. Amanda and I were indoors doing our holiday reading when the sleigh came back, so we didn't see who was in it, but when we went downstairs later there was a humming tension about the hotel, like the feeling you get when a violinist is holding his bow just above the string and the tingle of the note runs up and down your spine before you hear it. It was only mid-afternoon but dusk was already settling on the valley. We were allowed a last walk outside before it got dark, and made as usual for the skating rink. Coloured electric lights were throwing patches of yellow, red and blue on the dark surface. The lame man with the accordion was playing a Strauss waltz and a few couples were skating to it, though not very well. More were clustered round the charcoal brazier at the edge of the rink where a waiter poured small glasses of mulled wine. Perhaps the man with the accordion knew the dancers were getting tired or wanted to go home himself, because when the waltz ended he changed to something wild and gypsy sounding, harder to dance to. The couples on the ice tried it for a few steps then gave up, laughing, to join the others round the brazier. For a while the ice was empty and the lame man played on to the dusk and the dark mountains.

Then a figure came gliding onto the ice. There was a decisiveness about the way she did it that marked her out at once from the other skaters. They'd come on staggering or swaggering, depending on whether they were beginners or thought themselves expert, but staggerers and swaggerers alike had a self-conscious air, knowing that this was not their natural habitat. She took to the ice like a swan to the water or a swallow to the air. The laughter died away, the drinking stopped and we watched as she swooped and dipped and circled all alone to the gypsy music. There were no showy pirouettes like the girl from Paris, no folding of the arms and look-at-me smiles. It's quite likely that she was not a particularly expert skater, that what was so remarkable about it was her willingness to take the rink, the music, the attention as hers by right. She wasn't even dressed for skating. The black skirt coming to within a few inches of the instep of her skate boots, the black mink jacket, the matching cap, were probably what she'd been wearing on the journey up from the station. But she'd been ready for this, had planned to announce her return exactly this way.

Her return. At first, absorbed by the performance, I hadn't recognised her. I'd registered that she was not a young woman and that she was elegant. It was when a little of my attention came back to my mother that I knew. She was standing there as stiff and prickly as one of the pine trees, staring at the figure on the ice like everybody else, but it wasn't admiration on her face, more a kind of horror. They were all looking like that, all the adults, as if she were the messenger of something dangerous. Then a wom-

an's voice, not my mother's, said, 'How could she? Really, how
could she?'

There was a murmuring of agreement and I could feel the horror
changing to something more commonplace—social disapproval.
Once the first words had been said, others followed and there was
a rustling of sharp little phrases like a sledge runner grating on
gravel.

'Only a year . . . to come here again . . . no respect . . . lucky not
to be . . . after what happened.'

My mother put a firm hand on each of our shoulders. 'Time for
your tea.'

Normally we'd have protested, begged for another few minutes,
but we knew that this was serious. To get into the hotel from the
ice rink you go up some steps to the back terrace and in at the
big glass doors to the breakfast room. There were two men standing on the terrace. From there you could see the rink and they
were staring down at what was happening. Silver Stick and Square
Bear. I saw the thin man's eyes in the light from the breakfast
room. They were harder and more intent than anything I'd ever
seen, harder than the ice itself. Normally, being properly brought
up, we'd have said good evening to them as we went past, but
Mother propelled us inside without speaking. As soon as she'd got
us settled at the table she went to find Father, who'd be back from
ski-ing by then. I knew they'd be talking about me and felt important, but concerned that I couldn't live up to that importance.
After all, what I'd seen had lasted only a few seconds and I hadn't
felt any of the things I was supposed to feel. I'd never known him
before it happened, apart from seeing him across the dining room
a few times and I hadn't even known he was dead until they told
me afterwards.

What happened at dinner that evening was like the ice rink, only
without gypsy music. That holiday Amanda and I were allowed to
come down to dinner with our parents for the soup course. After
the soup we were supposed to say good night politely and go up
and put ourselves to bed. People who'd been skating and ski-ing
all day were hungry by evening so usually attention was concen-
trated discreetly on the swing doors to the kitchen and the pro-

cession of waiters with the silver tureens. That night was different. The focus of attention was one small table in the corner of the room beside the window. A table laid like the rest of them with white linen, silver cutlery, gold-bordered plates and a little array of crystal glasses. A table for one. An empty table.

My father said: 'Looks as if she's funked it. Can't say I blame her.'

My mother gave him one of her 'be quiet' looks, announced that this was our evening for speaking French and asked me in that language to pass her some bread, if I pleased.

I had my back to the door and my hand on the breadbasket. All I knew was that the room went quiet.

'Don't turn round', my mother hissed in English.

I turned round and there she was, in black velvet and diamonds. Her hair, with more streaks of grey than I remembered from the year before, was swept up and secured with a pearl-and-diamond comb. The previous year, before the thing happened, my mother had remarked that she was surprisingly slim for a retired opera singer. This year she was thin, cheekbones and collarbones above the black velvet bodice sharp enough to cut paper. She was inclining her elegant head towards the headwaiter, probably listening to words of welcome. He was smiling, but then he smiled at everybody. Nobody else smiled as she followed him to the table in the far, the very far, corner. You could hear the creak of necks screwing themselves away from her. No entrance she ever made in her stage career could have been as nerve racking as that long walk across the hotel floor. In spite of the silent commands now radiating from my mother, I could no more have turned away from her than from Blondin crossing Niagara Falls. My disobedience was rewarded, as disobedience so often is, because I saw it happen. In the middle of that silent dining room, amid a hundred or so people pretending not to notice her, I saw Silver Stick get to his feet. Among all those seated people he looked even taller than before, his burnished silver head gleaming like snow on the Matterhorn above that rock ridge of a nose, below it the glacial white and black of his evening clothes. Square Bear hesitated for a moment, then followed his example. As in her lonely walk she came alongside their table, Silver Stick bowed with the dignity of a man who did not have to bow very often, and again Square Bear copied him, less elegantly. Square Bear's face was red and flustered, but the other man's hadn't altered. She paused for a moment, gravely returned their bows with a bend of her white neck, then walked on. The silence through the room lasted until the headwaiter pulled out her chair and she sat down at her table, then, as if on cue, the waiters with their tureens came marching through the swinging doors and the babble and the clash of cutlery sounded as loud as war starting.

At breakfast I asked Mother: 'Why did they bow to her?' I knew it was a banned subject, but I knew too that I was in an obscurely privileged position, because of the effect all this was supposed to be having on me. I wondered when it would come out, like secret writing on a laurel leaf you keep close to your chest to warm it. When I was fourteen, eighteen?

'Don't ask silly questions. And you don't need two lumps of sugar in your café au lait.'

Father suggested a trip to the town down the valley after lunch, to buy Christmas presents. It was meant as a distraction and it worked to an extent, but I still couldn't get her out of my mind. Later that morning, when I was supposed to be having a healthy snowball fight with boring children, I wandered away to the back terrace overlooking the ice rink. I hoped that I might find her there again, but it was occupied by noisy beginners, slithering and screeching. I despised them for their ordinariness.

I'd turned away and was looking at the back of the hotel, thinking no particular thoughts, when I heard footsteps behind me and a voice said: 'Was that where you were standing when it happened?'

It was the first time I'd heard Silver Stick's voice at close quarters. It was a pleasant voice, deep but clear, like the sea in a cave. He was standing there in his rough tweed jacket and cap with earflaps only a few yards away from me. Square Bear stood behind him, looking anxious, neck muffled in a woollen scarf. I considered, looked up at the roof again and down to my feet.

'Yes, it must have been about here.'

'Holmes, don't you think we should ask this little girl's mother? She might . . . '.

'My mother wasn't there. I was.'

Perhaps I'd learnt something already about taking the centre of the stage. The thought came to me that it would be a great thing if he bowed to me, as he'd bowed to her.

'Quite so.'

He didn't bow, but he seemed pleased.

'You see, Watson, Miss Jessica isn't in the least hysterical about it, are you?'

I saw that he meant that as a compliment, so I gave him the little inclination of the head that I'd been practising in front of the mirror when Amanda wasn't looking. He smiled, and there was more warmth in the smile than seemed likely from the height and sharpness of him.

'I take it that you have no objection to talking about what you saw.'

I said graciously: 'Not in the very least.' Then honesty compelled me to spoil it by adding, 'Only I didn't see very much.'

'It's not how much you saw, but how clearly you saw it. I wonder if you'd kindly tell Dr Watson and me exactly what you saw, in as much detail as you can remember.'

The voice was gentle, but there was no gentleness in the dark eyes fixed on me. I don't mean they were hard or cruel, simply that emotion of any sort had no more part in them than in the lens of a camera or telescope. They gave me an odd feeling, not fear exactly, but as if I'd become real in a way I hadn't quite been before. I knew that being clear about what I'd seen that day a year ago mattered more than anything I'd ever done. I closed my eyes and thought hard.

'I was standing just here. I was waiting for Mother and Amanda because we were going out for a walk and Amanda had lost one of her fur gloves as usual. I saw him falling, then he hit the roof over the dining room and came sliding down it. The snow started moving as well, so he came down with the snow. He landed just over there, where that chair is, and all the rest of the snow came down on top of him, so you could only see his arm sticking out. The arm wasn't moving, but I didn't know he was dead. A lot of people came running and started pushing the snow away from him, then somebody said I shouldn't be there so they took me away to find Mother, so I wasn't there when they got the snow off him.'

I stopped, short of breath. Square Bear was looking ill at ease and pitying but Silver Stick's eyes hadn't changed.

'When you were waiting for your mother and sister, which way were you facing?'

'The rink. I was watching the skaters.'

'Quite so. That meant you were facing away from the hotel.'

'Yes.'

'And yet you saw the man falling?'

'Yes.'

'What made you turn round?'

I'd no doubt about that. It was the part of my story that everybody had been most concerned with at the time.

'He shouted.'

'Shouted what?'

'Shouted "No" '.

'When did he shout it?'

I hesitated. Nobody had asked me that before because the answer was obvious.

'When he fell.'

'Of course, but at what point during his fall? I take it that it was before he landed on the roof over the dining room or you wouldn't have turned round in time to see it.'

'Yes.'

'And you turned round in time to see him in the air and falling?'

'Holmes, I don't think you should ... '.

'Oh, do be quiet, Watson. Well, Miss Jessica?'

'Yes, he was in the air and falling.'

'And he'd already screamed by then. So at what point did he scream?'

I wanted to be clever and grown up, to make him think well of me.

'I suppose it was when she pushed him out of the window.'

It was Square Bear's face that showed most emotion. He screwed up his eyes, went red and made little imploring signs with his fur-mittened hands, causing him to look more bear-like than

59

ever. This time the protest was not at his friend, but at me. Silver Stick put up a hand to stop him saying anything, but his face had changed too, with a sharp V on the forehead. The voice was a shade less gentle.

'When who pushed him out of the window?'

'His wife, Mrs McEvoy.'

I wondered whether to add, 'The woman you bowed to last night', but decided against it.

'Did you see her push him?'

'No.'

'Did you see Mrs McEvoy at the window?'

'No.'

'And yet you tell me that Mrs McEvoy pushed her husband out of the window. Why?'

'Everybody knows she did.'

I knew from the expression on Square Bear's face that I'd gone badly wrong, but couldn't see where. He, kindly man, must have guessed that because he started trying to explain to me.

'You see, my dear, after many years with my good friend Mr Holmes . . . '.

Yet again he was waved into silence.

'Miss Jessica, Dr Watson means well but I hope he will permit me to speak for myself. It's a fallacy to believe that age in itself brings wisdom, but one thing it infallibly brings is experience. Will you permit me, from my experience if not from my wisdom, to offer you a little advice?'

I nodded, not gracious now, just awed.

'Then my advice is this: always remember that what everybody knows, nobody knows.'

He used that voice like a skater uses his weight on the blade to skim or turn.

'You say everybody knows that Mrs McEvoy pushed her husband out of the window. As far as I know you are the only person in the world who saw Mr McEvoy fall. And yet, as you've told me, you did not see Mrs McEvoy push him. So who is this "everybody" who can claim such certainty about an event which, as far as we know, nobody witnessed?'

It's miserable not knowing answers. What is nineteen times

three? What is the past participle of the verb *faire*? I wanted to live up to him, but unwittingly he'd pressed the button that brought on the panic of the schoolroom. I blurted out: 'He was very rich and she didn't love him, and now she's very rich and can do what she likes.'

Again the bear's fur mitts went up, scrabbling the air. Again he was disregarded.

'So Mrs McEvoy is rich and can do what she likes? Does it strike you that she's happy?'

'Holmes, how can a child know . . . ?'

I thought of the gypsy music, the gleaming dark fur, the pearls in her hair. I found myself shaking my head.

'No. And yet she comes here again, exactly a year after her husband died, the very place in the world that you'd expect her to avoid at all costs. She comes here knowing what people are saying about her, making sure everybody has a chance to see her, holding her head high. Have you any idea what that must do to a woman?'

This time Square Bear really did protest and went on protesting. How could he expect a child to know about the feelings of a mature woman? How could I be blamed for repeating the gossip of my elders? Really, Holmes, it was too much. This time too Silver Stick seemed to agree with him. He smoothed out the V shape in his forehead and apologised.

'Let us, if we may, return to the surer ground of what you actually saw. I take it that the hotel has not been rebuilt in any way since last year.'

I turned again to look at the back of the hotel. As far as I could see, it was just as it had been, the glass doors leading from the dining room and breakfast room onto the terrace, a tiled sloping roof above them. Then, joined onto the roof, the three main guest floors of the hotel. The top two floors were the ones that most people took because they had wrought-iron balconies where, on sunny days, you could stand to look at the mountains. Below them were the smaller rooms. They were less popular because, being directly above the kitchen and dining room, they suffered from noise and cooking smells and had no balconies.

Silver Stick said to Square Bear: 'That was the room they had last year, top floor, second from the right. So if he were pushed, he'd have to be pushed over the balcony as well as out of the window. That would take quite a lot of strength, wouldn't you say?'

The next question was to me. He asked if I'd seen Mr McEvoy before he fell out of the window and I said yes, a few times.

'Was he a small man?'

'No, quite big.'

'The same size as Dr Watson here, for instance?'.

Square Bear straightened his broad shoulders, as if for military inspection.

'He was fatter.'

'Younger or older?'

'Quite old. As old as you are.'

Square Bear made a chuffing sound and his shoulders slumped a little.

'So we have a man about the same age as our friend Watson and heavier. Difficult, wouldn't you say, for any woman to push him anywhere against his will?'

'Perhaps she took him by surprise, told him to lean out and look at something, then swept his legs off the floor.'

That wasn't my own theory. The event had naturally been analysed in all its aspects the year before and all the parental care in the world couldn't have kept it from me.

'A touching picture. Shall we come back to things we know for certain? What about the snow? Was there as much snow as this last year?'

'I think so. It came up above my knees last year. It doesn't quite this year, but then I've grown.'

Square Bear murmured: 'They'll keep records of that sort of thing.'

'Just so, but we're also grateful for Miss Jessica's calibrations. May we trouble you with just one more question?'

I said yes rather warily.

'You've told us that just before you turned round and saw him falling you heard him shout "No." What sort of "No" was it?'

I was puzzled. Nobody had asked me that before.

'Was it an angry "No"? A protesting "No"? The kind of "No" you'd shout if somebody were pushing you over a balcony?'

The other man looked as if he wanted to protest again but kept quiet. The intensity in Silver Stick's eyes would have frozen a brook in mid-babble. When I didn't answer at once he visibly made himself relax and his voice went softer.

'It's hard for you to remember, isn't it? Everybody was so sure that it was one particular sort of "No" that they've fixed their version in your mind. I want you to do something for me, if you would be so kind. I want you to forget that Dr Watson and I are here and stand and look down at the ice rink just as you were doing last year. I want you to clear your mind of everything else and think that it really is last year and you're hearing that shout for the first time. Will you do that?'

I faced away from them. First I looked at this year's skaters then I closed my eyes and tried to remember how it had been. I felt the green itchy scarf round my neck, the cold getting to my toes and fingers as I waited. I heard the cry and it was all I could do not to turn round and see the body tumbling again. When I opened my eyes and looked at them they were still waiting patiently.

'I think I've remembered.'

'And what sort of "No" was it?'

It was clear in my mind but hard to put into words.

'It . . . it was as if he'd been going to say something else if he'd had time. Not just no. No something.'

'No something what?'

More silence while I thought about it, then a prompt from Square Bear.

'Could it have been a name, my dear?'

'Don't put any more ideas into her head. You thought he was going to say something after the no, but you don't know what, is that it?'

'Yes, like no running, or no cakes today, only that wasn't it. Something you couldn't do.'

'Or something not there, like the cakes?'

'Yes, something like that. Only it couldn't have been, could it?'

'Couldn't? If something happened in a particular way, then it happened, and there's no could or couldn't about it.'

It was the kind of thing governesses said, but he was smiling now and I had the idea that something I'd said had pleased him.

'I see your mother and sister coming, so I'm afraid we must end this very useful conversation. I am much obliged to you for your powers of observation. Will you permit me to ask you some more questions if any more occur to me?'

I nodded.

'Is it a secret?'

'Do you want it to be?'

'Holmes, I don't think you should encourage this young lady . . . .'

'My dear Watson, in my observation there's nothing more precious you can give a child to keep than a secret.'

My mother came across the terrace with Amanda. Silver Stick and Square Bear touched their hats to her and hoped we enjoyed our walk. When she asked me later what we'd been talking about I said they'd asked whether the snow was as deep last year and hugged the secret of my partnership. I became in my imagination eyes and ears for him. At the children's party at teatime on Christmas Eve the parents talked in low tones, believing that we were absorbed in the present giving round the hotel tree. But it would have taken more than the porter in red robe and white whiskers or his largesse of three wooden geese on a string to distract me from my work. I listened and stored up every scrap against the time when he'd ask me questions again. And I watched Mrs McEvoy as she went round the hotel through Christmas Eve and Christmas Day, pale and upright in her black and her jewels, trailing silence after her like the long train of a dress.

My call came on Boxing Day. There was another snowball fight in the hotel grounds, for parents as well this time. I stood back from it all and waited by a little clump of bare birches and, sure enough, Silver Stick and Square Bear came walking over to me.

'I've found out a lot about her', I said.

'Have you indeed?'

'He was her second husband. She had another one she loved more, but he died of a fever. It was when they were visiting Egypt a long time ago.'

'Ten years ago.'

Silver Stick's voice was remote. He wasn't even looking at me.

'She got married to Mr McEvoy three years ago. Most people said it was for his money, but there was an American lady at the party and she said Mr McEvoy seemed quite nice when you first knew him and he was interested in music and singers, so perhaps it was one of those marriages where people quite like each other without being in love, you know?'

I thought I'd managed that rather well. I'd tried to make it like my mother talking to her friends and it sounded convincing in my ears. I was disappointed at the lack of reaction, so brought up my big guns.

'Only she didn't stay liking him because after they got married she found out about his eye.'

'His eye?'

A reaction at last, but from Square Bear, not Silver Stick. I grabbed for the right word and clung to it.

'Roving. It was a roving eye. He kept looking at other ladies and she didn't like it.'

I hoped they'd understand that it meant looking in a special way. I didn't know myself exactly what special way, but the adults talking among themselves at the party had certainly understood. But it seemed I'd over-estimated these two because they were just standing there staring at me. Perhaps Silver Stick wasn't as clever as I'd thought. I threw in my last little oddment of information, something anybody could understand.

'I found out her first name. It's Irene.'

Square Bear cleared his throat. Silver Stick said nothing. He was looking over my head at the snowball fight.

'Holmes, I really think we should leave Jessica to play with her little friends.'

'Not yet. There's something I wanted to ask her. Do you remember the staff at the hotel last Christmas?'

Here was a dreadful comedown. I'd brought him a head richly crammed with love, money and marriages and he was asking about the domestics. Perhaps the disappointment on my face looked like stupidity because his voice became impatient.

'The people who looked after you, the porters and the waiters and the maids, especially the maids.'

'They're the same . . . I think.' I was running them through my head. There was Petra with her thick plaits who brought us our cups of chocolate, fat Renata who made our beds, grey-haired Ul-rike with her limp.

'None left?'

'I don't think so.'

Then the memory came to me of blonde curls escaping from a maid's uniform cap and a clear voice singing as she swept the corridors, blithe as a bird.

'There was Eva, but she got married.'

'Who did she marry?'

'Franz, the man who's got the sleigh.'

It was flying down the drive as I spoke, silver bells jangling, the little horse gold in the sunshine.

'A good marriage for a hotel maid.'

'Oh, he didn't have the sleigh last year. He was only the under porter.'

'Indeed. Watson, I think we must have a ride in this sleigh. Will you see the head porter about booking it?'

I hoped he might invite me to go with them but he said nothing about that. Still, he seemed to be in a good temper again—although I couldn't see that it was from anything I'd told him.

'Miss Jessica, again I'm obliged to you. I may have yet another favour to ask, but all in good time.'

I went reluctantly to join the snowballers as the two of them walked through the snow back to the hotel.

That afternoon, on our walk, they went past us on their way down the drive in Franz's sleigh. It didn't look like a pleasure trip. Franz's handsome face was serious and Holmes was staring straight ahead. Instead of turning up towards the forest at the end of the hotel drive they turned left for the village. Our walk also took us to the village because Father wanted to see an old man about getting a stick carved. When we walked down the little main street we saw the sleigh and horse standing outside a neat chalet with green shutters next to the church. I knew it was Franz's own house and wondered what had become of his passengers. About half an hour later, when we'd seen about Father's stick, we walked back up the street and there were Holmes and Watson standing on the balcony outside the chalet with Eva, the maid from last year. Her fair hair was as curly as ever but her head was bent. She seemed to be listening intently to something that Holmes was saying and the droop of her shoulders told me she wasn't happy.

'Why is Silver Stick talking to her?'

Amanda, very properly, was rebuked for staring and asking questions about things that didn't concern her. Being older and wiser, I said nothing but kept my secret coiled in my heart. Was it Eva who pushed him? Would they lock her up in prison? A little guilt stirred along with the pleasure, because he wouldn't have known about Eva if I hadn't told him, but not enough to spoil it. Later I watched from our window hoping to see the sleigh coming back, but it didn't that day. Instead, just before it got dark, Holmes and Watson came back on foot up the drive, walking fast, saying nothing.

Next morning, Square Bear came up to Mother at coffee time. 'I wonder if you would permit Miss Jessica to take a short walk with me on the terrace.'

Mother hesitated, but Square Bear was so obviously respectable, and anyway you could see the terrace from the coffee room. I put on my hat, cape and gloves and walked with him out of the glass doors into the cold air. We stood looking down at the rink, in exactly the same place as I'd been standing when they first spoke to me. I knew that was no accident. Square Bear's fussiness, the tension in his voice that he was so unsuccessful in hiding, left no doubt of it. There was something odd about the terrace, too—far more people on it than would normally be the case on a cold morning. There must have been two dozen or so standing round in stiff little groups, talking to each other, waiting.

'Where's Mr Holmes?'

Square Bear looked at me, eyes watering from the cold.

'The truth is, my dear, I don't know where he is or what he's doing. He gave me my instructions at breakfast and I haven't seen him since.'

'Instructions about me?'

Before he could answer, the scream came. It was a man's scream, tearing through the air like a saw blade, and there was a word in it. The word was 'No.' I turned with the breath choking in my throat and, just as there'd been last year, there was a dark thing in the air, its clothes flapping out round it. A collective gasp from the people on the terrace, then a soft thump as the thing hit the deep snow on the restaurant roof and began sliding. I heard 'No' again and this time it was my own voice, because I knew from last year what was coming next—the slide down the steep roof gathering snow as it came, the flop onto the terrace only a few yards from where I was standing, the arm sticking out.

At first the memory was so strong that I thought that was what I was seeing, and it took a few seconds for me to realise that it wasn't happening that way. The thing had fallen a little to the side and instead of sliding straight down the roof it was being carried to a little ornamental railing at the edge of it, where the main hotel joined onto the annex, driving a wedge of snow in front of it. Then somebody said, unbelievingly: 'He's stopped.' And the thing had stopped. Instead of plunging over the roof to the terrace it had been swept up against the railing, bundled in snow like a cylindrical snowball, and stopped within a yard of the edge. Then it sat up, clinging with one hand to the railing, covered from waist down in snow. If he'd been wearing a hat when he came out of the window he'd lost it in the fall because his damp hair was gleaming silver above his smiling brown face. It was an inward kind of smile, as if only he could appreciate the thing that he'd done.

Then the chattering started. Some people were yelling to get a ladder, others running. The rest were asking each other what had happened until somebody spotted the window wide open three floors above us.

'Her window. Mrs McEvoy's window.'

'He fell off Mrs McEvoy's balcony, just like last year.'

'But he didn't . . . '.

At some point Square Bear had put a hand on my shoulder. Now he bent down beside me, looking anxiously into my face, saying we should go in and find Mother. I wished he'd get out of my way because I wanted to see Silver Stick on the roof. Then Mother arrived, wafting clouds of scent and drama. I had to go inside of course, but not before I'd seen the ladder arrive and Silver Stick coming down it, a little stiffly but dignified. And one more thing. Just as he stepped off the ladder the glass doors to the terrace opened and out she came. She hadn't been there when it happened but now in her black fur jacket, she stepped through the people as if they weren't there, and gave him her hand and thanked him.

At dinner that night she dined alone at her table, as on the other nights, but it took her longer to get to it. Her long walk across the dining room was made longer by all the people who wanted to speak to her, to inquire after her health, to tell her how pleased they were to see her again. It was as if she'd just arrived that afternoon, instead of being there for five days already. There were several posies of flowers on her table that must have been sent up especially from the town, and champagne in a silver bucket beside it. Silver Stick and Square Bear bowed to her as she went past their table, but ordinary polite little nods, not like that first night. The smile she gave them was like the sun coming up.

We were sent off to bed as soon as we'd had our soup as usual. Amanda went to sleep at once but I lay awake, resenting my exile from what mattered. Our parents' sitting room was next to our bedroom and I heard them come in, excited still. Then, soon afterwards, a knock on the door of our suite, the murmur of voices and my father, a little taken aback, saying yes come in by all means. Then their voices, Square Bear's first, fussing with apologies about it being so late, then Silver Stick's cutting through him: 'The fact is, you're owed an explanation, or rather your daughter is. Dr Watson suggested that we should give it to you so that some time in the future when Jessica's old enough, you may decide to tell her.'

If I'd owned a chest of gold and had watched somebody throwing it away in a crowded street I couldn't have been more furious than hearing my secret about to be squandered. My first thought was to rush through to the other room in my nightdress and bare feet and demand that he should speak to me, not to them. Then caution took over, and although I did get out of bed, I went just as far as the door, opened it a crack so that I could hear better and padded back to bed. There were sounds of chairs being rearranged, people settling into them, then Silver Stick's voice.

'I should say at the start, for reasons we need not go into, that Dr Watson and I were convinced that Irene McEvoy had not pushed her husband to his death. The question was how to prove it, and in that regard your daughter's evidence was indispensable. She alone saw Mr McEvoy fall and she alone heard what he shouted. The accurate ear of childhood—once certain adult non-senses had been discarded—recorded that shout as precisely as a phonograph and knew that strictly speaking it was only half a shout, that Mr McEvoy, if he'd had time, would have added some-thing else to it.'

A pause. I sat up in bed with the counterpane round my neck, straining not to miss a word of his quiet, clear voice.

'No—something. The question was, no what? Mr McEvoy had expected something to be there and his last thought on earth was surprise at the lack of it, surprise so acute that he was trying to shout it with his last breath. The question was, what that thing could have been.'

Silence, waiting for an answer, but nobody said anything.

'If you look up at the back of the hotel from the terrace you will notice one obvious thing. The third and fourth floors have balconies. The second floor does not. The room inhabited by Mr and Mrs McEvoy had a balcony. A person staying in the suite would be aware of that. He would not necessarily be aware, unless he were a particularly observant man, that the second-floor rooms had no balconies. Until it was too late. I formed the theory that Mr McEvoy had not in fact fallen from the window of his own room but from a lower room belonging to somebody else, which accounted for his attempted last words: 'No . . . balcony.''

My mother gasped. My father said: 'By Jove . . . '.

'Once I'd arrived at that conclusion, the question was what Mr McEvoy was doing in somebody else's room. The possibility of thieving could be ruled out since he was a very rich man. Then he was seeing somebody. The next question was who. And here your daughter was incidentally helpful in a way she is too young to understand. She confided to us in all innocence an overheard piece of adult gossip to the effect that the late Mr McEvoy had a roving eye.'

My father began to laugh, then stifled it. My mother said 'Well' in a way that boded trouble for me later.

'Once my attention was directed that way, the answer became obvious. Mr McEvoy was in somebody else's hotel room for what one might describe as an episode of *galanterie*. But the accident happened in the middle of the morning. Did ever a lady in the history of the world make a romantic assignation for that hour of the day? Therefore it wasn't a lady. So I asked myself what group of people are most likely to be encountered in hotel rooms in mid-morning and the answer was . . . '.

'Good heavens, the chambermaid!'

My mother's voice, and Holmes was clearly none too pleased at being interrupted.

'Quite so. Mr McEvoy had gone to meet a chambermaid. I asked some questions to establish whether any young and attractive chambermaid had left the hotel since last Christmas. There was such a one, named Eva. She'd married the under porter and brought him as a dowry enough money to buy that elegant little sleigh. Now a prudent chambermaid may amass a modest dowry by saving tips, but one look at that sleigh will tell you that Eva's dowry might best be described as, well . . . immodest.'

Another laugh from my father, cut off by a look from my mother I could well imagine.

'Dr Watson and I went to see Eva. I told her what I'd deduced and she, poor girl, confirmed it with some details—the sound of the housekeeper's voice outside, Mr McEvoy's well-practised but ill-advised tactic of taking refuge on the balcony. You may say that the girl Eva should have confessed at once what had happened . . . '.

'I do indeed.'

'But bear in mind her position. Not only her post at the hotel but her engagement to the handsome Franz would be forfeited. And, after all, there was no question of anybody being tried in court. The fashionable world was perfectly happy to connive at the story that Mr McEvoy had fallen accidentally from his window—while inwardly convicting an innocent woman of his murder.'

My mother said, sounding quite subdued for once: 'But Mrs

McEvoy must have known. Why didn't she say something?'

'Ah, to answer that one needs to know something about Mrs McEvoy's history, and it so happens that Dr Watson and I are in that position. A long time ago, before her first happy marriage, Mrs McEvoy was loved by a prince. He was not, I must admit, a particularly admirable prince, but prince he was. Can you imagine how it felt for a woman to come from that to being deceived with a hotel chambermaid by a man who made his fortune from bathroom furnishings? Can you conceive that a proud woman might choose to be thought a murderess rather than submit to that indignity?'

Another silence, then my mother breathed: 'Yes. Yes, I think I can.' Then, 'Poor woman.'

'It was not pity that Irene McEvoy ever needed.' Then, in a different tone of voice: 'So there you have it. And it is your decision how much, if anything, you decide to pass on to Jessica in due course.'

There were sounds of people getting up from chairs, then my father said: 'And your, um, demonstration this morning?'

'Oh, that little drama. I knew what had happened, but for Mrs McEvoy's sake it was necessary to prove to the world she was innocent. I couldn't call Eva as witness because I'd given her my word. I'd studied the pitch of the roof and the depth of the snow and I was scientifically convinced that a man falling from Mrs McEvoy's balcony would not have landed on the terrace. You know the result.'

Good nights were said, rather subdued, and they were shown out. Through the crack in the door I glimpsed them. As they came level with the crack, Silver Stick, usually so precise in his movements, dropped his pipe and had to kneel to pick it up. As he knelt, his bright eyes met mine through the crack and he smiled, an odd, quick smile unseen by anybody else. He'd known I'd been listening all the time.

When they'd gone Mother and Father sat for a long time in silence.

At last Father said: 'If he'd got it wrong, he'd have killed himself.'

'Like the ski-ing.'
'He must have loved her very much.'
'It's his own logic he loves.'
But then, my mother always was the unromantic one.

THE ADVENTURE IN
BORDER COUNTRY

Gwen Moffat

'What do you know of Cumberland, Watson?' Sherlock Holmes glanced up from his breakfast plate and I answered promptly.

'Sausages. They make excellent sausages in Cumberland. And there are the lakes. And daffodils. A pretty poem of Mr Wordsworth's—' And then I noticed the letter beside his plate. 'A case?' I asked eagerly. There had been no problem of note since November 5, when a certain Mrs Chaffinch took a meat skewer to her husband, dressed the body as a guy, and wheeled it in a perambulator through the East End to be consumed by a bonfire on the bank of the Thames. A simple affair for Holmes, although it had Lestrade stumped. Mrs Chaffinch had neglected to remove the buttons from her husband's old army tunic and they did not burn.

'What do you make of it?' Holmes passed the letter across the table. 'It was delivered by hand.'

Dear Mr Holmes [I read],

Some few years ago you resolved a problem for Sir Timothy Eamont who assures me your discretion is of the highest order.

I have come up from Cumberland to ask if you can assist my neighbour in a matter so delicate that the intrusion of police and newspapers could spell disaster for all concerned. I propose to call on you at eleven o'clock this morning.

Yours faithfully,
Clement Daw.

I shrugged. 'I assume he requires assistance for his own delicate problem. Blackmail, I shouldn't wonder. The man has become involved with a woman and has panicked.'

'It is intriguing,' Holmes murmured, and I knew he had not been listening. 'This is an articulate fellow, accustomed to command, but the script resembles that of a boy, and one more at home on the back of a horse than in the school-room. A self-made man, Watson, and labouring under strong emotion, not a rake who has formed an embarrassing liaison with his wife's maid. I look forward to eleven o'clock. Can it be possible that the tedium of Christmas is to be relieved after all?'

'I enjoy Christmas,' I confessed. 'Although this year the weather is hardly traditional.'

During the first half of December we had endured temperatures of such ferocity that a number of poor people had frozen to death in their unheated rooms. And when the cold did relent, a dank fog descended on us. Incarcerated in our sitting room, we had so far kept boredom at bay, Holmes applying himself to the study of bones in a paper recently published by the Royal Society while I was enthralled by a new book on monomania by Professor Ginsburg. Thus, with the fog outside and pungent tobacco clouds within, we occupied ourselves until that gloomy morning when Clement Daw's missive arrived.

The man himself appeared promptly at eleven, shown up by Billy the page. He was a big, hearty fellow with a strong nose and a thin but well-shaped mouth. He put me in mind of a prosperous yeoman farmer and he spoke loudly, like one accustomed to talk against the wind.

'I'm not going to waste your time, Mr Holmes,' he began, as soon as he was seated. 'Nor that of Dr Watson. I am a tobacco merchant and a widower. My two sons operate the business in Liverpool, allowing me to spend most of my time on my country estate, which is close to that of a Mr and Mrs Aubrey. It is on their behalf that I have made this journey, and it is necessary here to tell you something of our surroundings.

'Our houses front a lake and behind us wooded crags rise to a bleak moorland, the domain of sheep and grouse. There is a shooting box or cabin some three miles from Aubrey's house—' At this point our visitor checked and frowned, at a loss for words.

'The cabin features in your story?' Holmes prompted.

'That's the puzzle!' Daw cried. 'You see, Mr Holmes, Miles Aubrey has quite disappeared. He has not been seen since last Tuesday evening, when he told his wife he was going to the stables to look at a sick pony.'

'Six days ago.' Holmes was thoughtful. 'You searched of course. What did you find at the cabin?'

Daw said grimly, 'There was champagne on the table: an empty bottle and another a quarter-full. There was the remains of a game pie, and the bed had been . . . occupied. There was no sign of Aubrey.'

'What makes you think he had been there?'

'The champagne was from his cellar and the cook recognised her crust on what was left of the pie.'

'Why did you not go to the police?'

Daw slumped in his chair. 'There were two champagne glasses,' he said miserably. 'There is Mrs Aubrey to be considered and, indeed, her daughter. Minnie is only twelve. She is not Aubrey's child. Mrs Aubrey's first husband died of cholera in India. The poor lady is a sad example of the maxim that wealth cannot buy happiness. For she is an heiress: the only child of a Glasgow ironmaster. Widowed while still young, she remarried—' Again he broke off and glowered at us.

'And now the lady has lost this husband?' Holmes pondered his own question. 'What has been done to locate him?'

'When he did not come down to breakfast, Mrs Aubrey sent to see if he was indisposed, and discovered that his bed had not been slept in. She was not greatly surprised. She has confided in me and I knew that this was not the first time he had stayed out all night, and without warning. However, by afternoon, she began to worry, not least because he had taken no horse and no change of clothing, and it had snowed that morning. So she sent for me. I got up a search party but there was little we could do in the short space of daylight left. No one had seen Aubrey in the village, which lies two miles east of his house.

'At first light next morning we started a more organised search. We looked for tracks. I was leading the party that went to the cabin. Now the snow had started quite early the previous morning but there were no tracks about the place; the snow was pristine.'

'Which argues that he left before it stopped snowing,' Holmes put in. 'What of his drinking companion?'

Daw pursed his lips. 'The obvious person denies that she was with him, but then I am not adept at interrogation. Which is why I come to you, sir. We have to discover his whereabouts.'

'Do you suspect foul play?'

'It is possible. Our people are a rough, untutored folk, passionately loyal, but implacable in their hatred.'

'So,' said Holmes when our visitor had left, 'the disreputable Aubrey has at least one mistress in the locality, and someone has seen fit to avenge her dishonour?'

'Or the woman is with child and demands money as the price of silence.'

'Then she would be the victim.' Holmes reached for tobacco in the Persian slipper and started to fill his pipe. He glanced at the window. 'A visit to Cumberland promises escape from this climate and the ennui of Christmas. Moreover, there is the small matter of a fee, and Mr Daw is not without substance.' He glanced at the cheque left by our visitor to retain his services. 'Now why is it Daw who engages me to find the husband, and not the wife?'

'She shuns publicity.'

'So he comes to me knowing I shall be discreet? I have the impression that the lady is less keen to engage us than is this gentleman. There is an attachment? His concern is for her but he referred to her as "poor lady": a term more fatherly than romantic.'

'He will be considerably older. He has grown sons, her daughter is a child.'

'A girl of twelve can be precocious.' It was a statement out of context and I disregarded it. Holmes now lapsed into one of those periods of preoccupation which often assail him at the start of a case and which persisted until we were steaming out of London the following morning. We were alone, Daw having gone ahead the previous day. As the first pale ray of sunshine crept into the carriage he fixed me with a sharp stare and announced: 'The motive is not greed. It is the greedy person who has come to grief.'

'You think then that he has come to grief? He could have disappeared in order to escape creditors.'

'His wife would settle his debts. No, Watson, there is more to this than meets the eye. Daw may have it to rights with his talk of unbridled passions. We must not forget that Mr Wordsworth's pretty Lake District merges with the wild border country, where rapine and pillage were commonplace until a few generations ago. I suspect we shall find less of sparkling waves and dancing daffodils and more of Ruskin's "awful curtain of night and death" at the end of our journey.'

How right he was. In Cumberland the absence of fog served only to emphasise the harshness of the landscape. Other passengers alighting from our train and bound for a family Christmas, burdened as they were with packages and fat fowls, these good people seemed positively delighted to view the bleak lines of the mountains, indeed they even grumbled at the lack of snow.

Mr Daw had sent his carriage to meet us, and from the comfort of this, behind a pair of matched bays, I regarded the surroundings with some trepidation. I had thought Dartmoor a wilderness well suited to a savage monster,* but the Lake District was altogether more impressive. The lines of Dartmoor sweep and undulate but here the mountains loomed over us, rising above crags which themselves reared above timbered slopes so steep it was a marvel that any tree could find a purchase.

We had arrived late and the light was fading fast. As we drove westward the afterglow illuminated a vast horizontal mass that gleamed dully about its margin. 'The lake,' observed Holmes, 'and starting to freeze, I see. Now I wonder: did they drag the lake?'

The Hound of the Baskervilles

78

We passed through a village, doors and windows fastened against the frosty air, although a knot of children accompanied a pony that dragged a log along the frozen street. At the pony's head was a tall woman in a red cloak. In the light from a window we saw her face framed by dark curls and a scarlet hood: large, luminous eyes and sensual lips. I lifted a hand in salutation and she nodded casually, then, remembering her place, dropped a curtsey.

Leafless trees crowded the road and, after a couple of miles they stood back to expose parkland and a large house, its dimensions revealed by the disposition of its lighted windows. 'Aubrey's,' said Holmes. 'Daw's is the second house.'

The village boasted only a rude inn and Daw had insisted that we accept his hospitality. Upon arrival we were shown to adjoining rooms by a man-servant who informed us that his master was at Swithins, the Aubreys' place.

Nothing had been visible of the exterior of Daw's house other than the studded door lit by a porch light, but once inside we realised we were in one of those ancient buildings termed peel towers: relics of a time when even farmhouses had to be fortified against marauding Scots. Such was the servant's contention but I guessed that a similar tale would be told north of the border where marauding English would be the bogeymen.

The window of my room was heavily draped, the casement leaded with tiny panes, the walls over a yard thick. There was no fireplace and I wasted no time descending to the hall where massive logs flamed on the hearth. Holmes joined me and we were regaled with tea and scones until the appearance of our host. He told us that the search for Aubrey had continued but with no result, and that Mrs Aubrey asked that we should call on her at our earliest convenience. 'She is confronting the situation with courage,' he said. 'But then she must retain her composure for Minnie's sake.'

'The daughter is attached to her step-father?' Holmes asked.

Daw hesitated. 'They are not close. Aubrey is younger than his wife and he employs a playful air with the child which she seems to resent. I don't understand it.' He glanced at me, as if a doctor might divine the significance better than a detective.

'Perhaps he tries to get on a footing of equality with the little girl,' I ventured. 'To bridge the gap in age in order to be friends.'

'Quite.' Daw's expression was bovine in its lack of comprehension, which only echoed my own. Holmes, on the other hand, had a devilish gleam in his eye.

'Why are you so interested in Minnie?' I asked when we climbed the stairs after a robust dinner.

He paused at his door. 'I am looking forward to tomorrow. What are the two women like, think you: the lady and the daughter.'

I sighed. I was tired and he was being obtuse. 'Not two women, Holmes. One is a child.'

'Of course. To a physician she is a child. I forget.'

Swithins Hall presented a fine Georgian front that gleamed faintly pink in the morning light. The grounds were well maintained, conifers and hardwoods artfully dispersed on either side of the drive. No man in his senses would abandon this property voluntarily, an opinion confirmed upon our entrance. There were portraits by Reynolds in the hall, while furniture and opulent Eastern carpets spoke of good taste and the means to indulge it.

We were shown into a comfortable drawing room and a moment later the lady of the house entered. Helen Aubrey was neither beautiful nor imposing but we were seeing her at a disadvantage: meeting two strangers whom she knew were conversant with an embarrassing family secret. But although under great strain she bore herself with dignity. She was dressed in grey, her thick chestnut hair coiled about her small head and secured with tortoiseshell combs. She had a stubborn chin and a full and generous mouth. She smiled seldom but when she did, her face lit up—as when her daughter entered and came forward to be introduced.

Minnie was exquisite, with long blonde hair, clear blue eyes and a complexion like rose petals, heightened by a warm blush when she curtseyed to the visitors. I tore my eyes away from that damask skin to find myself observed with interest by Holmes. Meanwhile Daw was in a quandary, unable to broach the purpose of our visit in the presence of the child.

'How are your charges, Minnie?' he asked brightly. 'Minnie has quite a menagerie in the great barn,' he announced, his eyes pleading with us to solve this problem.

Mrs Aubrey knew what was required. 'You may go to the barn for a quarter of an hour,' she told Minnie. 'Your fur coat and hood, dear, and your warmest muffler—' She hesitated. 'Take Salkeld.'

'Salkeld?' The child looked astonished.

Mrs Aubrey said firmly, 'They tell me there is a tramp in the woods. I do not want you to go outside the house alone.' When she had gone her mother turned back to us. 'Events have made me nervous,' she confessed. 'We don't know who may be about the place.'

'A natural reaction,' Holmes said. 'And now perhaps we may have a few words before we visit your cabin. Tell me, madam, do you want your husband found?'

She started and her eyes widened. 'But that is why you are here! Not want him *found*?'

Daw was dumbstruck. Holmes was in no way abashed. 'There is the possibility that he has disappeared of his own volition. Threatened, perhaps?'

She collected herself and considered this. 'You mean, he has enemies?'

'If he has left of his own free will, would you wish him found?'

Her face set as if she were resigning herself to a further invasion of her privacy. 'It would depend on the circumstances,' she said bravely. 'I would most definitely want him *located*. If he were with a . . . friend, I would wish to be told. But,' she added quickly, 'I would not want him to know that he was discovered.'

'You know where he is, madam.'

'Mr Holmes, sir!' Daw was outraged. 'If the lady knew, you would not be here!'

'Quite. I apologise.' This time he did look chastened. 'My thoughts had taken a different tack.' His tone changed. 'Perhaps I may view your husband's rooms, madam. Meanwhile, with your permission, Dr Watson shall talk to the servants.'

'I will see to it,' she said evenly.

When she left the room Holmes drew me aside and whispered that I should speak to Minnie. By good fortune I avoided Mrs Aubrey and, following directions from a maid, I emerged from the rear of the house to cross a courtyard to the great barn. I found

Minnie on the upper floor, swathed in sealskins and crooning to a large white rabbit in her arms.

'What have you done with Salkeld?' I asked, scratching the animal's skull.

'I sent him to the tack-room,' she said calmly. 'There is no tramp, you know. My mama is frightened of shadows. No one can harm me on our own property.'

'Why is she frightened?' I pretended to study the rabbit with a clinical eye. 'I think this animal is a trifle overweight.'

'She is with child.'

My jaw dropped. 'The rabbit,' Minnie said impatiently. She placed it in its hutch and we moved to the next, where now a black rabbit hopped to the wire and begged for food. She opened the door and gave it some dandelion leaves.

'You were about to say who had frightened your mama,' I prompted. When this produced no response I went on, 'No doubt she is afraid that the person who attacked—' I stopped, appalled; I had been about to imply that her step-father had been murdered.

She said gravely, 'I understand Mama because of my animals. There is my cat, Tabitha, and *he* gave orders for traps to be set in the woods because martens take the pheasant poults, but Tabitha hunts in the woods, and I told him he was not to set traps. Mama feels about me as I do about Tabitha.'

I let her prattle on. Aubrey would not let her ride out with a groom, only with himself, whereas Mama insisted a groom accompany them because she said Aubrey was a reckless rider. He set traps, Mama ordered them to be taken up (Mama thought pine martens were beautiful and pheasants were silly, noisy birds). Mama liked eagles and falcons. He said they were vermin. He said Mama lived in fairyland and . . .

There was a step on the wooden stair. A young fellow appeared. 'Who art tha?' he shouted, glaring at me and approaching with menace.

'Now, Salkeld,' chided my young companion. 'This is Dr Watson. He is a visitor.'

The fellow apologised in his uncouth dialect and turned to his charge. 'Quarter of an hour, they telled. Ah, miss. Us maun go back. It's verra cold, tha knows.'

82

'One moment, Salkeld.' She moved along the bank of hutches, passing in leaves as I opened doors. 'Mama is *not* ill,' she persisted, as if arguing with me. 'She is sad because my papa died, and she is concerned about'—she glanced at the footman who turned his back in confusion—'about the estate,' she whispered. 'It is a heavy responsibility.' She regarded me solemnly with those cornflower eyes.

'Your mama looks remarkably well,' I said. 'And I should know.'

'I had forgotten you were a physician. Mama is quite well? She will not have to go away? Truly?'

With sudden horror I was aware that her mother might be suffering from some major disorder and here was I blithely assuring the child to the contrary. Her face fell as her eyes searched mine. 'You're not sure,' she said dolefully, and turned away. '*He* said you couldn't tell because it was inside her head.' She stamped her foot. 'I hate him! And he hates her. There!'

The footman was terrified and, scarcely aware of the action, he gripped her wrist. 'Away now, Miss Minnie, or us'll be in a fine mess.' He threw me a frantic look and almost pulled her down the stairs. I could hear her protesting staunchly: 'I *do* hate him because he says—' The rest was lost in the clatter of their boots.

I was unable to acquaint Holmes with the gist of this exchange, for no sooner did I emerge from the barn but I was caught up by the party setting off for the cabin. We were escorted by the coachman and two grooms, Daw having elected to remain with Mrs Aubrey.

Speech was impossible, first due to the angle of the path that climbed through the hanging woods behind the house, then by virtue of the hazards it presented as it traversed above sheer cliffs. We were equipped with alpenstocks, but even with their aid we were forced to watch our footing where streams had overflowed the path and frozen. Gullies between the crags were plugged by massive ice falls, green and bubbly, and treacherous as glass. In such places the local men chose a route some distance back from the edge, chipping footholds across the ice by means of their iron-shod staffs.

The cabin was a simple stone structure with a slate roof, the sparse dusting of snow about it trampled by hobnailed boots.

While the men waited outside, we entered and looked about us. After a moment Holmes said, 'Nothing can be as it was found; the champagne bottles have been removed, and the remains of the pie; even the bed has been tidied.'

On a bedstead, blankets had been neatly stacked to reveal a mattress from which the odd straw protruded. Holmes grimaced. 'A strange love nest for the master of Swithins Hall—but then, to a man driven by lust, the furnishings would be of little moment.' He went to the door and summoned the coachman: a responsible, middle-aged fellow. 'Is there a path to the village from here?' he asked.

'Yes, sir: two. A footpath less than two miles long, and an easier track for the ponies. That be rather longer. Both have been searched.'

'I have little doubt that the identity of the person who met your master here is common knowledge.'

'It wasna her!' The man blinked at the tidy bed. 'We asked her: first person us went to!'

'Her name?'

'Why, 'tis Rosie Yewdale. She lives below there, at Cunning Garth. But 'twasn't her this time, sir. And place were never left in such a state before'—he gestured at the cleared table—'keepers woulda let on. Master didna seem to care who saw—why, the lady coulda been with us!'

'Hardly.' Holmes's tone was dry. 'So if not Rosie Yewdale, who was here with your master?'

'I wouldna know that, sir.' He paused deliberately. 'I serve the mistress,' he said, meeting Holmes's eye with a hint of defiance. 'And now, by your leave, gentlemen, I must be getting back. The lady needs the men for to bring in the holly and such.'

'You propose to keep Christmas?' I cried. 'With your master missing?'

'He could be with a friend, Doctor. And the children must have their party. Mistress said as how the festivities was to go on as usual for the littluns' sakes.'

Holmes shook himself like a man emerging from a reverie and clapped his mittened hands together. 'We are keeping you from your duties, but before you go, show us the path to the village.'

We were directed to the start of a trampled track that descended easily, graded for horses. Here we could walk side by side, and I acquainted Holmes with the result of my talk with Minnie. He was less interested in her feeling for her step-father than her concern for her mother's health. 'Jealousy of a step-parent is not uncommon,' he murmured, 'but the suggestion that her mother is unbalanced is curious; the woman gave no indication of madness. And the girl had this from Aubrey? Dark waters, Watson.'

'Did the lady say more after I left?'

'She did not return after sending the butler to me—and he was as informative as the Sphinx. Nor did I learn anything from Aubrey's rooms except confirmation that he took nothing with him other than his normal outdoor clothing. No luggage, no toiletries, and we know he did not take a horse.' He stopped walking. 'What are those birds?' Two large black shapes beat by with heavy wings.

'Ravens,' I said. 'No doubt they have scented a sheep that has tumbled over the crags.' The birds were coming in to the crags beyond the cabin. 'They searched all along the foot of those rocks,' I reminded him.

He started walking again. 'First things first. I smell wood-smoke. Why did the fellow prefer to meet his paramour in that bleak hovel rather than in a warm house?'

At first sight the cottage had little to distinguish it from the cabin but the woman who answered our knock, bare-armed and glowing, exuded a vitality that was quite startling. I recognised her immediately: the dark curls, the lustrous eyes. It was the woman in the red cloak whom we'd passed in the village last night. She bobbed a curtsey in which there was nothing of subservience. In different circumstances I might have found her striking in her coarse country fashion but I had been seduced by the shy blonde beauty of little Minnie. In contrast I found Rosie's bold gypsy colouring alarming.

The house was filled with the delicious smell of herbs and roasting meat, and Holmes hung back from the cheerless parlour, suggesting we talk in the kitchen. She showed no surprise, had shown none at our arrival on her doorstep; one might almost have thought that she expected us.

We were seated at a scrubbed table where the meat sizzled in the oven and the fire-box produced a welcome heat. Without fuss she set about the making of a pan of mulled ale and to my astonishment asked whether we would prefer it flavoured with brandy or rum! Holmes glanced at me. It was a signal.

'You treat us like honoured guests, my dear,' I said in my avuncular fashion. 'A joint in the oven, brandy in the ale.'

She gave me a radiant smile. 'The mutton will not be roasted for an hour, sir, but if you will stay so long?'

'Thank you, Rosie, but I was admiring your style, not pleading for an invitation to dinner.' I pride myself on my rapport with women of the lowest rank. 'You keep sheep then?' I glanced meaningly at the oven.

'Oh, no, sir. The mutton is a present. As is the brandy. Folk are generous hereabouts.'

'They appreciate your value,' I said gallantly. 'You live alone?'

'Mostly, sir. I have no time for men about my feet.' She chuckled and her eyes danced.

Holmes said sternly, 'You do not seem greatly concerned at Mr Aubrey's disappearance.'

'Why should I be?' She was amazed. 'It is no business of mine.'

'You are his friend.'

'I would not be so presumptuous.'

He held her eye. 'Where is he, girl?'

'Why, with someone of his acquaintance?' She paused, seeming to gauge our reaction. 'He has gone away to escape the children at Christmas,' she suggested—and that did not ring true either.

'When did you see him last?' Holmes asked.

She looked at the brandy bottle, smiled slyly and said nothing. 'He gave you the brandy,' Holmes stated. 'And the mutton. Christmas presents?'

'He is very good to me,' she murmured.

'Tuesday night a week since?'

She shrugged and wouldn't answer, trying to assume the pose of the stolid peasant.

'Why did you go up there to him,' Holmes pressed, 'rather than he come here? This place is warm and cosy.'

' 'Tis Christmas and I have more callers than is customary, and unannounced. He wouldna want to meet one of his own servants here.'

Holmes tried another tack. 'How was he when he left you?'

'He was tired, and he had drunk a good deal of wine.'

'Was it your custom to leave the cabin in such a state: bottles, glasses, the remains of supper?'

She looked shifty. 'I woulda gone up on the morrow but I slept in an' then I left it 'til next day, and then the searchers was here asking had I seen him and o' course I said I hadna. They had to report back to Mrs Aubrey, so I said what they'd expect me to say.'

'If there has been foul play, who would you think responsible?'

She shook her head. 'I don't understand you.'

'How many men bring you meat and bottles of French brandy? There must be resentment of one who is so lavish.'

She threw back her head and pealed with laughter, firelight caressing the strong white throat. 'Bless you, sir! There are no such feelings in this house. I favour no one.' Of course not; others would bring her venison and pheasants—poachers all. 'There are the women,' she added, more soberly: 'mothers, sweethearts, wives.'

'Mrs Aubrey.'

She spread her hands in a gesture of helplessness and gave us a demure smile. 'What would you have a girl do? He is my landlord.'

'He is not her landlord,' Holmes said as we walked away, directing our steps towards the lakeside road. 'Mrs Aubrey owns the estate.'

'What's hers is her husband's,' I pointed out. 'But she would surely insist on the eviction of such a woman. It is not only her husband who is involved; think of the village youths, the disruption among families.'

'Aubrey would not allow her to be evicted. Not while she pleases him.'

I regarded the lake, the plum-coloured clouds lowered on ashen mountains. Flakes of snow floated gently to settle on the frozen mud of the road. 'We must be approaching them,' came Holmes's voice, bewildering me. 'The birds,' he explained. 'The ravens.'

'We are in for a blizzard. We must make haste for shelter.'

'Nonsense. We are on the road, not the high moors. Come, make a noise; if they are about we shall startle them. Mark where we put them up.' He strode forward, uttering shrill cries.

The ravens rose from the cliff with loud croaks, and they were joined by buzzards that soared above our heads, mewing like cats. Doves clattered through bare branches, a blackbird scolded—and Holmes was scrambling up the screes like a man demented. I sighed and followed. Normally I have no trouble with the old wound, but this ground was rougher even than Dartmoor. Beside Holmes I was an old crock. When I reached the foot of the crag he was nowhere to be seen.

The snow was now falling quite heavily. 'Holmes!' I shouted— and jumped as the response came from close above.

'Here, Watson.'

His head seemed to protrude from the rock some five yards above ground level. 'I have found Aubrey,' he said. 'Or rather, the ravens have.' I gaped at him, speechless. 'Stay there while I complete my examination,' he went on. 'Do not attempt to scale the face with your leg.'

He disappeared. I realised he must be on an inward-sloping ledge where the body had lodged. A few feet to the side was the base of one of those frozen waterfalls that festooned the gullies. Evidently Aubrey, his judgement clouded by his exertions and champagne, had attempted to follow the path instead of crossing the icy streams a discreet distance from the edge. One slip above those glassy cascades and nothing could stop his plunge into the abyss. I started to hunt through the withered undergrowth and after a few moments I gave a cry of triumph. There it was, most of it hidden by brambles but obvious when you knew it should be in the vicinity.

Holmes reappeared and, turning his back to the drop, he descended with agility, his eyes lighting up when he saw that I held two alpenstocks. 'Of course,' he breathed, 'it fell with him. He died immediately, by the by; the skull is shattered like an eggshell and all the limbs are fractured. There would be gross internal bleeding.'

He fastened his muffler to a tree to mark the spot and we slithered down the screes through snow which was now ominous in its intensity. 'So our task is completed,' I announced when we reached level ground. There was no response. 'There was nothing untoward about the body?' I persisted.

'Not about the body, but I found no knapsack. How did he carry two bottles of champagne, a pie, a joint of mutton and the brandy, not to speak of an alpenstock?'

'That is simply answered: Rosie used it to carry the meat and brandy to her cottage.'

He stopped and looked back. 'You cannot return to her now,' I said. 'Wait until the snow stops.'

'Go to Swithins and send a groom with a spare horse to the girl's cottage. Do not mention our discovery. I need to observe their reactions. Hurry, Watson, there is no time to be lost.' He bounded away, in a moment as insubstantial as a phantom.

Mrs Aubrey was supervising the decoration of the large room where the children's party was to be held. There was a spruce tree, mounds of holly and boxes overflowing with pretty baubles. She heard me out with disapproval but she was too well mannered to ask why Holmes should be at Rosie Yewdale's cottage. "Pursuing his enquiries" was how I put it. She ordered that a horse be taken to him immediately.

After the groom had left, I turned back to the stables, where a boy was sweeping out the empty stalls. 'I thought all hands were needed for the party,' I said pleasantly. He was a sharp-looking lad and he stood to attention when addressed.

'I had to saddle the ponies, sir. I shall go in to help when I finish here.' He followed my gaze to a handsome grey eyeing us through the bars of a box. 'That be Miz' Aubrey's mare: the prettiest horse at Swithins, and my lady be the best rider. Why, her even stuck on when Sheba there tried to throw her at back end.'

I considered the grey's intelligent eye. 'She doesn't look a nervous horse.'

'Her's steady as a rock, but what horse wouldna be startled at a shot fired by her ear?'

'What!'

He gaped and swung round, blundering against the side of the stall. 'Hold up there,' I said calmly. He stood rigid. 'Was it a poacher?' I asked. 'And you were told to keep quiet?' He muttered something. 'Speak up, lad.' I was sharp now.

'*I* said as it were a poacher.' He wouldn't meet my eye.

'And what did others say?'

'They searched the woods. It's said there were no poacher.'

'So who fired the shot?'

He looked on the verge of tears. 'They said she imagined it.'

I could get no more out of him and I went into the great barn and communed with the rabbits until Holmes returned, white as a snowman, and shed his outer garments in the stable. I was avid to know the result of his talk with Rosie but he hushed me. "Walls have ears," he whispered.

Mrs Aubrey received us in the drawing room. Daw was still there, as if she anticipated bad news and had need of support. Holmes told her simply that, as had been suspected, her husband had fallen from the lofty path. She sat stiffly, her face like stone, one hand pressed to her bosom. Daw took the other. 'We were afraid of it, my dear,' he said gently. He turned to Holmes. 'It is still a dreadful shock,' he added meaningly.

I rang the bell and when the butler appeared, sent him for brandy and water. At that the lady addressed me. 'Thank you, Doctor. And you, Mr Holmes. If you would inform Mr Daw of the location of the—of my husband, he will make arrangements.'

'I shall attend to everything,' he assured her. 'You must go and rest now. There is nothing to worry about.'

Holmes and I returned to the tower on a couple of trusty ponies, leaving Daw to oversee the removal of the body to the village to await the coroner. There was no sign of the road along the lake-shore but the ponies had no more trouble with it than if it had been marked by stakes. It was still snowing and we rode in silence. At the tower, changed into dry clothing and invigorated by hot toddies, we drew up to the roaring fire and regarded each other quizzically. 'So how did Aubrey carry all that food?' I asked.

Holmes nodded. 'The nub of the problem. Rosie is devious but her mind runs on one track. I asked her who reached the cabin first. She thought about her answer. She should not have needed to think. When she realised that she said quickly that it was herself, but her own long silence had rattled her, and subsequent questions were answered too fast. She betrayed herself. Did he take the knapsack away? I asked. She looked blank and then said she didn't know. It was not with the body, I told her, nor in the cabin, so it must be with her. She ignored this and asked where the body was. She appeared deeply shocked when I told her. I asked her to produce the knapsack and she claimed she did not know what I was talking about. I asked how she carried the mutton and brandy home on Tuesday night—and then, Watson, she thwarted me! She said that it was another night she was at the cabin; she had been mistaken, she said, and then confided that she had an addiction to drink and was often in an alcoholic stupor. I ignored that as an obvious lie and asked her where she was on the Tuesday night, thinking I had her to rights. She said she was home. Could that be substantiated? She looked at me boldly and said, "Oh, yes, sir, I was with one of the grooms from Swithins. All night." In fact, she held a party for several of the Swithins servants. The fellow that brought the pony for me bore her out. She has an unbreakable alibi—but that knapsack! Aubrey carried the food to the cabin in some container. Where is it? And why is it important?'

'But his death was surely an accident!' I exclaimed. 'He fell from the path.' Holmes was silent, staring into the flames. 'A stable lad told me something curious,' I told him. 'In the autumn Mrs Aubrey came in with a story that someone had fired a gun close by when she was riding, and her mare had nearly thrown her. No poacher was found. Pigeons flying up could have startled the mare, and the clatter they make might be misconstrued as a shot by an unbalanced mind. It is a symptom of monomania that the sufferer believes himself surrounded by enemies. What do you think, Holmes?'

'I think we must speak to Daw. He is as close to her as anyone.'

'Is he her lover?'

'No, a lover would be discreet. He took her hand quite openly when I informed her of her husband's death.'

A door slammed and the man himself came tramping into the hall, shedding snow and shouting for grog. He addressed us as he threw off his hat and cape. 'I sent up two of the most nimble fellows and they lowered the body with ropes.' He shook his head.

'To say I'm sorry would be hypocritical; I cannot but feel that man received his deserts.'

'He treated her abominably,' Holmes murmured. Daw looked at him sharply but at that moment the servant entered with a steaming jug and fresh glasses.

'I see they've been looking after you.' Daw regarded our depleted tray. 'But you will join me now in a glass of grog. Only the best Jamaica rum, gentlemen.'

Holmes accepted but refused to be diverted. 'Watson is making a study of monomania,' he said. 'A form of madness.'

'Servants' gossip!' Daw blurted.

'It is more than that.'

Daw's shoulders slumped. 'Aubrey was to blame. His recent behaviour would drive anyone mad. Rosie Yewdale! On his own doorstep! His wife's position was untenable. And Minnie. The child is sharp; it could not be long before it reached her ears. But there,' he cried. 'What could be done?' He became aware of our attentive silence and suddenly his whole demeanor changed and he beamed in great amusement. 'Minnie helped bring in the Yule log last week,' he began, for all the world as if to embark on a piece of family tittle-tattle. 'She caught a chill, and on the Tuesday Helen—Mrs Aubrey—kept her indoors. By Tuesday evening the child had a fever and her mother never left her side until Wednesday morning. How do I know? Because Minnie's room can be approached only through another, and that is occupied by her old nurse, who is a light sleeper. Moreover, she was wide awake during the night and she could see her mistress reclining on a couch by Minnie's bedside. There was a night-light. I know because when I called on Wednesday morning the nurse was coming downstairs to make her small charge a hot drink.'

'Where were you last Tuesday week?' Holmes asked.

Our host sighed. 'I supped with Sir Humphrey Spooner at Troutbeck and we played cards until three in the morning, when we went to our beds. I stayed the night there,' he added carelessly. 'Come clean now, Holmes; you suspect Aubrey was helped on his way to his much-deserved death, but how can you hope to prove it—and do you care? You have solved the riddle of the fellow's disappearance, you have earned your fee; what more do you want?'

'Resolution. I put up the fox, I have to run it to earth.'

'You will have plenty of time for it.' Daw was indulgent. 'They say the roads are blocked by great drifts. We shall have the pleasure of your company over the holiday.'

This was no disaster as far as we were concerned, and we were off to a good start when it transpired that we were invited to Swithins the following day, Christmas Eve, where we were to take tea and stay for cards and dinner.

It was four o'clock when we reached Swithins the following afternoon, travelling with Daw's men and their families, the babies swaddled in shawls. The riders took it in turns to break the trail for the road was deeply drifted.

Mrs Aubrey greeted us with raised chin and steady eyes. Minnie was at her side, enchanting in deep blue velvet.

We were served tea. The talk was of Swithins in summer, while I said something of my lighter moments in Afghanistan. There was no mention of Aubrey. Occasionally we heard bursts of merriment from a distance and shortly a buxom person entered, Minnie's old nurse, and took her away to the party.

'Minnie shall play hostess,' said her mother. 'We will join her later for distribution of the gifts.'

I found myself inexpressibly touched. An old warrior, a doctor, twice married (but childless)—'I should enjoy that,' I said eagerly, and Holmes glanced at me in surprise.

'Of course, Doctor,' said Mrs Aubrey. 'Everyone is invited.' The atmosphere was permeated with good humour. I could not help but feel that Swithins had lost not its master, but an incubus.

When the butler came to summon us we trooped out, Holmes with a gleam in his eye, and a jaunty step that had me puzzled; apart from the urchins of the Baker Street Irregulars, he has no interest in children. When we came to the room where the party was in progress, he settled himself against the wall near the big spruce tree and watched the proceedings keenly.

As for the partygoers, children from both estates and the village, they had eyes only for their gifts and their young hostess. Minnie was composed and clearly enjoying herself as she took the gifts from the young stable lad (scrubbed until he shone) and presented them with a few words for each recipient. Again I found myself ridiculously affected and, glancing away, caught Mrs Aubrey's eye. There was that in her look that was more than love, more than pride; there was a fierce watchfulness, a kind of triumph, and it sent a shiver through my bowels.

They had pulled back the drapes and I noticed Mrs Aubrey look towards a window. She stiffened and her expression resolved itself into one of unadulterated hatred. Rosie Yewdale was at the window, her brilliant face framed by the scarlet hood, her lips parted, her eyes alight with pleasure. She seemed fascinated by the Christmas tree, but now, as if feeling the fire of Mrs Aubrey's regard, she shifted her gaze, caught that obsessed glare, and was gone.

I was saddened. Whatever she was, Rosie was another childless soul, and for a moment I felt something like kinship. Christmas is a sentimental season.

Later that evening we dined on roast pork and hothouse fruits. Minnie was at table as a special concession but the ladies left us to our port quite early, Mrs Aubrey pleading the exertions of tomorrow. Daw was beginning to feel the effects of fine wines, and even I was not fully in command of my senses, nevertheless I did not fail to notice Holmes excuse himself and leave the room.

Within ten minutes he was back. Daw was approaching the climax of a thrilling fox chase and was caught up in his own excitement. I looked at Holmes's saturnine face and knew that something momentous had occurred. He was as smug as Pussy after finding a bowl of cream in the dairy. Where had he been? What had he seen—in ten minutes?

It was past midnight before he found the opportunity to tell me. We had returned to the peel tower, imbibed the smallest of nightcaps, not wishing to offend our host, and climbed the stair by the light of our candles. He hustled me into his room and I turned on him eagerly.

'Where did you go?'

'To my lady's chamber. And she was not alone.'

'She has a lover!' I was incredulous for Daw was with me.

'Not a lover, but one for whom she has great regard. There is love certainly, and passionate at that but they have it focused on a third person.'

'Holmes, it is too late for riddles. Who was she with?'

'Rosie Yewdale.'

I collapsed on a chair. 'Rosie . . . was . . . in Mrs Aubrey's bed-room? Doing what?'

'Talking pleasantly. I couldn't distinguish words, but I did not need to. It was enough to listen to the tones: like that of sisters or close women friends.'

'I don't believe it.' He said nothing. He would not lie to me. 'What is the explanation, Holmes?'

'Minnie.'

'That tells me nothing. I did see Rosie at the window watching the party—but I also saw Mrs Aubrey's face when she caught sight of the woman. I have seen a cobra rear and strike. It was like that.'

'Mrs Aubrey knew you were watching her.'

'She fabricated such an expression? You are telling me she is friendly with her husband's whore!'

'Rosie was hardly that, and most definitely not his friend.'

'Oh come, we have her word.'

'A red herring across the trail. Aubrey didn't chase after women, my dear fellow. That is a blanket story, believed by everyone, unwittingly encouraged by several, emanating from one person: the man himself, and that in order to disguise the truth.'

'What can be more foul than that a married man sought out trollops?'

'That he had a fondness for children.'

I should not have been so shocked as I was. I know such mon-sters exist—but not in great houses, not among people like our-selves. 'Minnie?' I breathed. 'He . . . he didn't . . . ' I could not go on.

'No. He was stopped in time.'

'By one of those two women after all? Or both in collusion?'

'Or three of them. As I came away from Mrs Aubrey's door I heard a rustle of skirts behind me and turned to see Minnie's old nurse enter the room.'

'Did she see you?'

'We shall know tomorrow.'

We were to know sooner than that. There came a knock at the door and our host was revealed, a greatcoat over an old-fashioned nightshirt. He regarded us in consternation. 'Helen is below,' he gasped. 'She wishes to speak with you, Holmes. What can it be? She rode here *alone!*'

'We will be with her immediately.' Holmes turned to me and I knew without his saying that the nurse had seen him. As Daw retreated I went to my room and retrieved my service revolver from my valise. It made a conspicuous bulge in my pocket but it might be as well to let our visitor see that we were not defenceless.

She was seated by the fire with Daw in attendance. He regarded us warily, and when she asked him to leave he refused. 'You will regret that you stayed,' she warned him. 'You will be hurt.'

'Nothing you have done will hurt me.'

'Oh, I have done nothing, dear friend.'

Ah, I thought, the evasions commence.

'I shall stay,' he said stoutly, and threw more logs on the fire. He brushed his hands and surveyed us: master in his own house, providing sanctuary for a lady (his lady?), offering defiance to any-one who threatened her. He gestured to chairs and we sat. Holmes turned to Mrs Aubrey.

'How much do you know?' she asked.

'About what—' Daw began—and she held up a hand. 'You will be shocked and distressed, Clement, but if you insist on staying, you must listen or we shall never be finished. And already it is Christmas Day,' she added, with a hint of a smile. 'I have much to do.'

Holmes replied to her question. 'You must assume that I know as little of recent events as I do about their origins, madam, al-though I can hazard guesses. It is obvious you knew nothing of Aubrey's true nature when you agreed to marry him.'

'Do you think for one moment I would have done so had I known?'

Holmes said calmly, 'He would have confessed that he had not led a blameless life where ladies were concerned. You thought marriage would reform him. He told you that Minnie needed a father.' Her eyes were wide. 'It is the standard cant of such men,' he assured her.

'That's what I said!' Daw interrupted.

'I married him.' Her tone was flat. 'And for a time he was most attentive, particularly to Minnie.' Daw let this go, poor fellow, in blissful ignorance of the horror to come. 'Then he started to absent himself for days at a time, pleading business in Glasgow or Liverpool. He was involved in shipping, he said—but said it so carelessly I was not meant to believe it. I came to suspect that he visited cities for other purposes.'

'I begged her to leave him,' Daw said. 'She wouldn't. I couldn't move her.'

'Swithins is my house,' she told us with dignity. 'I have responsibilities towards the people on the estate. I could not leave. But nor would he. He laughed at me. He said my suspicions were the result of a diseased imagination and he began to taunt me with what he termed was my steady deterioration into madness.' It was clear from his expression that Daw had not known of this; he made to interrupt but Holmes gestured for silence. 'To obtain proof of his perfidy,' she went on, 'I followed him to Glasgow, but I guessed I would be unable to follow him to his ultimate destination. I knew the hotel where he was staying however and I employed a private detective to track him from there. The result was devastating. I had expected a house of ill fame; what he discovered was so vile that he would not report back to me, would have relinquished his fee rather than tell me. I tracked him to his home'— she smiled grimly '—by employing a second detective. Thus I learned the truth about the man I had married.' She turned to Daw. 'He had no interest in women—except as mothers of little girls'—her voice dropped—'and as procurers.'

'What are you saying?' Daw was incredulous. 'Minnie?' He was floundering, his mind refusing to entertain the truth.

'He married me to be close to Minnie,' Mrs Aubrey went on coldly. 'He would have had me certified in order to become her sole guardian. It would be he who fired at me when I was riding, whether to kill me or as part of the fiendish plot to prove me mad, I do not know. After I went to Glasgow I told him I would no longer tolerate his presence under the same roof as Minnie. If he remained another day, I said, I would go to the police. The detective would be called as witness, not to speak of the person in Glasgow who provided the children. He defied me. He said that the detective would never appear in court, that this obscene trade

97

was operated by criminal gangs who would stop at nothing to prevent him. He said that the house he had visited would be abandoned long before the police reached it—in short, I had no proof. On the contrary, people had known for months that my mental health was deteriorating; my story was the ramblings of a madwoman, it could be nothing else. And then he told me something of his nature; he could do that, you see, he had nothing to lose. I was trapped.'

We were, all three of us, torn between horror and compassion. She gave us a thin smile. 'It was Minnie who saved my reason; I had to remain sane in order to protect her. In order to thwart him, at least temporarily, I moved her bedroom to one which could be approached only through another, and there I installed her old nurse—'

Daw had had enough. 'Why didn't you tell me?' he protested.

'You would have . . . confronted him.' The hesitation did not escape me. Daw would have killed the devil.

'Certainly I needed a friend,' Mrs Aubrey conceded. 'Nurse was too old, your emotions would impede your actions, Clement, moreover you could never dissemble. I needed a woman, one who was strong and clever and whom I could trust with my life. I went to Rosie Yewdale.'

'But she—how could you do that?'

'I said Aubrey was not interested in women except as mothers and procurers. Rosie loves children and, despite the disapproval of the village women, there are often children about her cottage. Aubrey had visited her, no doubt as part of the façade he presented to the world: that of the incorrigible rake, but his ulterior motive would be the children at that isolated cottage.' She shuddered, then pulled herself together and continued. 'Rosie did not believe my story so I told her that next time Aubrey visited her and his perceptions became clouded by drink, she was to steer him to the subject of children and mark what he said. A week later she came to me and asked what I would have her do.'

'What had he told her?' Daw was belligerent.

'I shall not tell you, nor anyone else.'

Holmes asked, 'What was Aubrey's reaction afterwards, when he realised he had betrayed himself to Rosie?'

'I said she was clever. He thought he had found an ally. Later, when he received a note asking him to meet her at the cabin, he went. The note said it had to be the cabin because she had taken a lodger. It also said they would discuss "the matter". The implication was that she was about to assist him in . . . what he did.'

'What did he take to the cabin?' Holmes asked.

She shrugged as if, on the threshold of her story's climax, she had lost interest. 'I did not see him leave. Minnie had a fever and I spent the evening and night at her bedside.'

'No matter. Rosie will tell us.'

'She did not go to the cabin either.'

'She implied to us that she did.'

'And retracted subsequently. In the first place she was protecting me because she thought it was I who went to the cabin— because it was I who directed her to send him the note and I who told her *not* to go. She retracted when she learned that I had not gone after all.'

'You had intended to meet him there?'

'I intended to be on top of the crags as he passed close to the edge. Yes, sir, I planned to kill my husband. I had gone to the cabin when Nurse and Minnie were helping to bring home the Yule log. I set the scene with champagne and the pie, and disordered the bed. I had told Rosie to entertain several men that evening and to make certain that one of them stayed the whole night.'

'Where did Rosie obtain the mutton and the brandy?' Holmes answered his own question: 'From you, of course.'

She nodded. 'So when he failed to return to Swithins, Rosie thought that I was responsible—and in a manner I was. I had arranged for him to be up there: at night, the path sheeted with ice, and himself far from sober, for he never spared the wine at dinner.' She stopped and leaned back in her chair, exhausted.

'An appalling story, madam; you have suffered beyond endurance. Fortunately none of us is called upon to pass judgement on your intentions to bring about his downfall because they failed?' There was the slightest question in his tone. 'He died by accident.'

It was four o'clock when we climbed the stair again. Daw was escorting Mrs Aubrey back to Swithins. She had insisted on returning; Minnie would wake early on Christmas morning. Outside our rooms I leaned against the wall, stupefied with weariness. 'I would say it was less of an accident than divine retribution,' I said.

My companion studied me, the candle flames flickering in a vagrant draught, then he turned, his hand to the latch.

'Holmes!'

'What is it, Watson?'

'You are not satisfied.'

'I am indeed.'

'It was an accident?'

'It was murder. The man was pushed.'

'Then which one? Rosie or the lady?'

'Or one of their alibis: the old nurse, the drunken groom in Rosie's bed? Not him; they would never trust a man. But the nurse was not drunk and she was wakeful. The lady, the nurse and the whore. There can be only one force more dangerous than a woman, Watson, and that is several of them working in league and all morally certain that they are in the right.'

'I believe they were.'

He nodded gravely. 'I agree with you, but would you—would I—have the courage to translate our belief into action? They live by a different code; can you imagine what they might demonstrate if they were criminal?'

THE ADVENTURE OF THE THREE GHOSTS

Loren D. Estleman

"Compliments of the season, Watson. I note Lady Feath-erstone retains her childhood infatuation with you. She thinks you twelve feet tall and two yards wide at the shoulders."

Scarcely had I entered the ground floor at 221 Baker Street and surrendered my outerwear to the redoubtable Mrs. Hudson when I was thus greeted by Sherlock Holmes, who stood upon the landing outside the flat we shared for so long. He wore his prized old mouse-coloured dressing-gown, and his eyes were brighter than usual.

"Good Lord, Holmes," said I, climbing the stairs. "How could you know I saw Constance Featherstone this morning? Her invitation to breakfast was the first contact I have had with her since the wedding."

"You forget, dear fellow, that I know your wardrobe as well as your wife does. I can hardly be expected not to notice a new muf-fler, particularly when it bears the Dornoch tartan. You told me once in a loquacious humour of your early romance with Constance

Dornoch. Who but she would present you with such a token in honour of the holiday? And who but a sentimental lady who still thought you taller and broader than the common breed of man would knit one so long and bulky that it wound five times round your not inconsiderable neck and stood out like the oaken collar of a Mongolian slave?"

I simply shook my head, for to remark upon my friend's pre-ternatural powers of observation and deduction would be merely to repeat myself for the thousandth time. Ensconced presently in my old armchair in the dear old cluttered sitting-room I knew so well, I accepted a glass of whisky to draw the December chill from my bones and enquired what he was up to at present.

"Your timing is opportune," said he, folding his long limbs into the basket chair, where with his hands resting upon his knees he bore no small resemblance to an East Indian shaman. "In ten minutes I shall hail a hansom to carry me to an address on Thread-needle Street, where I fully expect my fare to be paid by the Earl of Chislehurst."

I nodded, not greatly impressed, although Lord Chislehurst was a respected Member of Parliament and a frequent weekend guest at Balmoral and whispered about as the Queen's favoured candi-date for Minister of Finance. In the hierarchy of Holmes's clients, which had included a pontiff, a Prime Minister of England, and a foreign king, a noble banker placed fairly low. "A problem involv-ing money?" I asked.

"No, a haunting. Are you interested?"

I responded that I most certainly was; and ten minutes later, my friend having exchanged his dressing-gown for an ulster, warm woollen muffler, and his favourite earflapped travelling cap, we were in a hansom rolling and sliding over the icy pavement through a gentle fall of snow. Vendors were hawking roast chest-nuts, and over everything, the grim grey buildings and the holiday shoppers hurrying to and fro, bearing armloads of brightly wrapped packages, there had settled a festive atmosphere which trans-formed our dreary old London into a magical kingdom. In two days it would be gone, along with Christmas itself, but for the moment it lightened the heart and gilded it with hope.

"The earl is not a fanciful man," explained Holmes, holding on to the side of the conveyance. "A decade ago he acquired a money-lending institution teetering on the precipice of ruin and within a few short years brought it to the point where it is now universally thought of as one of the ten or twelve most reliable banking firms in England. Such men do not take lightly to ghosts."

I could divine no more detail than this, as very soon we pulled up before a gloomy old pile which I suspected had shown no great ceremony in its construction under George III, and to which the lapse of nearly a century and a half had brought little in the way of dignity or character. It seemed a most unlikely shelter for the institution Holmes had described.

Lord Chislehurst, to whom we were shown by a distracted young clerk, ameliorated to a great extent this disappointing impression. Well along in his fifties, he had yet a youthful abundance of fair hair, with but a trace of grey in the side whiskers and the gracefully swelling abdomen that instilled confidence in those who would trust their fortunes to the care of one so well fed, contained in a grey waistcoat and black frock. His broad face was flushed and his manner cordial as he exhorted us to make ourselves comfortable in a pair of deep leather chairs facing his great desk. I noticed as he made his way round to his own seat that he walked with a pronounced limp.

"I am doubly honoured, Dr. Watson, to welcome you to my place of business," said he, leaning back and threading his fingers together across his middle. "I have read your published accounts of Mr. Holmes's cases with a great deal of interest. As a writer, you may be intrigued to learn that my father toiled for many years as a clerk in the counting-house you came through just now."

"You have done well for yourself," I said truthfully.

"So my father might say. Despite the hardship, he was a jovial man, and would laugh long and loud to see his youngest child making free with the cigars in this office." He helped himself to one from a cherrywood box upon the desk and proffered the box, but we declined.

"Hardship?" prompted Holmes.

"The former owner was a fierce old dragon in his time, and pinched the halfpenny till it shrieked. Changed quite a bit in his last years, though, I'll be bound; saw the light, I suspect, as Judgement neared. His generosity to his employees after that made it possible for Father to arrange an operation that saved my life. I was a sickly child—a cripple, in fact. Unfortunately, the old banker overdid it, and wound up sacrificing those same sound business principles that made him wealthy. His fortunes declined even as mine ascended. He died in debt, and I acquired the firm the very week I entered the Peerage."

Holmes lit a cigarette. "An inspiring story, Your Lordship. Your letter—"

"The tea is not always sweet," he interrupted. "I had hoped to move the offices to more suitable quarters down the street next spring, but this South African mess has got all our foreign securities tied up. Against my better judgement, I have been forced to cancel this year's employee gratuities."

"Your letter mentioned a ghost."

"Three ghosts, Mr. Holmes. As if one were not sufficient." Our host's genial smile had vanished. "I have been visited by them the past two nights, and I must say it's getting to be a dashed nuisance."

"What happened the first night?"

"I was not greatly alarmed by it, thinking the business a bad dream caused by exhaustion and overindulgence. That day had been long and frustrating, beginning with more bad news from Africa in the *Times*, and complicated by a discrepancy in the accounts totalling forty-two pounds, which required that the transactions of the entire week be gone over with a weather eye by everyone on the staff. When the error was finally discovered and the correction made, the hour was well past seven. As is my wont, I stopped at the tavern round the corner on my way home, where I confess I had rather more than my customary tot of sherry. My wife, recognising my condition at the door, put me to bed straightaway.

"I slept as one dead until the stroke of one, at which time I awoke, or thought I awoke, with the realisation that I was not alone in my chamber."

"One moment," interrupted Holmes. "You do not share sleeping quarters with your wife?"

"Not since the early months of our marriage. I often sleep fitfully, with much tossing and muttering, and my wife is a light sleeper. I prefer not to disturb her. Is it significant?"

"Perhaps not. Please proceed."

" 'Who is there?' I asked groggily; for I was aware of a shimmering paleness in a corner of the room that was usually dark, as of a shaft of moonlight reflecting off a human face.

" 'The Ghost of Christmas Past,' came the reply. The voice was most solemn but youthful, and very much of this earth.

" 'Whose past?' I demanded. 'Who let you in?'

" 'Your past,' said the shade; and then some rot about coming along with him."

Holmes, settled deep in his chair with his lower limbs stretched in front of him and his eyes closed, said nothing, listening. His cigarette smoked between his fingers. As for myself, I felt my brow wrinkling. The narrative had begun to sound familiar.

"The rest is quite personal," the earl continued. "Vivid memories of my childhood, Christmas dinner with my mother and father and my brother Peter and my sister Martha, and Father going on about a goose, and what-have-you. Obviously I was dreaming, but I had the distinct impression of having travelled a great distance, and that I was peeping at all this as through a window, with the Ghost of Christmas Past standing at my elbow. It was all very strange, but nice, and sad as well. My parents are dead, my sister married and gone to America, and my brother and I have not spoken in years. We quarrelled over our meagre inheritance. I suppose it is not unusual to feel wistful over the happier days of youth. Still, it was an odd coincidence."

Holmes opened his eyes. "How was it a coincidence?"

"I had spent much of that trying day shut up with Richard, my chief clerk, going over the accounts. When at length the discrepancy was corrected, it seemed natural to invite him to join me in a glass of sherry at the tavern. He accepted, and we whiled away a convivial evening reminiscing about Christmases old and new. So it seems odd that I should dream about the very same thing that night."

"Not at all, Your Lordship," I put in. "Man is a suggestible creature. It would be far more unusual to dream about something that was not in one's mind recently."

"I think there is something in what you say, Doctor. Certainly it would help to explain the second part of my dream." The earl lit a fresh cigar, apparently forgetting the one he had left smouldering only half-smoked in the tray on his desk. "It seems I returned to my bed, for again the clock struck one and I found myself as I had previously, staring at a phosphorescence in the corner and asking who was there.

" 'The Ghost of Christmas Present,' responded a most remarkable voice, jolly and full of timbre, as of a man in the fullness of his middle years. Just this, and again the summons to come along.

"Now we were standing outside the window of a tiny flat in the City, witnessing what appeared to be a serious row between a young husband and his wife over money; something about not having sufficient funds to settle their bills, let alone celebrate the holiday. At the tavern, Richard had told me of a number of financial setbacks they had suffered because of unforeseen emergencies, but I had not perceived how serious the situation was until that moment. It appeared to threaten their union."

"Had you met his wife?" Holmes asked.

"I have not had that pleasure. However, he keeps a photographic portrait of her where he works. She is most comely."

"Women generally are, in photographs. What happened when the clock again struck one?"

Lord Chislehurst permitted himself a dry smile. "I should have been disappointed had you not seen the pattern. This phantom, who indicated through gestures that he was the Ghost of Christmas Yet to Come, was the most unsettling of all, and the picture he showed me of some future yuletide was bleak and hideous. I saw Richard's home broken, his wife, stigmatised by divorce, forced to make her living from the streets, even as Richard pursued a bitter and lonely existence as an unloved and aging bachelor. Worse, I saw my own neglected grave. Evidently I had gone to it without obsequy, my harsh and penurious business practises having ruined lives and left none to mourn my passing." He shuddered.

Holmes finished his cigarette. "In your waking moments, my lord, are you given to dwelling morbidly upon the subject of your future demise?"

"Never. I regard it as an inevitability, which to brood over is to squander what little life we have. This was what I told Lady Chislehurst when she brought up the subject of my last will and testament."

"Indeed?" Holmes lifted his brows. "Did this discussion take place before or after your dream?"

"Before. That very night, in fact. When I was late coming home from the tavern, she entertained various concerns over what might have befallen me, as wives will. When I arrived at last, she expressed relief, then scolded me as I was preparing to retire that I should be more careful, as the streets are not safe late at night for a man not in full possession of his wits, and that if I insisted upon placing myself in jeopardy I should make arrangements for the division of my estate before some footpad separates me from my watch and my life."

"A practical woman."

"Very much so. It is the quality which drew my attention to her in the first place. I met her when she came to work for me as a typist. Her suggestions for the improvement of the firm were inspired, and as she was of good family I soon realised that she was the woman to bring order to my existence away from the office. We were married within a year. From time to time, when the firm is shorthanded due to illness or personal emergency among the staff, she still comes in to help out."

"I assume she works well with Richard."

"They make an ideal team. Often I have seen them in conference, with many nods and expressions of agreement. But what has this to do with my ghosts?"

"Probably nothing. Perhaps everything. Let us return to this will. Were you persuaded to make it out?"

"My solicitor was in this morning. I signed the documents and Richard witnessed my signature. My wife is chief beneficiary, and Richard is executor; he is a reliable man, and the fee will come in handy should his financial difficulties continue."

"I commend Your Lordship upon his generosity. You had the dream again last night?"

"Yes, and I'm not certain it was a dream. I was cold sober, having gone straight home from the office without stopping at the tavern, and retired at a decent hour. A cup of tea with Lady Chislehurst before bed was my only indulgence. I shall not repeat myself, for the visitations were the same, including the redundant striking of the hour of one upon the clock, the shades of Christmases Past, Present, and Yet to Come, and the visions which accompanied them. This time, however, it was all much more vivid. I awoke this morning with the conviction that it had all been true. And there was something else, Mr. Holmes: the condition of my bedroom slippers."

"Your bedroom slippers?"

"Yes." He leaned forward, placing his palms upon his desk. "They were soaked through, Mr. Holmes, exactly as if I had been walking in snow the whole night."

This intelligence had a profound effect upon my friend. Face thrust forward now, his eyes keen and his nostrils flaring, he said, "I must prevail upon Your Lordship to invite Dr. Watson and myself to be your guests tonight."

The earl frowned—less perturbed, I thought, by the inconvenience of entertaining two unexpected houseguests as by the impropriety of Holmes having made the suggestion himself. "You deem this necessary?"

"I consider it of the utmost importance."

"Very well. I shall send a messenger to inform my wife."

"That is precisely what I must ask you not to do. No one must know that we are in residence."

"May I ask why?"

"Everything depends upon the outward appearance that your nightly routine remains unchanged. I assure you I am not being melodramatic when I say your life is in danger."

"But of what, Mr. Holmes? By whom?"

Holmes stood, ignoring this reasonable question. "I will need time to lay my trap. Will it be possible to ensure that Lady Chislehurst and your servants are all away from home this evening between the hours of eight and nine?"

"That should not be difficult. Our cook will have left by then, and our maid is away visiting relatives for the holiday. I shall suggest my wife call upon her friend Mrs. Wesley down the street. She was widowed last spring and faces a lonely Christmas."

"Excellent. Pray inform her that you are exhausted and will

probably have retired by the time she returns. Dr. Watson and I shall be watching from cover. Expect us immediately after she has gone. It is extremely important that you share none of these details with anyone, especially your clerk."

The earl agreed, and provided us with directions to his London lodgings, whereupon we moved towards the door. Upon the threshold I turned and said, "I should like to ask Your Lordship one question, a personal one."

"I have no secrets, Doctor."

"Is your family name by any chance Cratchit?"

He appeared surprised. "Why, yes, it is. I was born Timothy Cratchit. Did you read that in Brook's?"

"No, Your Lordship; in Dickens."

Lord Chislehurst scowled. "That meddler! I personally have not read his invasive little story, yet I cannot escape from it. Until I entered the nobility I could go nowhere without some new acquaintance hailing me as Tiny Tim, and thinking himself quite the clever fellow."

After we had been shown out of the counting-room by Richard, who seemed a personable sort, well groomed and dressed within the limitations of a clerk's salary, Holmes asked me the meaning of the last exchange. I was stupefied. "Surely you are familiar with Charles Dickens's 'A Christmas Carol'! Every English schoolboy has had the story force-fed to him each December."

"I was an uncommon schoolboy, and I haven't the faintest notion to what you are referring."

Briefly, in the hansom on the way back to Baker Street, I summarised that most English of Christmas tales and its unforgettable cast of characters: Ebenezer Scrooge, the miserly, holiday-loathing banker; Bob Cratchit, his long-suffering clerk; Cratchit's loveable, crippled younger son Tiny Tim; and the three ghosts who visited Scrooge and brought about his conversion to the season of love and forgiveness. Holmes listened with keen interest.

"I recall telling you once that it is a mistake to imagine that one's brain-attic has elastic walls, and that the time will come when for every new shipment of information one accepts, another must be sacrificed," he said when I had finished. "However, I rather think I have an uncluttered corner still, and it seems to me that literature would not be an unwise thing to deposit there. What one man can invent, another can subvert. If you and I are not careful tonight, Watson, your Mr. Dickens may well be an unwitting accomplice before the fact of murder."

"Whom do you suspect, and what is the motive?"

"Chiefly, I suspect Lady Chislehurst and Richard, the clerk. Whether their alliance is amorous or strictly mercenary has yet to be determined, but I am convinced they are in it together, and that Lord Chislehurst's estate is their object."

"But why the clerk? The wife is the sole beneficiary."

"It was he who planted the suggestion in the earl's mind which led to his Christmas Present vision of strife in Richard's household. Our client was not aware of his clerk's dire financial situation before their most timely conversation. There is nothing so effective as a little haunting, combined with a wife's reminder of one's fiscal responsibilities to his family, to bring a man to a contemplation of his mortality, and consequently his last will and testament."

"Are you suggesting Lord Chislehurst was mesmerised?"

"I suspect something even more ambitious and diabolical. You may count upon it, Watson, there is skullduggery afoot. I am reminded most acutely of that business at the Baskerville estate during the early years of our association. If there is a ghost involved here at all, it is Stapleton's."

At this point Holmes fell into a dark reverie, from which I knew from long experience he would not be drawn until the hour of our appointment with our endangered client. As we clip-clopped homeward through those streets laden with snow, the seasonal spirit was significantly absent inside that cab.

Big Ben had just struck eight, and the resonance of its final chime was still in the air when a well-built woman in her middle years bustled out the doorway of an imposing pile not far from Threadneedle Street and started down the pavement wrapped in a heavy cloak. This, I assumed, was Lady Chislehurst; and she had not been out of sight thirty seconds when Holmes and I emerged from the shallow doorway across the street where we had stationed ourselves five minutes previously.

Holmes did not ring the bell right away, but paced the length of the front of the building, swinging his cane in the metronomic manner he often used to measure distance. Presently he climbed the front steps with me at his heels.

The bell was answered almost immediately by our client, whose attire of nightcap and dressing-gown assured us he had followed Holmes's advice and convinced his wife that he was retiring. Once we were admitted to the rather dark and gloomy foyer, the detective repeated the procedure he had observed outside, pacing the room deliberately from the left wall to the right.

"An interesting building," he said when he was standing before the earl once again. "James the First, is it not?"

"James the Second, or so I was told when I acquired it from the Scrooge estate. It was a depressing old place, neglected and in disrepair. Lady Chislehurst has done much to improve it, although much remains to be done. The very first thing she did was to see to it that the hideous old door-knocker was removed. The lion's head frightened our nieces and nephews when they came to visit."

"It is admirable of you both to take the trouble to preserve the place. The loss of such an unusually substantial example of architecture would be a great tragedy. There is a discrepancy of six feet in the width of the building between the outside and the inside. One seldom encounters walls three feet thick so far past the medieval period."

"Indeed. I never noticed."

"I am always intrigued by how little attention we pay to familiar things, which are to us the most important. May we inspect your chamber?"

The earl led us up a narrow flight of stairs to a large room on the first floor, equipped with a huge old four-poster bed and a stone fireplace nearly large enough to walk into upright, with a bearskin stretched before it on the hearth. Above the mantel hung a huge old painting in a gilt frame of a medieval noblewoman languishing on the floor of a dungeon, with light streaming down upon her from a barred window high on the wall.

"An outside room," observed Holmes. "Do you not find it draughty?"

"No; the window was bricked in years ago."

"Convenient."

"How so, Mr. Holmes?"

"Darkness, of course. There is nothing less conducive to sleep than an unwanted shaft of light. Is that the corner in which you saw the apparitions? Yes, that is where they would be most visible to someone sitting up in bed. Where is Lady Chislehurst's chamber in relation to yours?"

"Just down the hall. Do you wish to see it?"

"That won't be necessary." He swung upon the earl, eyes bright as twin beacons. "Dr. Watson dabbles a bit in Jamesian architecture. Would Your Lordship object to conducting him upon a tour while I complete my inspection? I thought not. Thank you for your hospitality."

"Curious fellow, your Mr. Holmes," said Lord Chislehurst when we were in the gaslit hallway outside the room where Holmes could be heard rummaging about. "Is he always this unusual?"

"Usually."

"Do you know anything at all about Jamesian architecture?"

"Only that it is uncommon to find walls so thick, and I didn't know that until a few minutes ago."

He produced two cigars from the pocket of his dressing-gown and gave me one. "Curious fellow."

"He is the best detective in England."

We had smoked a third of our cigars when the door opened. Holmes appeared sanguine, as if he had spent the time stretched out upon the earl's bed. "There you are, Watson. Does Your Lordship have a spare bedroom?"

"I have several. Would you and the doctor like to share one, or would you prefer separate quarters?"

"With your permission, we shall share yours. I am suggesting that you sleep in the spare room."

"Whatever for?"

Holmes smiled and placed a finger to his lips. "As Dr. Watson has no doubt told you, my methods are my own and I seldom confide them. Pray do as I ask, and do not venture out under any circumstances. By morning I hope to have laid your ghosts to rest."

"See here, Holmes," said I when our host had left us alone in the room, "I have known you far too long to accept this nonsense

112

about architecture as an adequate explanation for keeping secrets from me. What were you about while I was out upon that fool's errand?"

My friend had removed his boots and stripped to his shirtsleeves and was making himself comfortable upon the big four-poster. "Forgive me, dear fellow. You know full well my weakness for theatrics. In any case your own mind is too active for you to continue to assist me in these little problems if I fail to occupy it. I have come to depend upon my amanuensis. What was lightning before Franklin arrived with his kite and key? Merely a pretty display."

My disgruntlement was only partly relieved by this academic apology. "What do we do now?"

"Nothing."

"Nothing?"

"Turn down the lamp, will you? There's a good fellow." Whereupon, in the dim orange glow of the lowered wick of the lamp upon the bedside table, he closed his eyes. Within moments his even breathing told me he was asleep.

I did not join him in the arms of Morpheus. Although nothing had been said, I knew from past experience that one of us must remain vigilant, and so I stayed awake in the room's one chair, feeling the reassuring solidity of my faithful service revolver in my pocket.

At length I heard the front door open and shut, and divined that Lady Chislehurst had returned from her visit. Presently, light footsteps climbed the stairs, paused briefly outside the room as if waiting for some sign of movement within, whilst I held my breath; then they continued down the hall, where the snick and then the thump of a door opening and closing told me that our client's wife had retired to her room. Then silence.

The night wore on. The room was chill without a fire, for which I was grateful, as it kept me alert. The shadows thrown by the nearly nonexistent light were monstrous, and in my imagination I peopled them with all sorts of mortal terrors.

I must have dozed, despite the cold, for I was suddenly aware of a pale light in a corner of the room where before there had been only darkness, and I had the impression it had been there for some little time. I started, and reached instantly for my revolver. However, a sudden sharp sibilant from the direction of the bed halted me. Holmes was sitting up, his attention centred on the light in the corner. His profile was predatory in its silver reflection.

As we watched, the light changed, assuming vaguely human shape. Now we were looking at a tall, gaunt figure seemingly wrapped in a cloak as black as the shadows that surrounded it. Its face was invisible in the depths of the cowl covering its head, but its skeletal wrist protruded from a loose sleeve, and as the image shimmered before us, its crooked, bony finger appeared to beckon.

My heart hammered in my breast. Clearly, this was the most frightening phantasm of the three that had been described to us: the Ghost of Christmas Yet to Come, with its cold, silent promise of a lonely grave for he who encountered it.

"Quick, Watson! The light!"

I hesitated but briefly, then reached over and turned up the lamp. Immediately the ghost vanished. I leapt to my feet, starting in that direction. Holmes, however, moved to the wall adjacent, which contained the huge fireplace. The grate was supported by an enormous pair of andirons of medieval manufacture, one of which he seized by its lion's-head ornament and pulled towards himself. There was a pause, followed by a grating sound, as of a rusted gate opening upon hinges disused for decades. Then the entire back of the fireplace, which I had assumed to be constructed of solid stone, slid sideways, exposing a black hollow beyond.

"A passageway!" said I.

"I surmised as much from the beginning. You will remember I remarked upon the discrepancy between the inside and outside measurements of the building. Hand me the lamp, and keep your revolver handy. Remove your boots. We don't want them to know we're coming."

I did as directed. Holding the light aloft, Holmes stepped over the grate and into the blackness, with me close upon his heels.

The passage was narrow, dank, and musky smelling. Once inside, Holmes exclaimed softly and lifted the lamp higher. A great metal contraption equipped with a glass lens stood upon a ledge at shoulder height. I smelled hot wax.

"It looks like a lantern," I whispered.

"A *magic* lantern." Standing upon tiptoe, Holmes reached up with his free hand, groped at the contraption, and slid a pane of glass from behind the lens. He examined it briefly, then handed it to me. When I held it up against the light from the lamp, I recognized the image of our old friend the Ghost of Christmas Yet to Come etched upon the glass.

"The image is projected through the lens when the candle is lit," Holmes explained. "When I examined the room earlier, I found a small hole in the painting above the mantel, just where the light streams through the window to fall upon the lady in the dungeon. That is where our ghost gained access to the room. When I found the mechanism that opens the fireplace, I knew my suspicions were correct. I daresay if we look, we shall find similar panes bearing the likenesses of the Ghosts of Christmas Past and Present as they were described to us."

"But Past and Present spoke to the earl!"

"It might surprise you to learn what a ghastly effect the echoes in a narrow passage such as this will lend to the human voice. But come!"

I was forced to hasten lest he outrun the light from the lamp. When I caught up with him several yards down that gloomy path, he was peering at a small bottle perched in a niche in the wall. Presently he removed it and held it out, asking me what I made of it.

"*Radix pedis diaboli,*" I read from the label. "Where have I heard that before?"

"Have you so soon forgotten the grim affair of the Tregennis murders, and the rather melodramatic title under which you published your account of them?"

I shuddered. " 'The Adventure of the Devil's Foot'! But the Devil's-foot root is a deadly poison!"

"It is also a hallucinogen in small doses. Small enough, let's say, to escape notice once it has been introduced to one's glass of sherry."

"Richard," I whispered. "Lord Chislehurst told us his clerk accompanied him to his tavern for a glass the night the ghosts first visited."

"I suspected him the moment the earl told us how Richard had taken him into his confidence about his financial situation. That, and the picture of Richard's wife in the counting-room, planted a suggestion in Lord Chislehurst's mind which under the influence of the root tincture came back to him in his dreams, convincing him that Christmas Present was allowing him a peep into his employee's private life."

"How do you explain the look Christmas Past gave him into his own childhood?"

"Christmas is a time of remembering, Watson. No doubt our client was reminded of his own impoverished origins, which sprang forth as a vision at the mere mention of the word *past*. Postmesmeric suggestion is a fascinating scientific phenomenon. I should like to know how Richard came by his expertise. It would make an interesting subject for a monograph."

"One moment, Holmes! His Lordship was haunted the same way last night, yet he said he came straight home from work. His clerk had not the opportunity to administer the drug again."

"But Her Ladyship did. He said himself he had a cup of tea with her before retiring."

"You're certain they're in it together? Richard and Lady Chislehurst?"

His expression was grave. "It was she who insisted her husband prepare his will without delay. She is the beneficiary, but Richard is the Svengali in our little melodrama. 'What evil one may do compounds when they are two.' They already have our unfortunate client walking in his sleep—mark you his sopping slippers! Who is there to say, when he is found some night murdered in an alley, that he was not set upon by some anonymous ruffian while in the somnambulant state?"

"Good Lord! And in the season of love!"

Holmes hissed for silence. Motioning for me to follow, he crept along the inside wall, and I realised belatedly that he was measuring the distance. Presently he stepped away as far as the outside wall would permit, scrutinising the other from ceiling to floor. He seized a stony protuberance and, with a significant nod towards the revolver in my hand, pushed with all his might. Again there was a grating noise, and then a section of wall eight feet high and four feet wide swung outwards upon a hidden pivot. Light flooded the passage. Together we stepped through.

We were in a chamber slightly smaller than Lord Chislehurst's, with a cosy fireplace, a bed piled high with pillows and canopied in chintz and ivory lace, a vanity, and a huge oak cabinet quite as old as the house, before which stood a tall, handsome woman ten years our client's junior, fully dressed and coiffed in a manner both expensive and tasteful. She appeared composed, but upon her cheeks was a high colour.

"Lady Chislehurst, I presume?" Holmes enquired.

"That is my name, sir. Who are you, and what is the meaning of this invasion?"

"My name is Sherlock Holmes. This is Dr. Watson, and unless I am very much mistaken, the gentleman hiding in the cabinet is named Richard."

Her hand went to her throat. She took an involuntary step closer to the cabinet. "Sir! You are impertinent."

At that moment, the door to the cabinet opened and a slender young man stepped out, whom I recognised as Lord Chislehurst's clerk. He was dressed entirely in black from collar to heels. I raised my revolver.

"That won't be necessary, Doctor. I am unarmed." He spread his dark coattails, revealing the truth of his claim. I returned my weapon to my pocket, but kept my hand upon it warily.

"I fled from the passage when the fireplace opened," Richard explained. "Not knowing who might be in the hall and fearful of compromising Lady Chislehurst, I took refuge in the cabinet. I thought perhaps it was the earl, and that we had been found out."

"Then you admit you were conspiring to murder Lord Chislehurst?" Holmes's tone was stern.

The woman gasped and swayed. Richard put out his arm to steady her. His face was white. "Good heavens, no! However did you form that conclusion?"

"Come, come, young man. There is the business of the will, the paraphernalia in the passage between the walls, and your own admission just now that you feared you had been 'found out.' I suggest you hold your defense in reserve for the Assizes."

"Thank you, Richard. I am quite well now." The lady relinquished her grip upon the young man's arm. Her expression was resolute. "I have been after Timothy for years to draw up his will. I saw no reason that the fortune he has worked so hard to build should be dissipated in the courts. To whom he decided to leave it was his own affair, but I thought it would be nice if he named Richard as executor.

"I have known Richard for two years. I don't think my husband realises how valuable he is to the firm, nor how much of himself he has sacrificed to its operation. This I know from what I have seen. Richard does not advertise his worth."

"Please, Your Ladyship," protested the clerk.

She smiled at him sadly, dismissing his plea. "When you work closely with someone, as I have with Richard when the firm was shorthanded, you learn things his employer doesn't know. Richard's financial situation is serious. Aside from his responsibilities as a husband, he has pledged to repay the many debts left by his late father, and his mother is seriously ill.

"Richard is the first member of his family to seek a career in business," she continued. "His father was a mesmerist upon the stage, and his mother was a magician's assistant. When I learned that he had inherited some of their skills, a plan began to form."

The clerk interrupted. "The plan was mine. Lady Chislehurst went along purely out of the goodness of her heart."

"You needn't claim credit," said she. "I'm proud of the idea. My husband is a good man, Mr. Holmes, but his order of values is not always sound. When the firm suffered, he should have chosen an area to practise economy that would not affect his employees. When he told me there would be no Christmas gratuities this year, I knew from experience I could not change his mind through talk. I decided instead to work upon his conscience. I suppose you know the rest."

Holmes appeared unmoved. "Your plan was dangerous. Any number of tragedies might have befallen him as he wandered in his sleep."

"That was unexpected, and alarmed me greatly." Her expression was remorseful. "Richard and I decided not to use the drug again. If the mere image of the Ghost of Christmas Yet to Come did not bring about the desired conversion, that was that."

"I am shamed."

"Timothy!" Lady Chislehurst turned to face her husband, who was standing upon the threshold to the hallway. None of us had seen him open the door, with the possible exception of Holmes, whose red-Indian countenance betrayed no reaction.

"I am shamed," the earl said again. His heavy face was tragic.

"I'm sorry, Timothy. It was the only way."

"I am not shamed for you," he said, "but for myself. Were I not so caught up in commerce, I would have seen what effect my measures to preserve the firm was having upon the people who work there."

His wife stepped towards him just as he strode forwards. He took her in his arms. "I'm sorry, Beth. Can you ever forgive me?"

"There is one way," said she.

"Of course." He looked at his clerk. "Richard, I want you in early tomorrow."

The young man was dismayed. "Tomorrow is Christmas Day!"

"All the more reason to start early, so we can count out the holiday gratuities, yours first. If we work hard we should be able to deliver them all by midday. Then you and your wife will join us here for Christmas dinner."

"Bless you, sir!"

"Bless *you*, Beth!"

"God bless us everyone!" I exclaimed.

Four curious faces turned my way.

"Surely you are more familiar with those words than most," I told the Chislehursts. "I am quoting His young Lordship from 'A Christmas Carol,' which Her Ladyship must have studied closely."

"I haven't read it in years. My husband doesn't approve of the story. I thought about it, naturally, but my real inspiration came when I discovered the secret passage and the equipment inside."

Holmes said, "Do you mean to say the apparatus was there already?"

"The magic lantern is an old model," explained Richard; "an ancestor, as it were, of the ones employed by the magicians with whom my mother worked. I replaced the bottle of hallucinative with one my father used in his act. The original would have been useless. It had probably been there thirty-five years."

"That is precisely when Scrooge lived here," reflected the earl.

"Well, Watson, what do you make of our little yuletide adventure?"

The next morning was Christmas. After I had breakfasted and exchanged gifts and greetings with my wife, I paid a call upon Holmes in the old sitting-room, where I found him enjoying his morning pipe.

"I should say Bob Cratchit was fortunate there was no Sherlock Holmes in his day," said I.

"Crafty fellows, these clerks. However, they are no match for a Lady Chislehurst. I perceive that package you are carrying is intended for me, by the way. The shops are closed, Mrs. Hudson is away visiting, and you know no one else in this neighbourhood."

I handed him the bundle, wrapped in brown paper and tied with a cord. "It is useless to try to surprise you, Holmes. It is a first-edition copy of *The Martyrdom of Man*, which you once recommended to me. I came across it in a secondhand shop in Soho."

He appeared nonplussed, a rare event. "I am afraid, old fellow, that I have no gift to offer in return. The season has been busy, and as you know I allow little time for sentiment. It is disastrous to my work." It may have been my interpretation, but he sounded apologetic. I smiled.

"My dear Holmes. What greater gift could I receive than the one you have given me these past twenty years?"

He returned the smile. "Happy Christmas, Watson."

"Happy Christmas, Holmes."

THE ADVENTURE OF THE CANINE VENTRILOQUIST

Jon L. Breen

Visits by apparent madmen to the old rooms in Baker Street were not infrequent. Some of these callers actually were mad and thus beyond the help of a consulting detective, while others merely seemed to be. Our visitor that blustery Christmas Eve I would quickly have consigned to the former category, but as he so frequently did, Sherlock Holmes disagreed.

We were in the midst of a splendid dinner from Mrs. Hudson's talented kitchen when we heard voices from the stairs.

"I must see Mr. Sherlock Holmes!" came a distraught masculine shout. "Only he can help me!"

The feminine voice of Mrs. Hudson tried to calm the lunatic in softer tones. Whatever she said was undistinguishable and did not serve to soothe our determined visitor, who burst through the door of 221B and implored Holmes's aid. Mrs. Hudson offered apologies, but, overtaken I suppose by a combination of the spirit of the season and the curiosity of a hound finding the scent of game on the air, Holmes offered food, drink, and the comfort of the fire.

In the confusion of welcoming our visitor, Mrs. Hudson's joyfully anticipated Christmas pudding was somehow forgotten. No comestible, however delightful, had the power to distract Holmes from the scent of a problem, but I am more devoted to the joys of the table—as well as averse to disappointing Mrs. Hudson. Still, I supposed, the pudding would keep until we heard this poor maniac's tale and arranged for his removal to an institution that could deal with his sad mental infirmity. After a few moments, our visitor had gathered himself enough to tell us, though not quickly, a lucid if fantastic tale.

"I have always enjoyed Christmas," he began, raising a cup of hot spiced cider to his lips. "The festival of Our Savior's birth marks my favorite time of the year, a time one can feel goodwill and good fellowship toward the fellow man who so sadly disappoints one the rest of the year, a time of conviviality and generosity and song."

His face brightened, then fell abruptly into indescribable gloom, the mercurial suddenness of the change making me all the more certain of his lunacy.

"But, gentlemen, one year ago tomorrow, events were set in motion that altered the whole scheme of my happy, productive life and reduced me to the ruined hulk you see before you."

A healthy, well-fed hulk beyond the wild eyes and troubled features, I reflected, not to mention one with a gift for florid exaggeration. My observational skills having been developed over the years, admittedly more through my long association with Holmes than the diagnostic lessons of my medical education, I was about to give voice to my impressions. But, as usual, Holmes struck first—and, I must confess, more strikingly.

"Pray continue, Mr. Marplethorpe. Dr. Watson and I are eager to hear your story."

"I can't express how much I appreciate—" Our guest broke off, looking perplexed. "But, Mr. Holmes, I fear in my agitated state, I neglected to tell you my name. Did I mention my name, Dr. Watson?"

"You did not," I verified.

"Forgive my rudeness. I am indeed Oliver Marplethorpe, the most miserable and beleaguered man in England. But you already knew who I was, Mr. Holmes. You called me by name, and I'm damned if I know how. I sent you no communication heralding my advent—indeed, who would be so presumptuous as to request an appointment for Christmas Eve? In my distress, I neglected even to offer a calling card to your landlady. You and I have never met before to my knowledge. While my name has given me some small notoriety, my likeness has never appeared in the press, and I am not given to delivering lectures or making other public appearances. I know my clothing is innocent of so much as my initials, let alone spelling out my entire name. So how in God's name did you know my name was Marplethorpe?"

With a damnably smug glance in my direction, Holmes said, "It's a matter more in my colleague's area than my own, Mr. Marplethorpe: literary style. Unless you are a verbal plagiarist, you used nearly the very same words describing your affinity for the Christmas season in an essay in the *Strand* two years ago. You must remember that charming piece, Watson. I believe one of your overwrought accounts of my own trifling exploits appeared in the same number."

Marplethorpe smiled sadly, as if viewing a forgotten time and place in his mind's eye. "Yes, I was proud of that essay, I must confess. But that is what the late Mr. Dickens would have designated a ghost of Christmas past, I fear. So many things have changed since then." He fell silent and seemed to drift off into a private reverie.

"Tell us your tale, Mr. Marplethorpe," Holmes persisted. "We shall lay your Christmas ghost if we can."

"Yes, of course, but where to begin? The writing life is not an easy one, as Dr. Watson must appreciate. I began beating on the doors of book and periodical publishers, figuratively I hasten to add, when I had not yet achieved one score in age. I persisted through my university years and after, subsisting mainly on the largesse of my generous but scarcely wealthy parents, both since unhappily deceased. For a number of cold seasons, I could have papered my walls with the rejections I received from the daily newspapers, the weekly and monthly magazines, the annuals, the book publishers. The support of a similarly minded circle of friends kept my spirits from falling into despair.

"But over the five-year period leading to last Christmas, I gradually accrued some measure of success. My essays became more popular with the readership of the better magazines; my reviews were more frequently solicited by the literary journals; my occasional poems and stories became steadily better received. Just thirteen months ago I was offered, and accepted, the editorship of *Vickery's Weekly*, a post that paid handsomely in prestige if only tolerably in currency. My income from all these sources combined had risen to the point where, still not yet thirty years of age, though I was by no means wealthy, I finally allowed myself to entertain thoughts of taking a wife, casting off the superficial freedom of bachelorhood for the more fulfilling responsibilities of family life. Most happily of all, I had at the ready a candidate to join me in this glorious venture. Miss Elspeth Hawley is her name, the fairest and loveliest creature to whom God ever gave life."

So he was not a madman but a professional writer—literary amateurs like myself are often quite ordinary and level-headed chaps, but those who attempt to scribble words on paper for a living are another matter. Even the sober ones often seem likely candidates for institutionalization. By now I had remembered the fellow's work: clever, often amusing, but deucedly long-winded. Impatient for him to get to the point, I was tempted to remind him that Holmes and I, unlike the editors he sought to please, would not pay him by the word. But Holmes was listening with rapt attention, as if treasuring every syllable.

Marplethorpe drained his cup of cider and said dramatically, "That brings us to Christmas last . . . but no, not quite."

I nearly snorted but restrained myself. I might have known we weren't there yet.

"In the year preceding the yuletide season of which I speak," our visitor continued, "I succeeded in placing an article on the art and history of ventriloquism with one of the better-paying monthlies. Perhaps you saw it."

"I did indeed," Holmes said. "Fascinating topic. Do you remember it, Watson?"

I confessed that I did not, and my negative response took me still farther away from the prospect of Mrs. Hudson's Christmas pudding. It put me in line for an exhaustive account of the fellow's research.

"As I'm sure you know," Marplethorpe droned, "the term *ventriloquism* refers to the art of making sounds appear to come from somewhere other than their actual source. 'Throwing the voice,' it is sometimes called. The term comes from two Latin words, *venter*, meaning 'belly,' and *loqui*, meaning 'spoken,' literally 'belly-speaking.' Popular wisdom has long held that the sounds issued from the ventriloquist's abdomen, though practitioners of the art assure me that is far from being a true impression, that in fact the sounds come from deep in the throat. Ventriloquism in one form or another dates back to ancient times through evidence found in Hebrew and Egyptian archaeological studies. The most famous ancient ventriloquist was the Greek Eurycles of Athens, who I believe specialized in bird sounds.

"The art could prove dangerous to its practitioners, witness the case of a magician in fourteenth-century France known as Meskyllene. He toured Eastern Europe with a wooden box as his prop. Audience members would be invited to ask questions, and the box would appear to answer them. Poor fellow was put to death for sorcery. That was too often the fate of early ventriloquists.

"Some of the most famous 'belly-speakers' of more recent centuries had a happier lot, serving in the royal courts of Europe, filling a kind of jester function I would imagine. Louis Brabant was the voice-throwing valet of King Francis I of France in the sixteenth century, and Henry King served in the same dual function to our own Charles I in the first half of the seventeenth. In the present day, of course, ventriloquism has become a recognized form of popular entertainment, a fixture of the music halls. I saw one chap who sat a wooden doll on his knee and appeared to have a conversation with it. He displayed remarkable skill and inventiveness and indeed was the inspiration for my article."

"The production of such an article must give you immense satisfaction," I said courteously, hoping he would move on to the point of his visit, whatever it might be.

"On the contrary, Dr. Watson," he said miserably. "I wish I had never heard of ventriloquism nor written a word about it. I mentioned my affection for Miss Elspeth Hawley, did I not?"

"Yes," I assured him quickly, hoping to head off more expressions of rapture.

"I fear one short sentence in my article of several pages incurred my beloved's wrath. I had pointed out, quite accurately, that fraudulent spiritualists often use ventriloquism as a method of producing disembodied voices, one of the types of bogus spirit manifestations that are their stock in trade. One of Elspeth's keenest interests is spiritualism, and she frequently attends seances with devoted enthusiasm, a foible I had always found amusing and, though certainly foolish, essentially harmless. My suggestion that the objects of her devotion could possibly be fraudulent filled her with anger. I did my best to explain that I had not said *all* spiritualists were of necessity charlatans. I sought to solicit her admission that at least some of the army of individuals hosting seances in this gullible day are out to dupe the naive and innocent, that in fact their activities should be deplored by no one more than the genuine spirit mediums on whom their activities bring discredit. But she would not be assuaged, and I feared our disagreement on this matter imperiled our pending marital happiness."

"What do you think of that, Watson?" Holmes asked me. "You know something of spiritualism, I believe."

"Poppycock," I muttered. "My literary agent has an interest in it. I can't imagine why."

"I had no belief in it, either," Marplethorpe hastened to reiterate. "But in trying to make my argument to Elspeth, I had to at least counterfeit an open-mindedness on the subject."

Our visitor had shifted from spiced cider to whisky, but the advent of the Christmas pudding seemed no nearer when he said, "That, I believe, brings us to Christmas last."

I bit back an ironic rejoinder.

"Elspeth and I were again on terms of concord and happiness when we gathered for Christmas at the country house of our friend, Charles Vickery. The gathering is an annual tradition. Charles is much the wealthiest of our circle, and indeed it was the literary weekly he publishes that gave my career part of its newly achieved stability. There are several regular guests at these functions, mostly those who like Elspeth and myself no longer had living parents or other close family near at hand when the holiday season comes. While the guest list has varied from year to year, Colin Ragsdale, another of my closest friends, has been a constant. Colin ekes out a living as an estate agent. He, Charles, and I were inseparable at university. We all had literary aspirations, and I remember remarking to Charles last year that the success he and I had achieved surely would soon be matched by Colin, whom I think we all believed, whether we said so or not, to be the most talented of the three of us.

"Charles Vickery is a man of generosity and kindness whatever the season, but he knows the art of keeping Christmas like no person of my acquaintance, and his home is annually a veritable lightning rod for the yuletide spirit. The towering tree, hung with shining baubles and candles and cloved oranges, the sprigs of heavily berried holly, the brightly wrapped gifts, the romantic lure of the mistletoe, the garlands on the mantelpiece, the yule log, the roasting chestnuts, the wassail bowl, and the food, oh, the glorious food, the succulent brown goose with its sage-and-onion stuffing, watercress garnish, brown gravy and gooseberry sauce, roasted potatoes arrayed around it; the glazed parsnips, the nuts, the dates, the mince pies—"

"And the Christmas pudding," I offered.

"Yes, yes, that as well, most memorably. I found the coin in my portion last year, and though I am not of a superstitious inclination, I was happy to take it as a harbinger of continued luck for the year to come. How gay we were those Christmas weekends with Charles, and how free of every care we were—or seemed." His face fell with such tangible sadness, I began to feel a tug of sympathy. However extravagantly stated, his desolation was very real.

"My friends had all read my ventriloquism piece, of course. It was only a small part of my prolific output for the year, but it was certainly the one that most captured their fancy. I had faintly hoped no allusion would be made to it during the Christmas weekend, since it remained somewhat of a sore subject between Elspeth and myself. But of course, with high-spirited friends, full of boisterous humor, I was resigned that the spectre of 'belly speaking'—not by that indelicate term in mixed company, of course—had inevitably to raise itself, probably as an elaborate practical joke of some sort.

"Christmas morning, we all exchanged our small gifts, one to another, an annual tradition attended by much laughter and affection. But when the gift exchange appeared to have run its course, I was informed that another gift was to come my way, one that was a token of esteem from all of my gathered friends. Charles led us into the drawing room, where an easel was set up with a white sheet covering the picture it held. I looked from face to face and saw only eager and good-humored expectation.

"With a flourish, Charles unveiled one of the strangest paintings I had ever seen. I must describe it to you in careful detail, Mr. Holmes, because the appearance of it, the very spirit of it, are central to my sad tale. It seemed at first glance cheerful and bright, a happy addition to a wall of art, but the more you looked at it, the more somber and troubling it came to appear.

"It depicted a man and a dog. The man was formally dressed, seated in a chair of rich scarlet fabric, the dog, a short-haired white terrier, lying on his knee. But closer inspection showed a blankness of expression on the man's face, a false brightness to his features, rather like a cartoon or a puppet. And when you looked closely, you could see that his jaw appeared to have a wooden hinge, like that on the ventriloquist's doll I had seen sitting on that music-hall performer's knee. The dog by contrast had a knowing intelligence to its features and far more character and personality in its face than its putative master. I mention the other details of the painting because they are important: a bright green handkerchief in the man's—or should I say man-sized doll's—pocket; a glittering jeweled collar around the dog's neck.

" 'Well, what do you think, Oliver?' Charles demanded, his twenty-five-December jollity not reduced a whit by the sight of the picture.

" 'It's . . . it's a remarkable piece of work,' I stammered, and I was by no means lying. However perverse its subject matter, it bespoke sound fundamental draftsmanship and a daringly original talent. That did not mean I relished the notion of hanging it on my wall and having to look at it every day, however. 'And who, may I ask, is the artist?' I inquired, looking without success for some signature on the canvas.

" 'An amateur,' Charles said, 'another of whose canvases you won't find if you comb every gallery in London.'

" 'A weekend painter,' agreed Colin Ragsdale.

" 'Is it someone here?' I ventured.

" 'You'll have to guess, Oliver,' said Elspeth playfully.

" 'And if I guess correctly, you will tell me?'

" 'No,' they all chorused as a single voice. 'It's from all of us, you see,' Colin explained, 'in celebration of your deserved success. The artist chooses to remain anonymous.'

"When the weekend was over, of course, I had no choice but to transport the thing back to my newly acquired rooms in Kensington. But I still didn't want that wise dog and man-doll looking at me day and night. Elspeth, however, insisted, stating that a refusal to hang it would be an insult to my friends. Perhaps, I ventured, I could keep it in a back room and take it out for hanging whenever one of them called. 'No,' she said, 'it must hang there all the time, to give you inspiration. You will grow to love it, Oliver.'

" 'And when we marry,' I inquired, 'are you prepared to live with it as well?'

" 'Certainly,' she said.

" 'And when will that wonderful event finally occur?' I inquired. Though definitely engaged, we had not yet set an official wedding date.

" 'It must be next Christmas,' she said, 'with our friends around us.'

" 'Must we wait so long?'

" 'Only a year. We can be patient. I am determined to be a Christmas bride.'

"Despite the long period of time, I was delighted to have a definite date finally set. I put aside my distaste and hung the painting in the sitting room of my flat, over the fireplace."

"You say Miss Hawley had no family?"

"No, she was an only child and her parents had died when she was ten years old and she was raised by a guardian. I and our circle of friends were her family, insofar as she had one."

"Pray continue your story."

"At first the year seemed to offer a continuation of my recent success. The editorial duties at *Vickery's Weekly* took a sizable part of my working time, but I still managed to continue placing articles and reviews in decent number, and my prices were rising as my volume lessened. Through January and February, I gradually achieved a kind of truce with the painting. I did not like it; I did not look at it more than I could help; but still it was not casting a pall over my life. In March, however, that began to change.

"For my birthday, Elspeth surprised me with a little dog. A kind gesture, you might say, and I would agree, but disquietingly the dog proved to be a white terrier identical in markings to the one depicted in the painting. I found it disturbing but realized that to say so would make me appear ungrateful and cause hurt to Elspeth.

"So, as lightheartedly as I could manage, I said, 'This lad is obviously the model for my Christmas painting. Tell me who the previous owner was and I shall identify the phantom artist.' She answered with similar lightness of tone but provided no information. When I asked her if the dog had a name, she said I should call him Eddie."

"Could Miss Elspeth Hawley herself have been the artist?" I ventured.

Marplethorpe shook his head. "I am certain not. We spent much of our time together, and she evinced no artistic proclivities. While my knowledge of her domestic arrangements certainly did not extend beyond the boundaries dictated by decency and propriety, I never associated any accoutrements of the artistic life with her. And if she had been keeping a terrier, I surely must have known.

"From the day that Eddie entered my household, my life began its unutterable descent. To begin with, I began hearing strange, faint voices in the night. 'Speak for me, master.' 'Sit me on your knee, master.' 'Take me to the music hall, master.' And if I looked for a source, the voice seemed to be coming from the terrier curled up at the foot of my bed!

"I confess I didn't take it seriously. From earliest childhood, I have had strange dreams. Indeed I have often been thankful for the spur they give my creativity. Thus I well know how easy it is to imagine bizarre, inexplicable things at night that seem to vanish in the light of day. The voices, I told myself, could only have been a dream, the deceptive product of a state somewhere between sleeping and waking. I surely could not blame the dog. Eddie was a good little fellow really and a welcome companion.

"But other manifestations were more troubling and harder to put aside. To put it bluntly, the painting began to change.

"First the change was subtle. The face of the man-doll had seemed blank and expressionless when I first saw it. But each time I looked at it now, it seemed to be taking on more character and feature. It began to look more and more like me. That it should resemble me was not so odd a notion; it would fit right in with the humor of my friends and of the mysterious artist, who I believed surely must be one of them. I told myself it was my imagination, that it had always looked like me, that this was part of the joke and I was only gradually coming to realize it. But each time I looked at the picture—and now I somehow felt compelled to look at it each time I entered the sitting room—it seemed the resemblance became more and more striking.

"The disturbance the painting was causing in me led me to avoid the sitting room. I spent more and more time at the desk in my study, even when I was not actively pursuing my writing and editing chores. This change of habits did not, as you might think, increase my productivity, however. It became more and more difficult to concentrate on my work. For the first time in my career, I began missing deadlines, and my hard-won reputation for reliability and professionalism began to erode. How can one keep his attention fixed on such mundane matters as writing and editing when he fears he is going mad?"

"Did you speak of this to anyone?" Holmes asked.

"Not to that point, no. Not when I could still attribute the odd happenings to my imagination. Not until I could no longer deny that either the manifestations were real . . . or I was descending into madness.

"One morning in early May, I left my bedroom and walked into the sitting room. On a small table near the doorway, the usual repository for gloves and items of mail, I saw a bright green handkerchief. I was puzzled, for I owned no such handkerchief, and I recalled having no visitor who might have left it. As I looked at it, it occurred to me it resembled the handkerchief the man-doll wore in the painting. Once again, my eyes were drawn unwillingly to the picture over the mantel, intending to compare them. But now there was no green handkerchief in the seated figure's pocket! It was gone!"

By now I was convinced my first diagnosis had been correct. The man was clearly out of his senses.

"Did you examine the painting closely, Mr. Marplethorpe?" Holmes inquired.

"Really, Mr. Holmes! How close an examination was necessary? It did not take any more than a glance to tell that something as striking as a bright green handkerchief was missing from the painting."

"You misunderstand me, sir. If we eliminate a supernatural explanation, which my training, experience, and personal philosophy require me to do, we must look for a natural one. If what you have told us is accurate, the only conclusion is that someone must have touched up the painting. Was there any sign of fresh or wet oil on the canvas?"

"My apologies, Mr. Holmes. That possibility did occur to me later, but in this first instance, I was too upset to notice."

"There were later similar events?"

Marplethorpe nodded. "A few weeks later, I awoke to find a jeweled collar had appeared around Eddie's neck. As soon as I saw it, I rushed to look at the picture, terrified of what I would find. My fears were realized. The dog in the picture now had no collar." He paused. "And, Mr. Holmes, there was no sign of fresh paint on the canvas."

"At what point did you tell someone about all these unusual occurrences?"

"I delayed for weeks, torn with indecision. Finally I invited a party of three to luncheon at my club. My intention was to share with them the singular happenings, take them up to my rooms to show them my evidence, and ask them if they could offer any possible explanation."

"And who were the three?"

"The three persons closest to me in the world, of course: Charles Vickery, Colin Ragsdale, and my own beloved, Elspeth."

"Had none of them been in your rooms since the first of these odd events?"

"No. Charles had been spending most of his time outside London, and Elspeth had recently expressed an increasing concern about visiting my bachelor quarters unchaperoned, though I hasten to assure you our relations were never other than completely proper. As for Colin, we often met for drinks and talk in Fleet Street pubs but for one reason or another had not visited each other's rooms in that period.

"It was not a happy gathering we had over lunch. My work for *Vickery's Weekly* had become erratic, and I knew Charles was concerned. My friends had perceived alterations in my personality for which I had offered no plausible explanation. I had always been regarded as a moody, volatile person, and it had been attributed to my artistic temperament, but lately my mercurial moods had become worse. Elspeth and I had quarreled over trivialities. Even Colin's insouciant manner was sometimes strained by my erratic behavior. And of course, as I told them my story, they could only think me as mad as you must think me now."

"Not at all," Holmes said, speaking for himself alone.

"I was glad finally to have told someone else about it, however, and of course, I knew once we got to my rooms and I showed them the painting, they would know I was not losing my senses. Then we could have a reasoned discussion of possible explanations."

"But when you arrived at the flat," Holmes ventured, "the painting had been restored to its original state."

Marplethorpe looked amazed at this, but it seemed quite an obvious deduction to me. Surely the poor man's friends would not share his delusion, and when they saw no change in the painting, he would no longer see it either.

"You are uncanny, Mr. Holmes. That is exactly what occurred. My first indication was when Eddie greeted us at the door. He did *not* have the collar around his neck, though I had never removed it. We moved into the sitting room and gazed at the painting. The collar was in place on the neck of the knowing dog; the green handkerchief was in the man-doll's pocket; and the face of the doll had returned to the wooden blankness we had seen on Christmas Day, with the resemblance to me erased. There was little I could say. I felt a fool, and yet I knew what I had seen. I determined to show them the handkerchief, but it was gone from my drawer. My friends departed with meaningless words of comfort, advising me to get some rest, not to work so hard.

"A note from Elspeth arrived a day later. She said she was taking a long ocean voyage with a distant cousin for her *own* peace of mind. Though she still claimed the greatest of affection for me, she begged to postpone our nuptials. And I thought her note was oddly impersonal in tone, as if she were attempting to distance herself from a situation beyond her understanding.

"Within a month, I had been discharged as editor of *Vickery's Weekly*. Charles was kindness itself, but said he had no other choice, that he would see what he could do for me when I regained my robust health. Sanity, he meant but did not say. The commissions for articles and reviews stopped coming, as if some tap had been turned off. I had to give up my Kensington accommodations and take cheaper rooms."

"And the painting?" Holmes inquired sharply. "What did you do with it when you moved to cheaper rooms?"

"Mr. Holmes, the very day I was to move, the painting vanished. I have not seen it since."

By this time, I could hardly contain my impatience with the fellow's tale. But Holmes merely said, "Certainly the painting vanished. It had to vanish. And the dog?"

"Still with me," Marplethorpe said. "My one consolation in a way. I cannot blame my miserable condition on Eddie. He's a loyal little fellow, more so than my supposed friends."

"Have you lost all contact with them?"

"I did not advertise my whereabouts when I moved. I heard nothing from any of them until this very day. And that is why I came to see you. I received a note in the post from Charles Vickery. He expressed regret he had failed to locate me until now, said all the old circle were already gathered at his country house, and assured me the celebration was incomplete without me. I feel drawn to go, Mr. Holmes, Charles's house parties having been such a happy part of my life, my old life in any case. And yet I feel a sense of foreboding at the same time. If *you* could come to Charles Vickery's country house, talk to my friends, investigate the odd occurrences, and perhaps come up with some reasonable explanation for them, the whole downward plunge of my existence might be reversed on the very anniversary of my unhappy decline's beginning."

It seemed to me that Marplethorpe was asking a great deal, but Holmes seemed to regard the request as a mere trifle. "Certainly, Mr. Marplethorpe, but first you must give us some directions."

"To Charles's country estate," he said, his face brightening with hope.

"Yes, but first to your old rooms in Kensington."

On occasion during my association with Sherlock Holmes, he asked me to represent him at some point in an investigation—the adventure of *The Hound of the Baskervilles* was one such instance. It was a flattering responsibility I always accepted with serious purposefulness. Thus it was that I attended Charles Vickery's Christmas celebration the following day. Holmes, who had swiftly departed the Baker Street rooms with Marplethorpe the previous night, did not explain why he could not appear at the Vickery house in person, merely admonished me to be on my guard.

By arrangement, a carriage met me at the railway station.

"A happy Christmas to you, sir," the coachman said. "Dr. Watson, is it?"

"Yes, and a happy Christmas to you."

"I had understood there were to be two passengers to the house, sir. Mr. Sherlock Holmes—"

"Mr. Holmes was called away on business related to an investigation," I said, quite accurately, as it happens.

Following a bracing if bumpy ride through the tree-lined countryside, I had my first view of Vickery's stately country house. The young man, I realized, must be wealthy indeed.

The host, who was waiting for me at the door to offer a hearty greeting, was a jolly and affable young man, who concealed his disappointment at my conveying of Holmes's regrets more successfully than had his servant. He assured me he was delighted to make me welcome. While his friendliness seemed quite genuine, the holiday gaiety was obviously somewhat forced. I detected an expression of concern in his eyes.

"Have you had any communication from Oliver Marplethorpe?" he asked.

"No, indeed, not since last evening," I said. "Do you mean to tell me he is not here?"

"No. When he telephoned last night, he advised me to expect him on the earlier of the two morning trains and to expect you and Mr. Holmes on the later. I was delighted and relieved to hear that he was coming. Oliver has not had the easiest of times in the past year. Indeed he unaccountably cut off all contact with those of us who most value him. When he asked leave to invite two additional guests as distinguished as yourself and Mr. Holmes, my delight increased. Imagine our disappointment and concern when he did not arrive this morning as expected. I had hoped he would prove to have accompanied you on the later train."

"I am as puzzled as you are, sir."

"Well, it's Christmas Day all the same, and we must celebrate as best we can."

The Christmas decorations proved as elaborate and festive as Marplethorpe had promised. In the shadow of an enormous tree thick with ornaments, I was introduced to several revelers of about my host's age, though they acted a decade younger. Several were clearly disappointed not to have the opportunity to meet the celebrated Sherlock Holmes, but only two of them seemed to share my host's deep concern about Marplethorpe.

Miss Hawley proved a comely young woman indeed. When smiling and vivacious, she undoubtedly could melt any masculine heart. Even in her current pale and distracted state, her amazing beauty shone through and her helpless desolation created an almost automatic desire to shield and protect her. That others felt the same was emphasized by the phalanx of young men that surrounded her. Seeing Elspeth Hawley for the first time made me feel all the more sympathy for Oliver Marplethorpe, madman or not. Next to the loss of her, the loss of income and literary reputation, even of sanity, might seem secondary.

"Dr. Watson," she said gravely, "I am heartened to know Oliver has made such a friend as you. But where can he be? What new misfortune can have befallen him to prevent his being here?"

"There are any number of explanations, Miss Hawley," I said, not really believing it. "I'm certain he will appear before the day is out, with an amusing story on his lips."

She shook her head distractedly. "How I wish I could share your confidence. But I feel things, Dr. Watson. I always have. It is an uncanny ability and not always a welcome one. Oliver is dead. I know it."

"Surely not, Miss Hawley. You must not lose hope."

"Thank you for your comforting words, Dr. Watson," she said, not seeming at all comforted. "You gentlemen will excuse me, I know. I must prepare."

Without revealing what she was preparing for, Miss Hawley drifted away. A moment later, my host introduced me to the third of the persons on whom it was my duty to concentrate my attention, Colin Ragsdale.

"Dr. Watson," the slight, red-bearded Ragsdale assured me, "I for one am even more honored to meet you than the absent subject of your remarkable stories."

"In that, you are most unusual, sir."

"In *many* ways he is most unusual," Charles Vickery said humorously, earning him a sardonically arched eyebrow.

"I cannot but ask," I said. "Why on earth would you rather meet me than Holmes?"

"Because of the value I place on the written word. While I am sure Mr. Holmes is a talented man, it is your accounts that have made him famous—and made him rich, I suspect."

"You flatter me, sir," I said, quite sincerely. "Holmes was already well known long before I put pen to paper."

"To thieftakers and villains, perhaps, but not to the general public."

"I suppose there is something in what you say."

"What a strange thing is fortune, Doctor," Ragsdale said reflectively. "If I had met you as recently as one month ago, I would have ascertained whether you were in the market for larger rooms, but happily I have left all that behind me." A shadow appeared over his face. "I believe I would be the happiest man in England at this moment, if I weren't so concerned for my old friend Oliver Marplethorpe. Where can he be do you think?"

"I had expected to find him here."

"And are you joining us for the seance, Dr. Watson?"

137

"A seance? On Christmas Day?" I cast a puzzled glance at my host. "It seems vaguely sacrilegious, somehow."

"Not to one who believes," Charles Vickery said. "I am not one such, I hasten to add, but Elspeth insists. And we all find it hard to deny Elspeth anything, especially on a day that once was intended to be her wedding day. She has brought her own medium for the occasion, and I have the delicate task of providing a suitable circle of participants."

"We must not laugh," Colin Ragsdale said gravely, "much as we might want to. Charles has to keep out the open scoffers—of whom I confess I would be one, were it not for my tender regard for Elspeth. We also must not have anyone likely to be too much affected by the proceedings. We don't want any deaths by fright, do we, Charles?"

"Nor any deaths at all," Charles said solemnly, apparently thinking of his absent friend. "Will you join us then, Doctor?"

To refuse would have been to ignore my duty.

We sat in a circle of six, our hands joined on a round table, the only illumination a series of candles on a side table and a fitfully burning fire on the other side of the very large and oppressively dark upstairs room. The sparsely furnished chamber was innocent of seasonal decoration and far from the noise of the Christmas revelers. Our group consisted, reading clockwise round the table, of Charles Vickery, Elspeth Hawley, myself, a Miss Cavendish, who was a contemporary of Miss Hawley and apparently a fellow believer in spiritualism; Colin Ragsdale, and the spirit medium, Madame Larousse, a tall, slender, heavily veiled woman whose French accent did nothing to counter my skepticism.

"Hear us, O spirits of the departed," she said, in a sort of chant. "We seek your wisdom and your comfort, you who have gone to the other side. Bring us your messages of advice and guidance."

The medium suddenly halted her chant, her head dropping forward in the dim light as if she had suddenly lost consciousness. Then another, higher voice, issued eerily from her mouth, its unaccented English in sharp contrast to her normal heavily Gallic tones. "I want to go home, master. I want to go home. Please let me go home, master."

The medium's head shifted from one side to another. We heard a new voice, and though the medium's lips moved, the voice seemed to issue from the corner of the room farthest from the table where we all sat.

"Eddie! Eddie!" the hollow voice cried, like a lost soul begging for release.

On my left, Elspeth Hawley's hand gripped mine harder. She breathed softly, "Oliver. Oliver, is it you?"

"Elspeth," the voice croaked. "I loved you, Elspeth, but Eddie took me away from you. Why, Eddie? Why?" The medium's lips were still moving, but surely even the most gifted ventriloquist could not throw her voice that far. "Eddie," the haunted voice continued, "what can your full name be? Is it Edgar or Edward or Edmund or Edwin? Tell me, Eddie."

The medium's head shifted violently to the other side and the high-pitched voice came again from her lips. "None of those, master, none of those. Eddie denotes not my name but my position in life. The position I took from you. I was your better, master. I was always your better. You knew that." With a sudden earsplitting shrillness, the medium shrieked out, "Editor! Editor! Oh, let me go home, master!"

I heard some creature skittering across the floor. The table rocked as one of our number broke the chain of hands and pushed back his chair. Miss Cavendish squeaked slightly and Charles Vickery uttered an exclamation. The lights in the room came up full and we saw Colin Ragsdale sitting, a horrified look on his face, a small white terrier leaping excitedly at his feet. Ignoring the dog, he rose from his chair and charged toward a black-clad figure in the newly illuminated corner.

"I should have killed you, Marplethorpe," Ragsdale roared. "And I will—!"

I leapt from my chair to intercept maddened Ragsdale, but the medium proved quicker, coming between the two of them and knocking Ragsdale to the floor with the skill of a practiced boxer. The French medium, freed of her veil, was none other than Sherlock Holmes.

*　　*　　*

139

Back in the rooms at Baker Street, I demanded of my friend why I had not been given more idea of what to expect.

"You could not have played your part as effectively, my friend, and I knew if I could fool an observer as keen as you, our quarry surely would not see through me."

Somewhat mollified, I inquired, "How did you get onto him?"

"Starting from the supposition that our client was telling the truth—and as you have pointed out, I was not the person to help him if he was not—I knew his tormentor had not only to be a gifted if secret 'weekend artist' but someone with access to his rooms. Since there was no wet paint on the canvas, there had to be multiple, nearly identical versions of the dog-ventriloquist painting extant, and there had to be some place to secret them near to where they were hanging, in a hidden closet or some other hiding place unknown to the occupant of the rooms. Only then could the nocturnal switches be made when needed. An intruder was also necessary to produce the voices Oliver Marplethorpe heard—and of course to steal the painting when Marplethorpe was to make his move to lesser quarters. Naturally Marplethorpe could not be allowed to take the picture with him, for the maddening effects could not be reproduced in his new quarters and having an unchanging version of the picture might cause him to reclaim his reason more quickly.

"Colin Ragsdale as far as we knew seldom left London, unlike Vickery or Miss Hawley. When I heard he had worked as an estate agent, I wondered if he had by any chance gotten Oliver Marplethorpe his new Kensington accommodations. When I learned that he had, the identity of the tormentor seemed clear.

"As we now know, Ragsdale was intensely jealous of Marplethorpe's success. He felt his own capabilities were greater, and yet he saw Marplethorpe getting all the writing assignments. Ragsdale also was in love with Miss Hawley, and here, too, Marplethorpe had outdone him. The appointment of Marplethorpe to the editorship of their friend's journal was the final blow. At that point, Ragsdale determined to bring Marplethorpe down, ruin him as a writer, get back everything he believed had been taken from him by his old university friend. What progress he had made toward winning Miss Hawley's affections I do not know, but he had recently been named the new editor of *Vickery's Weekly*, thus his reference to you of his recently improved fortune."

"Did the others know Ragsdale was the creator of the painting?"

"Certainly, but they didn't realize the nature of the macabre joke he had in mind. And the gift of the tauntingly named Eddie was also quite innocent on the part of Miss Hawley, who never suspected what Ragsdale was doing. They all liked Ragsdale, as indeed did Marplethorpe himself. They never suspected what vengeful bitterness simmered beneath the surface. Miss Hawley has confirmed that it was Ragsdale's careful manipulation that led her first to cease visits to Marplethorpe's rooms on grounds of propriety—it being essential to Ragsdale's plan that no one of their circle visit while the changes in the painting were being engineered—and later to postpone the engagement and depart on a holiday. One of his ploys was to convince her that her presence only made Marplethorpe's mental affliction worse, that it would be good for the poor fellow not to see her for a time.

"When Marplethorpe dropped out of sight, Ragsdale was delighted, thinking he'd seen the last of his ruined nemesis. But Vickery and Miss Hawley still had warm feelings for the unfortunate Oliver Marplethorpe and were determined to draw him back into their circle for the annual Christmas celebration. Ragsdale, of course, had to pretend to concur and join them in their search. When Marplethorpe and I arrived here by hired carriage in the early hours of the morning, we managed to attract Miss Hawley to her bedroom window. We related our plan of attack to her and she was happy to cooperate in our exposure of Ragsdale. I must say she was very surprised to hear Oliver Marplethorpe suggest a Christmas Day seance, but in the circumstances, she readily agreed to it, as well as to sponsoring my masquerade."

"And now they are again to be married," I remarked. "But Miss Hawley has given up the notion of being a Christmas bride and has agreed to settle for the New Year instead."

"Now then, Watson," Holmes said, "do my nostrils sense that much-delayed Christmas pudding?"

THE ADVENTURE OF THE MAN WHO NEVER LAUGHED

John H. Watson, M. D.
Discovered by J. N. Williamson

It was past the middle of December, in the year '94, that I woke one morning with a start and a distinct impression that some uncommon sound had disturbed my slumber. The clock on the mantelpiece indicated it was not yet seven, and I lay quite still for some seconds attempting to expel a vague presentiment of danger. My friend Sherlock Holmes rarely rose before I was ready for my medical rounds, but there was no question that he still had enemies whose dearest desire was his extermination. After all, it had been only the spring of the present year when Colonel Sebastian Moran had endeavored to slay Holmes with a powerful air rifle.

Persuaded that my fears were probably the product of having again read Charles Dickens's "A Christmas Carol" before falling asleep, I slid from bed, donned my robe, and tiptoed across the bedroom floor to the door. I opened it as quietly as possible and descended the stairs even more noiselessly to the sitting room.

"My congratulations, old fellow," a voice called. "You have single-handedly proved the contention that some aging faculties may improve in compensation for the deterioration of others."

"Holmes!" I cried as I stepped into the room. "You are already up and around."

"Very good, Watson." He glanced up with a wry smile. "Perhaps the acuity of your vision has not diminished to the degree I feared."

His remarks perplexed me. "My eyesight is normal for a man in his middle years," I said. I drew my robe more tightly round my waist as I walked toward my chair. "Or was that a jest, an allusion to my occasional failure to perceive things as swiftly as you do?"

"You are as astute as if it were midday," he murmured, and returned his attention to his previous activities.

Sherlock Holmes was seated cross-legged in the center of the floor, barefoot but wearing his favorite mouse-colored dressing gown. His hawk-nosed face was in profile and I marveled anew at his capacity for concentration so keen it rendered the rest of the world invisible.

Sitting, I saw several incoming letters were open to his left, another roughly half a foot to the front. Several sheets of his own writing paper and envelopes were to Holmes's right, while two of his letters were ready to be posted and he seemed in the midst of a third. I had no idea why he had not chosen to use the writing desk.

"You could apologize for waking me," I said with pique.

"And if I do not do so," Holmes answered, "you may be assured there is a reason for my apparent rudeness." His moving pen stopped for an instant. "I should think you would be pleased to find me with an amiable disposition. For years you have tried to wheedle me into assuming your relentlessly cheerful seasonal mood."

The thought passed my mind to say I had not realized he *was* cheerful, but the desire to ask Mrs. Hudson for breakfast combined with curiosity overcame the impulse. "To what may I attribute this phenomenon in you, Holmes? Have you been sought to investigate a scandal linked to one of the royal families of Europe?"

"Not at all," he replied, chuckling. "On the one hand, Watson"—he clapped his left palm on the stack of open letters, his right on his sealed envelopes—"I have two intriguing new correspondents for whom civility requires a response." He pointed to the letter separate from the others, a brow rising. "On the other hand is the prospect of a client whose problems may be marginally more challenging than their domestic nature implies. She will call on us within the hour."

"Just yesterday you complained about a complete dearth of cases," I reminded Holmes. "You cited, if memory serves, 'this endless period of Yuletide sentiment.' "

"So I did, Watson," he said agreeably. A long, pajama-clad leg shot out and he wriggled his pale toes. "But the special post only today brought the letter in question, knocking me up in the process. I daresay you were awakened in similar fashion, although it took you somewhat longer to break the spell of Morpheus."

"Ah!" I exhaled, nodding. "That is why you did not apologize for rousing me."

"Because I was merely the instrument of your inconvenience, not the cause," Holmes said. "Once afoot, I elected then to begin responding to my mail." He snatched up a letter to him, wafted it aloft. "Is the name 'Thomas Nast' at all familiar to you, Watson?"

I ransacked my memory. "Is he not an artist of some kind?"

"Precisely. Mr. Nast is an American newspaper artist whose cartoons have used satire to attack the New York politicians of what is termed 'Tammany Hall.' For some time we have exchanged letters of mutual regard. I see Nast as having cleverly extended the arm of the law, and he perceives me in the same light."

"And his present letter?"

Holmes, remarkably, chortled with glee. "He has accepted my proposed image for sketches he means to create depicting Father Christmas!"

"Congratulations, old friend!" I said sincerely. "But what image did you suggest?"

"My brother, Mycroft!" Holmes retorted, exuberantly pounding the floor with his fist and laughing. The mail on the floor bounced. "You yourself described his 'absolute corpulence,' his 'great bulk.' I recalled his wish to be of service to the government—in short, to others. And we are all mere children before my older brother's genius, or his size! Nast says he will add a beard and, in all probability, a smile! Come, what do you think of an old colleague who has reminded you of Ebenezer Scrooge now that he has made such a contribution to your precious Yuletide!"

I was at a loss to do more than add further congratulations. I added, "May I ask the identity of your second new correspondent?"

Holmes stretched his arms until he could lock his fingers round his toes. An affable gleam was in his eyes as he rocked lightly to and fro, exercising. "He is an extraordinary fellow who also lives in America, virtually in libraries, where he compiles lists. He haunts the files of old newspapers and other publications for oddities—anomalies of nature, and those of man."

"Odd chap." I fear I spoke hastily for I had heard Mrs. Hudson bustling around below us and I was eager to inform our landlady we were ready for breakfast. "I suppose he has other qualities you find interesting."

"Not one," Holmes replied immediately, freeing his toes and peering over at me with some annoyance. "I cited his single appeal to my intellect. In Charles Fort I sense a kindred spirit in some particulars. Fort is skeptical, understands that facts are what they wish to be and lack all flexibility. Well, it happens that I added to his collection of queer data which Fort calls 'damned.'"

I had gone to the landing, leaving the door ajar, and succeeded in signaling Mrs. Hudson. Now, closing the door, I returned my attention to my friend. "Good Lord, Holmes, why does the man call facts such a thing?"

He uncoiled from the floor like some magnificent jungle cat, brushing at his dressing gown before stooping to don his slippers. "Innumerable facts are despised by the close-minded, therefore effectually ostracized; ignored." He strode briskly to a shelf of his commonplace books and pulled out the volume labeled "K" in his own distinct penmanship. He held it out to me. "I sealed my letter to Fort. However, if you should like to see for yourself what obvious yet largely ignored fact I am sending him, do be my guest."

I opened the book, my gaze falling upon such entries as "Kaolin clay and its potential for concealing and preserving fingerprints," "Knights of the Golden Circle—link to the hooded Neal family victims?" and "Kisner and Koontz, outside the Valley of the Howl." I glanced at the detective. "For what am I looking, Holmes?"

"The town of Kottenforst, Germany," he called, seemingly about to resume his correspondence while seated at the desk. "It is a short distance from Bonn."

Leafing through the pages, I felt an honor had been bestowed upon me. Holmes often asked me to read telegrams and newspaper items aloud but rarely invited me to peer into his great, erratically organized commonplace books. Under the heading of KOTTENFORST I learned of an unrusted metal column called the Iron Man rising fewer than five feet from the ground and running some ninety feet deep—for *no* purpose anyone living has discovered! Amazingly, records of its existence have been found in writings from the late fourteenth century. "Plunging it through limestone and rock," Holmes's scrawl continued, "would have been virtually impossible five hundred years ago. Who put it there, and how? *Why* does 'the Iron Man' exist at all?"

There the entry ended and I turned to my friend with a mixture of inexplicable apprehension and irritation. "This is damned nonsense!" I exclaimed.

Holmes did not look up but simply patted his sealed letter to Charles Fort, not quite concealing his satisfied smile. I experienced a measure of relief when, a few minutes later, our reliable landlady tapped on the door with breakfast.

I ate silently while Holmes, at the desk, scribbled letters at a pace I knew from years of association would render his writing almost illegible to recipients unversed in his hand. He paused now and again to gulp hot tea or take bites from the slices of toast provided by Mrs. Hudson until they appeared to have been nibbled upon by tentative rodents. Finished at length with letters and meal, Holmes darted upstairs to dress for our expected caller.

I had just followed suit and rejoined Holmes in the sitting room when, with a great moan, he tumbled back on the sofa, forearm slung across his face.

"What is it, Holmes?" I cried, rushing to his side. "Are you in much pain?"

"Only the agony of one who can mark the difference between the profound and the superficial," he groaned. The message delivered by special post dangled from his fingertips, and that arm was outflung in despair. "Only the torment of a man who has been to the brink with Moriarty, outsmarted the second most dangerous man in London, and has destroyed his career by striving for perfection and reaching it. I cannot lie to myself about this matter or its simplicity."

He appeared to be seeking to hand me the letter and so I took and read it.

My dear Mr. Holmes:

I am well aware that you are accustomed to using your vast knowledge for personages far more important than my poor brother and me. However, I love Sydney with all my heart, and his mysterious disappearance means I have no one left to whom I may turn for guidance.

Briefly stated, the facts are that my brother's disposition changed greatly in a short period of time though he assured me he has done nothing wrong. Sydney was one who always loved me, and looked forward yearly to joining with other carolers at Christmastime. During the period of his change, he began avoiding me without animosity between us, and his vanishing convinces me he is in danger of some variety. I beg you to find and help him.

I haven't contacted the authorities because, despite my brother's spotless reputation as an aspiring author, some illness may have caused him to behave rashly. It may be of interest to read that Sydney, who took rooms in Montague Place since this all started, cannot smile or laugh.

A consulting detective such as you, Mr. Holmes, might be able to deduce my brother's whereabouts in a very short period and return expeditiously to matters of state.

The letter's writer mentioned the hour at which she would visit Baker Street, and signed herself Eleanor Chesterfield. I noted her address was on Mildenhall Road.

Sighing, Holmes was struggling into a resigned seated position. "What do you make of this, Watson?"

I studied the message closely. "They are doubtlessly impecunious since Montague Place has declined. The fact that the brother is attempting to become a writer makes it rather likely he has acquired debts which he has hidden from sister." I studied the letter line by line, even held it up to the light. "Poverty and debt often conspire to remove the smile from a man's face and turn him solitary."

Holmes said, tonelessly, "Is that all?"

"It's mere surmise, Holmes, but I would not hesitate to say the message is a most disciplined effort on the part of an aging maiden woman rendered virtually helpless by Sydney's absence." I shrugged. "If he is ill, it may be that the poor old soul has wandered off due to his mental infirmity. Do you follow my conclusions?"

"Only with peril, Watson." Holmes stood at the mantel examining his tobacco dottles from the previous day. As a rule he used them for his day's first pipe, but answering letters had preoccupied him this morning. "Both sister and brother lived on Mildenhall Road with its well-to-do residences until he moved, to be on his own. That deed, coupled with the decision to pursue a new career, suggests the thinking of a younger man. Not one afflicted with senility." He had his pipe going and his head was wreathed by pungent smoke. "At least your hearing has not suffered."

I was annoyed as I poured myself a final cup of tea and found it cold. "I suppose you deduce a great deal more from Miss Chesterfield's letter?"

"Quality means more than quantity in the art of deduction." Holmes crossed to the bow window, drew back the curtains, and peered out at Baker Street. "My client is a young, intelligent woman of considerable persuasion, accustomed to being her sibling's prevailing influence. Her reference to my skill at the outset and close of her missive demonstrates the former, her lack of understanding of his ambition the latter. The two resided together until the demise of their parents, who willed the property to them. I also know that Sydney has either led a double life throughout his adult years or is, indeed, strangely ill and in the depths of misery."

"It could be both," I said helpfully.

Holmes was lost in his track of thought. "It is embarrassment that prevented the lady from seeking official assistance. She preferred to contact no one about her brother's apparent disappearance until overcome both by sisterly love and the same sentimental attachment to this season which infects so many people each year."

"How can you deduce the latter, Holmes?" I asked.

"My dear fellow," he murmured, "what other conclusion is possible when Miss Chesterfield presents no reason for waiting to consult me, then does so suddenly by special post—early on a day when groups of carolers are beginning to move into the streets? It is clear she felt Sydney would return to his digs in time for the annual festivities, but her preference for privacy gave way to love and genuine concern." He released the curtain and went rapidly to his chair. "The same reasoning leads to the deduction that both of them lived in Mildenhall until their parents died, when, at last, he chose to pursue his literary career. An older man would have struck out on his own sooner." Holmes sat down, drummed his fingertips on the arms. "A carriage has arrived, Watson. We should hear the lady's footsteps on the stairs—*now*."

The unmistakable noise of woman's heels reached our ears simultaneously. My friend fell back in his chair, smiling and smoking. I was unaware he was listening closely enough to count the seventeen steps to our rooms until, before there was a rap, Holmes called, "Please, Miss Chesterfield—come in!"

The woman who entered did so before I was able to open the door for her. She stared at Holmes and then at me. "You have described Mr. Holmes exceptionally well," she said in genteel accents. As she allowed me to take her black winter coat, I saw that she was petite and fine featured, with blonde hair swept up from the neck. "I would have known you anywhere, Mr. Holmes."

"And I you, madam," my friend said, rising but briefly before falling back into his chair. He raised a single, golden hair doubtlessly plucked from the lady's letter. "Observe, Doctor, that Miss Chesterfield is some eight and twenty years of age. I take it your brother Sydney is not yet in his dotage?"

Her laugh, I confess, was that of a properly reared lady. "He is three years my junior. I become twenty-eight in June. Pray tell me what else you know about me, Mr. Holmes, and from what you accomplish your deductions?"

Holmes drew heavily on his pipe. "As to the latter, my sole sources of data are the letter you dispatched, and your person. As to the former, I informed Dr. Watson that your parents perished before your brother departed the home, that you imagined his problems not sufficient to keep him from a homecoming, and that you concluded his inability to smile or laugh lies near the root of his situation." Holmes's eyes narrowed. "I also have reason to think you fear for his sanity and what he may do, to others or to himself."

I was studying her refined features and saw her turn uncommonly pale. "Holmes, that is exceedingly direct and personal, even if you are correct."

"Yet he *is* correct, Doctor," Eleanor Chesterfield said, mustering a courageous smile I thought admirable. "The matter is both personal and delicate."

"Then I certainly commend your judgment in scorning the official police. And," Holmes added, "rest assured that what is spoken here will remain confidential." He pressed his fingertips together. "Comprehension, however, is my ally. Did your brother leave his family home because you disapproved of his ambitions or for any other point of contention between you?"

"Absolutely not, except I desired Sydney to consult a physician. Apart from that, I knew that the inheritance left equally to us finally gave him the opportunity to pursue his talents."

"Yet is it not curious for him to take rooms in a less comfortable residence?" Holmes relit his pipe. "Wouldn't Mildenhall have had a room suitable as a study?"

One of her pale hands fluttered. "I have no explanation for his choice apart from his impairment." She sat forward. "Sydney was never a jovial or sociable child and our father expressed his dissatisfaction clearly that my brother's aptitudes leaned more to the creative than to finance. Sydney was animated only with me, or in song. But even before he left home his moods had darkened. He denied anything was wrong even though he scowled and rarely spoke. Then, dwelling alone, his attitude seemed swiftly to deteriorate." Her voice faded and she appeared unable to continue.

"Please, proceed," Holmes said levelly.

"He refused most of my invitations," Miss Chesterfield resumed. "Several weeks ago, when he relented and came for dinner, I was obliged to make most of the conversation. Yet when he was otherwise amused by something I said to make him smile, his face remained expressionless, and . . ." She broke off speaking.

"You really must tell us everything," I said from my chair beside her, patting her hand.

She gazed desperately at Holmes. "Sydney was able only to make strange, grunting noises in lieu of laughter." She made the effort not to sob. "They sounded quite—*porcine*. He was aware of it, too, I'm sure. He averted his face, then leapt to his feet and bolted for the door. I have not seen or heard from him since then."

"Some questions of extreme importance," said Holmes. Erect in his chair, his authority could not have been denied. "On that evening, did your brother say or do anything whatsoever that was unmistakably irrational? In short, despite your concern that his condition might cause him to behave 'rashly,' is there a logical reason apart from the expressionlessness, inappropriate vocal sounds, or his leaving your house, to believe he was suffering a mental breakdown?"

"Why, no." A glimmer of hope restored some color to the lady's cheeks. "Furthermore, I know of no one he hates or fears, and I begged him to admit it if he had made some unwise investment, but he denied it." She paused. "The only peculiar statement he uttered was made while climbing into a carriage for the trip back to his rooms. 'Don't you know, sister,' he said, 'I'm the one person you cannot take at face value?' Then," Miss Chesterfield finished, shuddering, "he grimaced hideously as he was borne away."

151

My friend accepted a photograph of Sydney from a few years in the past, then mystified me with two last questions. He asked whether the brother sang tenor or baritone, and the name of the church that the family attended, which proved to be Saint Agnes in Cricklewood.

"Please locate him," Miss Chesterfield said while I held the door open for her. "Assure him I shall stand beside him whatever the nature of his problem."

"Find him, I shall, madam," Holmes promised from in front of his chair. "Perhaps just as 'expeditiously' as your letter so persuasively implored me to do. You may expect to hear from me."

When I no longer heard her heels striking the stairs, I turned to Holmes with some exasperation. "I cannot recall when you have sworn to solve a case, Holmes. Or for that matter, responded less warmly to a client's difficulties."

"But I did not promise Miss Chesterfield a happy Christmas, old fellow, merely to locate Sydney. He is plagued by an enigmatic malady, indeed." He was slipping into a topcoat. "As for the rest, I failed neither to observe that the lady is comely nor that you did, as well. Her attractiveness means little to me and does not make the case a fraction more challenging to me."

"May I inquire where you are going, Holmes?"

The door opened and he paused. "Why, I am going to church, Watson. I believe such attendance was a prominent element of the Christmas season before the giving of gifts and the consumption of certain fowl became *de rigueur*?"

And so for the next many hours I was alone with no patients on my schedule that day. I found all this irksome with so much leisure time bestowed upon me at such an early hour. I found a publication containing a medical paper I had meant to read, and settled into my chair. Entitled "The Psychic Mechanism of Hysterical Phenomena," the paper written by Dr. Freud and another Austrian, Josef Breuer, startled me by carrying Freud's sudden change of method in his treatment of hysteria. Rather than hypnotism, announced the article, the famed Viennese psychiatrist laid a foundation for analyzing a patient's psyche through something termed "free association."

I continued reading, attempting to absorb the pertinent points, until a mixture of lost sleep and the morning's excitement caused me to doze in my chair.

I awoke to music and straightened, knuckling my eyes. It took another instant to perceive both that Holmes was not present and the melodic noises came from a chorus on the street outside, singing carols. Squinting down from the window, I saw a goodly number of singers just two buildings away. Marvelous to discover, too, London was enjoying its first snowfall of the season!

Moments later, humming, I was dashing down the steps, pausing only long enough to ask Mrs. Hudson to put on hot chocolate for our music makers. Then I was out the front door, ready to greet them with my beaming audience of one and a baritone I had once believed rich enough for a life on the stage, a fact I had told no one.

Some sixteen singers of equal sexual character were completing a hearty rendition of "Good King Wenceslas" as they approached 221. Spying me through the flurries of this wintry late afternoon, the carolers began a particularly rousing "God Rest Ye, Merry Gentlemen," to which I now and then added my sonorous baritone. Most of the time, however, despite plummeting temperatures, I was happy to listen. The spiraling whiteness reminded me of lightning with its fury spent. Memories of this doorway, this house, also materialized in my mind's eye. Even while married, I had rarely been more than the distance of a telegram from Baker Street, and Holmes's adventures that were the nearest I would come again to the perils and thrills of the Fifth Northumberland Fusiliers and the Second Afghan War.

While the carolers sang a second chorus, Mrs. Hudson arrived with refreshments and a number of mugs. I had been rubbing my hands together for warmth and took a cup myself. It was then I noticed one tenor voice stood out above the others. His clear if rather insistent harmony on the line, "Oh, tidings of comfort and joy" made the fellow easy to locate. When they finished the carol and several of them shared Mrs. Hudson's capacious mugs, I was surprised when the tenor sidled over beside me. He was an elderly person with mutton-chop whiskers, robust enough despite rounded shoulders and a hitch in his gait. I supposed he desired to thank me for arranging a repast.

Instead, he gave me an audacious wink. "I really don't think you should be on the pavement without protection against the cold, Watson," he offered sotto voce. "You may perchance have observed it is snowing?"

I almost cried "Holmes!" but swiftly realized my friend must be in disguise on behalf of Eleanor and Sydney Chesterfield. "You did not leave home in disguise, Holmes," I said softly, impressed once more by his remarkable makeup skill.

"You were snoring too loudly when I returned from Saint Agnes church even to have heard the caroling group of which I have become the latest member had we practiced by the mantelpiece." He took my hot chocolate mug from my hand and drank the rest with his head thrown back, a gesture I had never seen Holmes make before. "This was our practice, by the bye—necessary because *I* am the replacement for young Mr. Sydney Chesterfield!"

"Your violin playing is masterful," I said, "yet I have no recollection of your singing. How can this possibly serve to locate your client's brother?"

Holmes put the mug back into my hands airily and wiped his lips with the back of his hand. "I may have a visitor before I return at the end of the early evening, old fellow, a gentleman with the sense to have wound a scarf round his face to guard against Jack Frost. Please admit him and ignore a surly or caustic disposition." In a louder, unfamiliar voice, he said, "Many thanks for the libation!"

All the carolers including Sherlock Holmes wished me season's greetings and were off to serenade Baker Street!

I spent the next hour or so completing an alert reading of the Freud and Breuer paper, then consumed a lonely evening meal. Of course, my thoughts reviewed the events of the day and I attempted to apply my professional training to the problems of our lovely client's brother and the symptoms we had heard described.

I recalled that it had been just six years ago, in '88, when Waldeyer-Hartz suggested the nervous system was built from separate cells with frail extensions. Disruption of them, I theorized, could account for an inability to smile or laugh. Some Italian had named the cells "neurons," the minute gaps between them—

My ponderings were interrupted by a strong, sharp knock at the door.

A slender man bundled from head to foot—a Scotch bonnet on top, a scarf concealing his face but for striking deep brown eyes, Navy frock coat buttoned at the neck to pinion the lower portion of the scarf, matching trousers, and boots—stood in the doorway. "Is this the residence of that arrogant dilettante," the chap demanded, "who thinks he can make a single appearance and lord it over the regular carolers?"

His hands were fisted, but this was not morning and John H. Watson may be depended upon in a pinch. "My friend is out, but expected shortly," I said evenly and stood back from the door. "I'm sure he would like to make your acquaintance, and explain. Come in, please."

He paused, then entered, his manner still truculent. "He won't like to see me, sir." Following my gesture, he took a chair. Perched on the edge, he glared up with outraged eyes. "Not even a member of Saint Agnes, but he told Mr. Calhoun, the conductor, he could 'sing rings around your last lead tenor'—right before the other singers! I wouldn't even know of the slander if a friend who was present hadn't come to me."

"May I have your coat and hat," I asked politely, "and your scarf?" Virtually certain the caller was Sydney Chesterfield himself, I was filled with medical curiosity to inspect his face. An idea occurred to me. "Something to drink?"

He gave me a curt shake of the head, relaxed, and leaned back. "My apologies for the rudeness. It's not your fault what a friend does." A heavy sigh. "Nobody can account for people's behavior, and that is why I am striving to become a writer. To understand their natures better."

"And your own as well, I trust?" Holmes stepped quickly through the door and strode across the room. Our guest did not leap up, as I had feared, because Holmes was conspicuously peeling off his mutton-chop whiskers and removing both white eyebrows and twenty years of age. Snapping to his erect, full height, he put out a hand to the younger man. "I am Sherlock Holmes, and the gentleman who admitted you is my colleague, Dr. Wat-

155

son." He lifted the artificial whiskers. "Perhaps you, too, would like to end the charade, Mr. Chesterfield? I doubt your face would alarm two gentlemen whose activities have left them fairly shock-proof!"

Chesterfield froze but he did not remove the concealing scarf. "How do you know me or my problems? Why did you deride my singing in front of the choir and join our caroling group?" His eyes narrowed. "Was my sister, Eleanor, here?"

Holmes, sitting, began a new pipe. "So many questions! Your sister engaged me this morning to find you. She was quite concerned and implied your enjoyment of caroling is so considerable you would not fail to participate unless a 'problem' made it impossible." He shrugged. "It was a simple matter to speak privately with your conductor, discover that a friend of yours was present who should know where you were, and—believing you could be taunted into showing yourself—express a scornful assessment of your vocal skills. I take it Mr. Calhoun was good enough to divulge my address?"

"I fail utterly to see what my well-being or interests have to do with either of you," Sydney said angrily. "But since your intrusion has gone this far, you may as well know that, living alone, I lost the last control I had of my facial muscles." He removed the Scotch bonnet, began to unwind the scarf. I had glimpsed the picture of him handed to my friend by Chesterfield's sister and found an amiably mustached face many women would have called handsome. Even knowing he was afflicted, I was unprepared for what I now saw in our guest chair.

He still had his mustache and was as fair as his sister. His features, however, were locked in a grimace that expressed depths of frustrated fury. That was not the worst of it. But for the flashing, wary eyes, Chesterfield's face might have been in the grips of rigor mortis. "You have suffered this condition increasingly," I began, "since you were a small lad. Is that not true?"

"It is," he agreed, surprise in his eyes. "However, my parents chose to think I was slow, sullen, given to dark moods, so I saw no physician and ceased to mention it." His lips moved sufficiently for him to speak clearly. "I disappointed Father so much that, when he died, our home seemed haunted. I could not stay and took inexpensive rooms rather than depend upon Father's money. Guilt over him made my writing progress slow, turned me resentful. I fear Eleanor thought I blamed her, when she was all I ever truly had." Tears shone in his eyes. "I knew no way to explain my need to discover if I could fend for myself, or that a friendship I formed with another caroler was—as *you* know, Mr. Holmes— with a young lady. And without her interest I should never have been able to survive without Eleanor, my church, or my caroling group."

I was taken aback when Eleanor Chesterfield was abruptly among us, and then I realized Holmes must have fetched her from Mildenhall Road. Without my noticing, he had signaled her to enter and now stood puffing beside the door, smiling watchfully and thinly.

"Sydney, I understand," Eleanor said, clasping her brother's hand."You clearly possess our father's independent streak." She stooped to kiss his forehead. "And I am eager to meet your lady friend when you decide the time is right." She turned prettily to Sherlock Holmes. "You, sir, are everything Dr. Watson has claimed you are! To think it was just this morning I consulted you for your assistance!"

"Well, well," Holmes said with a courteous bow, "I had the 'matters of state' you mentioned in your letter and had to work swiftly. It was instantly clear that your brother was a sensitive fellow with artistic tastes—a variety with which I am somewhat familiar. Such men cling dearly to their realms of talent, and guard them zealously. If Sydney knew a meddlesome stranger was speaking derogatively of his musical talent, he would emerge from the shadows to answer his critic—if he lived, of course."

Young Chesterfield clung to his older sister's hand. "I have been a vain fool, and two women have made that clear," he said. Sydney made a guttural sound in his throat that recalled Eleanor's accurate description of his attempt at laughter. "It is a pity I'm too much a fright to go caroling, yet it seems I still have my sister and a sympathetic friend. Name your fee, Mr. Holmes, and I shall pay it myself with gratitude."

"Ah, but this case is not over!" Holmes answered. "Dr. Watson's question to you about your condition's origins in childhood implies that he concurs." He motioned to brother and sister to sit, his pipe making a layer of smoke upon the ceiling. "When I found no evidence of criminality or madness on your part, Mr. Chesterfield, my logical conclusion was that something is amiss in the functioning of your brain or nervous system. They are man's most complex of organs and systems, and damage to either can topple even the giants among us as if we were intellectual saplings."

"You echo my thinking, Holmes," I said, meaning to mention my recent study.

"And yet, my dear fellow," Holmes continued, "your little records of my cases often suggest my intellect is 'cold'! In truth, intellect is that which makes each of us *most* human." He returned his gaze to our clients. "Watson is a practicing physician. You need not visit Harley Street in quest of medical assistance when, sir, a preliminary examination may be conducted without further delay." Holmes clapped my arm. "I have often placed my life in his hands, and there is no abler man!"

"How generous of you, old friend," I said. "The fact is, I have become aware only today of a course of treatment described by Dr. Sigmund Freud himself. There are no promises, but I think it is not unreasonable to surmise that, using this treatment, I might be able to return you to your group of carolers in time for next Christmas!"

When I had asked the young lady and Holmes to absent themselves briefly, I got my bag and gave Sydney Chesterfield his long-belated physical examination. Exactly as I expected, his health was sound and his problems lay elsewhere. I asked Miss Chesterfield and my friend to rejoin us, and presented my plan of treatment.

"See me regularly here, Sydney," I said while I tucked my stethoscope into place, "and I won't use hypnosis but the power of suggestion as Freud describes it. My intention is to encourage you to speak freely until we know your innermost memories, can deal with them, and you learn how to laugh or smile appropriately. Because I, too, am an author, I will discuss your writing efforts. The muscles of your face and mouth will, in my judgment, relax, and the rest will follow."

Brother and sister volubly expressed their appreciation. It was only when I had seen them out that I perceived Holmes had already wended his way to the writing desk. A trifle full of myself, I fear, I approached him in uncharacteristic bantering.

"Holmes, the young man was on the verge of paying your fee. You, however, volunteered my services and it appears now we are both out of pocket! A remarkable oversight, my dear fellow, for so astute a fellow as you."

"No oversight, Watson," Holmes said without glancing up from an envelope he was addressing. I noticed the name of his correspondent, Charles Fort. "I intended our deeds to be regarded as gifts. Those of the season, to be precise." His smile was fleeting. "I take it that you have no grave objections?"

I was taken aback and did not respond. A nod of my head indicated the envelope. "You remember mailing a letter to Mr. Fort today, I'm sure?"

"This is an addendum." He was scribbling the new letter as we conversed and he amazed me anew with the ability to come close to doing two different things simultaneously. "Fort will be fascinated by Mr. Chesterfield's peculiar infirmity. I wager he will discover further identical ailments, but never more than fifty to sixty in any given year. It is an observation of mine that nature repeats herself merely as a cautionary advertisement, but rarely places her notices haphazardly until the circumstances are dire."

With that, Holmes arose and glanced about the room. His new information for Fort was in its envelope, sealed and ready. "Did you happen to see where I left the disguise I used today?"

I pointed it out while he was again donning his coat. "Where are you going now, if I may ask?"

"Why, back to Saint Agnes in Cricklewood," Holmes replied, transforming himself once more into a robust but lame old man. "Your Freudian magic cannot be fulfilled immediately, and I am a man of my word. Mr. Calhoun called for a practice tonight, when we shall learn of tomorrow's schedule. I can scarcely let him down."

I peered at him in astonishment. "You are continuing to be a . . . a *caroler*?"

Sherlock Holmes paused at the door without reaching for the knob. "It is my commitment. And I might add, Watson, that Calhoun asked us to keep an eye and an ear open for an especially strong baritone."

I headed across the floor with alacrity, and my friend was holding my hat and coat out to me before I had taken more than a few paces. "I think it may be a happy Christmas, Holmes," I said.

"Or if not that," he said as we descended the stairs at a trot, "perhaps one that is marginally less tedious than the rest." We stepped out upon Baker Street and into swirling snow, and Holmes summoned a passing four-wheeler. "The game may not be afoot, my dear fellow, but at least *we* are!"

(With appreciation to Tracy Knight, Ph.D., for telling me about the extremely rare Moebius syndrome.)

THE YULETIDE AFFAIR

John Stoessel

FROM THE AUTHOR'S DESK

Conan Doyle always cast Dr. Watson as the traditional narrator, but even his series included a few accounts by Holmes. Those few were never as popular as Dr. Watson's, who sketched a profile of his amazing friend as he observed the clues invisible to others. Suppose, however, that Watson solved a mystery on his own? After all, giving a separate life to a biographer is fair play in mystery literature.

Actually, it is also long overdue. While Dr. Watson was not a master detective, he understood the discipline and mastered an equally challenging one of his own. In this alone, to say nothing of his patience and courage beyond the call of duty, I say Dr. Watson deserves his own moment of glory, one which would accent his talents without upstaging Holmes.

Picture Holmes and Watson sitting comfortably by the fire in Sussex. The time is December 1923, and the mail has arrived.

Watson reads a letter, then captures Holmes's attention. He ad-

161

mits with some shyness that he has a story to place in the second tin box. Holmes comprehends the situation immediately.

"An adventure of *your own,* Watson?"

"Yes, Holmes. I think the time has come to tell you. . . ."

Two Weeks Before Christmas

Sherlock Holmes was not at Baker Street when Inspector MacDonald stopped by. His hasty entry and brief greeting to Mrs. Hudson told me he had urgent business afoot. I also realised his wait could be long. Holmes seldom returned at a predictable time when he was on a case. I said so.

MacDonald waved his hand aside. "We can bring in Holmes later—if you think it's necessary. We need you, Doctor."

"*Me?*"

"Aye, at Saint Bart's. Lestrade's on his way there. He . . . he's pretty bad."

The gaslight shone on Mac's face then, and I could see his ashen colour. I took my bag at once, left a forwarding message for Holmes with Mrs. Hudson, and went with the inspector to the cab waiting outside.

"I doubt we'll need Holmes, Doctor. We have the rascal who knifed Lestrade. We need you because the regular staff is a wee bit overloaded from this influenza season. Lestrade was unconscious when the ambulance came, and I'm a bit worried about that. I thought it best to dash over here."

The big Scotsman had a curious way of understating current affairs, even when he was under strain. A new influenza and the winter season had come early to London. A fresh heavy snow had fallen, making it all the worse for the ill and infirm. Even now a driving sleet was pelting hard against the glass of the cab as we wended our way through the evening traffic. Christmas shoppers were in abundance: the Second Sunday of Advent had come and gone; it was now Wednesday, and Christmas was but a fortnight away.

My earlier Christmas cheer was replaced by worry for our friends at the Yard. Despite the friendly rivalry and differences of opinion, there were many cases I could name which required their police and warrant powers. Now they were friends in need. MacDonald was in a dark, quiet mood.

"How did it happen, Inspector? Who did it?"

"Vinny Shadwell!" exploded MacDonald in a rare burst of emotion. "I never thought he owned a knife! I wasn't there, but Constable Rance saw the scuffle. If Lestrade doesn't make it, I'll . . . I'll personally walk that little scarecrow up to the rope!"

"Mac, calm yourself! Lestrade's a robust man if there ever was one. I'll do my best, I promise—and here we are!"

Both of us half walked, half ran from the cab into the huge complex known as Saint Bartholomew's Hospital. I let MacDonald lead the way, and his cape fluttered in the still, antiseptic air as he glided through the white halls and dun-coloured doors. We stopped outside a room guarded by a few well-known friends. Tobias Gregson and Athelney Jones looked anxiously at me as I hurried past them. Lestrade lay very still in a single bed.

"Still unconscious! Well, let's see this wound now. . . ."

I tried to sound hopeful, but his colour was very pale. The knife thrust had entered the right side of his ribs and missed the heart area by inches. Since this was a police matter, the weapon was still in the room, which gave me a chance to see its length and potential depth. I mentally noted a possible three- or four-inch penetration. That was trouble. His pulse was weak, but steady. His lack of consciousness could be from shock, but I saw that the nursing staff had tried to bring him round with smelling salts, which should have worked. Why hadn't it? I did not know, but his breathing was laboured and shallow. I turned to MacDonald, who had brought in Jones and Gregson.

"Has he come out of it at all?" I asked. "Has anyone from the staff been here to see him?"

They all answered the first part in the negative. As for the staff, a nurse had come, applied some dressings to staunch the bleeding, and summoned a doctor. He promised to come soon.

"With this bleedin' plague, every hospital doctor is rare as gold," said Jones with a growl. "Take over, Doctor Watson. You know the ropes!"

MacDonald and Gregson muttered in agreement.

163

I know I should have asked about Lestrade's family. Had they been notified? This was what we called a battlefield decision in the Army Medical Corps. Since time was not on Lestrade's side, I decided to proceed. I tried exploring around the wound for hidden injuries, but found none. Aromatic camphor and ammonia smelling salts were handy, but Lestrade remained out cold. I looked for the floor nurse. MacDonald muttered something and left.

Two minutes later, there was a polite knock at the outer door. MacDonald came in, escorting Dr. Eden, a good man, but overworked. He was the one who had promised to come.

"Inspector MacDonald, please! *Every* patient is important to us, and the nurses did dress his wound! I can't see where Lestrade has been neglected—why, *hello*, John Watson! Nasty piece of business, what? Glad to have you here, old boy."

"I'm sorry, Dr. Eden, I should have contacted—"

"*Me*? For what, John?" Dr. Eden waved to the floor nurse. "Sister, if this man needs anything here at Saint Bart's, see to it, will you? Now the hospital is at your command, old boy, and I can deal with this epidemic."

As he left, there was a small commotion outside. Both of us left the room and came upon a couple of constables subduing a slender man in handcuffs with a torn coat. MacDonald came over with a dark look on his face and a raspy growl in his voice.

"Vinny Shadwell, you're in deep enough trouble! If ye' know any prayers, ye' best say them quick! Pray Dr. Watson got here in time!"

The slender man looked at me hopefully.

"You're *the* Dr. Watson from Baker Street?"

I nodded. Dr. Eden waved wearily to us and left. Shadwell tried to reach out to me, but was restricted by the handcuffs.

"Is Holmes with you?"

"No, I was called to Saint Bart's to help Lestrade. Holmes is away on another case," I said coldly.

I returned to Lestrade's bedside. I could hear Shadwell and MacDonald talking through the door. *It was a sad situation*, I thought, to see that little shadow of a man arguing with his captors and trying to talk his way out of trouble!

All my efforts with Lestrade produced no change. MacDonald was keeping Shadwell at the hospital for an ominous reason. If I couldn't save Lestrade, the charge would be murder, not assault. Gregson came in with a black look.

"Dr. Watson, that little twit's denying everything! That's not your problem, of course, but he says he never touched the knife! Is Lestrade any better?"

"No response yet, Gregson. The trouble with knife wounds are where they go, and how deep. I'm about to try to awaken Lestrade again, but keep Shadwell and Rance here. Unless he wakes up, I want every bit of information I can get."

Gregson cast one anxious look at his rival before he left, leaving the door ajar. I could hear the conversation drop outside as Mac-Donald and Gregson exchanged my news between themselves. It rose a bit as they resumed questioning Shadwell, who had a high, whining voice.

"I tell you I never touched 'im!"

"Right-o! That knife just appeared in his chest!" said Jones, who was even more cynical than Gregson. MacDonald spoke next. His Scottish accent heightened occasionally when he was under strain.

"Shadwell, I ask you to *conseedar* the consequences of your deed! Whatever ye' say will be noted and used against ye' in a court of law, but a man's dying in there, and you're our only suspect! What ha' ye' to lose by tellin' the truth?"

"But I *did* tell the truth! I had no knife!"

"Argh!" growled MacDonald. "If this man dies, ye'll hang!"

Suddenly, I noticed Lestrade's eyes flutter—he was coming conscious! Mac came in at that moment and Lestrade reached out and grabbed my arm with an intense look on his face. His voice was a mere gasp, barely audible, but clear enough.

"Wats—! Sha—d'll! S'a—rts!"

"*What*, Lestrade?" we said together.

"Sha—d'll? S'a—rts?"

"Shadwell's outside, Lestrade. We're talking to him."

Mac nodded grimly, went out again, and Lestrade faded away once more. Despite my best efforts, I was losing him. I looked at the knife, a wicked instrument designed to do harm with a minimum of effort. It was a common enough type, what a chef would call a fillet knife; long, narrow, and sharp as a razor. The blood smear was longer than I first thought—at least four inches long.

Over four inches, and this man was still alive? I could hear the Yard inspectors continuing to question Shadwell, and becoming more impatient by the minute. I had to explore the wound further, but I caught an occasional glimpse and heard them as I worked.

". . . I tell you I've *never* had a knife!"

"Oh, yes you *did*, Vinny Shadwell," said John Rance in an angry voice. "I've been in your neighbourhood for ten years! You used to scare the kids with a sticker."

That seemed to deflate Shadwell. I heard a weak rebuttal.

"All right, I did that when I was a bully in school, but I just scared them, I never hurt anyone! And I'd be off my chump to try anything against a Yarder!"

"A crime doesn't have to make sense, Shadwell," said Gregson.

"That's right," said Rance. "I know you said you ran *to* me after Lestrade went down, but I don't think you even *saw* me until I grabbed you. You were running away from the crime!"

"No, I wasn't! I tell you Lestrade was about to say something to me when he fell down. I never saw a knife in his chest until after you grabbed me and brought me back to him! Somebody else had to do it, it's *got* to be somebody else!"

MacDonald snapped at Shadwell.

"*Who?* No one else was *seen* near him between the time you ran and Rance brought ye' back, and that couldn't ha' been more than *thirty* seconds! I'm losin' ma' patience fast, Shadwell!"

The rest of the force glared at the suspect in sullen agreement. MacDonald started to say something more to him, then changed his mind. Jones was more vocal.

"Shadwell, we've pinched you before! What you say isn't worth the paper it's written on! Where's *your* witness?"

Shadwell was sweating now. He grasped at a final straw.

"What about Inspector Lestrade? *He* knows I didn't stab him!"

"If he says so—which I doubt very much—aye, you're a free man," said MacDonald. "But I've just been in to see him, and he mentioned your name. That's a dyin' accusation!"

There was a long silence, followed by the sound of a weeping man. It was then that I had my first doubts. *Why would a street tough suddenly turn soft if he knew he was guilty?* I came out of Lestrade's room; it was time for me to try surgery—nothing else was working. While the sisters were obtaining the cart used to transport the patient, I had a chance to see this man Shadwell once more.

As shabby as he looked when he was first brought in, he had become even more pathetic, like a rag doll with half the sawdust taken out of him. He was a small man who couldn't have weighed more than a hundred pounds. In truth, a knife was his logical weapon against a larger opponent, and the Yard obviously felt this was the whole case. I decided to try an idea of my own.

"May I see your hands, Mr. Shadwell?"

MacDonald, Gregson, and Jones looked at me in surprise. Rance was holding the man, but he relaxed his grasp enough to let him reach them over to me. The handcuffs clinked slightly as he rotated his wrists at my direction. I saw the patient cart coming down the hall out of the corner of my eye. Whatever I was trying had to be fast.

"Are you right-handed, sir?"

Shadwell nodded yes. Jones broke into the questioning.

"Doctor, I realise the wound is on the right side, but he still could have done it with his left hand! It doesn't take that much strength!"

Jones was right: it was no proof of innocence, and MacDonald gave me an annoyed look. Still, I had another thought and just enough time to ask it. The nurses were moving Lestrade onto the cart and looking my way. I nodded a "go ahead" order to them.

"Shadwell, did Lestrade say anything to you?"

"N-no, nothing—at least, nothing that made sense."

Jones interrupted again.

"C'mon, Doctor, we'll get the truth out of 'im at the Yard! Holmes couldn't save this bird from the rope!"

"Just one more question, *please*, Jones! What did he say?"

Shadwell looked more desperate than defiant.

"It . . . it sounded like 'carts' or 'sarts.' "

That was it! It had to be it! And not a moment too soon!

Lestrade was being wheeled past me towards the surgery room. I turned for one final moment before following him.

"Gentlemen, stay here—all of you! I have good reason to suspect Shadwell is as innocent as he claims. You should have my proof in half an hour!"

Everyone's jaw dropped, including Shadwell's. MacDonald found his voice and called out to me as I went down the hall.

"And Lestrade, Doctor?"

"Pray God he lives! But either way, I still believe Shadwell can be proven to be innocent! Don't touch that knife! There's an important piece of evidence on it!"

With that final shot, I ran to catch up to the nurses and Lestrade. Dr. Eden met me at surgery.

One hour later, Lestrade was in the post-operative recovery area looking much better, and Vinny Shadwell was swearing he was a changed man. He was so convincing that even Jones and Gregson warmed up to the reformed petty thief. MacDonald came in as happy as I've ever seen him.

"Lestrade verified everything, Doctor. You were as right as rain, and thanks to you, Shadwell, the Yard is twice in your debt! If it weren't for you and Dr. Watson, a good man would have died, you would have been sent to the hangman, and the Yard would have caused a grave miscarriage of justice."

MacDonald turned to me.

"How did you know what it *was*, Doctor? That was a bit of genius, realising how Lestrade fainted! He said so himself."

"So Lestrade did grab Shadwell for that reason?" I asked.

"Aye—exactly so!" exclaimed MacDonald. He turned to Gregson and Jones, who were staring at me. "You were right about the knife, too, Doctor! It *was* a piece of evidence in another case, and he hadn't had time to leave it at his office. It came out of his breast pocket when he fell, and he's lucky it didn't penetrate straight in!" MacDonald shuddered at the thought. "But how did you determine all that?"

"It was the wound's nature, Inspector—or rather, what it wasn't. Four inches into the chest cavity is fatal, and the knife stain was that long. What I *didn't* see confused the issue. All of us assumed the thrust was straight, because that is how a stabbing is done. Once I realised that was impossible, to quote Holmes, I had to reason what *was* possible. It was no mystery."

168

"Aye, Doctor. Holmes would say that was elementary."

"Humph! Yes, he would! As a doctor, I should have caught that diagnosis sooner than I did, but Holmes has experienced similar problems with tardy conclusions. It's the risk of a professional.

"What *none* of us saw was the type of bloodstain on the knife. If you look more carefully, you will notice Lestrade's blood on the blade near the tip—about an inch or so—but the *rest* of the stain is older and already dried. We were all being misled by a wound that wasn't there!

"That left the puzzle of why Lestrade *was* unconscious. He was *ill*, not injured. His windpipe was nearly closed. This wasn't the London influenza, but a fast-acting strain similar to diphtheria, and that's a killer disease! Dr. Eden called in a specialist just to be safe, but Lestrade responded well to pure oxygen. With his iron constitution, I daresay he'll be along in a week or two. Any other questions?"

Shadwell had one.

"Now that it's obvious, it seems so simple—the knife, I mean! How did you get on to that clue? It saved the day."

I reached into my pocket and pulled out a pen knife.

"This is a handy tool, but you can be assured it has stuck me a few times! It opens up, and all I have to do is bump into something—I have the scars on my leg to prove it. It just takes a moment of carelessness."

"Well," said Gregson, "you also said Shadwell was a hero, unknown to himself, Doctor. What did you mean by that?"

"Oh, that? He probably saved Lestrade's life."

Gregson and Jones looked popeyed at me. "How?"

"I'd like to know that myself!" added Shadwell.

"By slowing the fall! Lestrade fell forward and Shadwell broke the momentum. The knife caught the skin and changed the angle of thrust. Any other direction could have been fatal: that's my professional opinion, gentlemen. When Lestrade said 'sarts,' he was trying to say 'Saint Bart's,' but he could hardly breathe. He was asking Shadwell for help! You might have fled out of fear, Shadwell, but you were honest enough to stand by the truth, and that made a difference. Well, sir! You're a free man! Now you have another chance!"

Shadwell seemed to grow in stature as he spoke.

"Thanks to *you*, Doctor," he said. "It's a chance I'll not be wasting either. I can't pay you anything just yet, but I will—"

"Oh, no! That's not necessary. I was glad to be of service."

"But I *want* to do something. I need to prove to all of you that this isn't just some idle chatter!"

I was at a loss for words, but MacDonald was not.

"Hmm! If you really mean that, Shadwell, I know a position that needs filling. The pay isn't that much, but we need a good man at the jail."

"The jail?" he exclaimed. "What do you mean?"

"We call it rehabilitation, someone who can talk sense with the prisoners. Some are beyond reform, but many are not. I have always noticed they trust reformed lawbreakers better. We have a vacancy because our last man married and moved away from London. I'd be happy to recommend you—"

"Done!" said Shadwell. "Here's my hand on it!"

For two weeks I had delayed telling Holmes about Lestrade and Saint Bart's; I just didn't know what to say. Now it was Christmas Eve, and we were enjoying a nog and pudding at Baker Street when we heard a choir on the street below.

> *God rest ye, merry gentlemen, Let nothing you dismay!*
> *Remember Christ the Savior was born on Christmas Day!*
> *To save us all from Satan's powers,*
> *when we have gone astray,*
> *Oh, tidings of comfort and joy, comfort and joy!*
> *O-h ti-dings of com-fort and joy!*

It was Gregson, Lestrade, MacDonald, Shadwell, Jones, and Rance! You could hear the deep bass of Gregson and Lestrade booming the low notes, while Shadwell and MacDonald carried the high tenor. Rance and Jones filled in the baritone center. As they finished, we waved them in. Rance opened the lower door and up they all came, frosty, red, and cheery from the winter's cold. Holmes was talking to me as they came in.

"Watson, I *recognise* that new chap. He used to be a petty criminal in the Soho district. The Yard must be recruiting an irregular force of its own."

MacDonald introduced Shadwell to Holmes formally, and described his new position at Newgate Prison. The Yard was making progress in several cases, thanks to prisoner cooperation, and the jail's reform program was hailed as an act of justice tempered with mercy.

The caroling was also Shadwell's idea; he had sung in his youth. The normally gruff detectives had taken to it like ducks to water, and there was a favourable public goodwill in the local papers. Holmes nodded in agreement.

"My compliments, gentlemen, jolly good show! Music always makes better men of us! Sit down, warm your fingers, and have a bit of Christmas cheer!"

Lestrade sank into my chair, and Holmes looked at him more carefully.

"Lestrade, you look thinner. Did you perchance catch that illness that's been travelling around London?"

It was a precious scene. Lestrade gave me an appealing look, begging me to say *something*, or at least give him a clue. The balance of the force did their best to contain their amusement.

"Well," I said, "as a matter of fact I *did* treat Lestrade, Holmes. He had a rather nasty strain, but we caught it in time. I didn't think it was still that evident."

Holmes reached for his pipe, lit it, and sighed.

"I apologise, Watson, it's none of my business, but deductive reasoning never takes a holiday, and Lestrade *does* look pale. He usually prefers to stand, and I'd wager he has lost at least ten pounds. So what? Tomorrow will change that!"

There were good-natured chuckles all around.

"Yes, Lestrade," I said, "be sure to consume your share of the goose! You can take that as my personal prescription."

"Some pudding and brandy will also bring back your colour, Lestrade," added Holmes. "I have often wondered why Watson isn't a better detective! The art of medicine doesn't appear to be that different from the science of deduction. As a medical doctor, he has few equals, but in the subtle differences of detective science, he remains a better conductor of light than a source of illumination!"

This time there was an explosion of laughter.

"I say! What the devil was so funny about *that*? Have I *missed* something?"

I gave the men a precautionary look and winked at Shadwell.

"No, nothing at all, Holmes! I—ah, just made a face behind your back! No offence, my dear fellow—merry Christmas!"

"Oh, *really?* Well—merry Christmas to you too, Watson!"

"Aye! A bonnie good season to us all!" added MacDonald.

SUSSEX: CHRISTMAS, 1923.
A LETTER ARRIVES.

Dear Doctor Watson:

In response to your kind letter and request I am pleased to give you my permission to chronicle our brief adventure together. Your moment of brilliance became my moment of salvation, and I have never forgotten that wonderful long ago Christmas when my new life began. I plan to retire next year, write a little, and read some of your stories. If I could fit into one of them it would be an honour. May God bless your holidays, and all those yet to come! I am,

> Your most humble servant,
> Professor Vincent P. Shadwell,
> Queen Elizabeth College

THE ADVENTURE OF THE CHRISTMAS TREE

William L. DeAndrea

Over the years of my association with Mr. Sherlock Holmes, he strove constantly to present himself as the perfect reasoner, divorced from all human failings and concerns. And it is true that his perception and deductive abilities were unparelleled in at least the recorded history of our race; it is also true that Holmes was not devoid of those becoming and manly sentiments which distinguish the true English gentleman.

In perusing my notes, I see that I have already recorded a number of cases that illustrate my point, among them "The Adventure of the Yellow Face" and "The Adventure of Charles Augustus Milverton." There are others, recorded and unrecorded, that point in the same direction. Holmes scoffs, but I believe his ability to feel, albeit tightly controlled, enhances his genius as an investigator.

We were in our rooms at 221B Baker Street on the third day of winter of 1889, I reading the *Lancet*, and Holmes standing in the bow window scratching out tunes on the violin as he looked out at London. The weather had obliged the calendar by delivering at the advent of winter the first important snowstorm of the year.

The downy whiteness had muffled the usual bustle of the metropolis. I found it quite soothing, and it augured for a peaceful Christmas to come.

"I believe we are to have a visitor, Watson," Holmes said. "Two of them, to be precise."

"A case, Holmes?" I inquired.

I looked up to see him smile. "Bill collectors do not travel in the company of young ladies, and the charitably minded, collecting for a worthy cause, would stop at other doors than ours. I think we might safely say that these are potential clients come to see us."

I put away the *Lancet* and tidied up the area in which I had been reading. Soon Mrs. Hudson knocked to tell us that the visitors were Joseph Camber, and his daughter, Nancy.

Camber was nervous and embarrassed. He kept his hat, an old-fashioned high beaver, in his hands as he sat, and constantly turned it by the brim. He wasn't a tall man, but he was a muscular one, particularly in the arms and shoulders. His hair was brown, shot with gray. He was dressed for church, or for business, but he seemed uncomfortable in city clothes, as evidenced by the times he ran a finger around the inside of his collar.

The daughter was much more self-possessed. She was also brown haired, and she had a softer version of her father's strong features, rendering her handsome, rather than pretty. Still, she had an air of health and confidence about her that was most fetching.

"Good afternoon," said my friend. "I am Sherlock Holmes, and this is my colleague, Dr. Watson. Pray, how may we help you?"

Camber looked at his hat. "I feel a ruddy fool," said he. His accents marked him as a Highland Scot.

His daughter had the same soft burr. She laid a hand on Camber's arm and said, "Now, Father, we've come here. The decision has been taken."

"Ach. I know, but it *sounds* so daft."

"Perhaps I can help you get started," offered Sherlock Holmes. "You are the forester on the estate of the Duke of Balleshire in Scotland. You are left handed, and a widower, and you have come to consult me on a matter which will leave your mind no peace until you have got to the bottom of it."

The eyes of our younger visitor went wide with surprise; the elder visitor began to sputter. The only intelligible sounds he uttered were, "But how . . . ?"

Holmes gave the merest suggestion of a bow. "A trifling matter, really. The callosities on your hands are those of the man who wields the saw and the ax. Since your left hand is more heavily callused on the webbing of the thumb, that is the hand in which you hold the saw. As for being a widower, an outdoorsman will frequently seek the support of a woman in dealing with problems with which he is not familiar. Since your daughter is here with you instead of a wife, I assume that the lady in question is not available. Her having passed from the world was simply the most likely explanation. Am I perchance in error?"

"No, my Aggie's been gone these seven years. By gaw, I would have liked to have her advice now. She was never o'er thrifty with the givin' of it when she was alive, ye ken."

"Father!"

Holmes's amusement could be seen only in his eyes. "I'm sorry, Mr. Camber," said he, "but you shall have to make do with only my advice."

"How did you know about the Duke?" the daughter demanded. "And about how this has been preying on his mind?"

"Your father is wearing a stickpin in his cravat bearing the Duke's crest. Unless His Grace has developed a hitherto secret passion for woodsmanship, I knew your father must be in the Duke's employ, and that the pin is some sort of gift."

Camber nodded proudly. "Aye, man and boy forty years in the service of the duke and the old duke before him. The pin was given me from His Grace's own two hands Christmas last." His face turned grim. "Christmas in Scotland ye ken, is not the spectacle of it the Sassenach's make. We're more apt to save our celebrations for Hogmanay, when a man can see in the new year and get behind a wee nip or two. But His Grace's mother was from across the border, and he likes to keep the holiday in the ways she preferred. As a good servant, I've always done my best to help him, but this year it's landed me up to my ruddy ears in a mystery.

And as you say, it preys on my mind till I'm sleepless over it."

Holmes's nostrils had flared at the sound of the word *mystery*. The ineffable scent of that particular phenomenon was the breath of life to him.

"Indeed," said he, "I deduced as much when a member of such as canny race as the Scots would travel to London to consult me in the matter. I adjust my fees according to my interest in a case, Mr. Camber, but I do charge them."

Camber closed his eyes as though enduring great pain. "Ah, know it," he said with a sigh. "But I have no choice. The regular police, both in Scotland and here, laughed in my face. By gaw, we'll see who's laughing at the end."

"Now, please, tell me the details of your mystery. I know from the *Times* that the duke is keeping Christmas this year at his house in London. Does it have to do with him?"

Camber turned to his daughter. "You tell it, Nancy."

"Very well, father." She turned to us. "Yes, Mr. Holmes. We believe it does have to do with the duke. You see, His Grace spends alternate Christmases in London, and when in London, he follows the practice so many have adopted in emulation of the late prince consort. He erects in the hall of the building a Christmas tree. He supervises the hanging of the decorations and presents, and lights the candles himself."

"Yes. An invitation to the destruction of the house by fire, but I suppose it has its charm. How do you know of this?"

"I have the honor of being the personal maid to Lady Caroline, His Grace's eldest daughter."

"I see. Pray go on."

"In those years when His Grace celebrates in London, it is his pleasure to cause a tree from his own estate to be shipped up to town for decoration. A week or so before Christmas, my father selects the most robust and symmetrically formed tree of the proper size from among the large stand of Scotch pines on the grounds of the estate. He then makes preparations for the preservation of the tree in transit—something I do not understand, I'm afraid."

The outdoorsman shook his head in a gesture of dismissal.

"Earth and ice in alternating layers, with burlap between and canvas outside. It's really elementary."

I cleared my throat. "The workings of the expert mind," said I, "while perhaps seeming elementary to the experts themselves, do not always appear so to those who lack that expertise."

I had been wanting to say that for years.

"Thank you, Doctor," said Nancy Camber, "that expresses a thought I've never been able to articulate. In any event, my father made the usual trip out to the woods, marked the tree for cutting, then went to the railway station to make arrangements for a crate to ship the tree in."

"Upright and braced," said Joseph Camber decisively. "So that the branches might not be marred."

"But the next day, when he went with the horse and sledge to cut it and bring it away—"

"It wasn't *there!*" interjected Camber. "The ruddy thing was *gone*. I mean, I've heard of poachin', but I've never heard of anyone daft enough to poach a *tree.*"

"Is there any reason someone might want to do that, in any case?"

Camber shook his head. "I've been bruisin' my brain on just that question, Mr. Holmes. Pine is no good for firewood; too much resin, gums up the flue. Ye can make decent, rough-hewn furniture from it, but not from a tree small enough to keep in a house."

"You say you marked the tree. In what manner did you do this?"

"I just put a wee nick in the bark at eye level. It's easy to spot if you know what to look for, but it doesn't mar its decorative properties, ye ken."

"What did you do when you discovered the tree missing?"

"Well, I'll tell you, Mr. Holmes, I spent quite a while goin' back and forth between scratchin' my head and cursin'. When I left off doin' that, I did the only thing I could do. I found the next-best tree, and cut that and sent it to be shipped."

Holmes rubbed his chin. "Hmmm," said he. "Mr. Camber, your case presents certain elements of interest, and I think—"

"Oh!" said Nancy Camber. "Please, Mr. Holmes, forgive me for interrupting you, but we haven't got to the mysterious part yet."

"Oh," said Holmes in his turn. He began to fill his pipe. "I shall smoke if you've no objection. Pray continue."

"You see, sir, I prevailed upon my father to travel to London to keep Christmas with me. He is great friends with MacBurney, the duke's valet, and His Grace is rather fond of Father himself, so there was no problem about Father's staying with MacBurney in his room, and sharing our servants' Christmas fare."

"Then I took a notion," Camber said. For years, I'd been cutting the trees, but I'd never seen one in place. I reckoned this'd be my one chance to do it, so Nancy and MacBurney ganged up on the butler, a Sassenach named Havering, and he let me into the hall where the tree was."

"The hall is closed off before Christmas Eve," Nancy explained. "And no fire is lit there until then, to aid in keeping the tree fresh. Father went in and—"

"It was the *missing tree!* The very one that had been stolen in Scotland!"

"How can you be sure of that, Mr. Camber?" I inquired. "Your mark might have been copied after all."

"Dr. Watson," said he. "A medical man?"

I nodded assent.

"Do you deliver bairns, then?"

"Frequently," said I.

"Do you ever deliver more than one bairn in a day?"

"Of course."

"And if, at the end of that day, someone showed you one of the bairns, could you tell which one it was?"

"Of course."

"Well, Dr. Watson, trees are my bairns. I plant 'em when that's needed, and cut them down when that's needed. I watch 'em and take care of 'em, and spend my life around 'em. I made a study of that tree before I picked it. I'll take my oath that that is the same tree."

Holmes drew deeply of the aromatic shag in his pipe. "We'll take that established, then, Mr. Camber. Do you have any idea of what happened to the tree you cut and shipped?"

"Not a glimmer."

"Miss Camber?"

She looked surprised. "I? No, I have no idea at all. I am simply worried that someone is playing some sort of nasty joke on my father, seeking to spoil the fine relationship he and His Grace's family have always enjoyed."

Camber thumbed the top of his beaver hat. "Ah think this is summat much worse than a joke. It's mighty *expensive* for a joke, even for people of quality. *Ah* think it's some kind of evil plot, aimed at His Grace. He's quite an important figger in diplomatic circles, ye ken."

"Yes," Holmes said dryly. "I was aware of that." Holmes jumped to his feet. "Yes!" cried he. "The outré nature of this puzzle is quite refreshing. I shall investigate, Mr. Camber, and report to you at the earliest opportunity. You both remain at the duke's residence in Ounslow Square? Good."

"Well, now, Mr. Holmes," said Camber. "I don't—that is, I'm not a wealthy man."

"Don't worry about a thing, Mr. Camber. I shall leave you enough for bread and a ticket back to Scotland. On your way now. Charmed to have met you, Miss Camber."

When they were gone, Holmes threw himself into his seat and said, "For the first time, this looks as if it might be a tolerable holiday after all. What do you make of them, Watson?"

"Oh," said I. "They seem quite devoted to each other, and they are obviously sincere."

"Yes, Watson. You may trust me to notice the obvious for myself. What do you think of their story?"

"I hardly know what to think. At first blush, such machinations with an emblem of the festive season seem sinister, but has the final result been? The tree Camber wished to be in the duke's house is now in the duke's house, and an inferior tree is missing."

"Forget the inferior tree," said Holmes. "The inferior tree is now a pile of ashes, or flotsam in the Thames. What we must concentrate our attention on is how the original tree reached its destination on its own, like some vegetable version of a homing pigeon. And why."

"How are we to do that?" I inquired.

"Facts are the bricks from which deductions are built, Watson. Come, we go to seek facts."

179

We sought them in the Diogenes Club, that remarkable collection of unsociable men, who go there to read or eat or drink or relax in a comfortable chair, but who never, on pain of expulsion, allow one word of conversation to be passed one to the other.

Talking is allowed only in the Strangers' Room, and it was there we spoke to Holmes's elder brother, Mycroft. The corpulent elder brother was what he sometimes liked to describe as a "facilitator" for the British government. He had no title, nor even (so far as I knew) an office, but he seemed to know everything about any current crisis.

Mr. Sherlock Holmes informed his brother about Joseph Camber's mysterious story.

"Suggestive," said Mycroft Holmes.

"I found it so," averred his brother. "It is common knowledge that the duke moves, as my client says, in the 'highest diplomatic circles.' Is he engaged in anything of importance at the moment?"

"He is involved in something of the first importance. He is engaging in unofficial, preliminary talks concerning South West African mineral concessions with the Germans. The German government has brought Herr Stefan Geitzling over from Africa to begin the talks."

Mycroft Holmes pressed the tips of his fingers together and pursed his lips. "I need not tell you gentlemen that since the uniting of the German States under the kaiser, relations with that country have been strained, and the strain is felt most strongly in our respective empires. The problem under discussion may be a relatively trivial one, but if such trivialities cannot be worked out amicably, they will fester over time and, one day within our lifetimes, burst out into a horrible war."

I privately wondered what this had to do with Christmas trees, but I held my peace.

Holmes said, "I intend to call on His Grace this afternoon. I shall not, of course, allude openly to what you have told me, but I will keep it in mind. I answer for the discretion of Dr. Watson."

A rare smile disturbed the folds of Mycroft Holmes's face. "My dear Sherlock, I am quite prepared to answer for the doctor's discretion myself. Do, please, communicate with me again if you learn anything the government should know."

Holmes indicated he would, and we bade Mycroft farewell.

"Now, to Ounslow Square, I imagine," said I.

Holmes was already hailing a cab. We clopped along through the whitened streets. The weather seemed to have accelerated the rate at which the usual glumness and irritation of city life are replaced by goodwill as Christmas approaches. In this case, the cabbie seemed to be smiling even before he received his tip.

According to Holmes's wish, we alighted in the business area of South Kensington before proceeding to the square. Much to my surprise, he bade me wait on the sidewalk whilst he went into an ironmonger's shop, emerging a few moments later with a parcel wrapped in brown paper.

A butler at the duke's residence informed us that His Grace was in a meeting at the moment. Holmes asked that his card be brought in to him at the next opportunity, and asked if we might wait in the meanwhile.

The butler reluctantly assented.

In the event, we did not have to wait long. The butler returned, and asked us to accompany him to a room on the first floor. When we arrived, we saw it was fitted up as a conference room, with a large table in the middle of it. The table was littered with maps and charts and documents, some in English, some in German. Having no wish to surprise my country's secret affairs, I looked no further than that.

The butler began to announce us, but he had barely gotten our names from his mouth before a round, squat little man with an imperial beard and a monocle came forward and pumped my companion's hand vigorously.

"Mr. Sherlock Holmes, what an honor it is to meet you. Even in the Godforsaken desert, we have of your adventures read, as recorded by the so-good Dr. Watson."

He let go of Holmes's hand to pump mine for a while. "When we send for brandy and soda, and the so-good Perkins bring in to us the card of yours, I am beside myself with joy. I am neglecting my task, which is talking with my new good friend, His Grace, but I claim a guest's indulgence and say meet you I must do. And here you are."

"Here I am, indeed." Holmes turned to the duke, whose youthful face under a crop of snow white hair showed a not-quite-suppressed smile of amusement. "Your Grace, I do not mean to interrupt your work, but I wish to have a few words with you, on something of importance. A matter has come to my attention which concerns you."

"It's quite all right, Mr. Holmes. I believe Herr Geitzling"—here the round man bowed, still beaming—"and Herr Unter-meyer, his aide"—and now a handsome, blue-eyed young man with dark curly hair bowed—"were beginning to feel almost as stale as I do myself. That was why I rang for refreshment. May I be excused to talk to Mr. Holmes, Herr Geitzling?"

"You may on one condition be excused, Your Grace."

"Even now, *mein Herr*, you remain a tough negotiator. What is your condition?"

"That after your talk, Mr. Holmes and Dr. Watson to this room return and the brandy and soda share with us. Furthermore, we shall talk not about our business while they are here, but about their adventures."

The duke made a conciliatory shrug. "You must appreciate, Herr Geitzling, that Mr. Holmes is a busy man—"

"But not so busy that we cannot spare some time for such a distinguished visitor to our shores, Your Grace. We will be delighted to join you."

We repaired downstairs to the duke's study, a fine, masculine room of leather and books.

He told us to be seated, and took a chair behind a large square desk. "So, Mr. Holmes, what is the matter that needs my attention?"

"I believe your life may be in danger, Your Grace."

His Grace seemed as shocked as I was.

"I beg your pardon, Mr. Holmes. My life? In danger? From whom?"

"How important is the matter which you are discussing with Herr Geitzling?"

"Moderately important. I cannot go into details."

"That will not be necessary, for the present. Would events be dire if these talks were to fail?"

"Concealing nothing from you, Mr. Holmes, I don't think so.

Expensive, yes. Inconvenient, certainly. But dire? No. Nothing irrevocable here."

Then His Grace smiled slyly. "If the failure of these talks— which, by the way, I do not anticipate, they are going quite well, thank you—if the theoretical failure of these talks was to have a dire effect on anyone, it is likely to be Stefan Geitzling. His wife is a distant relative of the kaiser's. It is undoubtedly why he holds the position in Africa that he does. He certainly has no affection for the place, complains about it constantly. Still, he is a typical German, conscientious and painstaking. He knows his business."

"How about his aide?"

"Othmar Untermeyer is also painstaking and conscientious. He is a polite and self-effacing young man." Again, we saw the duke smile. "My daughter is quite taken with him. Really, Mr. Holmes. Your brother and I know each other well, and I am both flattered and honored by your concern, but this particular negotiation is not the sort of thing that leads one to fear for his life."

"Perhaps the danger comes from other quarters. Have you any personal enemies?"

"Only political ones. We don't assassinate each other in the House of Lords, Mr. Holmes. Not for some time, at least. *Please*, what has happened to cause your concern?"

"Information received. It would be pointless to burden Your Grace with the matter, especially since nothing can be found to substantiate it at this time."

"I'm sure your informant is mistaken," said the duke.

"Still, it is best to be thorough. Have I your permission to question the servants and the other inmates of the house?"

The Duke waved his hand. "You may have carte blanche, if it helps to resolve the matter. But before doing that, you must come and speak with Geitzling. Perhaps this will get a few more tons of magnesium ore per annum from him."

Holmes rarely agreed to socialize, but when he did he could be utterly charming, as he was on this occasion. This was perhaps helped by the fact that Herr Geitzling seemed to know every aspect of the detective's career, and be impressed by all of it.

"It is gratifying to know that my accounts are so well perused

183

in such a faraway place," I said at one juncture to a compliment of Geitzling's about my writing.

"It helps keep me to Europe tied," said he. "I have a duty, and this I do, but I miss home. Even here, I have the things I have not for two years had at Christmas. The snow, the promise of a roast goose, the smell of the *tannenbaum*. His Grace also the custom follows, and though he tries to keep it from me a secret, I can hardly wait to see it."

"How did you know that, Geitzling?" demanded the duke.

"Because in the nose I can smell it when I come in. It the lower hall pervades, and makes me feel as if I am already home."

"I hope," said His Grace, "you will think of this as your home while you are here."

Geitzling said, "His Grace has been so kind as to invite Herr Untermeyer, and Frau Geitzling and myself, to Christmas Eve keep with him here. It was Lady Caroline's idea."

I gave an involuntary glance at Othmar Untermeyer and saw on his face a young man's pride in his attractiveness.

Holmes took a last sip of his brandy and soda, rose, and announced that we must be off on further business.

Geitzling was crestfallen; His Grace, seeing how upset his counterpart was, had a suggestion. "Mr. Holmes, Doctor, if you've no previous plans, why don't you keep Christmas Eve with us as well? Then you can regale us all even with your adventures. It will be just a small gathering, but I fancy we'll generate some holiday cheer."

"We shall be delighted," said Holmes. "No idea could suit me better." He was, it seemed, giving free rein to his sentimental side.

The butler was summoned to show us out, but Holmes told him we had permission to roam the house and talk to those around. The butler conceded that His Grace had given him some such instructions, and left us to our own devices.

"Holmes, have we nothing to ask the butler?"

"Nothing. Come. Let me first retrieve my parcel in the hallway."

This done, we came to the locked door behind which stood the tree. I could now perceive that Geitzling had been right; there was a strong smell of pine even here, on the other side of a thick oak door. I remarked on this to Holmes.

"Yes, Watson, like the railway, you are frequently late, but you get there. Now, if you will just stand guard . . ."

From his pocket, he drew a skeleton key and put it in the lock. "Holmes!" said I. "You're not—"

"His Grace gave us carte blanche, remember?"

"Yes, but—"

I was talking to the oak panels of the door. Holmes was already inside. The pine scent that had been drawn out of the room with the opening of the door was nearly overpowering. Carefully, I put my ear to the door in an effort to perhaps hear what my friend was up to.

What I did hear was a soft, feminine voice saying, "Dr. Watson?"

I turned to see a lovely young lady of about one-and-twenty. She had a large quantity of blonde curls, and large brown eyes that dominated her rather pleasant face.

"Forgive my forwardness. Father told me you were here. I am Caroline Bentley." She gave me her hand.

"Lady Caroline," I said with a slight bow.

"Are you feeling well, Doctor?"

"I'm quite all right, thank you."

"Forgive me. I only ask because you were leaning against the door, I thought you might feel faint."

"No, Lady Caroline," said I. "Not at all. I was, um, investigating the source of the pine odor that Herr Geitzling was so enthusiastic about."

She laughed like tinkling bells. "Then, Doctor, you have sniffed out the truth, for in that room is the great tree sent down to us from Scotland. I can hardly wait to see it."

"Haven't you?"

"None of us has. It's part of the fun of the holiday—we trust the judgement of our forester implicitly. Othmar—that is, Herr Untermeyer—thinks it a charming custom."

"As do I, Lady Caroline," I said. I spoke, I suppose, louder than need be, for I wanted to make sure that Holmes heard us through the heavy door, and did not create an embarrassing situation by emerging while Lady Caroline was there.

"Father tells me you and Mr. Holmes will be keeping Christmas with us. I am so pleased."

"You and your father are very kind," I said.

"Not at all. We enjoy spreading the spirit of the season.

"Where is Mr. Holmes?" she asked.

"I can hardly say," I told her truthfully. "He stepped away for a few moments, and asked me to remain here."

Lady Caroline said that as much as she'd like to, she could not remain, and that she looked forward to seeing us again tomorrow evening. I watched her safely down the corridor, then knocked on the door to let Holmes know he might emerge if he chose.

He did so in a few moments, bringing with him another strong breath of pine.

"Excellent, Watson," said he. "You are by little and little overcoming your inherent honesty and developing a positive skill for indirection."

I sniffed. "I hardly know if I should thank you for *that*. Were your efforts successful?"

"Eminently. I have changed the nature of the trap; it remains for tomorrow evening to see who shall fall into it."

After a brief visit with our clients, to tell them the situation was well in hand, we returned to Baker Street.

That evening, Holmes as usual was maddeningly unwilling to discuss the case at hand. Only once did my opportuning avail anything. "I'm sorry, Watson, but you know how I dislike to explicate a case before it is completed. I shall only say that you should have sniffed out the solution for yourself."

"Confound it, Holmes. Are you or are you not drawing my attention to the strong pine odor that suffused the lower part of the house?"

"I am, indeed, Watson."

"What can one infer simply from an odor? I am not, after all, a bloodhound."

Holmes pulled his lower lip. "More to the point, you are a city-bred man. My people, as you know, were country squires. I know how a tree is supposed to smell."

I felt some of the old excitement; perhaps we were getting to the meat of the nut at last. "What was wrong with the smell, Holmes?" I asked.

"Nothing, Watson. Absolutely nothing. That was an especially intense whiff of the unmistakable fragrance of Scotch pine."

Before I was done sputtering, Holmes had picked up his violin. "I feel the spirit of the season upon me," said he, and he began playing "God Rest Ye, Merry Gentlemen."

There was but one more allusion to the case before we left Baker Street for His Grace's residence. Just prior to leaving, Holmes said, "It would be as well, Watson, to slip your revolver in your pocket."

"Holmes!" I cried. "On Christmas Eve?"

"Evil takes no holidays, Watson. Therefore, neither can those who would stop it."

We were greeted heartily by His Grace and Lady Caroline upon our arrival. The hall was now open, the tree revealed in all its green magnificence, the Yule log roaring in the fireplace. Holly was hung liberally about, and the tree had already been garlanded and hung with some ornaments. The duke invited us to join in the work of decoration, which, to my surprise, Holmes did.

"It is good, Mr. Holmes, we haff you to help the ornaments hanging, you are tall like Othmar, and can reach up high." Herr Geitzling was in high holiday spirits, frequently remarking that this was just like home, and constant in his attentions to Frau Geitzling, a woman as red and plump as her husband.

"I will get the candles," said Othmar Untermeyer. I had wondered how the candles were fixed to the tree so they wouldn't fall over, and, watching Untermeyer, I learned. He lit one candle and carefully softened the bottoms of the others letting the wax conform to the irregularities in the bark as he put them on. With his reach (he was, in fact, even taller than Holmes) he had little trouble placing the candles at the top of the tree, and he worked his way down, blowing out the softening candle and putting it on a lower branch.

"Lovely," exclaimed the duke. "Just lovely. We will light the candles after a holiday toast."

A servant came in with a tray of hot toddies. These were passed around, and the scent of the warm, buttered rum brought back holiday memories for me. I could see on the faces of the others that I was not alone.

His Grace raised his cup. "To friendship and happiness. To family and memories. To Her Majesty and the kaiser and all their subjects. To Christmas."

"To Christmas," we echoed, and drank.

Just then, the butler entered. He spoke a word to His Grace, then went to Untermeyer, with whom I was discussing the aseptic theories of Dr. Lister of Vienna. The butler told him there was a German person outside who needed to see him; some sort of emergency. Untermeyer in his turn made his excuses to the duke, and followed the butler.

As soon as they were gone, Holmes materialized at my side. "This is it, Watson. He will return in a moment and say he has to leave the party. Mark what he says, and leave a minute after he does. You have your revolver?"

"At the ready."

"Good man."

With that, Holmes himself slipped out of the room. Typically, he did it unnoticed by all save myself. And true to Holmes's prediction, Untermeyer was back in seconds, making apologies to the duke, then to the party at large. "A family emergency," he said. "I must go."

"Othmar, can I of service be?" asked Mr. Geitzling.

"No, sir, no. I wouldn't dream of spoiling your Christmas. I insist you stay."

He left. Now I was supposed to go. Not being surreptitious, like Holmes, not having a ready-made excuse like Untermeyer, I simply told Lady Caroline that I had to leave the room and would be back in a few moments. She was already missing Untermeyer, and barely heard me.

I headed for the front door and down the steps. Holmes was waiting, not quite invisible in the shrubbery.

"This way, Watson," he whispered. Following his finger with my gaze, I could see that two men were about halfway down the block. "Quickly now," he said.

"Do you recognize them?" he said as we closed the distance between us.

"The tall one is Untermeyer," I ventured.

"Indeed, and the other is Von Tepper, a notorious anarchist. Mycroft has suspected he has been secretly in London. He will be pleased to know we have captured him."

"We haven't done it yet, Holmes."

"Confidence, Watson, confidence."

We had now drawn quietly to within ten yards of our prey. Holmes drew his revolver; I followed his lead.

"Untermeyer! Von Tepper!" he barked. The men turned. "Your plot has failed," he went on. "There will be no explosion. The duke and Geitzling will not die. You will start no war between England and Germany. At least not *this* Christmas."

"You are wrong, Mr. Holmes," Untermeyer said. He sneered around a small black cigar. "Even now, His Grace is lighting the candles. When he gets to the last one I placed on the tree, he is doomed. They are all doomed. I am sorry about poor, foolish Lady Caroline. And I am sorry you will not be there to die with them."

"Sorry to disappoint you, *mein Herr*," said Holmes, reaching under his cape, "but I pulled the teeth of your little monster yesterday. He held up a parcel. "Quite an interesting device, the latest in high explosives."

"Herr von Tepper was responsible for procuring it. Well, you have spoiled our little plan. There will be other occasions."

"Not for you," said I.

"It does not matter. Others will rise until government and privelege have been done away with forever!"

"Indeed," said Holmes. "Your movement will need conspirators more intelligent than yourselves. Why did you select the very tree that Camber had marked for cutting?"

"Our allies in Scotland did that. It was done so that the tree would be acceptable to the duke when it arrived. We didn't know that the fool of a forester would come here to identify the thing." He took a puff of a cigar. "Or that he would consult you. He *did* consult you, did he not?"

Holmes gave a slight bow. "So you got hold of the tree, bored a hole through the back of the trunk and into a thick lower limb, packed that with explosive, and placed a sharp end of fuse through the remaining shell of wood for a candle to be placed on, a candle you would shorten by using it to soften the bottom of all the other candles. Did you think I wouldn't notice that the last candle stayed erect *without* having its bottom softened? I wasn't even forced to wait to see who made an excuse to leave the party early; I already knew you for the conspirator."

"How did you come to suspect the bomb?" Untermeyer had no air of a villain thwarted. He seemed honestly to wish to know where his errors had been.

"The tree was already suspect, thanks to Mr. Camber. The pine scent told me the rest. When you cut into a resinous wood like pine, you increase the intensity of the fragrance manyfold. I suspected something implanted in the tree even before I reached the duke's house. A breath of air within it, and the matter was settled. I had stopped at an ironmonger's shop and provided myself with an auger. A few seconds' work was enough to disarm your little toy. Here," Holmes said.

Then, to my astonishment, he tossed the parcel to Untermeyer.

The German mouth widened in a grin that was almost hideous. "Thank you, Mr. Holmes. I believe I know what you have in mind, and I shall avail myself of it." He puffed deeply on his cigar, causing the end to glow bright red. "However," said he, "I fear you underestimate the power of this new substance."

He took the cigar from his mouth.

Von Tepper screamed the only word I ever heard from him: "*Nein!*"

Holmes brought me to the pavement with a rugby tackle just as Untermeyer said, "See you in hell, Mr. Holmes," and touched the coal of his cigar to the parcel.

The blast felt like the kick of a spirited horse, and made my ears ring for a moment, but I was otherwise unharmed. Of Untermeyer and Von Tepper, nothing remained but a stain on the pavement.

"He *was* a fool," said Holmes. "Had he not the wit to imagine I would adjust the amount of explosive in the parcel?" He shook his head, and helped me to my feet.

"Come, Watson. We must go and spoil everyone's Christmas with the sad news that Herr Untermeyer and his friend have been assassinated by anarchists."

* * *

On Christmas Day in our Baker Street rooms, with Mrs. Hudson's wonderful goose inside us, Holmes puffing on the new pipe I had given him and I placing early engagements for next year into the leather-covered physician's pocket diary he had given me, Holmes finally deigned to discuss the events of the previous night.

"It takes but little imagination to see, Watson," said he, "that arresting Untermeyer and putting him on trial would be little better than letting his assassination plot succeed in the first place."

"In what way, pray?"

"The man wouldn't admit to being an anarchist; he was an employee of the German government. He would say he was following orders."

"But the Germans would deny it!" I protested.

"Which they would in any case. And our government, no doubt, would believe them. But the suspicion would remain, poisoning relationships, and adding to the already dangerous international tension. Mark my words, Watson, if war comes, it will be caused by just such a trivial incident as the assassination of a duke."

"Hardly trivial to the duke," I ventured.

"Quite so, Watson."

"And so you offered yourself, and me, though I hesitate to mention it, as bait to make it worthwhile for Untermeyer to kill himself."

"If you wish to put it that way."

"Strictly for patriotic reasons."

"Indeed. Mycroft is beside himself with the joy of it, I'll wager. My Christmas gift to him."

"You had no thought of Lady Caroline? She was well on her way to falling in love with that evil young man. You let her remember him as a martyr, rather than as a scoundrel who used her trust in an effort to kill her father and her."

"Well, Watson," he said in mock surprise. "So I did." Then, more somberly, he said, "I am sorry I could not prevent Christmas from becoming a time of sad memories for her. But we cannot be expected to pass miracles, eh, Watson?"

"Not that kind," said I. "Happy Christmas, Holmes."

"And the same to you, my dear Watson."

191

THE ADVENTURE OF THE CHRISTMAS GHOSTS

Bill Crider

It was the morning of the twenty-second day of December, a Sunday according to my notes, that Sherlock Holmes and I received one of the strangest visitors who had hitherto arrived at our lodgings at 221B Baker Street. I heard the man coming down the hall, and even before he had brushed past Billy, our page boy, and entered into our sitting room, I used the methods I had begun to learn from Holmes to reach a conclusion about our caller.

I deduced that he was not coming to give the greetings of the season to Holmes. I arrived at this conclusion because, although this was early in our association, I already knew Holmes to be the least sentimental and the least superstitious man I had ever known. Our halls were not decked with holly but with retorts and vials; there was not within our rooms the steamy scent of plum pudding but of the tobacco from our pipes mixed with the faint chemical odor of one of Holmes's experiments; the music Holmes occasionally played on his violin was of his own composing and was not remotely related to any known carol; and for Holmes, the idea of cattle bowing down in their stalls at midnight on the eve of Christmas was nothing more than the sheerest fantasy, laughable on its face. Logic was what Holmes believed in, rare as he considered logic to be in the world in which we lived.

Our visitor, as I have said, brushed past Billy and entered our room. He was a man of middle age, somewhat above medium height, well dressed in a dark suit and clean linen, with his hat firmly mounted on his head. His face was smooth shaven and strongly scored with lines that ran beside his mouth and down his chin as if he might have spent his life frowning perpetually. His face was ruddy, either from the intense cold outside or from his exertions, and his breath came in short gasps, as if he had run all the way to our rooms from his own.

"This gentleman—" Billy began, but Holmes waved to him to be silent, and Billy backed out of the room, closing the door behind him.

"Which of you is Sherlock Holmes?" our visitor asked, his voice rough with either emotion or the effects of the cold.

"I am," Holmes replied. "What brings you to us in such a rush and flurry of nervous agitation, having missed a deal of sleep into the bargain?"

"How did you know—ah, I see." Our visitor took a deep breath and let it out slowly. "I have been almost running, and it has taken my breath, so you know that I was in a rush to see you."

"That you are short of breath is true," Holmes acknowledged, and I was gratified to realize that I too had noted as much. "And your shoes are wet, with a rind of ice beginning to form on your pants cuffs," continued Holmes, "indicating that you stepped onto a crusted-over puddle rather than taking the time to pass around it. You shaved so hurriedly this morning that you missed a spot just below your right ear and another just below your nose. You have also nicked yourself at least twice, and there is a dot of blood on your right shirt cuff, no doubt from one of the nicks; you would surely have changed the cuff had you noticed it."

Our visitor looked down at his cuff. "I had heard of your methods, and you do not disappoint me. Yes, I would have changed cuffs had I noticed."

Holmes looked over at me. "Always look at a man's hands first,

Watson, and then his shoes and then the knees of his trousers. You will invariably learn something of interest."

"Quite so, Holmes," said I.

"As to your sleeplessness," Holmes went on, "I am sure that Watson has noted the way in which the pallor of your skin makes the black circles beneath your eyes stand out, a sure sign of sleepless nights."

"You are right," said Scrooge. "I have not slept well of late."

As usual, Holmes's analysis of the caller's condition seemed quite simple when he explained it, but I suspect that few men would have been able to reach the same conclusions from the clues that Holmes had observed.

"Now," said Holmes, "perhaps our visitor will have a seat and be so good as to tell us his name."

Removing his hat and seating himself opposite Holmes, the man said, "My name is Franklin Scrooge."

"Of Scrooge and Marley?" Holmes asked.

"The same. You have heard of my firm?"

"Certainly," responded Holmes. "As Watson could tell you, I have an interest in all the more sensational crimes of our little country. Isn't that right, Watson?"

It was of course true. Holmes, while his knowledge of ordinary things like literature and philosophy was virtually nil, had an immense store of facts at hand relating to sensational literature. He in fact seemed to have an intimate acquaintance with every appalling and dreadful crime committed within the last century.

Mr. Scrooge was puzzled. "I know of no crime in connection with Scrooge and Marley."

"Let me enlighten you, then," said Holmes. "I take it that you are related to one of the founders?"

"Yes. Ebenezer Scrooge was my uncle. My *great*-uncle, that is."

"And what of Marley?"

"Well, Marley died. That was the beginning of the whole confounded muddle in which I find myself. At least I believe that to be so."

"Let us not get our stories out of order," said Holmes. "Marley first. He died. Is that not correct?"

"Yes. Marley was dead. There can be no doubt about that."

"And how did he die?"

Mr. Scrooge started to answer. His mouth was halfway open. But then he closed it. "I . . . well, I don't believe that anyone ever said."

"No, I suppose not. And yet your uncle, your *great*-uncle, was his sole executor, his sole administrator, his sole assign, his sole residuary legatee, was he not?"

"I believe that is correct. But all that was long ago. What of it?"

"It is suggestive, is it not?" asked Holmes. "A man dies, and yet the cause of his death is never revealed. His business partner, the one who stands to gain the most—the one who stands to gain all—is never questioned. He was, as I understand the facts, a man quite well known for his avarice, and he inherited all the business." Holmes paused. "But, as you say, that was long ago. That is not why you came here. Why, by the way, *did* you come?"

I could see that Holmes had introduced the topic of the uncle, the *great*-uncle, to give our visitor some time to compose himself. He was now breathing quite regularly, and his face was composed. The lines beside his mouth, while still visible, had softened and receded into the flesh. He looked at me, then back at Holmes, sighed, and said, "Do you believe in ghosts, Mr. Holmes?"

Holmes gave a barking laugh. "I most certainly do not. Ghosts do not exist any more than other creatures of occult legend—vampires, say, or werewolves. To believe otherwise is utter lunacy."

Our visitor looked at the floor. "I was afraid that you would say so. You reject the idea out of hand?"

"Or course," Holmes responded. "And so you should as well."

Scrooge looked up and turned to me. "Dr. Watson?"

"Are you asking about my beliefs, or about my services as a physician? I do not generally treat nervous maladies."

"A malady I may have," said Scrooge. "I do not deny it. And yet I have seen . . . things."

"Ghosts?" asked Holmes.

"Yes, and worse than ghosts. Would you at least listen to my story? I do not ask that you believe it."

Holmes had little patience with people who presume they have seen things, ghosts in particular, and would ordinarily have told our visitor to leave at once. However, with no case of interest

195

having come his way of late, he had been idle for several days, and while he might not have hoped for much, he told Scrooge to continue.

"Thank you, Mr. Holmes! You do not know what I have suffered for the past two nights. It has been terrible, I assure you. But I must begin with my great-uncle, Ebenezer Scrooge. He was, as you seem already to know, the sole legatee of the late Jacob Marley, and when he took over as sole proprietor of the firm of Scrooge and Marley, a quite strange thing happened to him. It is the same thing that has been happening to me."

"The ghosts," said Holmes.

"Yes. The ghosts. My uncle was a greedy, grasping man, Mr. Holmes, but something happened that transformed him. It was the ghosts."

"Or perhaps his guilt over the untimely death of his partner."

"It could have been the effects of guilt. You see, when he went home one night, at just about this time of the year, he put his key into the lock of his door, and by chance he glanced at the knocker. But he did not see the knocker. He saw . . . Marley's face!"

Scrooge brought a handkerchief out of his coat and wiped his face, which had begun to perspire. I looked over at our fire, but it was burning low, and the room was hardly warm.

"When he looked again," Scrooge continued, "the knocker was merely a knocker again, and my uncle went inside the house and eventually went to bed. It was later that night that Marley's ghost appeared."

To my surprise, Holmes was leaning forward in his chair, his gray eyes a-gleam with excitement. "Did your uncle describe to you the process by which the knocker became Marley's face?"

"No. But that was not the strangest thing. When Marley's ghost appeared to him, my uncle . . . floated in the air of his room." Scrooge held up a hand as if to still a protest that neither Holmes nor I had made. "That is what he told me. And the air was filled with noise and numberless phantoms."

"And you believed his story?"

"That was forty years ago or more. I was quite young at the time, and impressionable, but even then I thought it was just a story. Especially when he told the rest, about the other ghosts that visited him, ghosts that helped him pass through the very walls of his rooms and out into the streets. Ghosts that helped him see the past and the future."

"And what became of these ghosts?" asked Holmes.

"One of them he smothered with an extinguisher cap, like a candle."

"A very small ghost," observed Holmes.

"It was not small. But it . . . dwindled somehow."

"And the other ghosts?"

"One of them simply disappeared. The other transformed into a bedpost."

"And your uncle insisted that he saw these ghosts? That he floated through the air, that he passed through the very walls?"

"He did."

I felt it was time for me to speak as a physician. "And what did your uncle have for dinner the night he saw these 'ghosts'? Could they not have been the result of a bit of undigested beef or a scrap of cheese? Perhaps a morsel of underdone fowl?"

"I would that it were so," said Franklin Scrooge, "and for a long time I believed that his visions were caused by nothing more, not that it mattered, for the visions, whatever might have been their cause, changed my uncle's life. They changed him from a miser into a philanthropist, from a skinflint into a virtual spendthrift, from one who believed Christmas to be a humbug into a man who loved that season more than any other. Previous to his seeing the ghosts, he tried to insist that his employees work even on Christmas Day, but that certainly changed. He had never had much to do with our family before that time, but from that Christmas forward he lavished us with his gifts and his attentions."

"So it seems that the results of his experiences were beneficial," I said.

"In his case, yes. But in my own . . ."

"Your own?" prompted Holmes, eyes gleaming.

"In my own case, I fear for my life. For, you see, the ghosts are now visiting *me*."

"Ah," Holmes muttered. "These are very deep waters indeed. Pray go on with your most interesting story, Mr. Scrooge."

I was so surprised that I am afraid I may have muttered some-

197

thing or other under my breath. Sherlock Holmes finding interest in a ghost story? It seemed incredible. Both Holmes and our visitor looked at me strangely. I smiled and said, "Yes, please do go on."

Mr. Scrooge resumed his tale by saying, "For two nights now, I have been visited by ghosts, or what I believe must be ghosts. Call them that or phantoms or apparitions—call them what you will. To me, they are ghosts."

"Hooded figures?" asked Holmes. "Gibbering, sheeted specters with eyes of flame? Describe them for us, please. And be as detailed as you can."

Scrooge shook his head. "They were nothing like the usual idea of ghosts. There were no sheets. They were more like the knocker on my uncle's door."

"The door knocker that became the face of Marley," said Holmes.

"Yes, exactly. Although in my case it was not a knocker. It was the doorknob."

"And what did it become?"

"The face of my great-uncle, Ebenezer Scrooge. It was strange, most horribly strange, but as I put my key into the lock of my door, the knob above my hand seemed to elongate, as if it were made of clay. And then it twisted itself into the very face of my uncle and floated before my eyes. Then it became a doorknob again."

"And for how long did it float before you?" asked Holmes.

"Why, I do not know," said Scrooge, as if this were the first he had thought of it. "It might have been a few seconds, or it might have been an hour. It has only just occurred to me, but I have no idea of the time that passed."

Holmes nodded as if he had suspected as much. "Please continue, then, Mr. Scrooge."

Scrooge passed a hand over his face and said, "Late that night, as I was preparing for bed, the curtains of my window began to sway and writhe. Eventually they assumed the shape of some kind of creature that I cannot really begin to describe. Somehow, I felt that the thing was speaking to me, and I opened the window. The creature passed outside and beckoned me. I knew at that instant that I could fly."

"But you could not, of course," Holmes said.

"No, although I must have tried. I have no recollection of launching myself through the window, but it seems that I did. I landed on the roof in a heap and slid for several yards over the rough shingles. I would have pitched into the street had I not been able to grasp the chimney and stop my progress. I managed somehow to crawl back to the window and pull myself shivering into the room. My nightshirt was damp, and I was extremely chilled. I got into my bed, but I was so terrified that I hardly slept.

"The next morning, I seemed a little better, and I did well throughout the day, conducting my business with precision and acumen. But that evening, at about eight o'clock, the gas flame in my room began to flicker and fade, and then it became the face of my father. It wavered in front of me and seemed to be trying to speak, but I heard nothing. That is, I heard nothing until I heard the tolling of midnight on the clock down the hall."

"The face hovered before you for four hours?" asked Holmes.

"So it must have been, although I could not give an accounting of the time. It might have been seconds, for all I knew of its passing. As I had the previous evening, I tried to forget the incident. I got into my bed, but I had not been there long before the room seemed to expand around me, getting larger and larger while the bed got smaller and smaller. Soon it was as if the walls had spread so far from me that I could barely see them. It was as if the room itself had become as large as all of London, or as if the bed and I had become as small as a pea. I believe that I must have screamed at that point, and when I did, the walls rushed inward upon me with the speed of a courser; but before they reached me, I fell asleep or into a faint."

Here our visitor paused once more to wipe his face with his handkerchief. He put it away and then said, "You must help me, Mr. Holmes. I fear that I am losing my mind or that the ghosts will somehow destroy me."

"In your uncle's case, did anyone else see the ghosts of which he told you?"

"No, or if so, he never told me of any witnesses."

"And has no one else seen the strange apparitions that appeared to you?"

"I am a widower," said Scrooge. "My wife died ten years ago, and since that time I have been a man of solitary habits and have lived alone. No one else saw what I have seen. But I know that I have seen it."

"I am sure that you know what you have seen," said Holmes. "And I will do what I can to help you."

I was astonished. Never would I have believed that Holmes could allow himself an interest in a story that seemed so fantastically unreal. Ghosts? Doorknobs that transformed themselves into faces? These were the very kinds of tales that Holmes abominated.

However, he seemed to have a genuine concern for our visitor, and he assured him that he would do all he could to assist him.

"You must, of course, be perfectly frank with me," he told Scrooge. "And you must answer all my questions, no matter how odd they may seem to you."

"I have heard of your methods, as I said. I will answer whatever you might ask."

"Good," said Holmes. "First of all, tell me about your place of business. How many employees do you have, and what is their character?"

"I employ seven men, including my clerk. All have worked for me for quite some time, five years at the least. The clerk, Timothy Cratchit, has been with me ever since I inherited the business from my uncle, and a more loyal employee I should never hope to have. His father served before him as clerk for my uncle just as faithfully. As to the others, their character is beyond reproach, with the possible exception of one Randall Tomkins, who is a fine man when sober but who on occasion is most decidedly *not* sober. On those occasions, which are unfortunately not infrequent, he does not appear at the firm of Scrooge and Marley."

"Very well," Holmes said, and I was gratified to hear his next question, which seemed to reflect his attention to my own earlier theory. "What meals do you eat, and where do you take them?"

"I rise early and break my fast with a slice of bread and an apple. I take lunch in the Bull and Boar, just around the corner from my office, and I often take dinner there as well, though there are other places where I dine when the mood is on me. Should I name them?"

"That is not necessary at present. Do you take tea?"

"Certainly. That is a daily ritual at the firm of Scrooge and Marley. Are you of the belief that some clot of cream or dab of biscuit is causing the appearance of these ghosts?"

"That remains to be seen. Tomorrow, Dr. Watson and I will visit you at your offices. As for today, I recommend that you go home and rest. Do not allow yourself any visitors. Should any come, simply tell them that you are unwell. I do not believe that your ghosts will visit you on a Sunday."

"I am afraid that you are taking me lightly," Scrooge said, mistaking Holmes's comment for a joke.

"On the contrary," said Holmes. "I assure you that I am taking you most seriously indeed. You have asked for my help and advice. If you do not choose to follow it, then I cannot accept your case."

Scrooge rose and settled his hat on his head. "I will do what you say. At what time will you arrive tomorrow?"

"As to that, I am not yet sure. But we will be there at one time or another. You may count on it."

"I will," said Scrooge, and then he left our quarters.

"I am most surprised at you, Holmes," said I when Scrooge was gone. "I had assumed that you had no curiosity about ghosts."

Holmes was rummaging round, searching for the Persian slipper where his tobacco was kept. "And you were quite correct in your assumption. Considering the fact that ghosts do not exist, it would be difficult to develop an interest in them. Ah, here it is."

He filled his pipe, and when he got it going to his satisfaction, he said, "We will be visiting the offices of Scrooge and Marley tomorrow afternoon. I am sorry to have presumed of you, Watson, that you would accompany me. I should have asked. But you will go, won't you?"

"Of course," said I. "I'm sure it will be as enlightening as any venture on which I have accompanied you."

"Good old Watson," said Holmes, a wreath of smoke surrounding him. "I knew that I could count on you. And you may want to take your revolver. It is best to be prepared."

"I hardly think that a revolver would be much use against a ghost," I said.

"Indeed," said Sherlock Holmes.

* * *

The next day was dark with clouds, and cold enough to crack stones. A thick, greasy fog slid around the buildings and rolled down the streets. Holmes and I spent the day indoors, I reading a book of memoirs written by one of my fellows from the Afghanistan campaign, Holmes going through his commonplace books and reading in some of the many volumes of chemical and criminal lore that he kept in a jumble about our rooms. Finally, at about half past three, he said, "It is time to pay our visit to the firm of Scrooge and Marley, Watson. Are you prepared?"

I patted the pocket of my jacket where I had secreted my revolver earlier in the day. "Yes, Holmes. I believe that I am."

We shouldered into heavy coats and wrapped our scarves around our necks. Holmes put on a traveling cap with earflaps, and I chose a black bowler. Both of us wore warm gloves.

What with the fog, the clouds, and the lateness of the hour, it was quite dark by the time we descended to Baker Street. The Christmas crowds were bustling about, but the people were subdued by the brutal weather, and the sounds of their voices were distorted by the thick murk. In the distance we could hear someone faintly singing a carol, and the gaslights were rosy gold smears.

"Do you know where we are going, Holmes?" I asked.

"To the firm of Scrooge and Marley."

"I meant the direction."

"I looked it up in my directory. It is not far from here, and I doubt that we can find a cab in this weather, so we must walk. Stay by my side, and you will not get lost."

Indeed it was the kind of evening on which one might easily get lost. The fog gathered around us so closely that I could hardly see Holmes's face, though he was but two feet from me at the most. The cold seeped in below the hem of my coat and crept up the sleeves.

"It hardly seems like Christmas." I remarked.

"Ah, but it will," Holmes said, "when Mrs. Hudson prepares for us a magnificent Christmas goose."

"Do you suppose there will be pudding as well?" I asked.

"I hope so," said Holmes. "But come along, Watson. We cannot dawdle."

He led me on at a goodly pace, but I was able to keep up and not lose sight of him. When we reached our destination, I was flushed and out of breath, but Holmes seemed to be breathing quite naturally.

"Here we are," said he, looking at the sign that appeared through the fog above the door. "Scrooge and Marley."

It was not a prepossessing building. The portion of the walls that I could see was streaked with soot, and the clammy stones were slick with little runners of ice. We went inside, and the atmosphere did not greatly improve. The walls were dark, the lights were dim, and the stove did not glow brightly, although I could detect that the chill in the air was not quite as profound as that outside the doors. Six men on stools bent over their account books at cramped desks.

"Our client seems to have inherited something of the frugal nature possessed by his great uncle," observed Holmes as he began to unwrap his scarf.

As he said this, Scrooge himself appeared from an inner office. "Mr. Holmes, Dr. Watson. I was afraid that you had forgotten our appointment."

"I do not forget appointments," said Holmes, removing his gloves.

"I am sure that you do not," said Scrooge. "At any rate, you have arrived just in time for tea. Will you take it in my office with me?"

Holmes nodded. "In a moment. Which of these men is Randall Tomkins?"

Scrooge indicated a portly man at one of the desks. His back was to us, but I had a feeling that he was listening to our every word.

"Watson and I would like to have a brief private conversation with Mr. Tomkins," said Holmes. "May we use your office before we take tea?"

"But the tea is steeping now," protested Scrooge.

"This will not take long. If you would be so good as to ask Tomkins to step in, Dr. Watson and I will go to your office now."

Without waiting for a reply from Scrooge, Holmes walked away. I, not knowing what else to do, followed him, and within seconds we were joined by Tomkins, whose portly physique was complemented by the red and pitted nose of the habitual toper. He was twisting his hands together as if he were washing them, and his eyes did not linger long in one place.

"Do you know me?" asked Sherlock Holmes.

"I . . . do not."

Holmes stared at him, his gray eyes hard.

"That is to say, perhaps I do. It isn't easy to say for sure, you know. It has been a while since our last meeting."

Holmes turned to me. "Tomkins and I have crossed paths in the past. He has reason to wonder about my being here, no doubt, considering his former career. I assume that you have changed, Tomkins?"

"Oh, yes, sir. No more of the old light-fingered Randall Tomkins, sir." He held up his right hand and his gnarled fingers. The thick knuckles indicated that he was afflicted with severe arthritis. "Just hard work and the occasional drink, but that's all there is."

"I am afraid that the drink is more than occasional," remarked Holmes.

Tomkins looked abashed. "In that you are right, but I am doing as best I can, sir. I do have an honest job, and Mr. Scrooge has been kind not to dismiss me when I backslid. I hope you're not about to get me into some difficulty with him, sir. This job is my salvation."

"I do not think that I am going to cause you any difficulties," said Holmes. "You may return to your desk, Tomkins."

"Thank you, sir," Tomkins said, backing out of the office.

"Is Tomkins involved in this, Holmes?" I asked. "Does he have something to do with the ghosts?"

"That is quite doubtful," said Holmes, though he had no time to tell me why, for Scrooge came into the office.

"Do you know Tomkins?" he asked. "He seemed to indicate that you were an old friend."

"I know him," said Holmes.

"That is a point in his favor, I'm sure," said Scrooge. "Are you and Dr. Watson ready now to take tea?"

Holmes rubbed his hands together. There was a definite chill in the air.

"Who will serve us?" he asked.

"Cratchit. He makes quite a delicious pot of tea."

"Ah, yes. The faithful Cratchit. Where does he make the tea?"

"There is a small gas burner in the back of the building near his office. Cratchit is a man who likes privacy, and he prefers to work away from the others here. But let me call him now."

He went out, and I said to Holmes, "I am not certain that I know where this is leading us. Can you see any evidence here of ghosts and apparitions?"

"None at all," said he. "But you should remember I did not expect to see any such evidence, considering that ghosts cannot and do not exist."

At that moment, Scrooge returned, followed shortly by a man whom I assumed to be Cratchit. He was small and bent and walked with a shuffling step. To my physician's eye he appeared to have been at one time a victim of some debilitating disease, which he must have overcome by no less than the most difficult of struggles. His wizened face was wreathed with a beneficent smile, and he said as he set the tea tray on Scrooge's desk, "God bless you, gentlemen, and the happiness of the season to you."

"Cratchit," said Scrooge, "this is Dr. Watson. And this is Mr. Sherlock Holmes."

Cratchit smiled and gave a slight bow. "I am most glad to meet you, sirs. I have heard something of your exploits, Mr. Holmes, but surely your talents are not needed here at the firm of Scrooge and Marley?"

"No need to worry yourself about that," said Scrooge. "Please do the honors, Mr. Cratchit, and pour."

As Cratchit reached for the pot, which was covered in a white crocheted cozy, Holmes said, "I believe that I might know something of your family, Mr. Cratchit. Do they not come from America?"

Cratchit drew back his hand. "Oh, bless us, no, Mr. Holmes. I have worked here with Mr. Scrooge for something more than thirty years, alongside my father for a great deal of that time, and my father worked for Mr. Scrooge's uncle long before I began here."

"But you have American relations," Scrooge said. "I know that your father mentioned them more than once."

"Bless me, yes," said Cratchit. "My own great-uncle, Samuel Cratchit. He was a rambling sort of a man, and left home before ever I was born."

"Quite the adventurer, to hear your father tell it," said Scrooge. He looked at Holmes. "Samuel Cratchit lived among the savage red Indians for years, panned for gold on the Pacific slope, and later went to the wilds of Alaskan Yukon, where he was supposedly mauled and killed by a grizzly bear."

"Yes, yes, Uncle Samuel was quite the frontiersman," said Cratchit. "Shall I pour, Mr. Scrooge?"

"Just a moment," said Holmes. "Dr. Watson, as you may know, has a habit of jotting down my own more sensational exploits for the public prints. Perhaps he might be interested in telling some tale or another about your uncle. You say he lived among the savages, Mr. Scrooge?"

"There is not much to the tale," said Cratchit. "He was adopted by them for some reason or another, but they were a peaceful tribe, and he grew weary of their simple life. Shall I pour, sir?"

"Please do," Scrooge said.

There were four teacups on the tray, and Cratchit filled them carefully, not spilling a drop.

"Milk?" he asked when he was done, picking up a delicate china pitcher. He poured as we requested, and then he said, "Sugar?"

When the tea was poured, we extended out hands for our cups, except for Holmes, who in an unexpectedly clumsy motion reached for one of several biscuits that lay on the tray. In doing so, he brushed his hand ponderously against Scrooge's cup, causing Scrooge to spill most of his tea on the tray, where it soaked into the biscuits and the cozy. It also splashed onto the arm of Scrooge's suit, and Holmes brushed at it with his napkin so vigorously that Scrooge dropped his cup to the floor where it shattered into several pieces.

"My word, Mr. Holmes," said Scrooge. "It is only a spot of tea."

Indeed it was, and I was taken somewhat aback to see how

Holmes was behaving. He was not normally so clumsy in his actions.

"Bless us all," said Cratchit, fairly hopping about in agitation. "Whatever shall we do for another cup? Mr. Scrooge never misses having his tea."

"He must do without it today, however, it appears," said Holmes.

He was still brushing at Scrooge's sleeve, and at that moment the napkin slipped from his fingers and to the floor. He bent to retrieve it, and as he raised up, he struck the edge of the tea tray heavily, upsetting another of the cups.

"I say, Holmes." I had been looking forward to having one of the biscuits, but it now seemed that I was not to have that pleasure. "Are you quite well?"

"I am fine, Watson, I assure you. I am sorry, Mr. Scrooge, that we will have to forgo the tea on this visit. Perhaps you can have Mr. Cratchit remove the tray before I do any further damage."

Cratchit was bent to the floor, picking up the pieces of the broken cup. He straightened and said, "Mr. Scrooge never misses his tea."

"Today he must," said Holmes firmly. "Mr. Scrooge?"

"You are right, of course," said Scrooge. "Remove the things, Mr. Cratchit. I can always have tea tomorrow."

Cratchit gathered everything onto the tray and took it from the room. With a backward glance and a halfhearted smile, he said, "God bless you all, gentlemen," and then he was gone.

"Well, Mr. Holmes," said Scrooge, "this has not proved to be a particularly auspicious meeting. I am afraid that you have done nothing to dispel the worry that afflicts me."

"On the contrary," said Holmes. "I have done everything to dispel it. You need not fear ghosts tonight or ever, Mr. Scrooge. I can say with some certainty that they will not appear to you tonight or ever again."

Scrooge's jaw dropped. "What? But how can you say that? You have done nothing here but upset my tea tray and break one of my cups!"

Holmes allowed himself a half smile. "That is how it may appear to you. It is quite different if seen through other eyes, however. Is that not so, Watson?"

I nodded my assent, although I had seen no more than Scrooge. I, however, was much better acquainted with Holmes than Scrooge, and I knew that if he said that no more ghosts would appear, then the matter was settled.

"Very well," said Scrooge. "But what if you are wrong?"

"I am not wrong," said Holmes. "You will sleep peacefully tonight and each night thereafter if your conscience is clear. I suggest you make a start to clear it by allowing a bit more warmth in your building." He turned to me. "Come along, Watson. Let us have one last word with Mr. Cratchit before we leave. He appeared most upset by my indelicate bumbling."

We left Scrooge scratching his head in puzzlement and made our way to the back of the building where Cratchit sat hunched over his desk in a cramped little room no larger than a closet. He turned with a jerk when Holmes entered.

I had to stand without the door, there being no room for me inside, but I could hear all that Holmes said.

"I know what you have done, Mr. Cratchit," said he. "And what your father did before you." Cratchit started to protest, but Holmes raised a hand to silence him. "There is no need to deny it. I have read something of Ebenezer Scrooge and his way of conducting business, and I have heard of Ebenezer's ghosts from his nephew. I am sure that what your father did, he did in hopes of working some kind of change in Scrooge, and in that, he was successful. But it was a dangerous course that he pursued, and you should never have chosen it for yourself."

"How can you know that?" asked Cratchit in amazement.

"Suffice it to say that I do know it. You must desist in your plans."

"But *this* Scrooge is embarking on a course that resembles that of his great-uncle," said Cratchit. "Have you not noticed the conditions here, the lack of warmth, the lack of light, the lack of cheer? God bless us, Mr. Holmes, Scrooge is well on a course to becoming his uncle."

"Be that as it may," said Holmes, "it is not your place to alter his life in the way you have attempted. You might try telling him the story of his uncle again. Perhaps he will see the similarities and change without your assistance. I have made one suggestion of my own to him, and I believe that he will pay me some heed."

Holmes took his gloves from the pocket of his coat and began to pull them on his hands. "But I must tell you, Mr. Cratchit, that if any harm comes to Mr. Scrooge, or if any more 'ghosts' appear to him, I will set the police on you."

Cratchit tried to smile but he failed. "I understand," said he.

"I am sure that you do," said Holmes. "Come, Watson. Let us go to Baker Street and see whether Mrs. Hudson has prepared our evening meal."

We left Cratchit sitting there, no longer hunched over his desk but staring after us with wondering eyes. He failed to bless us as we left.

Back in our rooms after a typically filling meal prepared by Mrs. Hudson, Holmes reached for his violin. I knew that if he began to play, I would never learn how he had known about Cratchit, and more than that, I would never learn *what* he had known. So before he set bow to strings, I said, "Tell me, Holmes, what made you suspect Cratchit in the matter of the ghosts?"

Holmes lowered the violin, holding it by his side. "There were no ghosts, Watson. That is the important thing to remember. Ebenezer Scrooge saw no ghosts, and his nephew saw none, either. We must begin at that point. There were no ghosts, so there must have been something else."

"But both Scrooges saw something," said I. "Ghosts or not."

"You should have listened more carefully to the present Mr. Scrooge's description of his great-uncle's visions," said Holmes. "He described them vividly, as he did the things he believed himself to have seen. Try to recall what he said. It was all quite suggestive."

"Suggestive of what?" I asked.

"Of the effects of certain mushrooms of the American southwest," said Holmes, "effects that are well known to certain red Indian tribes and their medicine men. They are often ingested for the visions they cause and are used in tribal religious ceremonies. One day I may write a small monograph on the subject."

"So that is why you asked about Cratchit's American connections."

"Yes. From the description given by Scrooge, I at once suspected the mushrooms, or something very like them, had been used. The elder Cratchit must have obtained them from his brother, Samuel, and he undoubtedly saved something of the remainder for use in the future if he ever needed it again. Though he did not, his son believed that the time had come to try the mushrooms, no doubt reduced to a powder, on our client."

"And that is why you asked where Scrooge took his meals?"

"That is true. I did not suspect, as you did, that the dreams were caused by some undigested bit of food. A man's stomach may or may not control his dreams, but it does not make him believe that he can fly."

"But what was that about Tomkins?"

"Whoever put the powder into the tea was quick of hand, and Tomkins used to be a sharp one at picking a gentleman's pocket. He is obviously no use at that trade now, judging from the appearance of his hand, and his fingers would not have been supple enough to drop the powder into the teacup, which is where it had to be placed. Cratchit would never have put it into the pot. He might have had to drink it himself in that case. I was watching carefully, and I saw him drop a dusty substance into Mr. Scrooge's cup this afternoon. That is why I so clumsily caused the cup to fall."

"But the taste of the tea," I said. "What of that?"

"The tea would not have been much affected, particularly not after the addition of as much milk and sugar as Mr. Scrooge received from the hand of Mr. Cratchit."

"You never fail to astonish me, Holmes," said I.

"That is one of your more endearing qualities," said he, and he raised his violin and began to play "God Rest Ye, Merry Gentlemen," the only song of that type I had ever heard him play, and one which he never played again.

THE THIEF OF TWELFTH NIGHT

Carole Nelson Douglas

"Nothing is more sinister, Watson," mused my friend Sherlock Holmes from the lofty prow of the bow window overlooking Baker Street, "than the city of London under a fresh coverlet of new-fallen snow."

I lowered my *Globe* to consider his remark. Christmas had come and gone, yet I still wallowed in the luxury of post-seasonal sloth, just as children sated on festivities, gifts, and plum pudding often do. My own laziness, however, had been abetted by rounds of adult conviviality centering on mulled wine, brandy, and other "spirits" of the season.

Holmes, however, did not much keep Christmas, being impatient with this annual enforced holiday from havoc, and keen for more adventurous pursuits the new year might bring.

"Sinister?" I repeated, hoping to gain the time to dust off my brain. Mrs. Hudson remained mistress of inventive post-holiday repasts, and I had hoped to digest my generous portion in peace. "What an odd way to describe a London that is the very image of a cozy Dickensian Christmas. I still expect to see moppets wrapped in red mufflers peering into snow-glazed shop windows."

"Is it odd?" Holmes took up my challenge by snapping his attention from the serene white scene outside to my innocent, half-drowsing form indoors.

"Perhaps you mean to say"—I was still rousing my brain for the effort that Holmes's apparently tangential remarks always required—"that fresh-fallen snow not only covers traces of soot and cinder, but the tracks of criminal doings. Even sharp-nosed Toby might baffle at a cold, white trail."

"Perhaps I do mean that." The mysterious twinkle in Holmes's eyes boded no good for any further dozing behind an unfurled newspaper.

"I have never known a man so unswayed by common sentiments," I remarked.

"Perhaps what leaves me cold, Watson, is not the sentiments, but the commonality of them. Or perhaps I have bittersweet memories of the season."

"Ah, yes. The small disappointments of childhood can rankle decades later." Despite our association of more than two decades, I missed no opportunity to probe my old friend's decidedly unspoken past.

"Not of *my* childhood, Watson, which I assure you was unremarkable." He turned to the window again. "Consider how Christmas snow, like a whited sepulcher, muffles not only the evildoer's tracks, but all sorts of the most unseasonal emotions. Insincerity is often the true hallmark of the holiday. How rare indeed is a holiday happy ending when crime is involved at this supposedly joyous time of year." Again he spun to confront me. "Have you forgotten our long-ago Twelfth Night dinner at Belleforest?"

"Of course I remember! I am not in my dotage yet, though we were younger then, and I was less stout. Fine house, splendid people, a delightful and traditional meal, if I recall rightly, crown roast of pork and Twelfth Night cake. . . . You were Bean King! And most oddly tolerant of the silly custom, considering your usual indifference to tomfoolery."

"The dinner would have delighted you more, Watson, had you realized that this occasion also served as the climax to one of my early cases. Or perhaps the anticlimax."

This had me sitting up and crinkling my paper as I hastened to set it aside. "I always wondered what your connection to the Oliver family of Belleforest might be. Now you say that more was happening there than I realized?"

Holmes's thin lips pressed together to forestall an additional comment, which no doubt would have been that such was often the case with me.

"And the Pea Queen!" Memory came tumbling toward me like a fresh-packed snowball. "As Bean King you were obligated to choose her ... and you selected that dreadfully common music-hall creature! What an awkward bit, the eldest son insisting that his most unsuitable fianceé attend a family affair, especially with strangers like ourselves present."

"That 'dreadfully common music-hall creature' was the most beautiful woman I have ever seen."

Now I had him! "Oh? I thought that the late Irene Adler held that honor." I glanced with mock reverence to the photograph of the stunning American opera singer, which Holmes kept in an honored place among his memorabilia.

He smiled. "Much to your chagrin, Watson."

"Irene Adler was exceptionally beautiful, I give you that—"

"Yes. Beautiful *and* clever. You will notice that I did not call her ... Twelfth Night predecessor clever, merely beautiful."

"Yet you can call that ... hussy ... more beautiful than Miss Adler, who for all her adventuring was certainly the soul of culture and refinement?"

"If steel is a standard of refinement, I agree, for the King of Bohemia himself said that Madam Irene's soul was thus constituted. As for the other woman, was she as fair? Assuredly so, Watson. Younger, but fair to the same measure that Mother Nature is unfair in bestowing such comeliness upon a single person. I am surprised that she did not strike you so; you are the connoisseur of feminine charms."

"As one, I must tell you, Holmes, that your powers of observation betrayed you on that occasion, or perhaps your memory does now. I recall that evening, and no 'case' came to its conclusion! As for the young woman, I admit that she had possibilities, else why was she on the popular stage, especially after hearing her sing

'Handsome Dick, the Muffin Man' at the family spinet after dinner? But that patently dyed parrot red hair . . . that dreadful tangerine-and–sky blue satin evening gown . . . and her lamentable vocal tone, like a violin sawed by an orangutan, not to mention her broad Bow Street diction."

Holmes shuddered slightly as I evoked the creature's raucous rendition of the old Cockney favorite.

"She was very young, not much past twenty, and a trifle obvious, I admit. Yet one must look beyond surfaces, Watson. Unfortunately, in the case of Miss Viola DeVere, I was a bit better than you at that. But we both were considerably younger then."

"Youth is no excuse, Holmes. Certainly it did not excuse Miss DeVere's lack of talent. Who has ever heard of her again?"

"Hmmm," Holmes agreed with maddening vagueness.

"What has occasioned this Twelfth Night reverie?" I demanded.

"I encountered young Sebastian Oliver in Pall Mall yesterday. Actually he is more nearly 'old' Oliver now. You will be relieved to know that he did not marry Miss Viola DeVere, but rather a lady of good family who is now the mother of his children."

My eyes narrowed. "Was that your 'case,' Holmes? That desperate family engaged you to uncloak the . . . er, memorable Miss DeVere as a fortune-huntress?"

"No. Young Mr. Sebastian Oliver sprung his shocking *mésalliance* on the family just after Christmas Day. They had no time to react to that disaster in the face of a far greater one. That fact alone should have led me instantly to the truth."

"Do not toy with me, Holmes! I am too old and cranky for holiday games."

"The 'case,' as you call it so dubiously, was indeed so inconsequential that I never found it necessary to mention. Your little *Strand* stories prefer to masticate more sensational meat. This minor matter had elements of both the beryl coronet and blue carbuncle cases without any larger aspect of political ruin, or at least the curiosity of grown men stalking Christmas geese through London to cut their throats aforetime."

"Yet this Twelfth Night dinner was part of a case?"

Holmes nodded, pausing at the mantel to shake some tobacco from the Persian slipper toe into his pipe bowl. Soon smoke was swirling about his head, the familiar, sharp features little aged from that evening decades ago. I eyed the paper I had set aside, startled to note the date: January 5, 1903: the Eve of the Feast of the Epiphany, observing the arrival of the Three Wise Men at Bethlehem. Twelfth Night.

Since medieval times, traditional rituals had celebrated Epiphany Eve. A song commemorated the Twelve Days of Christmas with both geese and golden rings. The Twelfth Night cake traditionally concealed a single almond, coin, or bean. This last, Holmes had been lucky, or unlucky, enough to find in his slice of cake that long-ago Twelfth Night, which made him Lord of Misrule for the evening. He might have relished that ancient title, but nowadays it was put in far less grandiose terms. Sherlock Holmes, the world's first and finest consulting detective, King of the Bean! I had forgotten that crowning indignity of the evening.

No wonder my friend happily let this case sink into the dark side of my memory. This Twelfth Night "cake of kings" bestowed temporary sovereignty on whoever found the baked-in trinket—along with the right to choose a consort for the night, in Holmes's case a Queen of the Pea. Kings and princes had bowed to this custom, so it was an honor. Still, I chuckled to recall my tall, dignified, intellectual giant of a friend meekly accepting his folderol kingship. In fact, I was relieved to hear that more had been going on that night. I had not known Holmes for very long in 1883; in retrospect, his behavior on that Twelfth Night had been most peculiar.

"It was called the 'Epiphany Emerald.'" His reflective voice emerged from a Vesuvius of smoke over the velvet-covered lounge chair. "Found on a warm January 6 in Brazil almost a century ago. Not an enormous stone, but truly fine emeralds rarely reach great size. Still, it was sufficiently impressive to become a family prize. The emerald was always brought from the vault for display during the Twelve Days of Christmas. Under a bell jar on the dining room sideboard, Watson, can you believe it? In the beak of a stuffed partridge in a pear tree. Around it day by day would gather the 'two turtledoves, three calling birds, four French hens, and five golden rings' of the song."

"Also the 'six geese a-laying, seven swans a-swimming, eight

215

maids a-milking, ten lords a-leaping,' etcetera. I remember now; these were all represented by small silver figures . . . except for the five golden rings, of course, which were of real gold. A costly custom."

Holmes shrugged. He never judged motives unless they were criminal. "The children loved it, and that is all the parents considered. Except that year, on Christmas Day, the emerald was missing from the partridge's beak. The Olivers were prosperous, but not wealthy. They had standards to uphold, but no governments would topple or suicides result should the Epiphany Emerald vanish. Yet they were disturbed to their souls, because the thief had to be a member of the household. Even the servants were on their second generation with the family."

"Why a household member? Presumably these convivial Olivers entertained mightily at Christmas, and many a guest saw the emerald on display."

"It was never identified as a true jewel, and easily would have been taken for paste. If you recall, the home was pleasant but not so grand as many we have entered during the course of our investigations."

In these latter years Holmes gracefully included me in the lustrous roll call of his cases, a courtesy that never failed to give me a glow of pride.

His points were unarguable. I remembered the display on the dining room sideboard, the usual shining Christmas clutter people set out in those days.

"I can't say that I even noticed the theme, just a lot of brassy gleam and a stuffed bird under a bell jar dome that collected dust, not emeralds, one would assume."

"Assumptions are the hobgoblins of a mediocre mind, Watson, as we well know by now. I must admit that I did not mention my real reason for being there to you. By the time you joined us for the Twelfth Night dinner, the matter was as good as solved. Only the Olivers' festive gratitude and dogged sense of hospitality encouraged me to join them for dinner and to bring a companion as well, for they insistently observed all Christmas traditions, and the table lacked the required twelve to consume the cake."

"That was my entire use in the affair? As a . . . receptacle for

216

Twelfth Night cake? Aha, that is why the awful DeVere woman was tolerated at table that night! Her mouth was needed for more than so-called singing. But . . . *she* must have done it! Taken the Epiphany Emerald. She was the only outsider—"

"Keenly noted, Watson."

"Then why was she allowed at dinner? They were all at dinner, the entire family. A servant, then, must have been unveiled and quietly removed by then."

"No." Holmes huffed on his neglected pipe to relight it, aggravating my patience. "I doubt that you could call the culprit a servant."

"Holmes, I warn you! I shall take notes and write a story if you are not more direct."

"Heavens, Watson, I am utterly cowed. I will *not* be portrayed as 'King of the Bean' in the popular press at this late stage of my career and life! Recall our cast of characters again, as if it were a play you witnessed years ago."

I nodded, my ruminative mind evoking a gracious home lit by the flicker of hearth fires and candles, a domestic landscape bristling with Christmas folderol, from Yule log to towering pine tree draped in paper flowers and tin soldiers.

Mr. and Mrs. Barnaby Oliver were the kindly, portly pater-and materfamilias so often found in domestic paintings. Their children were grown, except for the treasured moppet, Miss Antonia Oliver, all of eight and well pampered for it. Now, let me see, there had been twelve at table, including Holmes and myself: the Olivers; their eldest son Sebastian and his unspeakably unsuitable fianceé with a most pretentious name, likely a stage appellation, Miss Viola DeVere . . . and Miss DeVere's friend. Another outsider! I remember nothing of her, since unlike her companion she was quiet in every respect. Also present were the elder daughter, Olivia, and her husband, one Valentine Feste, if I recall correctly; the grandmother, the senior Mrs. Oliver; young Antonia on her most demure company manners; the younger son, Andrew, all of twenty. Indeed a dramatis personae one would hate to accuse, save for the forward stranger, Viola DeVere.

I reported my conclusions to Holmes, who nodded approvingly. "I assure you that I remember their names very well, Watson, for

I had the advantage of you. I was first called to the house on twenty-eight December, and had investigated the entire family inside and out by five January."

"A rather commonplace set of suspects, Holmes, who had opportunity to steal the jewel for years. Except for Miss DeVere. I would have looked first among the servants, no matter how long they had been in service with the Olivers."

"Oh, I overlooked nobody, not even little Antonia's pet monkey, Curio."

"A monkey?"

"Like certain birds, they have an eye for things that glitter and, unlike certain birds, have clever little hands that could tip open a bell jar."

"What about the scene of the crime, Holmes? Surely you gave it your first attention?"

"Indeed, from which I deduced that Maria, the under-housemaid, is myopic; that the elderly butler, Fabian, suffers from Reynaud's Syndrome; that a ginger cat is resident in the house and often engages in games of chase when that rapscallion Curio escapes his cage in Antonia's bedchamber. Also evident was the fact that Mrs. Valentine Feste was undertaking a severe diet, and that kindly, silver-haired Grandmother Oliver is a kleptomaniac."

"Goodness! One lowly sideboard told you all that?"

"Recall, Watson, that every family member, and nearly every servant, would approach a display on the dining room sideboard daily, whether at breakfast, luncheon, dinner, tea, or dusting-up time. You, of course, realize that I detected a trail of orange and black hairs along the sideboard cloth: cat and monkey at play. The butler's problem was evident in wax droppings on the same cloth around the candleholders. I diagnosed failing circulation in the fingertips, which would prevent him from feeling the warm wax as it dripped. Correct, Doctor? The housemaid's myopia is obvious. Not a smudge or a speck of dust besmirched the bell jar, yet the wax just inches away on the Chinese sateen was not removed. She obviously cleans each object at close range, but fails to observe the larger picture. Likely Mrs. Oliver overlooks her failings out of kindness. Also, the twelve lords a-leaping were only nine, three replaced by a fragrant brown shaving that identified itself to my nose as clove remnants. In her rooms I found the fresh orange pomanders the old lady studs with fragrant cloves for the holidays, the three absent leaping lords, a handkerchief embroidered with the scarlet letter *A* for Antonia, and a twenty-pound note folded to fit in a gentleman's wallet.

"The family swiftly excused the old dear, claiming the absent-mindedness of old age. Young Mr. Andrew Oliver's manner as he reclaimed the twenty-pound note was almost obsequious; he is obviously very short of funds and unwilling to tell his father why. As for the married daughter's regime of self-denial, so at odds with a holiday famed for the riches of the table, I found a crumpled handkerchief tucked between the wall and the sideboard, filled with crumbling fruitcake. No doubt her mother had pressed it upon her on Christmas Day, and she disposed of it as quickly as possible . . . her personal handkerchief was embroidered with the royal blue letter *O*. Doubtless she was responsible for Antonia's rococo *A* as well. God bless these merry embroiderers who must initial every piece of fabric within range; a child—nay, a monkey!—could have followed this trail."

"Then your conclusion was immediately forthcoming. I cannot understand why it had to wait until January fifth to be fully resolved. And I still say that the sudden introduction of the lovely but loud Miss DeVere into the family scene is most suspicious."

"Excellent, Watson! For one who went only to eat, not to observe, you showed early promise of deductive potential. I admit that for all my admiration of the lady's looks, I found her presence terribly wrong. But there was another instance of the younger Oliver's out-of-character behavior that Christmas. When the family solicitor was kind enough to suggest my services on the day after Christmas, *Andrew* Oliver insisted that they should engage the Pinkertons instead, and *Sebastian* seconded him."

"The Pinkertons are an American detective enterprise!" I objected in indignant British defense of my friend, "and cannot hold a Christmas candle to you."

"Thank you, Watson, but the Pinkertons did then—and do even more today—have agents at work in England and on the Continent. The Americans are everywhere nowadays, as you know. Yet such an unlikely source as young Andrew recommending this . . . rival investigation firm struck me as significant."

"Because he had good reason to discourage the use of a truly astute operative."

"Exactly, Watson, and my investigations beyond the family circle soon turned up a story older than Christmas: the prodigal son. Young Andrew, although not consorting with music hall wenches, had managed to amass staggering gambling debts."

"That, besides opportunity, Holmes, might explain the fact that the emerald disappeared on such a festive holiday. Gambling debts wait for nothing and no man. I cannot help but wonder if the puzzle had something to do with the Oliver family's mania for Christmas. From what you said, they did not omit a tradition. I even remember cut pine boughs twining the newel post and banister."

"Indeed. You remember more with every moment, Watson. We shall soon have you solving this case from the comfort of your easy chair, as I have been known to do."

"Pshaw, Holmes! Your conclusion is foregone. No point in my muddling my brains over something that is no longer an issue. Just tell me who the blasted culprit is."

"That which is not worked for is not worth the having."

"Oh, very well. If it amuses you. I still say some Christmas custom must be at the heart of it. What are there . . . Yule logs, trees . . . that's it! The jewel was not removed immediately from the house, but strung up like a piece of tinsel in plain sight on the tree!"

Holmes leapt up, puffing away like a great Western locomotive. "Wonderful, Watson!"

I leapt up myself, much regretting the shock to my settling dinner. "That is the solution, then?"

"No, my dear fellow, but it is a fine and devious suggestion. Where do you hide a jewel at Christmas? On a decorated pine tree. I of course examined every branch, which held only the traditional decorations, I fear. No Epiphany Emerald, no Koh-i-noor Diamond."

I had reseated myself. "Not on the tree. Humph. That's where I would have hidden it, removing it after the holiday spirit had tarnished and nobody paid much attention to the tree.''

"What other ideas have you?" Holmes posed by the mantel, enjoying himself immensely.

"Christmas cheer. I assume they had a wassail bowl."

"The wrong color, Watson."

"What?"

"Wassail is made from ale, wine, and spiced cider. One could have hidden a large topaz, or even a ruby, in the amber red fluid, but an emerald would visibly muddy the waters, so to speak. Green is too contrasting a color to hide in the holiday punch. Besides, given the Olivers' unrelenting hospitality, I'm sure the ladle often scraped the bottom of the bowl. I did look, Watson, finding the punch bowl tasty, but bare of bounty."

"So you considered that, too." I was encouraged by treading so closely in the master's footsteps. "What else? Snow? Sleigh rides? Carolers at the door—carolers invited in for a hot toddy!"

Holmes nodded slowly. "An invading, high-spirited group. A trip to the dining room wassail bowl. A stealthily removed mitten and a rosy-cheeked thief carries home a unique and valuable palm warmer. Possible indeed. Young Andrew clearly showed signs of living far beyond his means. Perhaps a confederate among the carolers had been alerted to the gem. Excellent theory, Watson. Quite . . . sophisticated."

"Were there carolers, Holmes?"

"Unfortunately, no. The first thing I asked. This was the infamous homegrown crime, I fear. One of our delightful Twelfth Night dinner partners was responsible."

"What of the son-in-law?"

"There you have touched upon an interesting history! Mr. Valentine Feste. I made discreet enquiries, of course, of the servants. A tall, nervous sort of two-and-thirty. Sandy hair, pale eyes. Thin as Master Andrew's wallet. Apparently a banker, but tight with his money, say the staff. Tightwads often have secret vices involving money, but I could uncover no gambling."

"A banker would have the connections to sell such a significant stone abroad."

"So would a banker's wife."

"You suspected Olivia? A plump, dark-favored woman, I recall, with an aging, sour look upon her face."

"Perhaps from her concealment of the fruitcake, and other delicacies before that."

"Exactly! You yourself pointed out that the woman was adept at hiding uneaten sweets, and such edibles are much larger than one gemstone. She would have mastered the skills to take and conceal the Epiphany Emerald."

Holmes drew his pipe from his lips and stared at me. "That did not occur to me, Watson, I must admit."

"You see! A simple family is never simple. Perhaps her pinch-penny husband had deprived Olivia of too much, such as money for a proper wardrobe, so that she resorted to collecting the family emerald as a consolation prize. Don't smile, Holmes. Any physician will tell you: diets drive women to strange extremes."

"And the taking of the absent emerald, after a placid history of untouched display for many years, certainly was a strange extreme."

"What other Christmas folderol? Plum pudding, I suppose."

"Oh, yes, the Oliver ladies—Grandmother, Mrs. Barnaby, and Mrs. Valentine—spent a full day before Christmas demonstrating the concoction and storing of these culinary Christmas jewels to young Antonia. On hearing this, I immediately hied to the cellar with a fencing foil from Barnaby's library wall to skewer these plump, bagged puddings on their pegs into Swiss cheese. I confess to a trifling excitation when I plunged in my point and pulled out a large greenish gold nugget—an exceptionally overgrown Turkish raisin. I also speared a quantity of Greek currants and candied fruit peel. Nothing so tasty as a missing emerald however."

"You destroyed the ladies' winter hoard of plum puddings! That is barbaric, Holmes. What did they have for dessert after you left?"

"Just desserts, Watson. Just desserts."

My stomach was protesting the massacre of the plum puddings with soft and, I hoped, undetectable growls. My body as well as my mind was growing keen on the guessing game. I changed my tactics.

"I take it that the culprit was revealed."

"Yes."

"And the Epiphany Emerald was found?"

"Indeed."

"And both before my arrival Epiphany Eve for the Twelfth Night dinner?"

Holmes paused, frowning. "Yes, so to speak."

"Then how can *I* say who took it, when I was only present on that occasion? If some under-servant was missing, how would I know?"

"I already said it was not a servant. It was someone at that table."

"Someone who was not being publicly challenged as the culprit. Why?"

"You were there, Watson! You have eyes and ears as well as an appetite. Think, and you will see the answer."

"Very well." I shut those eyes.

Now that we had talked so much about that blasted evening, I could evoke the scene as clearly as a painting on my wall. I had grown adept at marking details for my small excursions into print.

I saw old Fabian hunched over the sideboard, and nearsighted Maria dodging between us to lay precariously swaying soup bowls on our chargers. Neither had been dismissed, though both's duties revolved around the scene of the crime, so I dismissed them, as Holmes urged.

The elder Olivers occupied head and foot of table, with the capped, silver-haired grandmother on her son's right. I, and then Holmes, were seated next along the sideboard-facing length of the table; no accident, I do not doubt.

Across from us sat Olivia and Valentine, the very image of Jack Sprat and his wife, then Andrew. The disgraceful Viola DeVere was next to him, then Antonia, at her mother's right, which meant that the forward hussy sat nearly opposite Holmes. Perhaps that was why he named her Pea Queen; she was most convenient.

On Mrs. Oliver's left sat Miss DeVere's friend, who had been introduced, but whose name I did not recall, and whose appearance was even more of a mystery, since it was blocked by Holmes and Sebastian Oliver, who sat beside Holmes and opposite his lady love.

Viola DeVere was radiant—nay, as luminous as a Halloween

pumpkin in her tangerine satin gown fresh from the music-hall stage. A cheap violet cologne could not cover the odor of stale smoke and ale.

Young Antonia seemed a bit subdued by her gaudy and reeking neighbor, barely lifting her head from her plate unless offered some new course. Even a child could appreciate how unfit that DeVere woman was for this refined company. Her mother and brother were most solicitous of the child, both of what she ate and of her mood. Perhaps Antonia was not used to so many strangers at the family table, and certainly she was unaccustomed to the booming tones of Miss DeVere's Bow Bells voice.

"I'll 'ave some of that wine," she sang out to Fabian as he made his solemn rounds with the sherry that accompanied our soup. "Oooh, w'at a empty bowl of soupers we 'ave 'ere! All broth and no barley, just these ever-so-strange floating brown-like things. Look like button slices, they do."

"Mushrooms." Mrs. Oliver used the same martyred tone in which she might explain exotica to little Antonia.

"Fancy that! Not'ing more 'an cellar-sprouts, but cut so thin a body could starve on 'em. Well, bot'oms up!" With that she lifted a perilously full spoon to her painted lips and slurped consommé with the same bold musicality with which she sang. Even the slurp was off key.

I glanced at Holmes, expecting his keen musical sense to show mortal offense, but he regarded this performance with a certain amusement. I knew him to be a frequenter of the concert hall; at that moment I wondered if he harbored a secret taste for the music hall.

In the usual awkward silence that prevailed after one of Miss DeVere's pronouncements, I noticed that all present at the table—except the newcomer, who was thankfully silent if she sounded like her friend Viola—appeared oddly on edge. I had tried to peer around Holmes and Sebastian to view her, but she remained a silent and unseen dinner partner. No doubt she plied the stage, and her first name was Mignoncttc or some such nonsense. Could she be more than friend . . . a confederate? This I wondered in retrospect. Holmes had investigated the entire family and, while all were able and possibly motivated to take the emerald, this stranger I had little noticed could be the key to the crime! If so, it was most unfair of Holmes to imply that I could name the culprit.

"Miss DeVere's friend," I mentioned, opening my eyes to find Holmes back by the window, meditating on the snow-muffled street. "I barely recall her."

"An invisible woman," he agreed. "In marked contrast to Madam Viola. But she and you were the only total strangers present."

I bristled. "Are you saying that I was as nondescript as she on that occasion?"

"Nondescript? Never, Watson! But she was. A day later I could barely remember her face." His eyes narrowed. "What a fool I was in those days. At times, Watson, just at times."

"Yes, well, you were most unlike yourself that night. Not only did you not raise an eyebrow at the gauche Miss DeVere, yet you did raise a cry when you found the bean in the Twelfth Night cake, but you immediately named *her* Queen of the Pea, when almost any other woman present would have been far more suitable. It would have been gentlemanly, for instance, to give the honor to old Grandmother Oliver, or Mrs. Barnaby, or Mrs. Valentine, or even young Antonia."

"Yes, it would have been gentlemanly, but poor misjudged Miss DeVere deserved some credit for her role in unraveling the mystery."

"She betrayed young Andrew?"

"She betrayed no one but the thief, but I anticipated her. I got the credit, and she was Queen of the Pea, apt compensation for a theatrical personality, no doubt. Besides, she was the most beautiful woman I have ever seen, this was my only opportunity to crown a queen . . . and I was not yet thirty then."

"Holmes, this is so unlike you! You admit that another was a step ahead in solving the problem. You seem to admire this awful woman. And you still have not said who took the emerald and where it had gone to."

"I will say that Viola DeVere was the key."

So the woman was significant! Holmes had just let that fact slip. "Holmes, I have it. The DeVere woman was introduced to the family after the emerald had been stolen, and that is the key, is it not?"

He nodded, looking somewhat startled.

"And your manner indicates that some last piece of the puzzle was put into place at the Twelfth Night dinner."

Another nod.

"Then it is simple. The Epiphany Emerald was not stolen on Christmas Day."

"Indeed?"

"No. It was taken by Sebastian, not Andrew, and merely concealed somewhere. Sebastian, after all, was as eager as Andrew to avoid your services. Perhaps he put his younger brother up to suggesting other investigators. Then Sebastian introduced this appalling hussy to distract his family from your investigation. This Viola DeVere was not a serious fianceé to a love-besotted young Romeo. She was exactly what she appeared to be and acted completely in character. Sebastian had hired her in the role, but his real lady-love was Viola's supposed "friend," to whom he planned to slip the emerald at dinner, so she could vanish into the anonymous night from whence she came. Later, they would rendezvous, exchange the jewel, which he would sell and no doubt buy the doxy some trinket. And his family would rest easy and unsuspicious when he suddenly came to his senses and jilted Miss DeVere in favor of this more sedate female."

"Why would such a 'sedate' female be a music-hall performer?"

"I don't know; this is simply a theory. But I don't recall you unmasking the plot at the dinner. Was the byplay too subtle for my unsuspecting, and much misled, mind?"

Holmes laughed as he seldom did, in his odd, hearty, soundless fashion, coming over to collapse in the chair opposite me, still speechless with mirth.

"On my word, Watson," he finally managed to sober up enough to say. "You are the supreme fiction writer; in the past I have complained of this, of your embellishments to fact, but now to this I bow. A quite fabulous plot and, alas, wasted on this simple problem. Why need I bother solving cases, when you can resolve them in such an inventive manner, replete with embroideries of Lewis Carroll logic?"

"Then cease tormenting me and tell me what really happened. No doubt it was the footsteps of a gigantic hound on the sideboard scarf that led you to the family dog in conspiracy with the monkey, Curio, who was actually a trained accomplice to a thieving organ grinder from Ceylon!"

"Not so sour, Watson."

"You still have not said who took the emerald and where it had gone to."

"Gone to the cellar with the plum puddings, of course."

"But you skewered the blasted plum puddings, for nothing!"

"I was on the right trail, though. The Twelfth Night cake, remember the cake."

"How could I forget it? For dessert, first the cheese, riddled with 'portholes,' so to speak, the port wine in its many holes, was borne in. 'Stilton,' Mrs. Oliver announced proudly, 'precedes the crowning cake of the evening.' At which your queen-to-be cried out, 'Dessert without cheese is the kiss without the squeeze.' A most lascivious performance for a family dinner table. And then she winked! Luckily, she could not compete with the Queen of Cakes when it arrived. A lofty affair with thick sugar frosting and marzipan roses; it would take a dozen mouths to consume it at one go, and that is the point of a Twelfth Night cake, to be eaten fully at once so the trinket is discovered."

"This 'trinket' was emerald green and the size of a Brazil nut."

"The emerald? But how? And I did not see it."

"You were too busy eating your cake and trying to ignore my foolish new title and deliciously ridiculous consort. The only remaining question at that point was whose teeth would strike the Epiphany Emerald. Oddly enough, that honor fell to me, and then resulted in other, even more ludicrous honors, such as the title of Bean King."

"And, after that, you went to the sideboard to fetch the wine and personally refill everyone's glass, a most upstart social behavior, but I supposed then that a Lord of Misrule could do whatever he liked. You replaced the emerald at that time, didn't you, Holmes? And the family knew it. Why did no one remark upon the finding and restoration? Why was I left in utter ignorance for two decades?"

"No one wished to further upset the thief."

"Who was—?"

"Whose feelings would require sparing."

"Old Mrs. Oliver, the kleptomaniac, then. You said the family made excuses for her."

"Yes, but it was not she."

"Young Andrew? Prodigal sons are famous for being forgiven."

"Perhaps, but I doubt the Olivers could forgive the theft of the Epiphany Emerald. This case was child's play, quite literally. Who is traditionally excused of all mischief at Christmas?"

"Why . . . children, I suppose. Holmes! Not Antonia!?"

Holmes nodded in satisfaction. "You have found the right bean at last, Watson. Antonia had witnessed the women toss the raisins into the plum puddings and was duly impressed. When she heard about the hidden surprise in the Twelfth Night cake, she decided to cook up a surprise of her own. She took the emerald amid the Christmas Day flurry and kept it in her apron pocket until the cake batter was prepared some days after Christmas and stored in the cool cellar. A child's presence in a busy holiday kitchen is both tolerated and ignored."

"How was she able to take it without leaving a trace?"

"First, she was clever enough to do it before Maria dusted the dining room. She used a dining room chair, but needed to pull it out only the distance someone would to seat himself, so no telltale scratches marred the floor. And she did leave a clue: the clove flakes, but I attributed them to the maker rather than to one of the recipients."

"Surely Antonia heard the consternation about the emerald and would have confessed."

"The family wanted to spare her their suspicions of each other, so they kept her in the dark as much as possible."

"But when you arrived—"

"More holiday hullabaloo and strangers, as was Miss DeVere's presence. Antonia accepted the uproar; it was still the holiday, wasn't it, especially among the celebratory Olivers? Besides, the emerald was supposed to be a surprise. If she did realize the problem, her young mind only anticipated their greater surprise when the emerald was found."

"So that was why she was subdued at dinner! All had been discovered and she knew that her 'surprise' was a serious matter."

"Indeed. And that is why my discovery was so discreet; no one wanted to inadvertently reward her innocent childish mischief."

"And Viola DeVere was—"

Holmes chuckled again, like a rather young man. "Andrew's Pinkerton, grafted onto Sebastian. And a true performer as well, who couldn't resist taking the name of 'Viola' from Shakespeare's *Twelfth Night* for her impersonation in honor of the season."

"Then she was not as she seemed." My mind peeled away the gaudy gown, tawdry red hair, clownish face paint, and above all, the atrocious accent. The scales fell from my eyes. "You are right, Holmes, she was a beautiful woman, quite the most beautiful woman we have ever encountered, save for . . . Holmes! She was not . . . ?!"

"Let me just say that we have encountered the lady before, in another case . . . or, to be perfectly accurate, Watson, after." Holmes rose and rubbed his hands together, case closed. "Well, Watson, I believe that our mental exertions have by now exhausted Mrs. Hudson's splendid repast. Let us brave the fresh winter's day to view London's rare, pristine semblance. Then we may visit Simpsons-in-the-Strand for our own just desserts. I crave some Twelfth Night cake after all these years, and a splendid sherry."

I agreed with alacrity, but once I had donned my coat, paused at the door. "What of Miss DeVere's mousy friend, Holmes? Apparently she was no music-hall performer, after all."

"A true friend and an innocent, ignorant witness, present only to account for a slice of cake, like yourself, Watson. Unlike yourself, she was a personage of no importance, who has truly not been heard from again in our time. A respectable parson's daughter. A Miss Penelope Huxleigh, in fact. You will not find her in my index, Watson, I assure you."

And with that, Holmes hurtled down Mrs. Hudson's dark stairs with a young man's agility.

THE ITALIAN
SHERLOCK HOLMES

Reginald Hill

'Halloa! What's this,' said Sherlock Holmes, studying the sheet of paper he had just removed from a thick white envelope heavily embossed with a crest I did not recognise. 'I don't suppose you have ever attended an execution, Watson?'

'Indeed I have,' I replied, not displeased to be able for once to surprise my friend. 'As duty medical officer at a hanging in Afghanistan. Not my happiest memory of army life. Why do you ask?'

He tossed the sheet of paper to me.

'These Italians are an original race,' he said. 'This is surely the rarest Christmas entertainment a man was ever invited to!'

The news that Sherlock Holmes was wintering in Rome had spread through the British community like wildfire, almost eclipsing the rumour that the Prince of Wales, incognito, was dallying with an opera singer at Ostia. Had we so desired, we could have dined at the best tables in the city every night of Advent. But it was not for the social round that we had paused in Rome on our way north from Naples. I have met with few men capable of greater physical and mental exertion than my friend Holmes, but frequently once the occasion of such exertions has passed, a period of deep lassitude ensues in which that most brilliant of minds fades to the merest glimmer of consciousness in an all but moribund shell. For a few days after the conclusion of the affair of Ricoletti of the club foot and his abominable wife, which had taken us from the foetid cellars of the Camorra's Neapolitan stronghold to the smoking rim of Mount Vesuvius, I had hoped that the surge of energy success always brings would carry him safe across Europe to the healing solace of Mrs Hudson's traditional Yuletide cheer in Baker Street. But as we entered Rome he had suffered an almost complete nervous collapse and there had been nothing for it but to take rooms in a respectable *pensione* and bide out time till a quiet atmosphere and healthy diet should have worked their repairs.

Alas, in Italy the one is almost as hard to find as the other, and once the news of his presence had spread, I was hard pressed for at least ten hours of each day turning visitors from our door.

The written invitations, however, I admitted in the hope that something in them might spark an interest. But up till now they had all fluttered from his hand after the most cursory of glances. So to see him react with something of his old alertness to this latest invitation at first made my spirits rise. When however I reread the elegantly penned missive, my pleasure diminished somewhat.

My dear Holmes,

My delight at hearing from my good friend the British ambassador that you are presently in Rome was naturally tempered by learning of the reasons for your stay. May I join with all the honest men of Europe in wishing you a speedy return to health?

But even out of evil may come good, and though you may set it down to mere Romish superstition, forgive me if I see the hand of God in this (I hope) temporary indisposition of yours. How else am I to interpret your unforseeable presence in my city on the very day which sees the culmination of my first poor efforts to emulate your unique methods? I refer of course to the tragic case of the murder of my beloved uncle, Count Leonardo Montesecco. Tomorrow morning at nine-thirty, the foul assassin, Giuseppe Strepponi, will meet his richly deserved fate on the scaffold in the Piazza San Cassiano. I and a few interested friends will be gathering to witness this triumphant vindication of the laws of God and man, and I would be honoured if, health permitting, you and your companion, Dr Watson, would care to join us. If so, my carriage will collect you at eight of the clock.

With deepest respect from one who is honoured to inscribe himself your disciple and colleague,

The signature was a hieroglyph too elegant to be called a scrawl but too ornate for legibility.

'So what do you make of it, Watson?' asked Holmes.

'To invite us to watch some poor devil being put to death on the Eve of our Saviour's birth is such a monstrous piece of impiety,' I replied indignantly, 'that I can only hope the missive is a fraud.'

'No fraud,' he replied with a lively smile which cheered my heart. 'I know the coat of arms of the Montesecco family, and from what I recall of the hand and signature of Bruno Montesecco, the present count, the letter bears none of the inevitable telltales of forgery.'

'In that case,' I replied, 'it is an impudence as well as an impiety. I am sorry that such an ancient family has finally forgotten its manners. Will you dictate our refusal or shall I pen it myself?'

Now Holmes threw back his head and let out that characteristic cackle of laughter which I had not heard for many days and, despite my indignation, my heart grew lighter still.

'I think, dear fellow, in your present state of mind,' he said, 'that any reply from you is likely to be read as an invitation to pistols at dawn, or more probably a stiletto at night in view of your plebeian origins. No, I shall write myself and what is more, I shall accept the invitation with pleasure. When in Rome, Watson! But first ring the bell and summon up Signora Grillo to order some luncheon. Also I have some telegrams I would like to send.'

As he spoke he leapt to his feet in search of his neglected pipe, and the heavy shawls in which his narrow frame had been swathed, even though a roaring sea-coal fire turned the room into an oven, fell away. And with them fell the greater part of my resentment at Count Montesecco's invitation.

'Tell me, Holmes,' I said as we sat over luncheon, which I was pleased to note he wolfed down, 'how is it you came acquainted with this Count Montesecco? And why should he think the fate of this poor devil Strepponi should be of interest to you? And is it the custom of this country to treat executions as an occasion of social festivity? And does . . . ?'

'Stay, stay, my dear Watson,' he cried. 'Let me finish this excellent cutlet and I shall gladly try to answer your questions.'

Later as we sat before the fire, adding the sweet smoke of my Arcadia mixture to that of the coals, he began his explanation.

'I have never met the count in person, but he began writing to me early this year, before he had succeeded to his murdered uncle's title. From the style and manner of his writing, I put him down as the kind of young aristocrat who is rich enough to be idle but a little too intelligent to be satisfied with the customary recreations of his class. His restless enquiring mind, in search of some pastime which might satisfy his desire for activity without demeaning his self-esteem, chanced upon some of those infernal scribblings of yours about my cases, and having made his first deduction, which was that in England where we still set the standards for such things, it is possible to be a consultant detective without ceasing to be a gentleman, he decided to follow my example.'

'He must have a pretty large conceit of himself,' I observed.

'I think there can be little doubt of that,' replied my friend dryly. 'I think that in his very first letter he pointed out a couple of apparent deficiencies in my deductive processes which he very handsomely laid at the door of my inefficient chronicler rather than my inefficient technique.'

'The impudent puppy!' I snorted.

'Youth must be given its head, Watson,' said Holmes. 'I replied politely but coolly, not so much because of anything I found offensive in his manner, though I was always left aware, despite the flattering tone of his letters, that he was an aristocrat and I was not, but rather because I am sensible that my methods misapplied are as capable of causing serious damage as a surgeon's scalpel in the hands of a schoolboy.'

'But he persisted in the correspondence?'

'Indeed. A snub must be very blatant to penetrate the complacence of such an innate conviction of social superiority,' said Holmes. 'And I saw no reason to descend to rudeness. Then late in the summer I received a letter which was so full of the sheer excitement of investigation that it almost forgot to patronize! After bemoaning in previous letters the lack of such challenging crimes as seemed to be the commonplace of my life, he found himself actually present at the scene, indeed almost the occasion of one of Rome's most sensational murders. The fact that the victim was his uncle, the head of his own noble family, seemed almost inconsequential when set against the opportunity afforded him to investigate. Or perhaps he did not think it seemly to share a private grief with a stranger.'

'But from the sound of it, his investigation of the crime has met with some success?'

'So it would appear. His first letter on the subject, written the day after the murder, told me of a few preliminary deductions he had made and forecast complete success within twenty-four hours. I must confess I found his confidence smacked somewhat of arrogance.'

I concealed a smile. When it comes to an arrogant assumption of his own infallibility, Holmes can on occasion make the Holy Father *ex cathedra* sound like a bashful tyro.

'The next letter came hot on the heels of the first and proclaimed absolute triumph. The murderer was caught and all on account of Montesecco's insights. By now rather than asking advice, I felt he was with difficulty restraining himself from giving it. I sent a polite letter of congratulation. Since coming to Italy I have twice noted his name in the papers in connection with other investigations. They are calling him the Italian Sherlock Holmes! But as you know I have been too busy for more than a cursory interest. Now, however, fate has brought us close and I find I have a fancy to meet this prodigy. Who knows, Watson, he may be able to teach this old dog some new tricks, hey?'

'He would need to get up very early in the morning to do that,' I said loyally.

'From the sound of his invitation, that is one trick he has learned already,' said Holmes so merrily that I went to bed that night feeling more comfortable in my mood than for many a day.

Precisely on the stroke of eight on the morning of Christmas Eve the bell of our *pensione* was rung with a most imperious hand and a moment later Signora Grillo, our *padrona*, appeared to me in a state of great excitement to announce the presence of the Count Montesecco's coach. I summoned Holmes and was a little taken aback when on seeing me he burst into laughter and said, 'I hope the kernel is a little more fashionably shaped than the husk, Watson.'

Uncertain what local custom decreed was the acceptable garb for an execution, I had opted for comfort and was wearing my heavy Abercrombie with my long plaid scarf wound three times round my neck, my earflapped travelling hat pulled firmly on my head, and my legs cased in my stoutest boots. Holmes by contrast was clad in a light jacket and silk shirt, with a thin cloak thrown over his shoulders.

I said sternly, 'I may not know much about fashion, Holmes, but I have stood on more parade grounds than you and I think this wind which has rattled our panes all night will strike as cold in a Roman piazza as it would on Horseguards. I would advise you at the very least to change into your twill trousers.'

He looked a touch disconcerted and replied, 'You may be right, but it is too late to change now. Punctuality is the courtesy of kings. Hurry, or else we shall be late!'

I told him rather testily as we bowled along that as the execution was fixed for nine-thirty and nothing in this country ever seemed to start on time anyway, there was little need for haste.

'Indeed,' I concluded, 'I cannot imagine why Montesecco should request our presence so far in advance of his main entertainment.'

'Come now, Watson,' he said. 'Surely you know that it is not the execution but our presence which *is* the main entertainment.'

I brooded on this till, as we neared the Piazza San Cassiano, our progress became noticeably slower. Looking from the window, I became aware that we were not the only people drawn out on a raw Christmas Eve by the prospect of witnessing a man's death. There were many other carriages and also men on horseback, but the greater part of those flocking to the square were pedestrians with every conceivable variety of citizen represented, from sober, suited businessmen to the rag, tag and bobtail. The chill winter wind was pulling at hats and tousling hair and I said to Holmes, 'Now you may see why our presence was required so early. From the look of it, no latecomer will get to see more than the top of the scaffold.'

He did not reply but I saw him shiver and, reproaching myself for my triumphant tone, I started to remove my coat, saying, 'Here, Holmes, take this. You've only just risen from your sick bed and your lungs could easily take an infection from this raw, dank air.'

He smiled at me with real affection and said, 'Watson, you are more good-hearted than I deserve. Thank you, dear fellow, but I do not think that after all your sacrifice will be necessary.'

I looked out of the window and saw that we had passed the narrow entrance to the Piazza San Cassiano and were coming to a halt outside a haberdashery before which a liveried flunkey was waiting to bow us out of the coach, after which he bowed us through the shop doorway, down a passageway, across a mean and shadowy courtyard, through another door, up several flights of stairs, and finally, with his deepest bow of all, ushered us into a spacious room across which advanced a tall, handsome, moustachio'd man in his mid-twenties, showing dazzling white teeth in a wide smile.

'Mr Holmes!' he cried. 'Welcome. After so many letters between us, I am delighted at last to make your acquaintance in the flesh.'

'And I yours, Count,' said Holmes, taking his hand. 'May I present my dear friend and colleague, Dr John Watson.'

'Delighted,' I said gruffly. To tell the truth I was feeling distinctly uncomfortable. There were many other people in the room, of both sexes, all dressed most elgantly. The room was heated by a large stove and already I was beginning to feel overwarm, but my main discomfiture rose from my knowledge that I had seen no reason to wear beneath my topcoat anything other than a pair of balding moleskin trousers and the leather-patched Norfolk jacket which has accompanied me on so many outdoor expeditions.

'Dr Watson, the Boswell of the great detective!' cried Montesecco, wringing my hand warmly. 'It was through your writings that I first became acquainted with Mr Holmes's talents. You are the Vergil who has led me safe through the labyrinths of his mind.'

I cannot say I cared much for the flowery style of the Italian Sherlock Holmes and thought of pointing out that Vergil did most of his ciceroning in the circles of Hell. But Holmes, alert to both

236

my mental distaste and my physical discomfort, took my arm and urged me towards a window which opened onto a broad metal balcony, saying, 'I see we must brave the elements after all, Watson. Once again you have demonstrated that while I may lay some claim to superiority of insight, in matters of foresight, you are the master. The rest of us must shiver while you stay snug and warm.'

'I have provided cloaks for everybody,' said the count petulantly.

'Then we shall all be comfortable together,' said Holmes, stepping out onto the balcony.

All concern about my comfort or discomfort vanished as I took in the scene spread out below.

The house we were in stood at one end of the long and narrow Piazza San Cassiano, directly opposite the church of San Cassiano at the other end, some six hundred feet away. Already the square was full of people though not yet so crowded that they could not move freely about. It was a scene that an artist with our vantage point might have used as a model for a panorama of Bartholemew Fair. Hawkers hawked, tumblers tumbled, beggars begged, and the citizens of Rome strolled around in topcoats and tailcoats and long cloaks and short cloaks and some in no cloaks at all, wearing barely sufficient rags to cover their modesty. But all had that complacent air which says as clearly now as it must have done in Caesar's time, 'We are true Romans and may not be touched by any law but our own.'

At the very centre of the square stood the instrument of that law. Over the trough of a dry fountain had been erected the scaffold, a ramshackle jerry-built platform of uneven, unpainted planks some eight feet high, with a rickety ladder leaning against it, the ascent of which looked perilous enough to despatch a condemned man without troubling the waiting axe, which gleamed sinisterly, high in its towering frame. The polished and, I hoped, finely honed blade contrasted powerfully with the ponderous rusting mass of metal attached above to provide the motivating force necessary to drive the cutting edge through the bone and sinew of a man's neck.

The scaffold was ringed with foot soldiers, and a double line of them showed the route from the church by which the condemned man would be brought to his doom. The soldiers were stood at ease, which command is taken much more literally here than it would be by a similar escort from a British regiment. The men slouched, scratched, chatted with their neighbours, and even laid their weapons on the ground to stretch their arms in huge weary yawns, while their officers strolled around, smoking cigarillos and occasionally exchanging banter with some of the ladies of the town.

'Tell me, Mr Holmes,' said the count, who had followed us onto the balcony, 'have you ever had the pleasure of following one of your cases to this last extremity?'

'No, Count,' said Holmes. 'I am glad to say that in my country we have abandoned the practice of turning some poor devil's death into a sideshow.'

'You are indeed a people of great restraint,' murmured the count, not making it sound like a compliment. 'But there is a certain completeness, a roundness if you like, in seeing a matter out to the bitter end, particularly when, as in this case, the investigator was present from the very beginning.'

'Ah, you actually witnessed Strepponi committing the murder, then?' said Holmes. 'I should have thought that would have rendered my deductive methods somewhat redundant.'

Someone laughed behind us. The count turned and the laughter stopped. This was clearly a man who did not care for contradiction.

'I forget my manners,' he said. 'Come and meet my other guests.'

He and Holmes stepped back inside. I remained on the balcony, partly for comfort, partly because from this vantage I could take close note of the room and its inmates without my being noted.

It did not need my friend's sharp perception to remark that, though the room was elegantly furnished and made gay by the beribboned icons and silk-draped religious pictures with which these Papists mark the season of Christmas, its basic fabric was in an advanced state of dilapidation. I guessed that the count had hired the apartment purely as a vantage point for the execution and commanded his people to make it temporarily fit for fashionable society.

The first guest in line was in something of the same condition as the room. In his sixties, cadaverous of face and skeletal of frame, he was clothed in colourful silk and mohair and his long boney fingers were banded with diamonds and gold.

'No need for introduction,' said Holmes, offering his hand. 'Who could work within the law and not be acquainted with the famous Judge Pinelli? I trust Your Honour's respiration has improved from your recent voyage to the Holy Land on Count Montesecco's yacht?'

The man's jaw dropped like Marley's when he unwound his scarf in the famous Christmas story. Recovering, he said in fair English, 'I see the count has given you my curriculum vitae, Mr Holmes.'

'Not in the least,' replied my friend, smiling. 'As the principal trial judge, your likeness was in the newspaper cuttings which the count was kind enough to send me. As for the rest, your lip and jaw are slightly paler than the rest of your face, suggesting that you recently grew a moustache and beard during a period of exposure to wind and warm weather. From this I deduced a long voyage on a private rather than a public vessel, permitting you to indulge in not shaving without provoking the interest of other travellers. The count's evident gratitude to you for your conduct of the trial provoked me to guess that the vessel was his private yacht. And the enamelled medal you are wearing of Our Lady of the Rocks looks new enough to suggest recent visit to that particular shrine.'

'And the respiratory problem, Mr Holmes?' asked a handsome blonde woman of about forty, clad in the kind of loose flowing garment ladies are wont to wear when they become self-conscious about their spreading figures.

'Elementary, my dear Signora Masina,' said Holmes. 'I have heard the learned judge cough dryly several times since I entered the room. My good friend Dr Watson could have diagnosed much more precisely. But your pain at losing such a very dear friend is beyond mere medical remedy, and I think you are wise to have decided to go and live with your sister in America.'

As he spoke, he bowed in the direction of another woman, dark and slim and wearing a long grey dress of rather old-fashioned cut.

For a second Signora Masina looked disconcerted. Then she rallied and said, 'Now this is first rate, Mr Holmes. I daresay my likeness too appeared in the papers, but as for my sister and my debate about joining her in the United States, only a wizard could know of that. And don't tell me there's a family resemblance. As your proverb puts it, we are chalk and cheese!'

'The dark and the bright, two different kinds of beauty,' said Holmes with greater gallantry than I had suspected he possessed. 'The accent of your English suggests a period already spent in America. This lady's dress is of a style more popular just now in New York than in Rome. She wears a brooch and you a ring which look to have been set by the same hand perhaps fifty years ago. It could be that you have a common jeweller, but it's more likely that these are part of a set of jewellery divided on inheritance, and a mother is the most likely source of such a bequest. What would be more probable than that a sister should rush to your side at your time of grief and offer you a permanent home in the bosom of her family.'

'In other words, these deductions of yours are mere guesses, and your fame depends largely on folk tending to recall the few instances when you hit the mark and forget the many where you are wide.'

This came from the lady in grey who spoke English with a very pronounced Yankee drawl and had a cynical eye to match.

I waited to see how my friend's gallantry would survive this attack but the count came smoothly in.

'I think, Mrs Jardine, that the occasion of our meeting here today shows that there is rather more to our methods than mere guesswork,' he murmured. 'Mr Holmes, would you like to make a further display of your powers with regard to any other of my guests?'

This was clever, I thought. *Our methods* implied an equality of standing with Holmes while *a further display of your powers* suggested that such vulgar exhibitionism was Holmes's alone.

Holmes glanced at me ruefully. Perhaps the count had hit a nerve. Or perhaps he had recollected the solemnity of the occasion.

The introductions continued, confirming my impression that most of those present had some close connection with the murder of the last Count Montesecco. As well as Signora Masina and her sister, Mrs Jardine, there were present the family lawyer, Signor Randone; Captain Zardi, who had been in charge of the official investigation; Dr Provenzale, the attending medical officer; and a very beautiful young woman called Claudia Medioli, who stood in an ambiguous relationship to the count.

Even the trio of servants who were constantly on hand with hot chocolate, cold champagne and a variety of little sweetmeats, turned out to have been in the employ of the dead man and present in his house at the time of his murder. There were two maids, Violetta and Susi, and in charge of them Serge Rosi, who had been the old count's and was now the new count's majordomo.

Finally there was a group of some half dozen men standing a little apart who turned out to be representatives of the Italian press. Just as the introductions were completed, the door burst open and a young man of about the count's age entered. From his long unkempt hair, tied back in the peasant style, and his rather shabby suit, which stood out against the general elegance of the assemblage, I at first took him for another servant. But he came forward boldly, seizing a glass of champagne en route, letting his bright brown eyes run lightly over the other guests with a faintly mocking smile as he said in Italian, 'Sorry to be late, Montesecco, on such an illustrious occasion.' Then, switching to an accented but very correct English, he went on, 'And this must be the famous *British* Sherlock Holmes. How proud you must be that your influence now helps men to die in countries other than your own!'

Even allowing for the fact that he spoke a foreign language, this came close to being offensive, but Holmes merely held out his hand and said, 'I find no man's death an occasion for pride, Signor Chiari. Like yours, my interest is solely in *la verità*, the truth.'

For a moment the young man looked disconcerted, then the mocking smile returned and he said, 'So the count has warned you I am coming! Or are you going to claim it is the printers' ink on my fingers or the paper dust in my hair that helped you to make your conclusion?'

'I could hardly warn Mr Holmes of your arrival, as you were not invited,' said Montesecco coldly. 'But now you are here I will not deprive you of this chance to see how real justice works.'

Chiari bowed satirically. Holmes said nothing, but for once I needed no elucidation. It has long been his habit to study not only the English newspapers but also those of the main European capitals. 'The train and the steamship have made crime international, Watson,' he would tell me. 'It is no longer enough to know only what is going on in your own parish.' *La Verità* was an Italian weekly journal which I had often noticed lying around our chambers in Baker Street. All I knew of it was that its politics were radical, its style sensational, and its proprietor and principal reporter was Endo Chiari. I presume the magazine had at some time printed a picture of him, and of course Holmes never forgot a face.

Chiari now turned away from the circle that had formed around Holmes and the count and began a flirtatious conversation with Susi, the prettier of the two maids, till Rosi, the majordomo, sternly commanded her to go and fetch more refreshment. Outside in the square there was a sudden blare of a trumpet and everyone hurried out onto the balcony in case this signalled that events were going to start early. How anyone could spend a day in this country, let alone be a native of it, and still believe this was possible, I do not know! The trumpeter turned out to be some enterprising showman eager to attract customers to enter and view what he claimed to be the mummified and pickled remains of previous executed felons. The chill wind soon drove the others back indoors, but when they had retreated I found that Chiari remained. Perhaps his shabby suit was made of sturdier cloth than their finery, but he showed no sign of feeling the cold and leaned on the rail of the balcony, looking down at the growing crowd below with a mixture of sorrow and disgust.

'So, Dr Watson,' he said, 'and how shall you write of this spectacle you are to see here today?'

'I do not know that I shall write of it, sir,' I said shortly.

He turned his mocking gaze on and said, 'But surely you are the chronicler of all Mr Holmes's triumphs?'

'Whether this be a triumph or no, sir, is not for me to say. But it is certainly not one of Mr Holmes's.'

'You say so? The count certainly gives him a portion of credit. The name Montesecco does not yet have quite the same power to make the virtuous bow and the criminal tremble, and though it must irk him, for the time being at least he is content to pull in the same yoke as your master and let himself be called the Italian Holmes.'

I drew myself up and replied, 'Sir, you may say what you like about your fellow countryman, though as he is your host and it is his champagne you are drinking, I should have thought common decency demanded some restraint. But I would have you know that Mr Sherlock Holmes is not my master, he is my close and trusted friend, and I will greatly resent any further slurs on his character.'

He frowned and said, 'Is the truth then a slur in England?'

'On the contrary, sir. It is our lodestone,' I declared.

'Then let us without quarrelling about slurs accept this truth,' he said. 'The count has used your friend's reputation to help secure his own, and by his presence here today, Mr Holmes seems to confirm the close connection.'

I naturally resented the implication but when I peered back into the room and saw how Holmes, like all the others, seemed to be hanging on every word the count said as he described the course of his investigation, I began to wonder whether my friend's recent nervous debility had temporarily impaired his fine judgement.

This was the tale that we heard.

The murder had been committed early on the last day of August in the Montesecco *palazzo* on the Via di Monserrato. At eleven o' clock in the morning a terrible scream ('like the sound of a pig being butchered,' averred the maid, Susi, who came from country stock) was heard throughout the palace, bringing all who heard it rushing towards its apparent source on the first floor. Here they found Giuseppe Strepponi struggling to force open the door of Count Leonardo's study, which seemed to be locked on the inside. Rosi, the majordomo, was one of the first on the scene. He quickly produced his set of household keys, unlocked the door and he and Strepponi burst in to discover the count lying across his desk with his throat cut from ear to ear. The weapon, still lying on the desk, appeared to be an ornamental dagger honed to a razor edge, which the count used as a paper knife. Strepponi attempted to administer first aid, but it was far too late and the only significant result of his efforts was to cover himself with blood. Dr Provenzale was summoned and he confirmed what was evident to all present, that the old count was dead. The authorities were informed and Captain Zardi began his investigation.

Zardi, a laconic man with an upright military bearing, here took up the story. The key to the study was found on a marble plinth supporting a statue of Marcus Aurelius just inside the door. The central of the three windows was wide open and on the sill was the print of a bloody hand. The window opened onto the inner court of the palace, which was laid out as a formal garden. Up the wall grew an ancient vine, its thick, gnarled branches easily capable of bearing a man's weight.

From the courtyard garden there were many doorways and passages providing a wide choice of exits. Zardi immediately ordered a thorough search of the palace, but no fugitive was found, nor could any of the inmates recall seeing any stranger on the premises that morning.

Zardi now questioned Strepponi, who told him that the count had sent him away when he reported for duty at his usual time of ten a.m., saying that he would not require his services for another hour at least, as he was expecting his lawyer, Randone. Strepponi retired to his room on the upper floor. At five to eleven he came down and was just approaching the study door when he heard the scream from within. He rushed forward and tried to enter but found the door locked. He could hear sounds of movement from within but of course by the time Rosi arrived and unlocked the door, the room was empty, save for the dying old man.

Now Zardi applied all his energy to discovering who the visitor might have been. Everyone in the household had to account for his or her movements and very few of them, even among the servants, could produce witnesses to their movements in the half hour before the death. Only the young count, who had been with Signorina Medioli in the chamber immediately below his uncle's study, had a real alibi. On hearing the scream, he had rushed upstairs just in time to see his uncle dying in Strepponi's arms.

'I was naturally too stricken with grief for rational thought in the first hours after this tragic loss,' he said gravely. 'But once the flood tide of emotion had begun to ebb and I started to examine my new responsibilities as head of an ancient family, I knew that first and most urgent among them was to track down and deliver to punishment this foul assassin. I put myself, my wealth and my little store of wisdom at Captain Zardi's disposal. Naturally as a professional officer of the law, he received my offer of help courteously but coldly.'

He smiled at the captain, who gave a somewhat ambiguous shrug.

'But when I told him that I was a student of and in close correspondence with the famous Sherlock Holmes, whose services the experts of Scotland Yard are not ashamed to call upon, he showed the other side of his professionalism and immediately admitted me to the penetralia of his thought.'

'No fool, is he?' murmured Chiari in my ear. 'He learned quickly from your friend's experience that there is little advantage to be gained from making the police look like idiots!'

'You assume a great knowledge of Mr Holmes's mind,' I said frostily.

'Only what I have learned from your books,' he retorted. 'Listen and you will see how the count can triumph without appearing triumphant.'

'Captain Zardi had done all the groundwork,' said Montesecco modestly. 'All I was able to bring to the investigation were the reflexions of a quiet mind and a burning personal desire to see my dear uncle avenged. First I examined closely what it was that the captain had found outside and beneath the study window. This was most significant.'

He paused and right on cue, reminding me of myself, Holmes said, 'And what did these findings consist of?'

Montesecco paused for a perfectly judged beat of time, then, with a casual drama worthy of Holmes himself, said, 'Nothing. Absolutely nothing.'

Holmes nodded in approval.

'And of course you asked yourself, could a bloodstained man have climbed down the vine without leaving some traces on the leaves?'

'Precisely.'

'Perhaps he jumped,' said Holmes.

'There was no sign of anyone having landed on the ground with the kind of force such a leap would have entailed,' said the count. 'Also you will recall that I myself was in the room below with la Signorina Medioli. I am sure that one or both of us would have noticed the sudden descent of a human form past our window.'

'A fair deduction,' admitted Holmes. 'So where did your reasoning take you next, Count?'

'When you have eliminated the impossible, whatever remains, however improbable, must be the truth,' said this young pup with a nod in Holmes's direction which ackowledged the source of the maxim to those who already knew it without admitting it wasn't his own coining to those who didn't. 'If the murderer cannot have escaped via the window, then he must still have been in the room.'

'But the room was empty save for the murdered man.'

'On the contrary. From their own testimony, Rosi here and Strepponi did not pause on the threshold and take a quiet stock of what they saw. No, they rushed straight into the study. My uncle was dying but not yet dead. Rosi reached him first—is that not so, Serge?'

'Yes, Count,' said the majordomo. 'I flung open the door and for a moment we stood frozen on the threshold. There, silhouetted in the bright beam of sunlight which poured through the open window sat your uncle, the old count, his lifeblood streaming from his throat. Now I rushed forward with Strepponi close behind, and as I stood over your uncle, debating how best to proceed, the monstrous assassin pushed by me and took his victim in his arms, cradling his head on his chest and calling to me to summon the physician.'

It was clearly a speech he had made many times. I could imagine how very boring his friends and family probably found it after such frequent repetition!

Montesecco smiled at him approvingly and said, 'So you see, Mr Holmes, given that a man is not murdered until he is dead, there were two others in the study with the murdered man.'

This seemed to me so much chop-logic but Holmes appeared rapt.

'Continue, Count,' he said. 'This is quite fascinating.'

'See how the good teacher shares in his pupil's progress,' murmured Chiari.

'I suggest you wait a little,' I said with more confidence than I felt. 'The jails of England are filled with men who believed they could read the direction of Holmes's thought.'

'So. A miracle worker. And when he says, "That is the man!" are there any who quarrel?'

246

'It would take a very foolish or a very brilliant man to dispute the reasoning of Sherlock Holmes,' I said with some fervour.

'Such a reputation is like the Gorgon's gaze. You must be careful where you turn it,' he said enigmatically.

There was no time to examine his point. Montesecco was reaching the climax of his tale.

'I spoke to the doctor now and asked him if a man would scream after he had his throat cut. The doctor said he thought it unlikely that in such a circumstance a man would be able to produce the kind of noise that was heard throughout the household. I then examined the handle of the door on the outside and found traces of blood there. My suspicions were now thoroughly roused. I examined the key found by the statue of Marcus Aurelius and sure enough there were dried flakes of blood on it also. I asked myself if a man who had just committed a murder in the course of which his victim had screamed so loud that the alarm must have been raised would have been so composed that he would rush to the door, lock it, and place the key carefully where it was found, before escaping. Surely, even if he did have the presence of mind to lock the door, he would have left the key in the lock?'

'Perhaps,' objected Holmes, 'the door was locked before rather than after the murder.'

Montesecco looked at Holmes with just the expression of long-suffering exasperation I have seen on my friend's face when some plodding policeman is slow to take a point.

'Then why should there be blood on the key?' he said. 'No, everything was leading to the sole explanation which took account of all the facts. Question: why was there blood on the key? Answer: because the murderer had touched it after the murder. Question: why was there blood on the outer door handle? Answer: the same, because the murderer had touched it after the murder. Question: who had let out the terrible scream which roused the house? Answer: the murderer! You see his ingenuity. Strepponi, having slain my uncle, sees that his hands and cuffs are covered with blood. He rushes to the window, leaving a print there, then realising that it is going to be almost impossible to escape by that route undetected, he goes instead to the door, unlocks it, checks to be sure there is no one close outside, steps out, locks the door behind him, lets out that terrible scream, and starts rattling the door handle as if he is desperate to get in. Rosi appears, unlocks the door and rushes in. Behind him, Strepponi places the key by the statue, then rushes to his victim and takes him in his arms, partly to give himself a reason for being covered in blood, partly to prevent anyone else administering any aid which might have delayed my uncle's death. I immediately placed my findings in the hands of Captain Zardi, who then performed his duties with the vigour for which he is renowned.'

'Again, the sop to Cerberus,' murmured Chiari.

The captain nodded his appreciation and said in his bluff military manner, 'I meanwhile had interviewed all present in the palace, including Signor Randone, who told me he had just arrived for his appointment with the old count.'

'And I could not see how Strepponi should have imagined my appointment was earlier in view of the fact that it was arranged by himself in conjunction with my clerk,' interposed the lawyer.

'With this in mind, and after due consideration of the Count Montesecco's investigations,' resumed Zardi, 'I took the suspected man, Strepponi, into custody and searched his room. There I found correspondence of a threatening nature from Giulio Tebaldo, a well-known usurer, requiring immediate repayment of a large loan. When confronted, Strepponi admitted he had gone deeply into debt in order to purchase gifts for a certain lady with whom he had become deeply infatuated but without his feelings being reciprocated. Tebaldo, when interviewed, admitted that the evening prior to the murder he had sent a messenger round to talk to Strepponi. By messenger I understood him to mean thug. The messenger had returned with some items of jewellery on account, and a promise that Strepponi would be in a position to repay the balance within twenty-four hours.'

'And do we know the name of this lady?' enquired Holmes.

There was a silence. Then Claudia Medioli said, 'It was I. At first it was amusing, then he became a nuisance. Of course I returned his gifts but he kept sending more.'

'And did you tell your friend, the count?'

'No,' she said, her fine brown eyes downcast. 'His sense of honour would have required that he secured Strepponi's dismissal from his uncle's service. I was weak, and wished the young man no ill. How I wish now that I had spoken earlier!'

She wiped away a tear. Beside me, Chiari snorted derisively.

The count touched her arm comfortingly, then said, 'So now we had a motive. Strepponi approached my uncle for money. My uncle was a kind man, but he despised any weakling who let himself fall into the hands of the usurers.'

'Can't have had much time for his nephew, then,' muttered Chiari.

'But if my uncle could not help him living, Strepponi knew he could help him dead. In his will there was a generous legacy, token of my uncle's misplaced regard and more than enough to help him from his present troubles. Strepponi denied knowing of this, but Signor Randone was able to confirm that a copy of the will lay among my uncle's papers to which Strepponi as secretary had ready access. Perhaps my uncle in his disgust now threatened to remove him from his will.'

'This is possible,' said Randone. 'It was on a matter of his will that the old count had summoned me to see him.'

Montesecco frowned a little at this interruption, then resumed, 'So this egregious villain, finding himself in a desperate situation, did not hesitate to put his own security above the life of his noble benefactor, and slew him like a dog.'

There was a moment's pause, during which all the company save Holmes, myself and Endo Chiari showed signs of deep emotion. In some cases it looked likely to have burst out in the kind of loud lamentation these Latins are prone to, had it not been interrupted by a huge cry, half-welcoming, half-contumelious, from the mob in the square. Instantly all the guests crowded out onto the balcony, which creaked and groaned so much that I felt there was a real risk that we would all be precipitated to join the crowd below.

The cause of the uproar was the approach to the scaffold of a tightly bunched squad of foot soldiers, bayonets flashing in the wintry sunlight. In their midst, crouched low as if to conceal himself from the noisy mob, was a thin, shaven-headed man with a furtive, frightened expression whom at first I took to be the condemned prisoner.

'Why is he not manacled?' I enquired of Chiari.

The journalist laughed and said, 'You are mistaken, my friend. This is not Strepponi. This is the executioner who is held in such low esteem by the common people that they would subject him to his own foul craft if he dared appear without his armed guard.'

I glanced at my pocket watch. It gave ten minutes to the appointed hour. Could it be that in this matter alone, the Italians were untypically punctual?

Someone coughed. A small sound against the chatter of the guests and the tumult from the mob below as the executioner ascended his deadly machine. But it reduced all those on the balcony to silence as I had seen it reduce many other assemblages to silence during our long association, and every eye turned towards Sherlock Holmes.

'My dear count,' he said. 'My felicitations. To solve any murder requires the keenest of intellects, the finest of judgements. To solve a case with which you personally are so closely and painfully involved requires a dedication and a will almost superhuman.'

There was another huge roar from the crowd, mingled with a fanfare of trumpets. In the square the officers mounted their horses and unsheathed their sabres. The hundred or so foot soldiers lounging around seized their arms, fixed bayonets and cleared the corridor from the church, which in the relaxed atmosphere of the previous hour had been encroached upon by strolling pedestrians and pedlars of sweetmeats and cigar merchants. Then the bay of the mob suddenly declined to a single mighty gasp of superstitious awe, and many of them sank on one knee as out of the church emerged a macabre procession of priest and monks, some carrying banners, others, reliquaries, with at their centre two who bore above their cowled heads a huge, brightly painted crucifix on which hung an effigy of Christ, all draped in black hessian.

Holmes continued as if there had been no disturbance.

'Our art, Count, as you so clearly understand, is to select the single truth out of a wide array of erroneous possibilities, to refine what might be into what is. Above all we must not let ourselves be diverted from our purpose. A lesser man might for instance have wondered why, if Strepponi knew the lawyer's appointment was for eleven, he chose to include that particular lie in his story.

250

Or why, having had all of his expensive gifts returned from the *signorina,* he did not return them whence they came, getting the most part of his money refunded and thus clearing his debts. A lesser man, needing to confirm to himself that the death cry could not have emanated from the dying man, might have wasted his and the doctor's time by checking whether in cutting the jugular vein, the killer had struck so deep as to sever the vocal cords also. . . . '

He glanced interrogatively at Dr Provenzale, who looked confused.

'I presume also,' continued Holmes, 'that it was possible to tell from the direction of the death stroke whether the murderer was right or left handed . . . '

Another glance at Provenzale, another look of confusion.

' . . . and of course this information will no doubt have been cross-checked with the handedness of any suspected person.'

Outside there was another huge roar and all the kneeling spectators were back on their feet, craning to glimpse the last and most important player to arrive on this ghastly stage. As Holmes's long-time companion it has been my fate to see many murderers, so I know better than most that there is no distinguishing mark. But the pale-faced, slim, handsome young man who walked with his head held high at the centre of a squad of armed soldiers looked as little like one of the breed as any I have seen.

Chiari spoke, sounding puzzled.

'It seems to me, Mr Holmes, you are suggesting that perhaps the murderer might indeed have been in the locked room and made his escape through the open window as we all thought in the beginning.'

'Good lord, no,' said Holmes indignantly. 'How could I suggest such a thing when the count has proved it impossible? To climb down the vine without leaving traces of blood on the foliage defies belief. And while it might be argued that a man could leap down onto the hard-baked earth without leaving an impression, fortunately the count himself, and Signorina Medioli, were in the room below. And still more fortunately, despite the fact that the full blast of the sun's heat must have been on their window (for was

251

it not pouring directly into the study above?), they had broken with the custom of the country and had the protective shutters wide open.'

I saw several of the journalists exchange speculative glances at this juncture. What was Holmes up to? I wondered.

'And the blood on the key? And on the outer door handle?' said Chiari eagerly. 'Are you equally well persuaded of the accuracy of your pupil's deductions?'

'Naturally. That any other of the people entering the room in the hustle and bustle of those dreadful minutes after the discovery might have unknowingly become stained with the old count's blood and inadvertently transferred it to either the key or the handle is a possibility incapable of proof and therefore to be discounted.'

'That it is incapable of proof surely means it is also incapable of disproof,' said Chiari.

'Come, come, Signor Chiari, one pupil among your countrymen is quite enough for me to take on at a time,' murmured Holmes.

Below, a huge cheer signalled that the condemned man had successfully negotiated the perilous ladder to the scaffold platform. The black-draped Christ had been brought to a halt directly before him and his eyes were steadfastly fixed on the effigy. To a non-Papist it seems a tasteless pantomime, but I found myself praying it brought the young man some comfort.

'So you have no doubt that this poor fellow about to lose his head is guilty?' demanded Chiari.

'His guilt is between his judge on earth, who is here with us, and his judge in heaven, who I also believe is here with us,' said Holmes solemnly. 'All we can know for certain is that a good man on the brink of a new life with the lady of his choice has suffered a most terrible wrong which not only deprived him of his future happiness but also robbed the son he perhaps hoped to have of a name and a role, perhaps even of a country.'

Suddenly everyone was looking at Signora Masina, who was flushing tremendously while her sister was staring at Holmes with pale anger.

'But happily no act however foul is without good as well as evil consequences, and this particular deed has brought earlier than was dreamt possible a new, young heir to his title and fortune with many years ahead in which to prove how much he merits them.'

He bowed towards the count, who looked uncertain how he should react to this somewhat ambiguous compliment. But he was saved the trouble of reply by a deathly silence falling on the square, which drew all our attention as much as the previous noise.

Strepponi was kneeling beneath the knife. His head rested in a hole in a cross plank. Another plank with a matching half circle removed from it was fitted over his neck. A priest made the sign of the cross over him. The executioner bent to a lever. And the next moment with a rattle like the passage of a metal-rimmed wheel over a cobbled street, the knife descended and the severed head fell forward into a leather basket. From this the executioner plucked it and, holding it by the hair, displayed it to the mob, prior to fixing it on a pole to be left as a target for the crows and a warning to the criminals of this great city.

It was all over in a few seconds and immediately the crowd began to disperse, save for some morbid souls eager to take a closer look at the headless body.

Our party all streamed back from the balcony to the room where fresh bottles of champagne awaited. Signora Masina and her sister did not pause but left immediately. I saw the judge and Zardi and Falcone and the doctor in a close group, deep in conversation. The count and Signorina Medioli stood close together but exchanged no words. And all the journalists were crowding around Sherlock Holmes, who raised his hand to command silence and said, 'Gentlemen, please. You have your own Italian Sherlock Holmes to question. And in Signor Chiari I believe you may have your own Italian Dr Watson to chronicle his exploits.'

He smiled at Chiari, who glanced at me with an expression eloquent of apology, then turned back to Holmes, who pulled on his cloak and said, 'As for me, I am too fatigued to talk. And besides, my good friend Watson and I have a train to catch.'

This was the first I had heard of this and at first I took it for a mere excuse to make a rapid departure. But half an hour later, with scarcely time to draw a breath let alone use one in idle conversation, I found myself seated in plush comfort in one of the most ornately decorated railway coaches I had ever seen, rattling northwards out of Rome.

'But our luggage, Holmes!' I had gasped as I was hurried aboard.

'All taken care of,' he said with that air of knowing far more of things than I do which I find so insufferable. I determined not to feed his complacence by asking questions about our travel plans. Instead as we relaxed and lit our pipes, I turned back to our morning's adventure, about which I was still greatly curious.

'Holmes, what you implied, most ungallantly I may observe, about the Signora Masina, that she was . . . *enceinte*, do you believe it true?'

'I should have thought a medical man could tell at a glance,' he replied. 'Sixteen to twenty weeks, I should have said.'

'And you believe this to have been the old count's child?'

'I would hope so. But no need to worry about her. She is going to America, where no doubt she will be presented as a grieving widow. And I do not doubt the new count has been most generous in making a settlement to take care of the upbringing of his bastard nephew.'

'Who would, if the old count had lived to marry, have been the legitimate heir,' I said slowly.

'Indeed,' said Holmes.

'And it is almost entirely as a result of young Montesecco's investigation including the evidence of his own *inamorata* that Giuseppe Strepponi was condemned?'

'Evidently.'

'Holmes,' I said, horrified. 'What have we done?'

'Explain yourself, my dear chap,' he said, affecting puzzlement.

'Everything you said towards the end of our visit seemed to me to imply a possible refutation of the count's logic. Now you seem to be suggesting that he more than anyone had an excellent motive for killing his uncle.'

'I cannot argue with you there,' said Holmes complacently.

'Then how can it not trouble you that even as you made your comments, that poor young fellow, Strepponi, was being hauled up onto a scaffold and executed within your very sight?'

Now Holmes threw back his head and laughed, a sound which

would have struck me as callous had it been emitted by any other man.

'My dear Watson, rest easy. I cannot say how much the unfortunate secretary may have been egged on to the murder by his connection with Claudia Medioli. That is for Zardi and perhaps the Roman press to discover. But I can assure you that Strepponi was guilty, and probably commited the crime very much as the count worked out.'

'But how can you be sure after the way you undermined his deductions?'

'Oh, never doubt it, his *deductions* deserved to be undermined, but his *conclusion* was I believe correct. Partly because, (a) he probably knew that Strepponi was the killer from the start, and (b) if it had not been correct, he would not have dared involve me. But principally because the execution took place on time.'

'I'm sorry, I don't understand. I know these Latins are sadly deficient in their timekeeping, but I do not see how you draw such a remarkable conclusion from a single instance of punctuality!'

'Then you must learn to understand as well as pity and patronise these poor benighted foreigners, Watson. To these Romans, death by execution for no matter how foul a crime does not mean eternal punishment for the criminal. No, even the vilest creature may, after serving his time in Purgatory, be admitted to the grace of God, which passeth all understanding, even mine. But not if he goes to his death unconfessed and unshriven. Wherefore the young man Strepponi was taken into the church of San Cassiano on his way to the scaffold. Had he refused to make his confession, the execution would have been delayed until sunset, so determined are these merciful priests that the condemned man should have every chance of grace. So when the execution of one who was reputed to be a devout young man takes place on time, it may be assumed that he has made a full and free confession of his guilt.'

'And had he not confessed?'

'Then the case would have been altered,' said Holmes grimly. 'So a guilty man has been sent to his Maker. All that I wished to ensure was that this mountebank of a would-be detective should not be able by misuse of my reputation to send other, perhaps less guilty men to their dooms. I believe there are at least two already languishing in jail as a result of his so-called deductions. I trust once our friend Chiari, and some of the other pressmen also, have their say, these will be released, and any other attempt by the count to interfere with justice will be greeted by indignation and derision!'

'Holmes, you are a marvel,' I said. 'And not the least marvellous thing is that we should be sitting on this train heading heaven knows where.'

'Why, where else should a man head at this time of year but home?' my friend replied. 'We shall travel nonstop across the face of Europe and not stop until we are safe in Baker Street. I have telegraphed Mrs Hudson that we are coming, so, though you may eat it late, you will not after all be deprived of her famous goose, which I know you value so much.'

'But, Holmes,' I said. 'Nonstop, you say? How may that be?'

'Because this is a Special,' he said.

'A Special? All the way to England? But that must be costing us a king's ransom!' I said alarmed.

'Possibly. Fortunately we have a king, or one who will be a king, to pay for it. It is not our Special but His Royal Highness, the Prince of Wales. You may recall I was able to do him a trifling foolish service some years ago, and he said if ever he could be of use to me, I had only to let him know. Hearing that he was at Ostia, and guessing that he would not disoblige Her Majesty, his mama, by spending the whole of Christmas out of the country, I telegraphed him via the embassy. He is not the man to forget a promise. So rouse yourself, Watson. We are to take lunch with the prince in half an hour, and I hardly think you will want to appear looking like a municipal rat catcher! One thing you may neglect to take with you, however.'

'What's that?' I asked.

'That infernal notebook of yours. This part of the tale you will not be able to tell for a hundred years!'

The Christmas Client

Edward D. Hoch

It was on Christmas Day of the year 1888, when I was in residence with Mr. Sherlock Holmes at his Baker Street lodgings, that our restful holiday was interrupted by the arrival of a most unusual client. Mrs. Hudson had already invited us to partake of her goose later in the day, and when we heard her on the stair I assumed she was coming to inform us of the time for dinner. Instead, she brought a surprising announcement.

"A gentleman to see Mr. Holmes."

"On Christmas Day?" I was aghast at such a thoughtless interruption, and immediately put down my copy of the *Christmas Annual* I'd been perusing. Holmes, seated in his chair by the fireplace, seemed more curious than irritated.

"My dear Watson, if someone seeks our help on Christmas Day it must be a matter of extreme urgency—either that, or the poor soul is so lonely this day he has no one else to turn to. Please send him up, Mrs. Hudson."

Our visitor proved to be a handsome man with a somewhat youthful face, though his long white hair and the lines of his neck told me he was most likely in his mid-fifties. He was a little under six feet tall, but slight of build, with his fresh face giving the impression of extreme cleanliness. Holmes greeted him with a gentle handshake. "Our Christmas greetings to you, sir. I am Sherlock Holmes and this is my dear friend Dr. Watson."

The man shook my hand too and spoke in a soft voice. "Charles Lutwidge Dodgson. I am pleased to meet you, sir, and I-I thank you for taking the time to see me on this most festive of days."

As he spoke I detected a slight stammer that trembled his upper lip as he spoke. "Please be seated," Holmes said, and he chose the armchair between the two of us. "Now tell us what brought you out on Christmas Day. Certainly it must be a matter of extreme urgency to keep you from conducting the Christmas service at Christ Church up in Oxford."

Our slender visitor seemed taken aback by his words. "Do you know me, sir? Has my infamy spread this far?"

Sherlock Holmes smiled. "I know nothing about you, Mr. Dodgson, other than that you are a minister and most likely a mathematician at Oxford's Christ Church College, that you are a writer, that you are unmarried, and that you have had an unpleasant experience since arriving in London earlier today."

"Are you a wizard?" Dodgson asked, his composure shaken. I had seen Holmes astonish visitors many times, but I still enjoyed the sight of it.

Holmes, for his part, casually reached for his pipe and tobacco. "Only a close observer of my fellow man, sir. Extending from your waistcoat pocket I can see a small pamphlet on which the author's name is given as Reverend Charles Dodgson, Christ Church. Along with it is a return ticket to Oxford. Surely if you had come down to London before today the ticket would not still be carried in such a haphazard manner. Also on the front of your pamphlet I note certain advanced mathematical equations jotted down in pencil, no doubt during the train journey from Oxford. It is not the usual manner of passing time unless one is interested in mathematics as a profession. Since you have only one return ticket, I presume you came alone, and what married man would dare to leave his wife on Christmas Day?"

"What about the unpleasant experience?" I reminded Holmes.

"You will note, Watson, that the knees of our visitor's pants are scraped and dirty. He would certainly have noticed them on the train ride and brushed them off. Therefore it appears he fell or was thrown to his knees since his arrival in London."

"You're correct in virtually everything, Mr. Holmes," Charles Dodgson told him. "I left the mathematics faculty at Oxford seven years ago but I-I continue to reside at Christ Church College, my alma mater."

"And what brought you to London this day?"

Dodgson took a deep breath. "You must understand that I tell you this in the utmost confidence. What I am about to say is highly embarrassing to me, though I swear to you I am innocent of an-any moral wrong."

"Go on," Holmes urged, lighting his pipe.

"I am being blackmailed." He paused for a moment after speaking the words, as if he expected some shocked reaction from Holmes or myself. When he got none he continued. "Some years ago, when the art was just beginning, I took up photography. I was especially fond of camera portraits, of adults and children. I-I liked to pose young girls in various costumes. With the permission of their parents I sometimes did nude studies." His voice had dropped to barely a whisper now, and I noticed that his frozen smile was slightly askew.

"My God, Dodgson!" I exclaimed before I could help myself.

He seemed not to hear me, since he was turned toward Holmes. I wondered if his hearing might be impaired. Holmes, puffing on his pipe as if he'd just been presented with a vexing puzzle, asked, "Was this after you had taken holy orders?"

"I sometimes use 'Reverend' before my name but I am only a deacon. I nev-never went on to holy orders because my speech defect makes it difficult for me to preach. Some-sometimes it's worse than this. I also have some deafness in one ear."

"Tell me about the pictures. How old were the girls?"

"They were usually prepubescent. I took the photographs in all innocence, you-you must realize that. I photographed adults, too, people like Ellen Terry and Tennyson and Rossetti."

"With their clothes on, I trust," said Holmes with a slight smile.

"I know what I did was viewed with distaste by many of my acquaintances," our white-haired visitor said. "For that reason I abandoned photography some eight years ago."

"Then what is the reason for this blackmail?"

"I must go back to 1879, when I published my mathematical treatise *Euclid and His Modern Rivals*. Although the general public paid

259

it little heed, I was pleased that it caused something of a stir in mathematical circles. One of the men who contacted me at the time was a professor who held the mathematical chair at one of our smaller universities. We became casual friends and he learned of my photographic interests. Later, af-after I'd ceased my photography, he apparently did some picture taking of his own. I was at the beach in Brighton this past summer when I met a lovely little girl. We chatted for a time and I asked if she wouldn't like to go wading in the surf. I carried some safety pins with me and I used them to pin up her skirt so she co-could wade without getting it wet."

I could restrain myself no longer. "This is perversion you speak of! These innocent children—"

"I swear to you I did nothing wrong!" he insisted. "But some-how this former friend arranged to have me photographed in the very act of pinning up the little girl's skirt. Now he is using these pictures to blackmail me."

"What brought you to London today," Holmes asked, "and what unpleasantness brought you here to seek my help?"

"The professor contacted me some months ago with his threats and blackmail. He demanded a large sum of money in return for those pictures taken at the beach."

"And what made him believe that a retired mathematics instruc-tor, even at Oxford, would have a large sum of money?"

"I have ha-had some success with my writing. It has not made me wealthy, but I live comfortably."

"Was your Euclid treatise that successful?" Holmes chided.

"Certain of my other writings . . ." He seemed reluctant to con-tinue.

"What happened today?"

"The professor demanded that I meet him here at Paddington Station, with one hundred quid. I came down from Oxford on the noon train as instructed, but he was not at the station to meet me. Instead I was assaulted by a beggar, who pushed me down in the street after handing me an odd message of some sort."

"Did you report this to the police?"

"How could I? My rep-reputation—"

"So you came here?"

"I was at my wit's end. I knew of your reputation and I hoped you could help me. This man has me in his clutches. He will drain me of my money and destroy my reputation as well."

"Pray tell me the name of this blackmailer," Holmes said, picking up a pencil.

"It is Moriarty—Professor James Moriarty."

Sherlock Holmes put down his pencil and smiled slightly. "I think I will be able to help you, Reverend Dodgson."

It was then that Mrs. Hudson interrupted us with word that the Christmas goose would be served in thirty minutes. We were welcome to come down earlier if we liked, to partake of some holiday sherry. Holmes introduced her to Dodgson and then a remarkable event occurred. She stared at him through her spectacles and repeated his name to be sure she'd heard it correctly. "Reverend Charles Dodgson?"

"That's correct."

"It would be a pleasure if you joined us, too. There is enough food for four."

Holmes and I exchanged glances. Mrs. Hudson had never even conversed with a visitor before, to say nothing of inviting one to dinner. Still, it was Christmas Day and perhaps she was only being hospitable.

While she escorted Dodgson downstairs, I whispered to Holmes, "What's this about Moriarty? You spoke of him earlier this year in connection with the Valley of Fear affair."

"I did indeed, Watson. If he is Dodgson's blackmailer, I welcome the opportunity to challenge him once again."

We said nothing of our visitor's problems during dinner. Mrs. Hudson entertained him with accounts of her young nieces and their occasional visits to Baker Street. "I read to them often," she said, gesturing toward a small shelf of children's books she maintained for such occasions. "All children should be exposed to good books."

"I couldn't agree more," Dodgson replied.

As we were finishing our mince pie and Mrs. Hudson was busy clearing the table, Holmes returned to the subject that had brought Dodgson to us. "If you and Professor Moriarty were casual friends, what caused this recent enmity between you?"

261

"It was the book, I suppose. Moriarty's most celebrated volume of pure mathematics is *The Dynamics of an Asteroid*. When I followed it with my own somewhat humorous effort, *The Dynamics of a Particle*, he believed the satire was aimed at him. I tried to explain that it dealt with an Oxford subject, a contest between Gladstone and Gathorne Hardy, but he would have none of it. From then on, he seemed to be seeking ways to destroy me."

Holmes finished the last of his pie. "Excellent, Mrs. Hudson, excellent! Your cooking is a delight!"

"Thank you, Mr. Holmes." She retreated to the kitchen while he took out his pipe but did not light it.

"Tell me about this cryptic message you alluded to earlier."

"I can do better than that." He reached into his pocket and produced a folded piece of paper. "This is what the beggar gave me. When I tried to stop him he knocked me down and escaped."

Holmes read the message twice before passing the paper to me:

On Benjamin Caunt's day,
Beneath his lofty face,
A ransom you must pay,
To cancel your disgrace.

Come by there at one,
On Mad Hatter's clock.
The Old Lady's done,
And gone 'neath the block.

"It makes no sense, Holmes," was my initial reaction. "It's just some childish verse, and not a very good one."

"I can make nothing of it," Dodgson admitted. "Who is Benjamin Ca-Caunt?"

"He was a prizefighter," Holmes remarked. "I remember hearing my father speak of him." He puzzled over the message. "From what I know of Moriarty, it would be in character for him to reveal everything in this verse, and challenge us to decipher it."

"What of Caunt's lofty face?" I asked.

"It could be a statue or a portrait in a high place. His day could

262

be the day of his birth, or of some special triumph, or perhaps the day of his death? I have nothing about the man in my files upstairs, and it will be two days before the libraries are open."

"And what is this about the Mad Hatter?" I inquired.

Mrs. Hudson had returned from the kitchen at that moment and heard my question. "My niece prefers the March Hare, Mr. Dodgson," she told him. "But then little girls usually like soft, furry animals." She walked over to the little bookshelf and took out a slender volume. "See? Here is my copy of your book. I have the other one, too."

She held a copy of *Alice in Wonderland*.

Holmes put a hand to his forehead, as if pained by his failure. "My mind must be elsewhere today. Of course! You are the author of *Alice* and *Through the Looking Glass* under the pseudonym of Lewis Carroll!"

Charles Dodgson smiled slightly. "It seems to be an open secret, though it is something I neither confirm nor deny."

"This puts a whole new light on the affair," said Holmes, laying down his pipe and turning to Mrs. Hudson. "Thank you for refreshing my memory." He looked again at the message.

I puzzled over it myself before turning once again to our client. "Moriarty must know of your writing, since he makes reference to the Mad Hatter."

"Of course he knows. But what does the message mean?"

"I believe you should remain in the city overnight," Holmes told him. "All may come clear tomorrow."

"Why is that?"

"The message speaks of Benjamin Caunt's Day, and he was a prizefighter—a boxer. Tomorrow, of course, is Boxing Day."

Charles Dodgson shook his head in amazement. "That is something worthy of the Mad Hatter himself!"

Mrs. Hudson found an unoccupied room in which Dodgson spent the night. In the morning I knocked at his door and invited him to join us for breakfast. Holmes had spent much of the night awake in his chair, poring over his books and files, studying maps of the city and lists of various sorts. Dodgson immediately asked if he had discovered anything, but my friend's answer was bleak. "Not a thing, sir! I can find no statue in all of London erected to the boxer Benjamin Caunt, nor is there any special portrait of him. Certainly there is none in a lofty position as the verse implies."

"Then what am I to do?"

"The entire matter seems most odd. You have the blackmail money on your person. Why did not this beggar simply take it, instead of giving you a further message?"

"It's Moriarty's doing," Dodgson insisted. "He wants to humiliate me."

"From my limited knowledge of the good professor, he is more interested in financial gain than in humiliation." Holmes reached for another of his several guidebooks to the city and began paging through it.

"Have you ever met Moriarty?" our visitor asked.

"Not yet," Holmes responded. "But someday—Hello, what's this?" His eyes had fallen upon something in the book he'd been skimming.

"A portrait of Caunt?"

"Better than that. This guidebook states that our best-known tower bell, Big Ben, may have been named after Benjamin Caunt, who was a famous boxer in 1858, when the bell was cast at the Whitechapel Foundry. Other books attribute the name Big Ben to Sir Benjamin Hall, chief commissioner of the works. The truth is of no matter. What does matter is that Big Ben, the clock, certainly does have a lofty face looking out over Parliament and the Thames."

"Then he is to meet Moriarty at one o'clock today—Boxing Day—beneath Big Ben," I said. At last it was becoming clear to me.

But Charles Dodgson was not so certain. "The Mad Hatter's clock, meaning the watch he carried in his pocket, told the day of the month but not the time."

Sherlock Holmes smiled. "I bow to your superior knowledge of *Alice in Wonderland*."

"But where does that leave us?" I asked, pouring myself another cup of breakfast tea. "The number one in the message must refer to a time rather than a date. Surely you are not to wait until New Year's Day to pay this blackmail when the first line speaks of Benjamin Caunt's day. It has to be Boxing Day!"

"Agreed," Holmes said. "I suggest we three travel to Big Ben and see what awaits us at one o'clock."

The day was pleasant enough, with even a few traces of sunshine breaking through the familiar winter clouds. A bit of snow the previous week had long since melted, and the day's temperature was hovering in the low forties. We took a cab to Westminster Abbey, just across the street from our destination, and joined the holiday strollers out enjoying the good weather.

"There's no sign of anyone waiting," I observed as we walked toward Westminster Bridge.

Holmes's eyes were like a hawk's as he scanned the passersby. "It is only five to the hour, Watson. But I suggest, Mr. Dodgson, that you walk a bit ahead of us. If no one attempts to intercept you by the time you reach the bridge, pause for a moment and then walk back this way."

"Do you have a description of Moriarty?" I asked as Dodgson walked ahead of us as instructed.

"He will not come himself. It will be one of his hirelings, and all the more dangerous for that."

"What should we look for?"

He seemed to remember the poem. "An old lady, Watson."

But there was no old lady alone, no one who paused as if waiting for someone, or attempted to approach Charles Dodgson. He had reached the bridge and started back along the sidewalk, stepping around a small boy who was chalking a rough design on the sidewalk.

It was Holmes whose curiosity was aroused. As the boy finished his drawing and ran off, he paused to study it. "What do you make of this, Watson?"

I saw nothing but a crude circle drawn in chalk, with clocklike numbers running around the inner rim from one to thirty-one. An arrow seemed pointed at the number twenty-six, the day's date.

"Surely no more than a child's drawing," I said.

Dodgson had returned to join us and when he saw the chalked design he gave a start of surprise. "It's the Mad Hatter's watch, with dates instead of the time. Who drew this?"

"A young lad," said Holmes. "No doubt paid and instructed by Moriarty. He'll be blocks away by now."

"But what does it mean?" Dodgson asked.

" 'Come by there at one, on Mad Hatter's clock,' " Holmes quoted from memory. "There is no time on the clock, only dates. The phrase 'on Mad Hatter's clock' must be taken literally. You must stand on the chalk drawing of the clock."

Dodgson did as he was told, attracting the puzzled glances of passersby. "Now what?"

It was I who noticed the box about the size of my medical bag, carefully wrapped and resting against the wall to the east of the Big Ben tower."What's this?" I asked, stooping to pick it up. "Perhaps they're your pictures."

"Watson!"

It was Holmes who shouted as I began to unwrap the box. He was at my side in a flash, yanking it from my grasp just as I was about to open it. "What is it, Holmes?"

"One o'clock!" he yelled as the great bell above our heads tolled the hour. He ran several steps and hurled the box with all his strength toward the river. He had a strong arm, but his throw was a good deal short of the water when the box exploded in a blinding flash and a roar like a cannon.

Two strollers near Westminster Bridge had been slightly injured by the blast and all of us were shaken. Within minutes police were everywhere, and somehow I was not even surprised when our old friend Inspector Lestrade of Scotland Yard arrived on the scene about fifteen minutes later.

"Ah, Mr. Holmes, they said you were involved in this. I was hoping for a peaceful holiday."

"The Christmas box held an infernal machine," Holmes told him, having recovered his composure. "I glimpsed a clock and some sticks of dynamite before I hurled it away. It was set to go off at one o'clock, exactly the time that Mr. Dodgson here had been lured to Big Ben."

Lestrade, lean and ferretlike as always, stepped forward to brush a speck of dirt from my coat. "And, Dr. Watson, I trust you weren't injured in this business."

"I'm all right," I answered gruffly. "Mr. Dodgson here was the target of the attack, or so we believe."

People were clustered around, and it was obvious Lestrade was anxious to get us away from there. "Come, come, here is a police carriage. Let us adjourn to my office at Scotland Yard and get to the bottom of this matter."

I was concerned for Charles Dodgson, who seemed to have been in a state of shock since the explosion. "Why should he want to kill me?" he kept asking. "I was willing to pay him his hundred quid."

"Professor Moriarty is after bigger game than a hundred quid," Holmes assured him.

"But what?"

The police carriage was pulling away as Lestrade shouted instructions to the driver. Holmes peered at the vast number of bobbies and horse-drawn police vehicles attracted by the explosion. "You have a great many men out here on a holiday."

"It's Big Ben, Mr. Holmes—one of London's sacred institutions! We don't take this lightly. It could be some revolutionary group behind it."

"I doubt that," Holmes responded with a smile.

He said no more until we had reached the dingy offices at Scotland Yard. "Our new building will be ready soon," Lestrade informed us a bit apologetically. "Now let us get down to business."

Charles Dodgson told his story somewhat haltingly, explaining how he'd come to Holmes on Christmas Day after being roughed up at Paddington Station. He tried to treat the episodes with the young girls with some delicacy, but Lestrade gnawed away at the story until he grasped the full picture. "You are being blackmailed!" he said with a start. "This should have been reported to the Oxford police at once."

"More easily said than done," the white-haired man responded. "A hundred is not a bad price to save my reputation and my honor."

It was here that Sherlock Holmes interrupted. "Surely, Lestrade, you must see that the plot against Mr. Dodgson is merely a diversion, a red herring. And if it is a diversion, why cannot the bomb at Big Ben also be a diversion?"

"What are you saying?"

"We must return to Moriarty's cryptic message. All has been explained except the final two lines: 'The Old Lady's done / And gone 'neath the block.' "

"A nonsense rhyme," Dodgson insisted. "Nothing more."

"But your own nonsense rhymes usually have a meaning," Holmes pointed out. "I admit to a sparse knowledge of your work, but I know a great deal about London crime. I ask you, Lestrade, which Old Lady could the verse refer to?"

"I have no idea, Holmes."

"Robbing an old lady would be akin to blackmailing a retired Oxford professor. Unless it was a particular old lady."

Lestrade's face drained of blood. "You can't mean"—his voice dropped to a whisper—"Queen Victoria!"

"No, no, I refer to the playwright Sheridan's quaint phrase, *The Old Lady of Threadneedle Street.*"

Lestrade and I spoke the words in the same breath. "The Bank of England!"

"Quite so." Holmes said. "The Big Ben bombing brought out virtually all the police on duty today. The financial district, closed for the holiday in any event, is virtually unguarded. I would guess that at this very moment Moriarty's men are looting the Bank of England and escaping back through their tunnel *'neath the block.*"

"My God!" Dodgson exclaimed. "Is such a thing possible?"

"Not only possible, but probable for Professor Moriarty. Lestrade, if you will bring me a large-scale map of the area, I will show you exactly where to find this tunnel."

"If you do that," said Dodgson, "you are truly a wizard."

"Hardly," Holmes said with a smile. "If you are tunneling under a street between buildings, you naturally would choose the shortest route."

Less than an hour later, while I watched with Holmes and Dodgson from a safe distance, Lestrade's men took the tunneling bank robbers without a struggle. Moriarty, unfortunately, was not among them.

"One day, Watson," Holmes said with confidence. "One day we will meet. In any event, Mr. Dodgson, I believe your troubles are over. All this blackmail business was a sham, and now that you have made a clean slate of it to the authorities there is nothing to be gained by blackmail."

"I cannot thank you enough, sir," the white-haired author said. "What do I owe you for your services?"

"Consider it a Christmas gift," Holmes announced with a wave of his hand. "Now, if I am not mistaken, you have just time to catch the next train back to Oxford. Let us escort you to Paddington Station and wish you an uneventful journey home."

THE ADVENTURE OF THE ANGEL'S TRUMPET

Carolyn Wheat, ASH

"Really, Watson," Sherlock Holmes exclaimed in a deprecating tone as he peered over my shoulder, "the affair you have chosen to chronicle can scarcely be termed an adventure. I did little more than sit in a drafty courtroom listening to an interminable series of lies. Indeed," he went on, "my brother Mycroft could have solved the case perfectly well without ever leaving his chair at the Diogenes Club."

"But, Holmes," I protested, "without your presence in the case, an innocent young woman would surely have hanged. And the fact that you managed to clear her name even though you were not called in until the eleventh hour is the most remarkable fact of all. Surely such circumstances qualify as an adventure of a particularly intellectual sort."

"Perhaps you are right," my friend agreed with a sigh. "I fancy I played a small part in the satisfactory outcome of the affair of the angel's trumpet. And the case itself was not without points of interest and even of instruction."

The events that precipitated Miss Charmian Carstairs's trial for the murder of her grandfather began in December and culminated in the week in which Christmas festivities were at their height. During that time, Holmes and I were engaged in a most delicate business on the Sussex downs; we knew little of the events which would later catapult my friend into one of the most bizarre cases of his distinguished career. Thus it was not until some six months had passed and the young lady stood in the dock facing a charge of murder that the affair thrust itself onto his consciousness.

"Yes, Watson, you are correct," Holmes remarked, seemingly apropos of nothing. My friend and fellow lodger lounged upon the sofa in an attitude of extreme languor, wearing his purple dressing gown and smoking a pipeful of the most unpleasantly aromatic tobacco ever imported from Virginia. I had lately finished reading the morning papers, which lay scattered at my feet.

"It is a terrible business," he went on, speaking in low, drawling tones, as if the very formation of words were too much for him, "this murder of a grandfather by his newly discovered granddaughter. One would think the natural bonds of filial piety would overcome even the most mercenary motives, and yet we see the young woman in the dock."

"But, Holmes," I protested, "I have said nothing concerning the case in question. How ever did you know I was contemplating that horrible business?"

"You had lately put down the morning paper, which carries a very full if only marginally accurate account of the affair. You then directed your gaze at the miniature of your own grandfather, which reposes upon the secretary. You proceeded to heave a sigh. Surely the meanest intelligence could ascertain that you were thinking of the Carstairs case and wondering how any grandchild could be so unnatural."

"Yes," I admitted. It seemed absurdly simple now that Holmes had explained the reasoning behind his remark. "It appears a wholly cut-and-dried affair, does it not? There appears no room for doubt that Charmian Carstairs poisoned her grandfather immediately upon being informed that she was to be his sole heir."

"No room for doubt indeed, Watson, and yet I fancy the barrister defending Miss Carstairs will exert himself to the utmost to obtain an acquittal."

"Mr. O'Bannion is celebrated for his eloquence," I remarked. "Some call him the Great Defender."

"He is equally well known," my friend amended, with a touch of acerbity, "as 'that confounded Irishman.' "

I have seldom attempted to duplicate my amazing friend's ability to deduce facts from the most insignificant of details, but I attempted a foray into such a deduction on this occasion. "You have had dealings with Mr. O'Bannion, I take it."

"Excellent, Watson," Holmes replied. "I have not wasted my talents on your education after all. Yes," he continued, his face becoming grave, "I had the misfortune to be in the witness box when Mr. O'Bannion was counsel for the defense. I gave my evidence in a most straightforward and logical manner, while he proceeded to twist and obfuscate and generally obscure the truth. In the end, he was responsible for the acquittal of the most accomplished jewel thief in London."

"Well," I replied stoutly, "he will have his work cut out for him if he intends to do the same for Miss Carstairs."

The doorbell rang. As it was still quite early in the morning, I raised an inquiring eyebrow. "A client, at this hour?"

"Pray instruct Mrs. Hudson to send the visitor away, no matter what his name or how urgent his errand," Holmes said in a voice that brooked no disagreement. "I have worked night and day for the past fortnight and am disinclined to exert myself on another case at the moment."

Mrs. Hudson led the visitor into the room. His curly brick red hair and humorous face marked him an Irishman; his severely cut black coat and trousers marked him a professional man.

"Mr. Holmes," the visitor began, "you must help me. A young lady's life depends upon it."

"And you are . . . ," I inquired, drawing myself up and glaring at the man who would command my friend's services without so much as stating his name.

"Why, Watson," Holmes cried, "I cannot believe your obtuseness. Surely you recognize our visitor from the accounts you have lately read in the *Globe-Dispatch*. For he is none other than the legal pettifogger who succeeded against all reason in convincing a jury of twelve good men and true to disregard my testimony, the man who held me up to ridicule before that same jury, the man who holds the fate of Charmian Carstairs in his dishonest hands."

The Irishman bowed as if Holmes's words were the most fulsome compliments. He smiled broadly and finished the introduction.

"Kevin O'Bannion, at your service, sir," the Irishman said, turning his attention to me. There was but a hint of brogue in his speech; he had taken a first at Oxford and could speak when he chose with an accent worthy of the Archbishop of Canterbury.

"At my service, indeed," Holmes scoffed. He waved the visitor away with a petulant hand. "Pray remove yourself from my doorstep at the earliest opportunity, Mr. O'Bannion. I have neither the time nor the inclination to bandy words with you."

"I've not come here to bandy words, Mr. Holmes," the barrister cried, his florid face reddening. "My visit here is a matter of life and death to the young woman I have the honor to represent."

"Life and death, indeed," Holmes replied. He jumped from the sofa with remarkable agility for someone who had appeared so lacking in energy, and stood before the fire, rubbing his hands. "Your client will most assuredly hang if she is convicted of murdering Sir Wilfred."

"Mr. Holmes, she is innocent," O'Bannion replied. He placed a large hand over his heart and repeated the words in thrilling tones that would have done justice to an organ. "She is innocent, sir, as God is my witness."

"Well," Holmes replied briskly, "that must make a nice change from your usual clientele."

The Irishman's ruddy face fell with comic swiftness. "You must help me, Mr. Holmes. Only you can unravel this tangled skein of evidence and help me prove that Miss Carstairs did not poison her grandfather."

"You seek my help?" Holmes inquired in a tone of injured acerbity. "You seek the help of a man you described to a British jury as 'an interfering, meddling amateur?' "

O'Bannion had the grace to blush. As he was very fair of skin, the blush was a deep rose that suffused his entire face. Although he dressed like a Regency dandy, his features and build were those of a common hod carrier.

"Mr. Holmes, I beg of you," he said earnestly, "do not refuse Miss Carstairs the aid she requires because of ill feeling between us."

Holmes raised a single eyebrow. "Ill feeling? Do you think permitting a criminal to go free rouses in my breast nothing more significant than ill feeling, sir?"

The Irishman waved away Holmes's words and said, "Come, Mr. Holmes, all I ask is that you and Dr. Watson attend the trial and listen to the evidence. I confess I can make nothing of it that will help my client, and yet I am convinced that she did not poison her grandfather."

"She is the sole beneficiary of her grandfather's will," Holmes pointed out. "He had but lately altered that will in her favor, disinheriting his other relations. She alone had the motive to poison Sir Wilfred."

"Mr. Holmes," the barrister proclaimed, "I would stake my not inconsiderable reputation on the fact that that pure, sweet angel did nothing of the kind."

It did not require the powers of a Sherlock Holmes to deduce that the celebrated barrister had fallen victim to the spell of the fairer sex. I found myself looking forward to meeting the object of O'Bannion's admiration.

Holmes knotted his brow in thought. "I will admit," he said at last, "the case presents some features which are not entirely devoid of interest."

"But, Holmes," I cried, "the trial begins this very morning. How is it possible to conduct a proper investigation six months after the murder?"

"There is, I fear, no question of an investigation, Dr. Watson," the Irishman explained with an air of apology. "I daresay I should have sought your assistance sooner, but only now do I realize the overwhelming extent of the evidence against my client. I urge you to come to court and hear the testimony, to suggest lines of questioning I may pursue on cross-examination, and to assist me in conveying to the jurors a true explanation of the baffling events that occurred on the night of December twenty-second last."

"Do you mean to suggest," I inquired, my breast swelling with indignation on my friend's behalf, "that Holmes investigate this crime six months after it has occurred, with no opportunity to visit the scene of the crime or to interrogate witnesses directly?"

O'Bannion had the grace to look abashed. "I agree the case is a difficult one," he began, "but under the circumstances—"

"Difficult?" I repeated. "It is more than merely difficult, man. It is impossible!"

Holmes turned his attention from the fire; for the first time since the unsatisfactory conclusion to the curious affair of the Cypriot banker and the seven pug dogs, the light of battle gleamed in his dark eyes.

"Impossible, Watson?" he echoed. "Surely nothing is impossible where human intelligence is applied."

Less than an hour later Holmes and I sat in a drafty room in Holloway Prison. Seated across from us at the plain wooden table was a spirited young woman with glossy black hair and speaking gray eyes. She wore a shapeless gray smock and was without adornment of any kind, yet her face was as exotically lovely as a tropical flower growing against all odds in an English garden.

"Miss Carstairs," Holmes began, "I have agreed to place my small talents at the disposal of your attorney." He nodded at O'Bannion, who stood in a corner, arms folded, having agreed with bad grace to remain in the background while Holmes questioned his client. "But before I undertake to examine the evidence against you, I wish to hear your story from your own lips."

The young woman nodded. "It is a story well known to the newspaper-reading public by this time, I believe," she said, "but I will recount it as briefly as I can."

Her voice was low and well modulated, marred only by her American accent, which tended to flatten the vowels and elide some of the consonants. "I was born in California," she began, "but my father came from England. He was the son of the late Sir Wilfred Carstairs, but he and my grandfather quarreled, so he immigrated to America when he was a young man. He traveled extensively and held a great number of jobs in the West. Sowing his wild oats, Mother always used to say."

"Your mother was an American?" Holmes inquired.

Miss Carstairs nodded. "Her people were French," she explained. "Her name was Madeleine Duclos, and her father owned a vineyard in the Sonoma Valley. When my father married her, he went to work for Grand-père in the winery. Papa was very fond of growing things, and became great friends with Mr. Burbank in Santa Rosa."

The expression on Holmes's face was one of disappointment. "Then your father had nothing to do with gold mining?" he inquired. We had but lately made the acquaintance of a lady from San Francisco named Hatty Doran, and Holmes had been quite taken with her accounts of claim jumping in the American West.

"Really, Mr. Holmes," Miss Carstairs replied with evident amusement, "you have formed the most outlandish ideas about my homeland. I live in a fertile valley studded with lovely little towns and crisscrossed by farms and vineyards. There may be gold in the mountains," she went on, "but for us the gold is on the vines. California will someday produce the best wines in the world."

Holmes said nothing to this extraordinary boast, but a quirk of his mouth indicated serious doubts about the young lady's knowledge of vintage wines.

The dark Mediterranean eyes took on a faraway cast. "I miss my home," she said with a simplicity that touched me deeply. "I miss the scent of redwood trees at night. I miss the sunshine gleaming off the grapevines. I miss the blue skies and the cool mornings and the misty fog between the hills. I don't know how you can bear to live in this damp, gloomy place—but then, of course, you have never seen California."

As the only place on earth that might be considered damper and gloomier than England was Kevin O'Bannion's native land, I doubted the Irishman's evident infatuation with his client would bear fruit unless the man was willing to consider expatriation.

"Your father never renewed contact with his family, Miss Carstairs?" Holmes asked, bringing the conversation back to the terrible events of December 22.

The young woman shook her head. "No," she replied sadly. "It was the dearest wish of his life that he would someday be recon-

275

ciled with his father. Indeed, he talked of it often, particularly during the Christmas season. He told me all about the grand Christmas feast his family prepared every year. All the servants and tenants would be invited into the dining hall, where glasses of wine would be poured and a toast drunk."

The girl's face glowed when she talked of her father. "Papa loved California," she said, "but he was always a little bit melancholy at Christmastime. He wished more than anything else for a real English Christmas like the ones he'd known as a child."

"Your father did not live to fulfill this wish," Holmes said with deliberate bluntness.

Charmian Carstairs shook her head. "My parents died when their carriage plunged off a narrow road into a canyon near our home," she explained.

"When your parents died, you wrote to Sir Wilfred," Holmes continued. His elbows rested on the scarred table between us and the young lady; his slender fingers were steepled. "Pray tell me what made you do that."

"I thought my grandfather should know that his son was dead," the American said. "And I was curious. I wanted to know my father's family in the same way I knew my mother's. I suppose I was searching for a part of myself."

"Sir Wilfred's reply to your letter included an invitation to visit him in London," Holmes prompted.

"Yes," the young woman replied. "I was to stay a month, through the Christmas holidays."

"It would appear you and your grandfather became quite fond of each other," remarked Holmes.

The pale face lit with pleasure. "Oh, yes, Mr. Holmes," she said with enthusiasm. "We took to each other at once. He loved hearing me talk about Mr. Burbank's work and about the interesting plants we have in California. And I enjoyed spending time in the conservatory with him."

"You brought him several treasures from your native land," Holmes said. "That was most kind of you."

"I brought dates and dried figs and walnuts—I could not bring fresh fruit, of course. And I brought cuttings and seeds from Mr. Burbank."

"There were seeds from the plant known as 'angel's trumpet,' were there not?"

The young woman nodded. "Its botanical name is *Datura sacra*. It is, strictly speaking, not a native of California. It was introduced from Mexico, and it is very showy. The blossoms are quite large and they hang from the branches like great golden trumpets. Grandfather particularly requested that I bring him seeds so that he could grow his own angel's trumpet in his conservatory."

I entered the conversation for the first time. "The seeds are quite poisonous," I remarked. "Were you aware of that fact when you brought them from America?"

"Of course," she replied. "Any competent horticulturist knows the properties of the plants she works with. Angel's trumpet is related to jimsonweed and nightshade. The entire plant is toxic, but the seeds are particularly so."

Holmes turned to the barrister and explained, "The toxicity of *Datura sacra*, commonly known as sacred datura, results from the presence of the alkaloids hyoscyamine, atropine, and scopolamine."

O'Bannion nodded. "The celebrated Dr. Hopgood is expected to testify for the prosecution," he replied glumly. "I do not anticipate that his testimony will be favorable to the defense."

"He is England's premier toxicologist," I remarked. "I shall be quite interested in what he has to say."

"The symptoms of datura poisoning are particularly horrible," Holmes remarked, in a manner that might have been considered callous by one who did not know him. "The sufferer feels a dryness of mouth and a great thirst. The skin reddens, the pupils dilate. The patient suffers hallucinations and disturbed vision. The pulse races, the patient grows increasingly delirious and may appear insane. The final stages involve convulsions and then coma and death."

The young lady's face paled; she swayed slightly, but did not flinch. "Mr. Holmes," O'Bannion cried, abandoning his post in the corner and rushing to his client's side, "kindly remember that you are speaking to a lady."

The lady in question was made of sterner stuff than her defense counsel believed; she waved away his protests and said in a calm tone, "Indeed, the plant is called *Datura sacra* because the natives of Mexico use it in their rituals. Taken in minute quantities, it produces visions. Taken in larger quantities, it produces death."

"It is a horrible way to die," I remarked.

"It is a death no man should endure," Holmes replied. His eyes remained fixed on Charmian Carstairs's beautiful, exotic face.

"It is a death I did not cause," the young lady said with calm firmness.

"And yet you profited from it," Holmes persisted. "You were your grandfather's sole heir, and you were aware of that fact because the late Sir Wilfred announced the change in his will to all at the dinner table the night before he died."

"He said something of the kind, but I didn't believe he really meant to do it," she protested. "I thought if I talked to him, he might change his mind. I had no need of his money; my father left me well off and my *grand-père* in California promised me a share in the family vineyard as my dowry when I marry. So I had no need of Grandfather Carstairs's money, and I was sorry to see the true heirs cut out of the will."

"Were you, Miss Carstairs?" Holmes asked with palpable disbelief. "Had Miss Letitia Carstairs and Mr. Cyril Carstairs been so good to you that you felt obliged to intercede on their behalf?"

"No, on the contrary, they were horrid to me, as you well know," she replied with a show of that spirit one associates with the daughters of the former colonies. "Miss Carstairs referred to me as 'a baggage' and Mr. Carstairs called me an 'Amazon from an uncivilized country.' But they had lived with Grandfather for years and had expectations of him, and I didn't think it was right for them to be left with nothing."

"But before you could discuss the matter with your grandfather, he died by poisoning," Holmes retorted. His tone was so palpably skeptical as to border on the offensive. O'Bannion, who stood next to his client in an attitude of protectiveness, bristled but remained silent.

"Yes, but I had nothing to do with his death!" the young woman cried. Tears sprang into her eyes; she turned her face away and said, "If you do not believe me, then leave me alone to face my fate in the courtroom. I can endure this questioning no longer."

"Mr. Holmes, this is enough!" the barrister cried. "I did not invite you here to badger my client but to help her."

"And what of the box, Miss Carstairs?" Holmes inquired with deadly gentleness. His eyes bored into Charmian Carstairs's face; he ignored totally the indignant Irishman.

"What then of the box and the things it contained?"

The lovely oval face paled and the large, dark eyes widened as the young woman gazed earnestly into my friend's face. "As God is my witness, Mr. Holmes," she said in a low, thrilling voice, "I knew nothing of that box, nothing at all."

"And yet you brought it to your grandfather," Holmes persisted.

"I brought it," the young lady whispered at last. "I brought it, but I was ignorant of its contents. I did not know what that box contained until the morning my grandfather's body was discovered in the study. And even now, Mr. Holmes," she continued, her eyes pleading for understanding, "even now that I know what items were in the box, I still do not know what they mean."

"And what of the legend on the box itself?" Holmes persisted. "What of the letters O.G.D., which appeared on the cover? What do they signify?"

The Irishman could stand it no longer. He drew himself up and signaled his client to say nothing. "Mr. Holmes," he said in ringing tones that resonated through the bare room, "it is clear from your cross-questioning technique that the bar lost a valuable asset when you chose to exercise your talents elsewhere. You would have made a fine prosecuting counsel. But the fact remains that my client will have to answer such questions as Sir Bartholomew Anders chooses to put to her when she testifies in court. I will not have her subject to cross-examination twice."

Once again, O'Bannion's client refused to shield herself behind her defender's skirts. "I had never seen the box before," she explained. "I found it among my father's effects, along with a letter indicating his desire to send the box to his father should they ever reconcile. And so I brought it when I came from America." She drew a ragged breath. "Please, Mr. Holmes," she begged, "find the meaning of the things in the box and I have no doubt you will find the person who killed my grandfather. But as God is my witness, I did not know, Mr. Holmes. And I did not kill my poor grandfather, whom I had grown to love very much."

"Not the most promising of defenses, Mr. O'Bannion," Holmes commented as we stepped into the misty spring air after leaving the prison.

O'Bannion said nothing, but his expressive face indicated a profound gloom. "Mr. Holmes," he said in a tone heavy with irony, "I thank you for a most instructive morning. I now feel the case against my client is even more daunting than I believed before I enlisted your aid."

He stepped into the street and raised his hand as a signal to passing cabdrivers. Holmes followed; the three of us piled into a hansom.

"You need not continue with this case," O'Bannion said, "since it is obvious you have no belief in my client's innocence of the charges against her."

"My beliefs signify nothing," Holmes replied in a mild tone. "It is the evidence and the evidence alone which should be examined. I have every intention of continuing with this case, and of hearing that evidence from the mouths of the witnesses."

The Irishman appeared less than pleased by this intelligence, but he instructed the driver to take us to the Old Bailey with all possible speed.

The first witness for the prosecution was our old friend Lestrade. He took the oath with an air of pompous determination, as if to say he was a plain man who would speak plain truth no matter what questions fancy Irish lawyers might think up to ask him.

Sir Bartholomew Anders, an impressive figure in his silk gown and immaculate white wig, elicited from Lestrade the particulars of his career in the Metropolitan Police Force. He then asked Lestrade to elaborate upon his part in the events of December 22 last.

"I was called," Lestrade said, warming to his subject under the prosecutor's friendly interrogation, "to the house of Sir Wilfred Carstairs by the butler, who said his master had been locked in his library since the night before. I proceeded to assist the butler in opening the door, which had been locked from the inside."

There was a stirring in the crowd at these words; next to me, a man leaned over and murmured something, then pointed a bony finger at the prisoner in the dock. Charmian Carstairs stood still as a statue, dressed in her plain prison gown, regarding the events in the courtroom with a detached air, as if watching the trial as a mere spectator.

"When we succeeded in opening the door," Lestrade continued, "I saw the body of Sir Wilfred lying on the floor beside his desk. He appeared to have died in a horrible convulsion," the inspector intoned, "and so I arranged for a doctor to be sent for. The doctor said it looked like poison, so I instructed the servants to give an account of the events of the night before, with particular emphasis upon what was eaten and drunk in that house."

Beside me on the hard pew of the first row of spectators, Holmes leaned forward intently. He seemed to make a mental inventory of the testimony, and nodded with satisfaction when Lestrade stated, "In the opinion of the chief toxicologist, the poison was administered in a cup which sat on a small table next to Sir Wilfred's desk."

The cup itself sat on a corner of the table used by the prosecuting attorney. It was a large silver cup of medieval design, almost a chalice, of a type rarely seen in our modern age. But Charmian Carstairs had spoken of an old-fashioned Christmas with ceremonial toasts; perhaps this cup was a family heirloom used to drink the health of the season.

Lestrade was permitted, over O'Bannion's vigorous objection, to testify that the means of death was a little-known plant poison whose Latin name was *Datura sacra*.

"And was there a time when the seeds of the datura were found in the house where Sir Wilfred died?" the prosecuting counsel inquired. He directed his gaze at the prisoner as he spoke, as if silently accusing her with his eyes.

"I obtained a warrant and searched the whole house from top to bottom," Lestrade replied. "In the bedroom occupied by the accused I found a box containing datura seeds along with a note and a picture," he went on.

Holmes pulled a small notebook from his pocket and sat poised to take notes; there had been speculation regarding the contents of the mysterious box in the newspapers, but none of the accounts had contained a definitive list of the items therein.

Crown Counsel handed Lestrade a piece of paper; he identified it as the note he'd found in the box in Charmian Carstairs's room. It was marked and entered into evidence; Lestrade was asked to read its contents into the record.

The tension in the courtroom was palpable. Lestrade held the piece of paper in his hand and in ringing tones read the words thereon: "When the angel's trumpet sounds, then shall you cross the abyss."

There was no sound in the crowded courtroom; all who heard the words were struck by their ominous intent. Sir Wilfred Carstairs had ingested those poisonous seeds and he had indeed "crossed the abyss" from life to death.

"And the picture?" Sir Bartholomew persisted. "Can you describe for the jury the picture you also found in the box that contained the seeds and the note?"

"It was of the Last Trump," Lestrade said. He shifted in the witness box; he had been standing for the past half hour.

Beside me, Holmes drew in a sharp breath. "I must see that picture," he muttered. "And the note as well."

"It showed the Archangel Michael," Lestrade explained, "blowing a golden trumpet and summoning the souls of the dead to judgement. Under the picture was the single word: Judgement."

Once again all eyes in the courtroom turned to Charmian Carstairs. Once again, she stood immobile as a marble effigy, her beautiful, exotic face expressionless.

The picture was marked and entered as well, then passed among the jurors. One or two of them handled the small rectangle and passed it along, but most looked up from the pasteboard to the young woman in the dock, shaking their heads as if in no doubt as to her guilt.

Charmian Carstairs claimed to have no knowledge of the items in the box she had carried from California, but to the jurors, as to everyone else in the courtroom, the contents of the box signified a day of reckoning for past wrongs. And the young woman on trial was the daughter of a man disinherited by his father, a man who might well have imbued his child with the desire for revenge and instructed her in the means to take her grandfather's life.

At a signal from Holmes, O'Bannion rose and requested a recess. It was granted; within moments we sat in a small paneled conference room with the barrister, who paced the floor with ill-concealed impatience.

"I must see the picture in question," Holmes began. O'Bannion nodded and dispatched an assistant to fetch it. "And I have questions I should like answered."

"Have you an idea, Mr. Holmes?" the Irishman asked with an almost pathetic eagerness. "Have you discerned a pattern in this seemingly incomprehensible testimony?"

"I have a glimmer," Holmes replied. "I feel it is imperative to know the exact contents of Sir Wilfred's study. Were there objects besides the fatal cup on the small table next to the desk? And what lay upon the desk itself? Was there a book, and if there was, what did it contain?"

O'Bannion drew in a long breath and regarded Holmes as one might a dangerous animal. "Mr. Holmes," he began, "the putting of questions to a witness on cross-examination is considered an art in my profession. One does not ask questions in order to obtain information, particularly information which may be detrimental to one's client."

"Mr. O'Bannion, I assure you," Holmes replied, his tone grave, "the answers to these questions could be vital to the discovery of the truth."

"The truth?" O'Bannion's voice rose in disbelief and his words took on the rhythms of his native land. "Is it the truth you're after wanting, Mr. Holmes?" He pulled a white handkerchief from the sleeve of his gown and mopped his brow. "It was a dark day indeed when I sought help at your door, Mr. Holmes," he muttered. "The truth, is it? God help me and my poor young lady now."

The assistant returned with the picture of the Last Judgment. Holmes studied it; I looked over his shoulder. It was an ordinary picture, with bright colors and crude lettering.

"I hadn't realized the late Sir Wilfred was a Roman Catholic," I remarked, hoping to hear a word or two of praise from Holmes for my deduction. The picture was not one a worshiper of the

Church of England would have carried in his Book of Common Prayer.

Holmes grunted. "This card is no relic of the Church," he replied, his tone grim.

"Do you recognize it, then?" I asked.

"Is it important?" O'Bannion demanded.

"It is of the utmost importance," my friend replied. "Indeed, its significance cannot be overstated."

The butler, Reginald Bateson, was the next to testify. He attested to the fact that there had been a small, intimate gathering at Sir Wilfred's house on the evening of December 21. In celebration of the Christmas season, a toast had been drunk, with Sir Wilfred raising the medieval cup to his lips. The house had been decked with holly and ivy; it was truly the old-fashioned English Christmas Charmian Carstairs had been promised.

On cross-examination, O'Bannion asked the butler about the curious items on the table next to Sir Wilfred's desk.

"A queer lot, they were, that's certain," the butler replied. "There was a sword that usually hung over the mantelpiece, along with a stick and the drinking cup and a gold coin."

"Let us," O'Bannion suggested, "take these items one by one, shall we. Please tell the jury about the sword, Mr. Bateson."

Crown Counsel objected, but His Lordship permitted the question. The butler puffed himself up like a turkey cock and proceeded to satisfy the court's curiosity.

"It was a family heirloom," he explained. "A sword from the time of Cromwell, it was. Hung over the mantelpiece from the time I first came into service, it did. And the day after Sir Wilfred died, there it was on the table with the other items."

"And the stick?" O'Bannion continued.

"A walking stick," the butler stated. "A plain staff, such as a man might take on a tramp through the woods. Brought from the country, I daresay, though I'd never seen it before that morning."

"Can you describe the cup, Mr. Bateson?"

"Old-fashioned, it was," replied the butler. "Like something out of the Middle Ages. A heavy metal cup with no handle. Never seen the like myself, but there it was on the table with the other things, plain as day."

"Please tell us about the coin," O'Bannion urged.

"Well, now, I'm not altogether certain it was a coin," the man said, shaking his head. Next to me, Holmes leaned forward in the pew, his eyes alight.

"What do you mean by that?" O'Bannion asked. There was a slight frown between his eyes. "It was either a coin or it wasn't, Mr. Bateson."

"I mean it wasn't money, not proper English money, any road," the butler retorted. "It was gold, right enough, just like a sovereign, but no picture of our queen on it. Just a queer design, a star, like."

Holmes leaned forward in his place with a suddenness that had one of the bailiffs rushing toward him. He held up a warning hand, then pulled a piece of paper out of his breast pocket and scribbled a note. He handed the note to the bailiff and pointed toward O'Bannion. The attendant took the note and walked to counsel table.

O'Bannion had all but finished his questions, but he read the note and raised his eyes to the bench. "If I might ask one more question, Your Lordship?" he asked.

His Lordship glared, but nodded assent. "Very well, Mr. O'Bannion."

"How many points did the star have, Mr. Bateson?"

The butler frowned. "It had five points. Five, but there was something queer about the star. It was crooked-like."

O'Bannion thanked the witness, but it was clear to me he had no idea what the man had said that was important. Yet next to me, Holmes nodded and smiled as if he'd just heard the name of the true murderer.

The next witness was the deceased's nephew, a foppish young man who claimed to have taken his uncle's change of will with equanimity.

"Where there's life, there's hope," Cyril Carstairs said jauntily. "He couldn't very well change his mind and put me back into the will once he was dead, now could he?"

285

Holmes stirred in his seat, then stood and made for the door. I followed.

"We must visit the house where Sir Wilfred died," Holmes insisted. "I cannot confirm my hypotheses without a glimpse of the study where the events took place."

"But, Holmes," I protested, "we shall miss the testimony."

"That young man knows less than Miss Carstairs about what happened," Holmes replied with some acerbity. "No, Watson, we shall do our client more good by going to that house than we could by any other means."

Sir Wilfred's London house was a large, airy Georgian mansion situated near Green Park. In the absence of the butler, the door was opened by a housekeeper, who invited us to enter. Holmes asked to be directed to the library; the housekeeper inclined her head and led us along the hallway in silence.

The library was crammed with leather-bound volumes, some of which looked to be of great antiquity. Holmes ran his slender fingers along the leather bindings. Then he gave a cry and pulled a volume from the shelves. "Here it is," he cried, brandishing it aloft in triumph. "I knew I should find it. We must take it to O'Bannion at once."

"What is it, Holmes?" I asked. "What single book could possibly explain these bizarre events?"

"It is called *The Book of Thoth*," Holmes replied. "It was written by a man called Aleister Crowley, and it is the bible of an organization known as the Order of the Golden Dawn."

"O.G.D.," I said, repeating the letters on the cover of the box Charmian Carstairs had brought from America. "Then O.G.D. stands for Order of the Golden Dawn. But what is this order, and how is it connected with the murder of Sir Wilfred?"

"It has nothing whatever to do with his murder," Holmes answered, "but it has everything to do with his death."

There was a japanned box on top of the desk, next to an elaborately decorated inkwell with a design on it of a cross with a rose in the center. Holmes opened the box and drew out a square object wrapped in black silk. He lifted the silk away with a flourish and revealed an oversized pack of cards.

"I hadn't realized Sir Wilfred was a gambler," I said. "Perhaps he was murdered by someone to whom he owed money."

"These are not playing cards, Watson," my friend said. He turned over the deck; instead of ordinary suits and numbers, these pasteboards were painted with bizarre designs. The one Holmes showed me was of a man hanging upside down, a golden aureole around his head. It was a grotesque image, but its horror was soon surpassed by the other images Holmes revealed in the deck: a man lying facedown with ten swords sticking out of his back; a woman with a blindfold holding two crossed swords; a tower struck by lightning. The most unnerving card of all portrayed Death on a black horse.

"What do you think you are doing here?" an imperious voice said. I looked up, startled, to see a formidable woman standing in the doorway. She was of an age with the late Sir Wilfred, and the way she bore herself told me she must be the deceased's sister.

"Miss Carstairs," Holmes began, "I must apologize for presuming to enter your brother's study. I had thought you were attending the trial, or I should have begged your housekeeper to make you aware of my presence."

"If you had, Mr. Holmes," the old woman replied stiffly, "I should have had her deny you access. My home is not a place where riffraff may come whenever it pleases to satisfy its curiosity."

"I am here for a far different purpose than that, Miss Carstairs, as you must suspect if you know my name," Holmes replied in a tone that might almost have been called gentle. "I am in search of evidence that will support the defense contention that your grand-niece did not murder your brother."

The old woman sniffed. "Then you have come on a fool's errand, Mr. Holmes, for no such evidence exists. That girl killed my poor brother and no amount of fiddling by that Irishman is going to help her escape the fate she so richly deserves. She will die on the gallows, Mr. Holmes, and justice will finally be served."

"You did not approve of your brother's change in his will, did you, Miss Carstairs?"

"I make no secret of the fact that I considered my brother besotted on the subject of his granddaughter," the woman announced. "She had no manners whatsoever, no pretense to gentility. I sincerely hoped my brother would recover from his infatuation with this uncivilized young woman who was the product of the most ill-advised union two people ever entered into."

"What about the gathering on the night your brother died, Miss Carstairs?" Holmes inquired, changing the subject with an abruptness that caught me by surprise. "You were the hostess, I believe."

"It was a gathering in honor of the season," the lady replied dismissively.

"Yes, but which season were you celebrating, Miss Carstairs?" Holmes persisted.

"I do not know to what you are referring, Mr. Holmes," the woman replied, but there was a spark of fear in her eyes.

"I refer to the season," Holmes said. "I refer to the reason for your gathering. I refer to the night upon which your brother died. It was a celebration, and the house was decorated with the traditional holly and ivy, but was it in point of fact a celebration of Christmas?"

The old woman raised a trembling hand to her throat; she fingered a brooch which fastened her collar. In the center of the brooch was a rose, and in the center of the rose, a small cross. The design was similar to the one on her brother's inkstand.

"You will leave my home at once," she said in a shaking voice, "or I will summon the police."

"I shall leave, madam," Holmes answered with a bow, "but I shall take with me this book and these cards, for they are vital pieces of evidence that must be laid before the court without delay."

"There are one or two points to which I should like to draw your attention," Holmes said. We sat in the small paneled conference room, the japanned box and *The Book of Thoth* resting on the table between us.

"I should be grateful if you did, Mr. Holmes," the barrister replied, "for a less promising series of accounts I have seldom encountered."

"Have you ever heard of the Order of the Golden Dawn?" Holmes asked. O'Bannion shook his head; it was clear he was as much at sea as I myself.

"It is a branch of the Rosicrucian sect," Holmes went on. I parsed out the meaning of this new term, and a chill went through me as I realized Rosicrucian meant "rose cross." I remembered the brooch the elder Miss Carstairs had worn at her throat, and the strange design on Sir Wilfred's inkwell. Both were variations on the theme of cross and rose.

"The Order of the Golden Dawn, which is an offshoot of the Rosicrucians, bases its belief system upon the Tarot. Those were the cards we found in Sir Wilfred's desk, Watson."

"And the curious items on the table, Holmes?" I cried. "What can they have to do with this strange business?"

Holmes set the deck of gaily painted cards on the table and spread them in a fan-shaped array. He reached in and pulled one out, then held it up for us to inspect.

The card showed a young man wearing a red robe, holding one hand aloft and standing before a table. On the table were four items: a stick, a sword, a chalice, and a coin.

I shivered; the table in Sir Wilfred's study was an exact duplicate of the table depicted in the strange card.

"This is the Tarot card known as the Magician," Holmes explained. "The four items on the table represent the four suits of the Tarot deck: swords, wands, cups, and pentacles."

"The five-pointed star!" O'Bannion exclaimed. "The gold coin with the star was a pentacle."

"Precisely," Holmes agreed.

"But what is the meaning of all this?" I cried. "Why should Sir Wilfred place such objects on his table?"

Holmes answered my question with a question. "Watson," he asked, "what was the exact date upon which Sir Wilfred died?"

"Why, early in the morning of December twenty-second," I replied, astonished that my friend should have forgotten so elementary a fact. "Three days before Christmas."

"No, Watson," Holmes admonished, with a shake of his head. "Sir Wilfred did not die three days before Christmas. He died instead on the holiday he had chosen to celebrate in its place: the winter solstice, which occurs between December twenty-first and December twenty-second. He hid the pagan symbols of that holiday beneath the trappings of an English Christmas, but the true meaning of holly and ivy precede the Christian era in England.

He invited others of his sect to partake of the holiday, and when they left, he embarked upon his own initiation as an adept, setting forth the items on the table and ingesting the sacred seeds."

"Then there was no murder after all?" O'Bannion exclaimed.

"There was no murder," Holmes repeated. "The late Sir Wilfred was an adept of the Order of the Golden Dawn, and as such, he aspired to an even higher state of spiritual knowledge and power. He prepared his study for a ritual that would take him, in the words of the note, 'across the abyss.' "

"Then the abyss does not refer to death, Mr. Holmes?" O'Bannion inquired; the relief in his voice was almost comical.

"In a way, it does," Holmes answered. His face was grave. "Do you know why the angel's trumpet is known as the sacred datura?" he asked. I shook my head, as did O'Bannion.

"Because it produces a type of mania that is believed to be conducive to spiritual visions."

Holmes stood and began to pace the small room. "I have read accounts of shamans who have ingested the seeds of the sacred datura," he went on. "They fall into a deep trance and appear to be dead. Then they rise from the dead and claim to have witnessed extraordinary visions and to have obtained occult knowledge. It is my belief that Sir Wilfred took the seeds of his own free will, seeking to 'cross the abyss' from worldly to otherworldly knowledge. The note was indeed written by Miss Charmian Carstairs's father, but it was not a symbol of revenge, but of a spiritual bond between father and son."

"But what of the angel, Holmes?" I cried. "Surely the angel with the golden trumpet must be a Christian symbol?"

Holmes shook his head. He lifted a slender hand and moved the Tarot cards about. At last he lifted one and showed it to me. It portrayed an archangel blowing a trumpet while gray figures emerged from their coffins. Underneath the card was written the single word *Judgement*.

"It is a card of the Tarot deck," Holmes stated. "Lestrade had never seen it before; he assumed it was a Christian picture."

"But, Holmes," I protested, "the brooch Miss Letitia Carstairs wore was of a rose and cross; do you mean to imply that she, too, was a member of this Golden Dawn? And if she was, why did she not come forward and make the truth of the ritual known to the police?"

"That question is easily answered, Watson," Holmes replied with a grim smile. "Mr. O'Bannion can tell us what happens to an heir who is convicted of murdering the testator."

"She would be disinherited," O'Bannion explained, "and the inheritance would pass to the residuary legatee."

"I think you will find that Miss Letitia Carstairs occupies that position in her late brother's will," Holmes said. "She not only hated her grand-niece, she intended to keep her brother's fortune for herself by refusing to explain that Sir Wilfred took the datura seeds of his own free will."

The testimony of Sherlock Holmes in the trial of the American heiress was a nine days' wonder. Kevin O'Bannion's motion to dismiss all charges against his client was granted amid much clamor in the courtroom. The headlines in the morning papers trumpeted the news of the Great Defender's latest courtroom triumph to an admiring public.

To Kevin O'Bannion, she was always *the* woman.

Or perhaps not. Holmes and I attended the opera last night (the incomparable Goldini was singing), and who should we see in a box but the Great Defender himself, escorting a lady whose raven hair and large gray eyes were reminiscent of the California poppy he had defended with such skill. But a closer look revealed her to be a pale copy of her American predecessor, whom I later learned had taken the first boat for New York as soon as she was released from prison.

We received a case of wine only last week. It bore a label showing rolling hills and the name Duclos Winery, Sonoma Valley, California. Holmes proclaimed the vintage, which bore the improbable name zinfandel, undrinkable (without actually tasting it), solely on the grounds that no vintage produced in the New World could possibly please an educated European palate. I, on the other hand, sampled a glass with last night's chop and found it most satisfactory, if a trifle young and forward, a quality that renders it not unlike the daughters of the great republic from which it came.

ABOUT THE AUTHORS

As the creator of historical mysteries with her Charlotte and Thomas Pitt novels, *Anne Perry* is indisputably one of the world's most popular mystery writers. She lives in a small fishing village on the remote North Sea coast of Scotland.

Barbara Paul has a Ph.D. in Theatre History and Criticism and taught at the University of Pittsburgh until the late seventies when she became a full-time writer. She has written five science-fiction novels and sixteen mysteries, six of which are in the Marian Larch series. A new Marian Larch will be out in 1997, titled *Full Frontal Murder*.

Gillian Linscott is the author of six mysteries featuring suffragette Nell Bray. The latest, *Dead Man's Sweetheart*, will be published in 1996. Formerly a parliamentary reporter for the BBC, she currently writes full time. Linscott lives with her husband, also a writer, in their three-hundred-year old cottage in Herefordshire, England.

Gwen Moffat was born in 1924. She is a crime novelist living in the English Lake District. A mountaineer, she sets her stories in the backwoods, from the Scottish Highlands to the Rockies and southwestern deserts. Her series characters are the urbane and formidable Miss Pink, and Jack Pharoah, ex-Mountain Rescue, prickly, and battered by family disasters and a bad fall.

Loren D. Estleman is the author of thirty-seven books, including the Amos Walker detective series, several westerns, and the Detroit historical mystery series: *Whiskey River, Motown, King of the Corner, Edsel,* and *Stress.* His first Sherlock Holmes pastiche, *Sherlock Holmes vs. Dracula,* has been in print for eighteen years.

Jon L. Breen has written six mystery novels, most recently *Hot Air* (1991), and over seventy short stories; contributes review columns to *Ellery Queen's Mystery Magazine* and *The Armchair Detective;* was shortlisted for the Dagger Awards for his novel *Touch of the Past* (1988); and has won two Edgars, Two Anthonys, a Macavity, and an American Mystery Award for his critical writings.

J.N. Williamson is a titular-invested member of the Baker Street Irregulars, and has been since he was nineteen. A long-time Holmes fan, he started writing and publishing articles on Sherlock Holmes when he was fourteen. A full-time writer now, he has thirty-seven novels and over one hundred and fifty short stories to his credit, as well as editing the acclaimed four-volume anthology series *Masques.*

John Stoessel has been a chemist, musician, scientific consultant, and investigator before turning to writing, particularly about Holmes and Watson. He has written three mystery novels, *The Vatican Affair, The Oyster Affair,* and *The Vladivostok Affair,* and is currently finishing *The Great Western and Atlantic Affair,* all featuring Holmes and Watson with classic Victorian backdrops. John lives in Duluth, Minnesota, with his wife and four children.

William L. DeAndrea has won three Edgar Allan Poe Awards from the Mystery Writers of America, for the novels *Killed in the Ratings* and *The Hog Murders* and for the reference work *Encyclopedia Mysteriosa.* He lives in Litchfield County, Connecticut, with his wife, mystery writer Jane Haddam, and their two sons.

Bill Crider is the author of more than twenty mystery, western, and horror novels as well as numerous short stories. *Too Late to Die* won the Anthony Award for favorite first mystery novel in 1987, and *Dead on the Island* was nominated for a Shamus Award as best first private-eye novel.

A multi-genre author of thirty-two novels, *Carole Nelson Douglas* writes about the only woman to outwit Sherlock Holmes, Irene Adler, in four novels beginning with *Good Night, Mr. Holmes*, a *New York Times* notable book. She trades deerstalker for cat-ears to record the cases of feline sleuth Midnight Louie, winner of two 1995 Cat Writers' Association awards: best cat novel for *Cat in a Crimson Haze*, and a special short story citation.

Reginald Hill has written more than forty novels, including the well known Dalziel and Pascoe series. He has won the Crime Writers' Association Gold Dagger for best crime novel of the year, has been shortlisted for the MWA Edgar, and in 1995 was awarded the CWA Cartier Diamond Dagger for outstanding contribution to the genre. He lives quietly in Cumbria, England, with his wife, Pat; their cats, Pip and Matty; and his conscience.

Edward D. Hoch, past president of the Mystery Writers of America and winner of the Edgar award for best short story, has published nearly eight hundred short stories and forty books. His stories have appeared in every issue of *Ellery Queen* since 1973. He and his wife live in Rochester, New York.

Carolyn Wheat's fourth Cass Jameson mystery, *Mean Streak*, was published in May 1996. "The Adventure of the Angel's Trumpet" introduces Cass's spiritual ancestor in the person of barrister Kevin O'Bannion (a cousin of John Dickson Carr's Patrick Butler). An Adventuress of Sherlock Holmes, Carolyn's investiture is The Penang Lawyer (Hound).